The Creatures
of Celtic Myth

The Creatures
of Celtic Myth

BOB CURRAN

ILLUSTRATED BY
ANDREW WHITSON

CASSELL&CO

To Michael and Jennifer, for their faith in their father
BC

Dedicated to the ones I love: My mum, sister and Catriona
AW

First published in the United Kingdom in 2001 by Cassell & Co
Previously published in hardback in 2000

Distributed in the United States of America by Sterling Publishing Co. Inc.
387 Park Avenue South, New York, NY 10016-8810

A CIP catalogue record for this book is available from the British Library

ISBN 0-304-35898-3

Designed by Richard Carr
Edited by Sarah Widdicombe

Printed and bound in Slovenia by Delo Tiskarna,
arrangement with Korotan Ljubljana d.o.o.

Cassell & Co
A Member of the Orion Publishing Group
Wellington House
125 Strand
London WC2R 0BB

Contents

Introduction 6

GIANTS 12
WALES: In the Hall of Yspaddaden Pencawr 14
BRITAIN: The Dance of the Giants 19
CORNWALL: The Slaying of Old Denbras 24

DEMONS 28
SCOTLAND: The Hoodie's Bride 31
IRELAND: St Brigid's Bell 36
BRITAIN: The Wild Hunt 40
BRITTANY: The Midnight Washerwomen 46

FAIRIES 52
SCOTLAND: The Laird of Gesto 54
IRELAND: The Trip to London 58
ISLE OF MAN: The Prisoner of Garwick Glen 62

MERFOLK 66
IRELAND: The Sea-Bride 68
BRITTANY: The Sunken City 73
CORNWALL: The Mermaid of Zennor 77

MONSTERS 84
IRELAND: The Last Serpent 86
ISLE OF MAN: The Buggane of St Trinian's 90
SCOTLAND: The Water-Bull and the
Nightmare Horse 97

HALFLINGS 100
IRELAND: The Love of Aoibheall 102
ISLE OF MAN: The Changeling 109
BRITTANY: The Lady of the Forest 114
BRITAIN: The Green Children 122

SOLITARY FAIRIES AND SPRITES 132
BRITTANY: The Fairy of Lanascol 134
IRELAND: Bridget and the Leprechaun 139
CORNWALL: The Tolcarne Troll 143

WITCHES, WIZARDS AND WISE WOMEN 148
BRITAIN/WALES: The Madness of Myrddin 151
SCOTLAND: The Brahan Seer 158
IRELAND: The Death of Biddy Early 163

ANCIENT HEROES 170
BRITAIN: The Sword in the Lake 172
IRELAND: The King of Rathlin's Daughter 180
WALES: The King of the Otherworld 185

Select Bibliography 190

Index 191

INTRODUCTION

In 225 BC, a fierce battle occurred near the Italian seacoast which was to have dramatic implications for the culture of much of western Europe. The Battle of Cape Telamon was between the forces of the Roman Empire and a massive army of a people known only as the Celts.

The actual origins of the Celts are uncertain, but it is highly possible that they were an amalgam of ancient tribal groupings who had emerged from beyond the Alps and were now making inroads into Roman territory. The Romans probably first heard of them around the fourth century BC (some historians estimate their presence in Italy as even earlier) when they ousted another ancient people – the Etruscans – from settlements in the valley of the River Po away to the north and began to settle there. It would be wrong to think of them as a wave of barbarian invaders, for by the time they arrived in north Italy they already had a developed and complex culture.

It is also erroneous to think of the Celts as a unified race in the conventional sense. They were probably a confederation of peoples who had come together for specific purposes – defence, religious worship, trade and industry – and had gradually come to share a cultural identity. They did not describe themselves as 'Celts' (although the word *keltoi* was to be found in their tongue, meaning 'secret' or 'hidden'); rather, the name was a nick-name given to them by the Mediterranean cultures and meant the 'hidden people', due to the fact that they did not write anything down concerning themselves or their history.

A fiercely territorial people, the Celts built their settlements all along the Po Valley and roughly divided their time between warfare and agriculture. The land on which they lived and worked played a significant part in their lives not only in a temporal sense, but in a religious and a cultural way as well. For the Celts, the land was a living, breathing thing, peopled with invisible spirits and forces, and their entire way of living was built around the seasons of the year – the Great Wheel of Nature, which incessantly turned in the Celtic mind and by which the days were measured.

In the Po Valley, the nomadic Celts had more or less become settled farmers. Soon, however, they were ranging further south and beginning to menace Roman cities in the Italian midlands. Frequent campaigns were waged against them by the Roman authorities, but with little success, as the Celts were still regarded as fearsome warriors. The defining moment, however, came at Cape Telamon.

In many ways, Telamon was a stroke of luck for the Romans. The powerful Celtic army found itself unexpectedly caught between a strong Roman force from the Sardinian campaign against the Carthaginians, which was marching south from Pisa, and another equally fearsome military expedition moving northwards along the Etrurian coast. Desperately, the Celtic generals tried to pull together their rather haphazard forces – comprised of a number of tribal groupings all under their own individual commanders – in order to take on this pincer-like threat. They were unsuccessful, and at Telamon the Celtic army was decimated. The myth of Celtic superiority in battle was dashed for ever.

The victorious Roman legions pursued the Celts into their heartlands, most notably the Po Valley, which they scoured. Faced with military might, the Celtic peoples were now forced to make a response. Some stayed and tried to negotiate with the victors (in 224 BC, one year after Telamon, we hear of Celtic ambassadors in Rome trying to sue for peace), but the Romans were not all that accommodating. In 223 BC, they pillaged the lands of individual tribes, their generals returning laden with booty and captives.

The majority of the Celts, however, fled. Some moved to the east, where they sacked Delphi, passed through what is now the Czech and Slovak Republics, and established a Celtic state on the plains of Asia Minor. This was Galatia – taking its name from a Roman term for the Celts, the Galli – and when the Apostle Paul wrote his famous Letter to the Galatians, he was writing to a predominantly Celtic Church.

Most of the Italian Celts fled to the west, where they were to have a profound effect upon the culture and learning of the lands which they occupied. They established settlements in Iberia (Spain), Gaul (France) and even North Africa. Some kept on travelling, until they reached an area which the Greeks called Cassiterides and the Romans, the Pretanic (or Tin) Islands. We know this place today as the British Isles. It was here that the Celts settled in large numbers and began to clear the indigenous forests and turn their hands once again to agriculture.

Language was important to the Celts because they were, primarily, a people with an *oral* (not written) tradition. Julius Caesar believed that their leaders and holy men forbade them to write anything down for fear it would fall into the hands of their enemies, who would then know their strengths and weaknesses and could plan accordingly. Whether or not this is true, the Celts left very little written material about themselves. They did, nevertheless, leave a wealth of spoken information, through poems, epic stories and folktales. These were the traditions which they had probably brought with them from a time before they settled in Italy, and that they had adapted to the new lands in which they found themselves.

The lands to which the Celts came were not exactly empty. Already there were a number of 'aboriginal' peoples living there and these the incomers either conquered or (more probably) absorbed into their overall structure, for the Celts were a highly adaptive people. With these aboriginals came traditions that the Celts quickly amended and claimed as their own.

Already the Celtic language was beginning to fracture and split. In fact, it divided into two distinct linguistic forms. The source of the separation is thought to have been the sound *qw*, which one section – the Goidelic Celts – pronounced as a hard 'q' and subsequently as a 'c', and the other – the Brythonic Celts – pronounced as a soft 'p' sound. The Goidelic linguistic group formed the basis for the Irish, Manx and Scottish tongues, while the Brythonic formed another important language block: Welsh, Cornish and Breton. Giodelic is said to have been the oldest form of Celtic tongue, with the Brythonic being closely related to continental Celtic (which was called Gaulish). However, although the language split, many of the stories remained the same but now took on new characteristics associated with the language blocks into which they fell. Thus, the Irish and Scottish heroes shared common attributes which were determined as much by the language of the storytellers as by the geographical nearness of the two countries.

Soon other elements were to infiltrate and change Celtic culture. The first such element we might describe as being the 'foreign Celt'. Some of those Celts who had originally fled eastwards to avoid the Romans now began to drift westwards again following the collapse of the Roman Empire. They had been displaced by other peoples from the east, and they came to the lands of the west as invaders. They still retained a Celtic culture, but it was a culture which had been adapted and modified by their sojourn in places such as Turkey and Greece. This was reflected in the tales which they told and the form that those stories took.

Some of these invaders came from around the headwaters of the Danube (and were sometimes known as the Dana, a possible origin for the name Tuatha de Danan in Ireland) and from along the Ruhr, and they were quickly incorporated by conquest and intermarriage into the settled populations of areas such as Gaul, Scotland and Ireland. Other invaders were to come after them – Germanic peoples such as the Saxons and Jutes who swept down from the north, bringing elements of a culture which was totally alien to the Celts. Following them came the Vikings from the frozen lands of Scandinavia, who brought with them a highly developed mythological and folkloric culture. Of course, not all the Vikings were simply raiders who attacked and fled again;

many of them actually settled in Celtic lands and became integrated into Celtic society, becoming known as 'foreign Gaels' – a curious hybrid of the two cultures.

All these invaders left an impact on the beliefs, traditions and folktales of the Celtic people. What we might term the 'pure Celt' was rapidly becoming an entity of the past, as their society changed and adapted. But there was still one last invader to come which would change the Celts profoundly and for ever.

This invader did not come with a sword or war band; rather, it came with a book. It was not a conquering army smashing all in front of it, but a philosophy and a religion. This was Christianity, and it spread from Rome, now a religious capital instead of a military one.

The Christian faith slowly turned the Celtic world upside down. The complex beliefs and traditions which the people had held, amended and developed were now termed 'pagan' by the followers of the new creed. However, this didn't mean that the Christian Church dismissed them entirely – indeed it could not, since they were so deeply ingrained within the Celtic psyche; rather, the Church itself adapted and amalgamated them into its own theology. Thus wells at which spirits had been worshipped for many centuries suddenly became 'holy wells', dedicated to the memory of some saint; feasts which the Celts had observed since time immemorial suddenly became 'holy days' or 'pattern days', which were an integral part of the Church calendar. The Celtic Christian Church of the west, with its base in Iona rather than in Rome, actively maintained many 'pagan' traditions within its overall structure and teaching until the Synod of Whitby in AD 664. The Christians did, however, bring one development which was to impact greatly upon the tales and stories that had been passed down.

Despite all their cultural development through contact with other peoples, the Celts still remained a population with a predominantly oral tradition. Stories, histories and poems were passed from one generation to the next largely by word of mouth. Christianity changed all that, because the monks and missionaries of the early Church were, above all, literate men. And writing, particularly the writing of the monks, was to alter the traditional Celtic stories as never before.

Initially, the monks wrote on religious themes in their isolated monasteries – expositions of the Bible and biographies of the early Church Fathers – but gradually they turned their attentions to the Celtic-based mythologies and folktales of the areas in which they were working. For the first time, many of these traditional stories were written down. But there is one thing to be remembered: the monks who wrote them were *not* faithful and impartial recorders of the stories that they heard. They had their own agenda, and it was a religious one.

Once again, the tales and traditions of the Celtic peoples were modified, usually to fit in with a Christian perspective. New elements were introduced, and many of the formerly 'pagan' tales now became moral fables, extolling the benefits of a virtuous life. Those spirits which had been worshipped as deities by the Celts now metamorphosed into 'demons' within a Christian context – demons who were defeated by the powers of the faithful and the holy. Stories concerning early saints now featured as prominently as those which concerned ancient heroes – indeed, many of the formerly non-Christian heroes found themselves transformed into holy men by the stroke of a monkish pen.

Nevertheless, many of the more pagan elements did survive within the written texts, especially in Ireland, where both the oral tradition and the Celtic bias to Christianity appear to have been very strong. Collections of works such as *The Cattle Raid of Cooley*, *The Annals of Ulster* and *The Book of Invasions* served to retain the Celtic consciousness in as near pure a form as could be expected, given the religious climate. There may well have been other written collections, too, in other Celtic lands, but these have undoubtedly been lost to history.

The writings of those early monks formed the basis of the great Myth Cycles which have been passed down to us. But the oral tradition was also passed down. The *seanchi* (men of lore) and professional poets and storytellers, who traced their descendancy from the great Bardic schools which had maintained history, poetry and storytelling as their disciplines, were to be found in many rural areas. They passed on, by word of mouth, much of the folklore pertaining to the area round about. They were also responsible for remembering the genealogies of the families who came and went on the land. This fitted in well with the ancient Celtic connection to the land and gave the people a place on the territory which they owned.

Thus Celtic tradition became a mixture of both the written and the spoken word. In an ancient *Annals*, the great myths were told, while from the lips of the country storyteller more rural, personalized tales were passed on. Both traditions preserved a corpus of lore which had come down, in various shapes and forms, from the days of the early Celts. Across the years, both began to blend together into a heady mixture which fused legend and history, and it was impossible to understand one without also understanding the other.

With the coming of what many have called the 'modern age', much of this lore began to slip away. The fireside storytellers, singers, historians and poets were replaced by the television and global network news. No longer were people concerned with the traditions of their local community – they were more interested in the 'big picture' that spanned the entire world. Modern transport and communications systems began to break down the old geographical distinctions with their individual traditions and draw them into one homogeneous mass. Admittedly some of the old lore was still produced in books, but these tended to be dismissed as 'infantile' or 'quaint', and not as the accumulated history of the perceptions of the Celtic people. Modern society, it was argued, had become far too sophisticated to see the world as those in former years had perceived it.

Thankfully, that view is gradually changing, and once again people are looking to the old lore and ways of their Celtic forefathers. Even the high realms of academia now pay deference to the past, with the introduction in many universities of 'Celtic Studies' as part of their overall curriculum. This is usually a combination of Celtic-based literature, poetry, history, drama and folklore, and is proving very successful. Gradually, too, communities are coming to realize what they are throwing away by not retaining any of their Celtic heritage, and local schemes and projects are being developed to resurrect the early kinship with the land. Publications have also begun to appear which explore Celtic history and folklore. Which brings us to this volume.

It would be extremely difficult, if not impossible, to try to cover the entire expanse of the oral and written traditions that have been passed down from one Celtic generation to another. Nevertheless, they have clearly influenced the perceptions, histories and literature of the Celtic peoples. While not attempting to produce a definitive collection of mythology and folklore, I have tried to look at some common themes which appear within the traditions of what we might call the 'western Celtic empire' – those lands of the west which were populated by fleeing Celts. I have grouped these themes under the general heading 'Celtic Creatures', since most of them feature some sort of realized facet of the tradition. Under various individual headings, I have tried to show how such traditions may initially have come about, and how they may have been amended and transformed by later elements and events, not least by the advent of Christianity.

The book will, hopefully, give a taste of the varied tapestry of the Celtic imagination and perspective. It draws from both the written and the oral traditions which underpinned (and, in some cases, continue to underpin) Celtic society. The tales themselves can be read as individual stories, or can be seen as windows on to the richer and more complex world of the Celtic mind. As such, the book can offer only a tantalizing glimpse of how the ancient world must have looked to our Celtic forebears and how they interpreted it. Turn each page, then, and prepare to be dazzled by the myriad wonders which shaped the fundamental thinking of the Celtic age.

Giants

N THE YEAR 1828, while sinking a foundation for a new pulpit at the east wall of Ballywillan Church, near Portrush, County Antrim, in the north of Ireland, a group of workmen unearthed a man's skull. It was approximately three times the size of a normal human skull, with long and pointed teeth suggestive of cannibalism. The workmen were so terrified that they called the local rector in to bless the relic and reburied it at 'a considerable depth', where, presumably, it still lies today.

Around 1900, miners working the tin mine at Pedeen near St Just in Cornwall dug up the thighbone and armbone of a gigantic man which had been trapped in a layer of clay. Deciding not to tempt fate, they left the huge remains where they were. Similar stories are to be found in both Brittany and Wales.

Legends of giants – whether as individual beings or as races of supernaturally large creatures – abound across the Celtic world and many of them have found their way into the general folklore of western Europe. Tales of Jack the Giant Killer (originally based on an early legend of the British Celts) and the flesh-eating ogres of fairytales show just how pervasive the motif of the giant can be. There is something in all of us which fears the towering figure and booming roar of the titan.

Of course, the psychologist may explain this giantophobia as some sort of repressed childhood fear of adults, but surely there is something much deeper in our consciousness – some ancient and long-buried race memory, maybe? Certainly there is written evidence that giants once walked the world – stories of the Annakim and Raphim in the ancient Holy Land (their most famous son was Goliath of Gath) appear in the Bible. But were giant races more widely scattered than we suspect?

The frequency with which giants appear in Celtic myth would seem to suggest that there were races of immense beings living in the west as well. But we must be careful here, because the ancient Celts had a tendency to

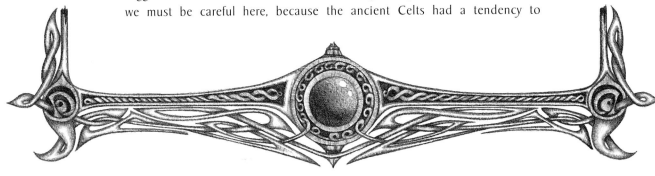

exaggerate the exploits of ordinary men to almost supernatural proportions. Thus some of the 'giants' of Celtic legend may be nothing more than mighty warriors – but not all of them!

For the ancient Celts, the giants were the first inhabitants of the western world, leaving evidence of their passing in the great megaliths and rock formations which they had supposedly erected. In some legends, they were the remnants of the Nephilim – a gigantic and barbaric race which had been all but destroyed by the Flood; in others, they were descended from Noah's 'evil' son Ham; yet other sources state descent from his youngest son, Japheth. Whatever their origins, they arrived from Africa in the second millennium before Christ to take possession of the empty lands of the west. Their king was known as Albion – incidentally, the oldest known name for Britain – and was the son of an ancient sea god whom the Romans called Neptune. He is said to have reigned for several hundred years, fathering many children, who spread out across the Celtic countries.

These were the forerunners of the Cornish giants under Cormoran, Lord of St Michael's Mount, against whom Brute, an early king of the Celts, led a number of expeditions, and also of the titans, who transported the pillars of Stonehenge from Ireland to England upon the whim of King Vortigern. Some were highly skilled and clever, as evidenced by Fionn MacCumhaill, the wily Irish giant; others were stupid and only a little above animals in their intelligence, living in caves and wearing animal skins – traditionally, these were early Cornish giants. All such stories hint at a long-buried recollection of a vanished race who shared the developing Celtic world with their smaller and weaker neighbours.

As human civilization spread across the world, the time of the giants began to recede. Now few in number, they were easily defeated by the fabulous figures of

mythology and conquering heroes of ancient romance. Gradually, they retreated to remote valleys and deep caverns, leaving behind their mighty stone constructions, scattered across Celtic lands, as the sole proof that they had ever been there.

A vibrant and youthful Christianity, surging across Celtic countries, saw the giants as the monstrous face of a pagan past and imbued them with horrific qualities – child-eating, wife-beating, murderous intent and so on. They were quickly absorbed into fairytales, and their prehistoric and folkloric basis was rapidly forgotten.

And yet, somewhere in the dark recesses of the Celtic mind, the giants still lurk. We should not dismiss them too lightly – they are, after all, the first recorded inhabitants of our world upon whom all traditions agree.

In the Hall of Yspaddaden Pencawr

It is always difficult to know how much one Myth Cycle has influenced another. Between the first and fifth centuries AD, the Celtic mythology of Britain was undoubtedly in contact with the highly developed belief systems of Rome, and each may well have been exposed to the supernatural nightmares of the other. Similarly, the Vikings, who later raided through the Celtic lands, may well have brought their own gods and demons with them to mingle with the visions of those whom they fought. Certain images, therefore, jointly persist in all these traditions – the most famous being that of the one-eyed giant. Polyphemus the cyclops is the titan from Mediterranean fable who captures Odysseus and his crew, while Odin, the All-Father, is the monstrous one-eyed Norse god who ranges through the skies at certain times of the year, seeking out those whom he can reward or punish according to their worship or neglect of him.

The figure of the one-eyed giant appears in Celtic tale as well. Indeed, the Irish once believed their country to have been occupied by such creatures – the Irish Celts called them Fomorii. The Fomorii were hideous beings, mostly with either one eye or one leg and were totally evil. Their king was Balor, son of Buarainech, known in legend as 'Balor of the Evil Eye'. The gaze of his single eye was so malevolent that it destroyed whomever it gazed upon. According to Irish legend, Balor was eventually destroyed by his own grandson, Lugh, at the Second Battle of Magh Tuireadh.

The Fomorii, however, were not the only one-eyed giants in Celtic lore. Perhaps one of the most fearsome of the race was the flesh-eating Welsh cyclops, Yspaddaden Pencawr. The name itself simply means 'Chief Giant', and Pencawr was believed to be the last king of a tribe of cannibalistic titans which had inhabited prehistoric Cymru (Wales). Unlike Balor, Yspaddaden Pencawr's glance was not fatal, but the giant was extremely wise and tricky. Stories of this ogre once dominated Welsh folklore but perhaps the best known is the romantic fable of Culhwch and Olwen.

Having refused to marry the daughter of his own step-mother – the sorceress Goleudydd – the Welsh hero Culhwch is cursed by the witch so that the only woman he can marry is Olwen, daughter of Pencawr himself. Culhwch has to go to demand Olwen's hand from the monster – that is, if his prospective father-in-law doesn't eat him first! Pencawr has an insatiable appetite for young heroes and it has been widely prophesied that, like the Irish Balor, his own grandson will slay him. Therefore, Culhwch doesn't expect a warm reception at Pencawr's underground mountain fortress.

Together with some other Celtic heroes who have joined with him from the court of his cousin, Arthur of Britain, Culhwch enters Pencawr's stronghold, slaying the giant's watchdogs and gatemen in the process. There, in the manner of all heroes, he confronts Yspaddaden...

YSPADDADEN PENCAWR WAS VERY OLD - perhaps even older than the mountains that formed the walls of his stronghold. He was also very big. Standing in the half-light of the gloomy chamber which was the giant's hall, Culhwch was conscious that Pencawr towered above him as much as the height of a tall tree and about the width of a stone dyke. The creature was also very fat, and as he moved slightly he appeared sluggish. He lolled, huge and bloated and seemingly incapable of sudden movement, on the rock throne in front of the hero, his one eye closed and with a great thread of saliva – thick as a rope – falling down from a corner of his mouth and into the tangle of his beard. On either shoulder sat a dwarf-like creature, each with a tiny pole in its hand, ready to roll up the mighty eyelid like a blind so that the giant could see his visitors.

All around Pencawr's throne the hall was dark and dreary, and a palpable chill crept from the rocky stone walls and seeped into Culhwch's bones, making him shiver. Nevertheless, he took a step forward, and as he did so, several shadows in a far corner of the hall appeared to move with him. Pencawr's men-at-arms, no doubt, who would strike down the hero and his companions at the slightest signal from the monster.

The giant appeared to be asleep. His great head had fallen forward a little way on his chest, and a deep and booming breath came in sporadic gasps, like the rise and fall of the sea-tide. And yet Culhwch knew that this could be merely a trick. Giants were notoriously sly and devious beings, and Yspaddaden Pencawr was the worst of them all. He might simply be waiting for the hero to come within reach of his great tree-like arms before snatching him up to devour him. It was as well to be extremely cautious when dealing with such a monster. Culhwch moved his foot and heard a discarded bone crunch beneath his heel – though whether it was human or animal, he couldn't tell.

'Yspaddaden Pencawr!' Culhwch's voice stirred up echoes within the mountain chamber. Behind him, he heard Bedwyr draw his blade from its scabbard and knew that his friend was wary of the giant's soldiers, who were already moving forward in the darkness behind the rock-throne. Pencawr stirred slightly and the rhythm of his breathing changed. The tiny creatures on his shoulders scuffled in an attempt to raise the huge eyelid.

'Who speaks?' asked Yspaddaden Pencawr. His voice, deep but old-sounding and creaking from long years of disuse, was like the screeching of a massive and rusting iron gate. Culhwch didn't answer. 'I hear a voice,' went on the giant, as his eye was slowly opened. 'I think it is a human voice, for it is like the irritating drone of a bee in the early summer. Who is the bold mortal who has been admitted to my chambers?' He moved a huge and taloned hand threateningly on the armrest of his throne. Culhwch moved into a dusty shaft of sunlight, but kept his hand resting on the hilt of his sword.

'Know me then, Pencawr!' he said defiantly. 'I am Culhwch ap Cilydd and I am here to crave a special boon from you!' The giant shifted his head forward but, because of his size and girth, he was unable to move very far. The rays of the sun, falling from a window above, caught and highlighted his jowls and for the first time Culhwch actually saw the face of the monster.

Pencawr's countenance was certainly broad and bloated like his body, but it had an evil craftiness about it. It was lined and wrinkled with the giant's immense age, but also with all the wickedness of the world. Ragged strands of hair hung about his cheeks, and his jowls were practically hidden by a massive growth of iron-grey beard which stretched down his middle, to be tucked into his belt. The beard was badly stained with the blood of the victims which Pencawr had devoured. The sight was enough to freeze the heart of any champion, but Culhwch stood his ground.

'A manling!' exclaimed the giant. 'And a bold one too! Approach me then,

Culhwch ap Cilydd, and ask your boon. If it is in the gift of Yspaddaden Pencawr, then I will consider it. If not, then you must be on your way, manling, ere I devour you and your comrades. I've not eaten for three weeks now and I begin to feel hungry for human flesh!' Boldly, Culhwch took another step forward and almost gagged at the reek of the giant thing before him. By now, the dwarves had raised the eyelid and Pencawr's single eye blazed darkly down on him, full of malice and ancient menace.

'I have come to ask for the hand of your daughter, Olwen, in marriage, Pencawr. Know that because of a curse put upon me by my stepmother, Goleudydd the witch, I can marry no other. Therefore, giant, grant me my boon and let me depart.'

There was silence for a moment, then the hall was filled with a rumbling laugh, like the mutter of far-away thunder. Yspaddaden Pencawr threw his ancient head back in great mirth and the dwarf-things clung to his shoulders for dear life.

'Rash manling!' the giant gasped. 'You are either a true hero or an utter fool to approach Yspaddaden Pencawr with such a request! Know you not that it is forbidden by ancient law for the sons of Adam to marry among the spawn of the giant kind? Know you not of the prophecy, widely broadcast throughout Cymru, that I am to be slain by my own grandson? And yet you approach me and ask for the hand of Olwen, my only child? Be gone before my mood changes and my hunger consumes you!' Raising a taloned hand from the arm of the rock-throne, he made a dismissive gesture in the air, and the shadows of the men-at-arms moved closer. Culhwch, however, was not to be turned.

'Olwen is the only girl that I can marry, Pencawr,' he cried, his voice stirring up sinister echoes through the mountain fortress. 'Therefore give me your blessing, or I and my comrades will kill you. Be assured that those who travel with me are heroes one and all' – and he beckoned into the shadows for his friends to step forward. Bedwyr and Menw both stepped into the shaft of sunlight, their swords already half-drawn. 'Here are Bedwyr and Menw, both champions from the court of Arthur of Britain. I trust you have heard of them, for if you have you know that I am in heroic company. And there are others of equal valour waiting in the shadows beyond who are more than a match for you or your warriors. Should any evil befall me, they are well able to avenge my death. Therefore I ask you again, Pencawr – grant me the hand of your daughter and let us all depart this place. The alternative is your own death.' The giant's laughter had died away and now only faint whisperings of it reverberated from the cold walls. Yspaddaden Pencawr seemed to be considering the proposal.

'Your comrades are indeed well known to me,' he rumbled at last. 'And you speak persuasively for a manling. But we of the giant-brood will not be hurried. I have not lived for near a thousand years to be rushed into a decision by a mere human. Return in three days, Culhwch ap Cilydd, and I shall give you my answer. Those are the words of Yspaddaden Pencawr. Now trouble me no further this day.'

Seeing that there was nothing to be said, Culhwch motioned to his companions and they turned back towards the great doorway into the hall.

'I shall return for my answer in three days, Pencawr!' cried the hero. 'Depend upon it!' But the giant seemed to have lost interest in the exchange and appeared to be asleep once more. His head had fallen forward on his chest again and his breathing had become regular. And yet, in the flitting shadows of the hall, Culhwch could not see whether or not his single eye was closed. Slowly and carefully the hero and his comrades moved backwards towards the door, their eyes firmly fixed on the giant. Only when he had reached the great doorpost did Culhwch turn around to leave. As he did so, the hall rang with a shout.

'Culhwch! Look out!' Bedwyr sprang forward and pushed him out of the way as a great spear – thick as a tree trunk – buried itself in the wood of the door. Green and poisonous venom dripped from its deadly spike and ran down to form a small pool on the stone floor. This had been destined for Culhwch's back! He turned around and looked back into the hall.

Yspaddaden Pencawr still sat on his rock-throne with his head lolling forward on his huge chest and appeared to be asleep. Had he thrown the spear? Or maybe it was one of the shadowy men-at-arms from the darkness behind the throne?

None of the heroes could be sure, but they all knew that Pencawr was a deadly and tricky creature. Swiftly, Bedwyr pulled the spear from the oaken door and, raising it above his head, hurled it back at the inert form of the giant. The weapon clanged off the rock-throne, catching the ogre a glancing blow on the knee as it did so. The mountain hall rang with the great roar of Yspaddaden Pencawr as the giant struggled to full wakefulness. Culhwch and his companions ran for the door.

A similar exchange takes place in three days' time. Pencawr refuses to give a definite decision and tells the heroes to come back. A spear is thrown after Culhwch as he departs and is hurled back, catching the giant in the chest. At a final exchange, Culhwch drives the spear into the giant's single eye. The blinded ogre then agrees that the hero can marry Olwen but only if he performs 13 extremely difficult tasks. Furthermore, there are 26 subsidiary tasks to be undertaken in order to accomplish the original 13. With the help of his comrades, supernatural personages and allies ranging from tiny ants to magical thunderstorms, Culhwch performs every one of the tasks and marries Olwen. Yspaddaden Pencawr is eventually slain by his own grandson, thus fulfilling the prophecy. The date of Pencawr's death is given, according to some legends, as 'one hundred years before the arrival in Cymru of Dewi Sant' – St David.

The Dance of the Giants

Despite the frightening folklore that surrounds them, there can be little doubt that Britain was inhabited by a powerful and gigantic race, long before the coming of the first Celts. Evidence of their existence is to be found everywhere, from the naked hill figures at Cerne Abbas in Dorset and Wilmington in Sussex to the ancient grave of the ogre Ascapart near Southampton.

The early Celtic kings, of course, made war against them in an attempt to drive them into the sea and take their lands. The Trojan king Brutus, great-grandson of Aeneas – who is said to have been exiled from Greece after the Trojan War and to have ruled Britain as King Brute several years later – mounted frequent campaigns against the giants of Cornwall. These were primitive and brutish beings who were, nevertheless, extremely fierce and managed to hold out for many years against these expeditions, under a wily king named Cormoran. In the end, Cormoran himself was driven into the sea and drowned at St Michael's Mount. His body was given to Irish mercenaries who had aided Brute and was shipped back to Ireland, where it may still lie. A documentation of these early giants is given by the medieval scribe Geoffrey of Monmouth – the writer who, incidentally, declared Albion to be the first king of the giants.

Subsequent Celtic kings (as well as some Roman rulers) also fought campaigns against groups of giant men and against individual titans at various locations right across Britain. However, the giants were by now rapidly declining in numbers and were unable to mount any proper defence against such attacks.

It was reputedly a Romano-Celtic monarch of southern Britain, King Vortigern, who defeated the last of the giant-kind around AD 425. These were two gigantic brothers, descendants of the Cornish brood, who lived in the hills to the south of the ancient settlement of London and frequently menaced the people there. Their names are given as Gog and Magog, although certain writers simply refer to one giant named Gogmagog who stood 18 feet tall. Vortigern apparently hunted down these two titans like wild animals and brought them in chains and in a cage into London.

This story is, for the most part, completely false. To start with, there seems to have been no such ruler as Vortigern. The name, however, comes from the root *vawr-tighern*, which simply means 'Great Ruler'. He was probably an early Celtic overlord in the style of the Irish Ard-Ri or High King. Certain scholars have identified him as a Romano-Celtic monarch who took the name Vitalinus and consolidated much of the southern reaches of Roman Britain (to the Cornish border) under his rule. In popular legend he fought monsters, wizards and giants, defeating the brothers Gog and Magog – who were little more than savages – in a mighty battle.

Interestingly enough, Vortigern is alleged to have betrayed Celtic Britain to the Saxon king Hengist and allowed him to overrun the country. For this, he was driven out of his own kingdom and, according to Welsh legend, wandered hopelessly from place to place.

The greatest monument to Vortigern's reign, is said to be Stonehenge, which was originally in Ireland and was known as the 'Dance of the Giants' having (allegedly) been raised by Irish giants. On a whim, Vortigern had the mighty structure transported to Britain as a commemorative marker to those who had died fighting the giant-kind. And, as a jest on his part, the king had the two captured giants – Gog and Magog – do this for him...

At last the gates opened, allowing the procession to enter the town, and the crowd surged forward. First came Vortigern himself, riding on a pure white steed. The king, fresh from the battle against the giants, was still bedecked in battered armour and looked weary. Nevertheless, he had a dusty regal splendour about him.

'The gods bless you, King Vortigern!' An old women broke free from the throng and approached the passing horse. Her cry was taken up by others in the crowd. 'May the gods bless you, great king, for saving our town from the giant-kind!' Vortigern smiled in his beard and acknowledged their thanks with a regal wave of his hand. Behind him, on a black thoroughbred, rode Aurelius Ambrosius, second son of the murdered King Constantine and 'magister' of the town of London. He was a thin man, youthful-looking despite his advancing years, and his face lacked the narrow slyness which characterized that of the king. He, too, acknowledged the cries of the people with a thin smile which crept gradually across his beardless face.

Behind their leaders rode a battalion of horsemen from Vortigern's Pictish guard – the wild, tattooed men from the far north. Their heads were shaven almost to the point of baldness, save for a single ponytail of hair which hung from the back of their skulls down on to their shoulders. Each rider carried a long spear hung with gory trophies and the fetishes of the northern tribes.

Vortigern held up his hand, and the leading part of the procession drew to a halt just inside the gates.

'People of London!' The king's voice brought the sounds of the crowd to silence. 'Your king and his warriors have fought a lengthy and bloody battle against the giant-brood which have menaced your town these many years.' He paused significantly. 'And they have been victorious. Many of the giants have been slain. I myself slew a giant-dam with two whelps suckling at her breast – aye, and her brutish mate forby.' The crowd cheered wildly. Vortigern raised his hand once again to quieten them. 'As a token of your king's mighty and historic victory, I have spared the last two of the creatures – perhaps the last of their kind in Britain – and have brought them here in chains in order to commemorate our great triumph over their kind. Never again will the giants menace the town of London. This Vortigern swears to you now.' He made a dramatic gesture towards the still-open gates, where a number of the Pictish horsemen had gathered. 'Behold! The last of the giants!' All heads turned.

There was a movement in the gateway. Several more Pictish riders came through and then, trundling slowly on huge wheels, came a great wooden cage, mounted on a low platform and drawn by a team of straining bullocks. It was the tallest of all cages, its bars made of solid oak and coated with a kind of pitch for added strength. The people pressed close to see.

Within the cage stood two great, shadowy figures who watched the crowd that milled around with savage and hostile eyes. They were massive beings, bigger than the Picts who rode on either side of the lumbering wagon. The largest of them pressed his face against the bars of the cage and roared, showing long, dagger-like filed teeth. He was half-naked – wearing only a set of hairy breeches, almost completely bald-headed, and with the skin of his upper torso tanned by long exposure to the fierce sun. His face was twisted into the most horrific contortions, from the midst of which two yellow eyes surveyed the crowd with an undisguised brutality. His companion was much more hairy, a lank and greasy mane hanging down almost to his shoulders and a massive beard covering his lower jaw. He, too, wore hairy trousers, but the upper portion of his body was covered with a thick matting of dark hair, making him look more like an immense ape than a sentient being. Both giants were bound with heavy iron chains, which clanked loudly as they moved on their bedding of straw within the cage. The chains were fastened to a huge iron ring, firmly fixed into the centre of the wooden floor.

Muttering among themselves, the crowd pressed forward to see. The bald-headed giant raised a talon-like hand and swept it through the bars of the cage. Men and women drew back, screaming loudly as the massive paw swiped through the air above their heads, and several of the Pictish guards dismounted and ran quickly forwards, striking at the mighty arm with their spears. Several of the shafts drew blood and, howling in pain, the giant withdrew his hand back between the bars.

'Behold the brutes!' shouted Vortigern above the resultant din. 'Look how they fume and and strain to be free, like the senseless animals that they are! Their names are Gog and Magog and they are indeed the last of the giant-brood in this land. See how savage they are, full of venom and fury. Were I and my soldiers not here, they would undoubtedly break free of their chains and escape their prison and devour you all.' The crowd gasped. Vortigern waved them to silence. 'Fear not, for even the giant-kind must bend the knee before Vortigern, king of all the Britons.' He gestured to several of the Picts who stood by the side of the cage. The Pict captain raised his spear and thrust it between the bars of the cage, catching the hairy giant in the side. With a clank of chains, the massive creature drew back. Vortigern rode closer to the cage while the crowd muttered among themselves, obviously impressed by their king's boldness.

'Bow down!' commanded Vortigern in a loud voice. 'Bow down before your master, you savage, witless oafs!' The giants looked at him almost uncomprehendingly with their yellow eyes. 'It is Vortigern who commands you.' The Picts prodded their longest spears between the bars, driving the giants hither and thither across the cage's straw-covered floor, restrained by the heavy chains which were attached there. The hairy ogre pawed at the air, trying desperately to stretch beyond the confining bars of the prison, while the other simply rattled the edges of the cage, howling loudly against the air. The crowd screamed and threatened to break and scatter, but Vortigern motioned them to stay where they were and they obeyed, while the giants continued to roar and fume.

Vortigern's horse bucked and reared a little as it caught their scent, but the king reined it in and it stayed still, whinnying nervously. At last, exhausted by their struggles, the two massive beings cowered well away from the king, their great heads bowed. The crowd cheered wildly. Vortigern, not wishing to get too close, waved his sword threateningly in the air and returned to where Aurelius Ambrosius was waiting.

'See how they love me!' he hissed out of the corner of his mouth. 'I am their king and they are grateful. I can use that gratitude to my advantage – these oafish giants will ensure my undisputed rule in Britain!' The magister regarded him warily. He knew that Vortigern was especially devious and tricky – he suspected the king and his Pictish cohorts of killing his own father, but so far he could prove nothing.

'They are restrained now,' he whispered, 'but they will not always be so. What plans do you now have for them, King Vortigern?' The monarch merely smiled unpleasantly in his beard.

'Something which will ensure that my reign is well remembered long after I am gone. A lasting monument to my greatness and to my defeat of the giant-kind,' he said softly. A puzzled frown crossed the magister's brow.

'What do you mean?' The king leant closer, and Aurelius could smell the stink of sweat and sour wine from under his tattered armour.

'You have heard of the Dance of the Giants?' he asked. Aurelius nodded slowly.

'Isn't that an old legend – a great stone circle on the side of the Killaurus Mountains in Hibernia [Ireland], supposedly raised by the last of the Hibernian giants?' he asked. 'I recall my father, who visited that bleak country, telling me about it but I've never seen it myself.' Vortigern nodded, his wolfish smile widening slightly.

'Indeed, it's as you say – the last massive giant-ring. They say that the stones were carried from Africa by the first giants to come to these islands and, as such, are sacred to the giant-brood.'

Vortigern motioned his still-drawn sword in the direction of the cage, where the two ogres continued to peer threateningly through the bars. The crowd had regained a little of its composure and were edging curiously forward again. 'These creatures will be easily cowed once I have turned my Pictish warriors on them, and when they are I shall send them to Hibernia to bring back the circle and assemble it once more on the Great Plain at Salisbury. This will mark the supremacy of mankind over the giants and immortalize my reign. All who will wonderingly gaze upon such a mighty circle in future ages will also remember King Vortigern! And it will have been raised by the last of the giants.' The magister nodded slowly.

'A great scheme, Majesty,' he said, 'and a wonderful monument. But are you sure that these monstrous beings can be so easily cowed?' He hesitated. 'And are you certain that they are indeed the last of their kind?' For the first time, Vortigern's composure seemed to slip a little.

'Once my Pictish troops have finished with them, they will obey me,' he replied, but his voice implied hope rather than certainty. 'Their only sovereign will be

Vortigern. And I am sure there are no further of their kind living on these islands.'

By now several bolder members of the crowd had drawn close to the sides of the cage, in which the two giants were still cowering. A tall man, well muscled and tanned, pushed a long piece of wood against the bars of the cage, rattling them in a great show of bravado.

'Ho, Gog! Ho, Magog!' his voice rang in the air, making the Picts nearby start forward. 'You are not so powerful now!' From inside the cage came a faint rumbling like far-away thunder. Gog, the bald-headed giant, made a sudden, darting movement, his fist striking at the oaken bars of the cage with unimaginable force. The wood splintered, sending shards hurtling outwards, and the gigantic hand of the confined titan swept over the heads of the crowd, who stumbled back, shrieking. Trailing fingers caught around a young woman, lifting her aloft, while the palm caught the man with the stick and carried him with it. The Picts ran forwards, their spears striking at the great arm. The hand swung back, knocking a Pictish captain aside as though he were a doll.

Above in the air, there was a crack as the spine of the man was snapped like a twig and his body was discarded in the dust. It fell with a horrid, bloody sound at the feet of the Picts, who were still ramming their spears into the newly created hole in the side of the cage, trying to drive the titan back. By now Magog had also become excited and had grasped the screaming girl, dragging her inside the cage. The two monsters bent over her, obscuring her body from view, and the screams ceased. The hulking figures of the giants bent over her and the day was filled with the horrific sounds of feeding. The Picts crowded all around the cage and the crowd was suddenly silent.

'Well, King Vortigern?' asked the magister softly. 'Can they indeed be cowed?' Vortigern toyed with the reins of his horse, and when he spoke his voice was strained and anxious.

'They will be cowed!' he promised after a pause. 'Giants will not be the masters of men! So swears Vortigern!'

In the end Vortigern did tame the two fierce giants and sent them, with a large contingent of Picts, to Ireland to bring back the Dance of the Giants. The results of their labours can still be seen on Salisbury Plain in the form of Stonehenge. Gog and Magog were kept in chains at Vortigern's palace, which occupied the site of Guildhall in London, until their death many years later. However, their likenesses were later carved at the entrance to Guildhall by medieval stonemasons, where they stood as guards over all who entered. Indeed, these effigies were still recorded as being carved on the side of Guildhall in 1413, during the reign of Henry V, but were destroyed in the Great Fire of London in 1666. So, even the very images of the last giants in Britain have now long since passed into history.

CORNWALL

The Slaying of Old Denbras

Although Vortigern was supposed to have destroyed the last of the British giants – and, by implication, the last of the Celtic giants as well – there is no doubt that several of them continued to live in remote parts of the country until medieval times. In the far north, on the Shetland island of Unst, two savage and gigantic brothers – Saxi and Herman – threw rocks at all who came near the shores of their island as late as the early 1100s. The names of these two giants may owe something to the Viking occupation of the Shetlands, but in Orkney their brother – the man-eating Cubbie Roo – was unquestionably Celtic.

Well to the south, the giant Tom Hickathrift was said to dwell in Hertfordshire during the reign of William I (1066–1087). By this time, the perceptions of the giant-kind may have been changing, for Tom appears to have been an extremely benign creature, anxious to help his neighbours when he could. His name may come from Hiccafrith, a patron-god of the Celtic Iceni who controlled the area in pre-Christian times. Like his successor, Hiccafrith was a giant, but was charged with looking after his worshippers and ensuring that no harm befell them.

The Isle of Man was also inhabited by a fearsome race of barabaric giants who had to be expelled by the wizard Merlin at the request of King Arthur.

But it was in Cornwall, long the home of the Celtic giant-kind, that the titans continued to live longest, stretching their influence in that part of the country well into the early Middle Ages. Although apparently smaller than their great forefathers, these giants were still treated with awe and terror by those who lived around them, and their names

have long passed into Cornish legend – the Giants of Trecrobben, Giant Wrath of Portreath, the deaf-and-dumb Dan Dynas of Castle Treen. By this time, of course, Christianity was spreading across the Celtic world, and the giants were often absorbed into Christian mythology as the last vestiges of a dark and pagan past. Nevertheless, there is evidence that the general perceptions of the creatures was slowly changing. Giants, after all, were no longer masters of the Celtic countryside and had to live among the expanding humankind. To do this, they often had to co-operate with their human neighbours, and many ancient tales begin to reflect more kindly giants working as builders and farmers.

Those titans who refused to compromise, and clung to their former and barbaric ways, retreated from the developing centres of humanity into remote valleys and deep caves, and within mighty and brooding castles. The image of the fairytale ogre was already taking shape within the Celtic consciousness. Nevertheless, some shared memory of the titans as an older race – perhaps the original inhabitants of the world – still lingered in the deep recesses of the Celtic mind, as many of these Cornish giants bear the epithet 'Old' in front of their names to acknowledge their undoubted antiquity: Old Pengersec, Old Gall and so on. Many of these beings were remarkably dull and stupid – witness the Giant Bolster of Chapel Porth, who propositioned the virtuous St Agnes and easily fell foul of her feminine wiles.

From time to time, of course, problems still arose between human- and giant-kind, and every now and again a hero was called upon to sally forth to defeat an ogre and reassert human supremacy...

THERE HAD ONCE BEEN a multitude of giants living in Cornwall, but towards the end of the twelfth century only a handful of them remained. Those that were left were smaller than the giants of old, but still twice the size of ordinary men. These were the descendants of the true Celts, the old masters of the world, who had ruled in those lands long before men had looked from their caves. But now their time was passing.

The most fearsome of those that still remained, however, was Old Denbras of Towednack, who had built his castle on the very edge of the old main road which ran between Market-jew (an old name for Marazion) and St Ives. He was a fear-some creature, standing over 15 feet tall in his mighty boots and with a girth the size of a small mountain, made all the more terrifying because this ancient ogre spent much of his later life in great idleness and gluttony. His hair was like a stretch of wild heather on the hilltop, russet but streaked with grey, while his teeth were worn down to the gums due to the grinding down of bones of humans and animals, he was rumoured to have trapped along the road. He was said to have married innumerable times, but none ever saw any of his wives again – it was supposed that the giant ate them as soon as he tired of them. Few locals ventured near his fortress because of his reputation for cannibalism. But there were strangers to the district who were unaware of the giant's terrible reputation.

One of these was a lad named Tom Trithick, who lived a good distance away. Tired of his mother's endless complaining about his idleness, he decided to set out for the town farthest away from her scolding tongue – which happened to be Market-jew. Arriving in the town, he found employment almost immediately. The mayor at that time was a brewer and as Tom was a big, hulking boy, he hired him to take a cartload of beer to a tavern in St Ives. All went well for the first part of the journey. Tom stopped near Cowlas to help a number of men who were raising a fallen tree on to a wagon in order to take it to timber a church that they were build-ing. Because he was such a strong lad, he was able to lift the tree trunk on to the cart without any sign of strain at all.

Not many miles further on, Tom Trithick found the main road blocked by a great hedge which appeared to have grown right across it. In the centre of the growth was a large wooden gate that was securely locked with a great chain and padlock. The hedge grew from the walls of a large fortress which stood close to the roadside, its walls of such a height that they could only have been built by a giant. It was the stronghold of Old Denbras of Towednack.

'Well,' said Tom to himself, 'it ain't right that such a selfish old rogue of a giant should build his hedges across the highway and enclose the commonlands round about. He's got his gate locked up right where the road goes through and that ain't right either. What right has he to stop honest people going and coming from their work? I've a good mind to break the gate down and drive right through!' And, taking out an axe which he kept in the cart in case of robbers, he began to attack the gate in the centre of the hedge. The sound of splintering wood and smashing timbers, together with the barking of the giant's dogs, soon woke Old Denbras, who was slumbering on the other side of the castle wall. Drowsily, he put his great head over the parapet and looked down.

'Who's makin' that noise?' he demanded in a throaty roar. 'Is it a stump of a boy wi' a wagon o' beer? Es beer fer me?' He gave a booming laugh. 'Soon will be, fer I'll take it as a toll for boy to get through to Market-jew!' Tom looked up at him.

'You're welcome to a drink if you let me pass,' he told the giant, 'but these barrels are bound for a tavern in St Ives and not for the likes of no scruffy giant!'

The giant's head ducked beneath the parapet and the gate of the castle opened. Filled with fury, Old Denbras lumbered out. He had in one hand a large elm tree, stripped of its leaves, which he intended to use as a club, and in the other he held a rusty sword with which he swiped at the air in a threatening manner.

'You're an impudent stump for a mortal!' he snarled. 'You know who I am? Old Denbras of Towednack, that's who!' Tom never flinched.

'I don't care if you were the king himself!' he said, raising the axe a little way. 'You've no right to block the public road down which the common people travel and start charging them a toll for going about their business! If it's a fight you want then a fight you shall have.' Tom had always been a reckless sort of a boy. Boldly, he raised the axe to take on the giant's attack.

He need not have worried about fighting Old Denbras, for the giant was old, slow and clumsy. He swiped the tree-club in front of him with great, regular strokes, like a man mowing corn, and Tom was able to leap nimbly out of the way. He darted below the giant's thrust and struck at the old ogre with his axe, catching him just below the knee. The blow caught Denbras off balance and he stumbled forward and fell to the ground, sending up a shower of small stones. The giant lay where he had fallen, groaning loudly to himself, then Tom would courteously help him up and the two would have a drink of beer from the cart – and when they had drunk sufficiently, they set to at each other again.

Soon the old giant began to tire and signalled that he wanted an end to the fight. With one final push of the axe, Tom sent him reeling backwards into the hedge. It was meant only to be a playful jab, but it had disastrous consequences. As Denbras wearily slumped back into the growth, a large sharpened stake, which the giant himself had placed there, speared his great body. With a loud and dispairing cry, Denbras fell forward with a crash that was heard in St Ives and which shook the ground beneath Tom's feet. The giant's blood and gore ran like a crimson river around his legs, and the dying cries of the ogre boomed and echoed in the land all around. There was nothing Tom could do to stem the great gash in Old Denbras's side – he used cloths and even great pieces of earth, but all to no avail. The only thing which made the giant stir was a cask of ale, pressed close to his lips. Only then did the dying titan open his eyes and look at Tom. He hoisted himself up on one of his great elbows.

'Truly,' he sighed faintly, 'you are a Cornishman, for only a true Cornishman could slay one such as I in a fair fight. I have no sons to come after me and so I name you as my sole and rightful heir.'

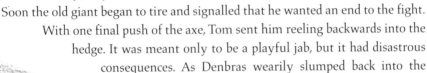

Demons

The first Celtic settlers in western Europe regarded the lands they came to with a mixture of reverence and awe. For them, the countryside was the abode of powerful and primeval spirits, whose slightest whim could destroy their settlements, spoil their hunting or ravage their crops. Such spirits were everywhere. They dwelt in rocks, trees, mountains and wells, and were continually watchful of the puny human tribesmen who now established themselves on lands which had once been theirs. These forces rapidly became the ancient gods of the Celtic world, worshipped by the tribesmen as they put down stable roots in the western world. As gods, they were strongly linked in the Celtic mind to the land and to wild and untamed nature, and they were worshipped in a number of forms – both inanimate and animal – for thousands of years.

The earliest gods of the Celts were capricious beings, either exchanging favours for obedience, sacrifice and subservience or else destroying those who stood against them. Offerings and sacrifices were continually made to them so that the hunting would be good, the ground would be fertile or no sudden storms would devastate the crops or the settlement. Their rites of worship were controlled by druids and shamans and were often extremely bloodthirsty, but it was better to obey than to be destroyed. For example, in the north of Ireland a child was sacrificed each year to the river goddess Banna, so that the river which bore her name (the Bann) would not flood the countryside round about. Not even the might of the Roman Empire could stand against these ancient beliefs, although there is much evidence that in the areas of Rome's occupation, Roman and local Celtic deities tended to merge together to form new entities which contained elements of both. It was a form of religious compromise.

After the fifth century AD, however, the position began to change slightly. Christianity, a new and expanding force in the western world, was beginning to sweep across Europe from its base in the imperial city of Rome. The new religion appeared to have little room for the pagan forces of the past. Of course, the ancient Celtic gods did not go away – they were far too ingrained within Celtic society for that! Christianity dealt with them in two ways. First (as the Roman Empire had done before), it adapted these deities into its overall religious framework, turning some of the early gods into saints and their shrines and wells into holy places; or second, it denounced them, demonizing them and their worshippers.

Sometimes, the distinction between the two was rather blurred, for while Christianity often denounced the use of, say, pagan wells, its priests still officiated at them, declaring them to be 'holy' and dedicated to 'saints' within the Christian canon. The Irish Church, for example, recognized the ancient shedding of animal blood in its feast of St Martin (11 November), when each house was required to shed the blood of a living animal in honour of the saint (a practice elsewhere often denounced as 'demonic'), while in 1656 the Dingwall Presbytery, 'findeing among uther abhominable and heathenishe practices, that the people in that place were accustomed to sacrifice bulls at a certain tyme upon the 25 of August, which day is dedicate, as they conceive to St Mourie as they call him... and withall their adoring of wells and uther superstitious monuments and stones', also condemned this similar practice.

Such worship, including the spilling of blood (upon which demons were said to feast), later became viewed in the context of 'deviltry', as orthodox Christianity took a tighter grip on the minds of the people. The gods of the Celtic pantheon became the 'demons' of the expanding Christian faith (the Greek word *diamon* from which it derives simply meant a supernatural force or spirit).

The orthodox view may well have had its roots in the increasing monastic regimentation in the medieval west. It may also have been due to the decline of the particularism of the Celtic Church and the advance of Roman dogma, as the Church in Rome rigidly established its teachings and authority in Celtic lands (as evidenced by the great councils such as Rath Breasail in Ireland in 1111 and Rheims in France in 1148).

To the mind of the medieval *religieux*, ancient powers lurked everywhere in the guise of demons and under the direct control of the Devil himself. God's people had to be alert to their wiles, for they had now assumed the undisputed characteristics of the Enemy of Mankind. Some wandered about the world invisibly, others took on a number of familiar shapes

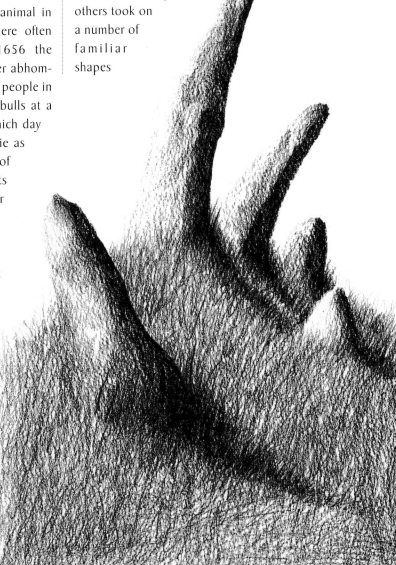

in order to deceive mortals. Yet evidence of them was apparent everywhere in the landscape. A great standing stone on the horizon was the symbolic finger of some primal deity; the thin cry of a wolf in the forest was the call of a malignant spirit; the unexplained disturbance on the river marked the passing of some pagan force – all seeking to divert God's children from the true and righteous path.

Nowhere was the existence of demonic forces more evident than in the writings of the hermits and recluses who sought sacred contemplation away from the wiles of the world. These Fathers were continually tempted by natural forces and urges which manifested themselves in various forms – every one diabolic. The thoughts of these anchorites served only to strengthen the resolve of the militant Church against the forces of the dark.

And yet the pagan worship which had characterized early Celtic society lingered on in the hearts and actions of the people to whom the clerics ministered; 'demonic' tradition still bubbled beneath the surface of everyday life. In the Scottish Highlands, milk was still poured on to special hallowed ground as a libational sacrifice at the Dobby Stane; in Brittany, wine and food were still left at the tombs of the dead as an offering to Ankou, the Breton Lord of Death; in Lewis and Islay in the Western Isles, within living memory, casks of beer were broken into the incoming tide as an offering to Shony, the Celtic sea-god.

Celtic festivals of undoubted antiquity such as the Lammas Fair are still carried on, although much of their original significance has been lost in a welter of commercialism and trading.

Like their Catholic counterparts, the Protestant Churches also railed against the ancient 'demonic powers'. As late as 1699, an old man was arraigned before the Kirk Session in Elgin, Morayshire, on a charge of idolatory because he continually raised his cap to a certain stone in the locality. In 1774, Thomas Pennant remarked regarding several sacred places in the west of Scotland associated with the 'demon king' Mhor-Ri (Great King) that 'if a traveller passes any of his resting places, they never neglect to leave an offering... a stone, a stick, a bit of rag'. Doubtless, in many rural areas these so-called 'demons' were still accorded the respect which they once enjoyed and were regarded with reverence by the people there.

Even today, few country-dwellers will linger overlong in certain places – for example, within the stone circles or ancient earthen forts which still litter some parts of the Celtic world – for fear of spirits, powers or 'fairies' which might be lurking within them. These are the last refuges of the 'demons' which once alternately protected and tormented the land – demons whose legacy certainly reaches across the centuries from pre-Christian times, and which are even yet condemned by the holy Christian Church. Perhaps we still might do well to fear their long shadows!

The Hoodie's Bride

The notion of crows as either the symbol of death or the symbol of protection occurs frequently among the ancient Celts, but also in other civilizations as well. Indeed, the image of the crow may actually have crossed between the Celtic world and others.

For example, in 345 BC, the household of Marcus Valerius Corvus (Marcus Valerius the Raven) adopted it as their symbol and incorporated it into their family. This was based on a legend concerning Marcus Valerius himself. According to this tradition, Marcus fought in a hand-to-hand battle with a Celtic chieftain who disabled him and was about to deliver the killing blow when a crow descended from the sky, pecked at the chieftain's face and shielded the Roman with its wings. This was taken to be a symbol of victory by the house of Valerius, who took the bird as a 'good luck' symbol. However, as the historian Henri Hubert has commented, no similar story occurs in the entire Latin tradition and it is highly probable that it was 'borrowed' directly from the Celtic tradition – particularly an episode in the ancient Irish epic *Tain Bo Cuailnge*, in which the goddess Morrigu attacks the Ulster hero Cu Chulainn, who has spurned her love, in the guise of a crow. Further such 'crossovers' are attributed to Roman writers such as Livy whose histories, it is suggested, are partly made up of Celtic traditions and stories.

Marcus Valerius Corvus was not the only war-leader to adopt the motif of the raven into his family. When Imhar the Landwaster, the son of Harald, Norse (or Hiberno-Norse) king of Dublin, attacked and devastated the island of Raghery (Rathlin) in 1045, legend states that his banner bore the insignia of a crow as a god of death and destruction. (Imhar's other cognomen was, of course, Imhar the Raven.) North Irish tradition also speaks of other Viking (or part-Viking, part-Irish) pirates who fought and slew beneath the standard of the crow.

It may have been from the Vikings and from the Hiberno-Norse traditions that the Scots of the outlying Western Isles took on the crow as a symbol of evil. This combined the old Celtic notion of the crow as the representation of the goddess of death with the destruction and slaughter wreaked by the Northmen. The crow, especially the hooded crow (or 'hoodie'), was greatly feared and distrusted all through the Isles and the Western Highlands as a bird closely connected with the forces of Celtic darkness.

It was quite easy, then, for the Church to transform this belief into one which directly connected the crow with the Devil and his minions. In certain traditions on the western Scottish seaboard and in the Isles, hoodies drank blood (not an outlandish belief, since crows were frequently seen with bloodied beaks on the battlefield after a conflict), placing them in roughly the same context as vampires. This was not the only connection. It was widely believed in places such as Orkney and Shetland that hoodies could take on human form as and when they pleased, although they usually chose to take the form of crows after dark when they went about their unholy business. In both the Inner and Outer Hebrides, tales abound of young girls who marry handsome boys only to find that they travel about at night in the guise of hoodies in order to drink blood. Any children born of such a union are usually carried away by the hoodies as their own.

The following tale comes from Islay, just off the Scottish coast – it was reputedly first recorded from a Cowal woman, Mrs Ann McGilvray, in 1859 – and it reflects the strange half-world in which men and hoodies existed side by side...

A farmer on Islay had three good-looking daughters. Indeed, they were so good-looking that they had many offers of marriage from men from all over the Islands and from Kintyre as well, but they turned them all down. One day they were waulking (tramping) clothes by a river when a hoodie alighted on a stone nearby. It spoke to the eldest.

'Arragh! Will you wed with me, farmer's daughter?' The girl gave the bird a disdainful look.

'Be gone!' said she. 'For a hoodie is an ugly creature and with the voice of the Devil forby. I'll not wed with you.' And the hoodie flew off. But it came again the second day when the girls were waulking once more. It spoke to the second daughter.

'Arragh! Will you wed with me, farmer's daughter?' But the girl took the same stance as her elder sister.

'Begone!' she told it. 'For the hoodie is a horrid creature and with the stare of Beelzebub forby. I'll not wed with you.' And the hoodie flew away. But it was back again the following day, alighting on the rock near to where the girls were waulking. It spoke to the youngest.

'Arragh! Will you wed with me, farmer's daughter?' The girl considered.

'Aye,' she answered, 'I'll wed with you, for the hoodie is a bonny creature and with enough magic about it to look after its own.' And so it was settled, and they were married the following day in the old style of the island – a handfast marriage and without the benefit of clergy. Soon after the marriage, the hoodie took her to his house in a wild part of Islay.

'Now,' said the hoodie, 'would you prefer me to be a hoodie by day and a man by night, or a man by day and a hoodie by night?' The farmer's daughter didn't even have to think.

'I'd wish you a man by day and a hoodie by night,' she told it. And so it was settled, and each day the farmer's daughter had a handsome young man by her side but by night he became a hoodie. In that guise, he travelled all over the Islands, even as far as Pabbay and the Uists, drinking the blood of bairns sleeping in their cots as he went, but the farmer's daughter knew nothing about it. The house in which they lived was a grand one and she wanted for nothing, for as she had imagined the hoodie had enough magical powers to look after its own. For a good while she lived very happily.

At the end of nine months they had a son. One night when everyone was in bed and sound asleep, there came the most beautiful music around the child's crib and the bairn was taken away by a hoodie. The young mother wept and told her husband when he returned in the morning, but the child was a hoodie-bairn and rightfully belonged among his own kind, and so he could not, or would not, do anything.

At the end of nine months they had another son. This time everyone kept watch every time the bairn slept. One night, however, the beautiful music sounded again and it was so soft and so melodic that it put everybody in the house to sleep. And a hoodie came and took the child away.

The young mother was distraught, and when her husband returned in the morning she pleaded with him to bring her child back to her. But he shook his head.

'I have flown over Tiree and Mull,' he told her, 'and over Rum and Canna. I have even flown as far as the grey slopes of the St Kilda islands in the north where the women sleep still wrapped in their shawls, but nowhere did I see a trace of the child. He has been taken far away and you had better forget him.' And he could not, or would not, do anything further.

At the end of nine months, they had yet another son. And this time when the bairn slept a tight watch was kept on him. But the same thing happened as before. One night, the beautiful music sounded and everyone in the house was lulled to sleep. And the child was stolen away by a hoodie.

This time, the young mother was almost demented. When her husband returned the following morning, she threw herself upon him and would not let him go until he had done something about getting her children back.

'Go to your own people wherever they are,' she begged, 'and tell them to release all my children.' And though he reasoned with her, she would not be consoled or pacified. At last he gave in and summoned his grand coach to take her to meet with his own kind. She climbed into the coach and was whisked along at such a rate that she soon lost all notion as to her bearings. The country outside might have been another part of Islay, it might have been Scotland, it might have been Ireland or some other country altogether.

'Is it far to go and meet with your people?' she asked her husband. But he didn't answer and she asked again.

'Far enough!' said he, and would say no more. The coach went on at great speed, and when they had been travelling for a good while her husband leaned across to her in the carriage and asked, 'You haven't forgotten anything, have you? You have all your things about you? It might be the worse for you if you've left anything behind.' And the young girl looked among her things.

'I've forgotten my coarse comb,' she answered. And at that, the grand coach suddenly disappeared and the girl was sitting astride a withered stick. And, looking up, she saw that her husband had changed into a hoodie which flew away with a loud 'Arragh!'

So there was the farmer's daughter, lost in a strange country and with no idea where she might be. The only thing she could do was to follow the hoodie and see if she could catch it. Then she would make her husband reveal to her where her children might be. She followed him on to the top of a nearby hill, but when she got there the hoodie was in the hollow, and when she got to the hollow the hoodie was on another hill.

This way, she followed him all day until night was coming on and she was very tired. But she had nowhere to sleep. Then, away through the gathering dark, she saw a light from the window of a house and made towards it. Looking in through the window, she saw a wee lad asleep in a narrow bed and a woman spinning beside him. The young girl's heart went out to the boy, for he was very fair and bonny-looking. She rapped at the door and the woman of the house brought her in, gave her something to eat and invited her to rest. The hoodie's wife slept until daybreak.

The next morning she was up and on her travels again. Thanking the woman of the house, she took a bit of breakfast and set out on the road to search for the hoodie. She searched from hill to hill, and indeed from time to time she saw the hoodie, but, as before, when she was on the hill the hoodie was in the hollow, and when she was in the hollow the hoodie was on another hill. Soon another day had passed and she was very tired. She was still no nearer catching the hoodie and finding her children, but she was very tired. As dark drew on, she saw another light shining through the gloom. It came from the window of a house and, running quickly, the hoodie's wife was soon at it. Looking in through the window, she saw a wee lad asleep with a woman sitting beside him sewing clothes. Again, the girl's heart went out to the child, for he was a bonny bairn and he slept so peacefully. She rapped at the door and the woman of the house let her in, gave her something to eat and told her to lie down and rest. This the hoodie's wife did, and she slept till sunrise.

The next morning, after a morsel of food, she was on the road again in search of the hoodie. And this day was just the same as the day before – sometimes she would see the hoodie on the hill and at other times in the hollow, but she could never catch up with it. And soon night came and she arrived at another house. There was another wee lad, lying asleep, and a woman beside him darning socks. Once again, she was brought into the shelter and warmth. The woman took pity on her and told her that the hoodie had only just left.

'This is the last time that you will see your husband,' she went on. 'If you want to catch him, you mustn't fall asleep.' She gave the hoodie's wife a seat beside the fire and then she and the boy went to bed. The girl tried to stay awake, but she was

very tired, having walked all day, and was soon dozing off. And, as she dozed, her husband came into the room in his human form. Gently, he tried to remove her wedding ring from her finger, but he fumbled and dropped it with a clang on the hearthstone, waking her up. As she came out of her sleep, he immediately changed into a hoodie once more and flew away with a loud 'Arragh!' The girl started and made a swipe at him, catching at a dark feather from his tail as she did so. He dropped the feather and flew away, leaving the girl very distraught behind him, for she knew that she'd lost the final chance to find her children. Hearing the noise, the woman of the house came down and, seeing the girl in such a state, took pity on her.

'I know where he has gone,' she told the girl. 'He has gone over the Hill of Poison, which no mortal can climb without horseshoes on both their hands and feet. Also, you will not be able to climb it unless you are dressed as a man.' And so the woman dressed the hoodie's wife as a man, and told her to go to the smith and learn how to make horseshoes for herself. She did this, and learned so well that she made horseshoes for her hands and feet in no time. Then she went over the Hill of Poison and into a town beyond, only to hear that her husband was about to marry the laird's daughter.

There was a horse race in the town that day to celebrate the wedding and everyone wanted to go to it, especially the laird's cook. Thinking the hoodie's wife to be a stranger man in the district, he approached her and asked if she would cook the meal for the wedding guests so that he might go to the race. She agreed, and cooked up a big pot of broth for the guests. Before it was served up, she looked carefully to see where her husband – the bridegroom – was sitting, and as she carried his portion to him she dropped both the ring and the feather into his bowl. With the first spoonful he took up the ring, and with the second, the feather.

'Bring me the cook that has prepared this broth,' said he, and they fetched the laird's cook, but the hoodie-bridegroom shook his head. 'That's not the cook that made the broth,' he said. 'I'll not marry until the true cook is brought.' And so they fetched his own true wife to him and he recognized her, for whatever spell he had been under was now broken. Together, they went over the Hill of Poison and she threw the horsehoes behind her while he followed. And, as they went home, they collected their three sons from the houses that they had already passed. That was the way of it, and the young girl lived with her family ever after – as happy as any girl could be when married to a hoodie!

The motif of the comb which the girl forgot and which cast the spell on her hoodie-husband appears in many other ancient Celtic tales and beliefs. For instance, the Banshee of Ireland is supposed to arrange her hair continually with a bone comb. There is also a stone at Dunrobin Castle in Sutherland which carries the engraving of a comb, together with other curious devices, which has never been satisfactorily explained. Combs have also been found together with querns in prehistoric burial mounds, suggesting that the implement may well have had magical connotations.

St Brigid's Bell

As we have seen no animal, or bird, embodied the dark side of the natural forces more than the crow or raven, with its rasping voice, black plumage and quick, intelligent eyes. Small wonder, then, that the ancient Celts regarded it with some fear.

Crows were usually associated with death and battle in the Celtic world. This is not surprising for, following the carnage and slaughter of warfare, crows often dropped from the skies to feed upon the bodies of both the dead and the nearly dead. According to ancient writers, European battlefields were often black with feasting crows, filling the blood-soaked air with their horrid squalling as they fought over succulent pieces of human flesh.

The mythology of the Celts connected crows with Badbh, the goddess of battle and slaughter. These birds, which were usually scald or Royston crows (hooded crows), became both her embodiment and her emissaries, and indeed her name denoted 'crow' among the early Celts. All across the Celtic world, she was known by a variety of names, or as part of a group of war-goddesses – Nemhain, Macha or Madb (She Who Intoxicates) and, most importantly, Morrigan (Phantom Queen). It was as Morrigan that she combined the fundamental elements of warfare and sexual conquest which seemed to be inextricably linked in the Celtic mind. As Morrigan, too, she was the sorcerous shape-shifter who would often take on the form of a wild creature, most usually a crow – she is described in Celtic literature as 'battle crow' or 'battle raven'. This is also true of Badbh Catha, the great battle raven who presided over fire and the bloody violence of warfare.

Not even the Romans could stamp out the linkage in the Celtic world between crows and the goddess of battle and sexual intoxication. In Romano-Celtic Gaul (France), a raven goddess called Cathubodua served much the same function as the Badbh/Morrigan. Here, an element of prophecy also seems to be included, and this reflects the idea that Morrigan was now coming to be seen as a prophetess or oracle. Indeed, seeing a flock of crows as one rode to battle was invariably considered to be an omen of ill-luck as far as Celtic warriors were concerned. The hag-like Badbh, in the guise of a crow, had the power to cast an evil spell upon them which would ensure their defeat and perhaps even their death if she so chose. Thus, the Badbh/Morrigan translates from being a goddess to a shape-changing seeress/witch.

Naturally, such pagan thoughts were anathema to the developing Christian Church. The crow, symbol of the Badbh/Morrigan, the Celtic war-goddess, now became the symbol of the Devil himself. It had drunk of the Devil's spittle, so ran Christian folklore, and this had scalded its throat, bringing about its harsh, cawing cry. The blackness of its feathers represented the black, scaly hide of the Evil One, and its darting eyes were always on the lookout to snatch the souls of the worthy for its dark master. The medieval mind, in which diabolical forces were continually abroad in the countryside, transformed these dark birds into demons themselves. It was hardly surprising, then, that certain witches chose the birds as their 'familiars' (attendant spirits) and that they frequently appear in medieval artwork as the epitome of evil. Only the power of a holy man – such as St Patrick – could stand against them. Indeed, it was the function of such saints within the Mediterranean Christian tradition to defend their flocks from these demonical wiles.

In the fifth century AD, not long after the Blessed Patrick had come to these shores, demons came out of the east in a great cloud and lit on all the lands of Ireland. They came in the shape of black crows – but bigger and more vicious than any normal bird.

It was said that it was the goodness of St Patrick himself which brought them. The saint had been fasting and praying for 40 days and 40 nights on the top of Cruachan Aigle (Croagh Patrick – now one of Ireland's holiest mountains) in order that the Christian religion might take hold in such a pagan land. The forces of darkness beyond the ocean had therefore sent a horde of demons to blight the country and so thwart the holy man's sacred purpose. They lit on the land, tearing up the seed that the farmers had planted; they tore the rushes from the roofs of the houses; they attacked the babies as they slept in their cradles and the animals as they grazed in the fields. There was no driving them away, for as soon as anyone struck at them, they faded away like shadows or black smoke but soon returned again, more angry and vicious than ever. The people of Ireland were at their wits' end and did not know what to do, for the demon crows had settled all across their land like a foul blight.

At last they went to the saint, still meditating high on Cruachan Aigle, and asked him for his help. Indeed, the Blessed Patrick knew of their coming, for he had been tormented by the crows himself as they wheeled and cawed around the sacred mountain, sending up a dreadful din which distracted him from his prayers. On hearing the plight of the people, the saint prayed long and hard that the demonic blight should be lifted from Ireland, but the powers of evil were very strong in those days and the numbers of demons seemed only to increase, darting about the top of the mountain and screaming ever more loudly.

Wearing only a chasuble (the sleeveless long white gown of ancient priests), Patrick went to the very lip of the rock on the topmost part of the mountain and shook his crozier at the crows, hoping that it would drive them away, but still they wheeled and darted overhead and merely laughed mockingly at him for his impotence. He struck at them with the sacred rod, but they simply turned to puffs of greasy smoke and drifted out of his reach. By now the air was so full of dark birds that neither the saint nor any man in Ireland could tell if it was day or night, and the mantle of their evil lay across the land like a black blanket. Patrick then threw holy water from a sacred well at them but with little result, for they crowded and flapped all the thicker and the sound of their mockery grew ever louder.

Now St Patrick tried something else. He sang maledictive psalms at them and this seemed to have at least some effect upon the awful host. They flew back to the seashore, but they did not leave Ireland. They tormented the settlements along the coast and attacked the men in their boats as they fished. As the day wore on, they returned to Cruachan Aigle to taunt the saint once more. Three times did Patrick sing his psalms at them, three times he drove them away, and three times the demons returned to mock him with their cawing.

By now a holy anger had come upon Patrick, a religious fury that was so great he could scarce contain it. Lifting a holy bell which he had with him to summon the faithful to prayer, he rang it fiercely to drive them away. In fact, so furiously did he ring it that every man, woman

and child in Ireland heard its tones, and echoes of it sounded far beyond the Sea of Moyle, in the lands of the Caledonians (Scotland). And yet, so great were the pagan powers that the ringing of the bell had little effect on them, and they cawed and shrieked all the more at his feeble efforts to get rid of them. In frustration, St Patrick threw the bell at them, but it missed entirely and fell down the mountain, bouncing and cracking as it went. In the end, it hit against a great stone and a huge crack or gap appeared in its side. The demons howled and cackled in triumph, and filled the airs above Ireland with the beating of their dark wings.

The saint was now utterly exhausted and could do no more. He fell, weeping, on the mountainside while the demons danced and dived above him. He wept until the front of his chasuble was sodden with his tears. And, as he wept, the Blessed Patrick prayed, long and sincerely, that the scourge might be lifted from the land. He wept for so long that eventually God took pity on the lone saint and answered his prayer.

An angel was finally sent to minister to Patrick and to drive away the demons which tormented him. The crows flew, screaming in terror, back across the sea to the lands from whence they had come, and were replaced by doves and beautiful white birds which circled the mountaintop and sang sweet melodies. At last St Patrick raised his head, to see the last of the demons vanishing into the east like a black cloud over Clew Bay. And God's angel consoled him and cleansed his chasuble. No demon came to the land of Ireland after that for a period of seven years, seven months, seven days and seven nights.

The bell which St Patrick had thrown at the demons to drive them away lay, untouched, well hidden among the bushes at the foot of Cruachan Aigle until it was found, many years later, by the followers of St Brigid. They took the bell and partly repaired it, and it was hung in Brigid's convent at Cil-Doaire (Kildare – literally, 'Church of the Oaks'). It hung there for some time, but was subsequently lost. During its time in Kildare the bell was known as Brigid's Gapling (on account of the crack in its surface) or St Brigid's Bell, and it was said that if it could be rung, it had the power to drive away demons. Maybe that is why there are so few devils in the holy island of Ireland.

The tale of a powerful bell being used as a defence against diabolical forces is not unusual in Celtic countries. As Christianity firmly integrated itself among the Celtic tribes, great veneration was paid to sanctified objects such as bells and croziers, and they were often accorded super-natural powers – such as the ability to ward off demons – thus showing the order and supremacy of the Church over the pagan forces of darkness and chaos. In Scotland, for example, St Drostan's Bell in Aberdeenshire was said to have the power to expel devils and to still the elements, while in the Great Glen, Merchard's Bell was believed to have similar powers. In fact, as late as the nineteenth century, bells were rung from church towers in parts of Brittany and in Wales to ward off electrical storms and lightning.

The Wild Hunt

Crows were, of course, not the only wild creatures to have demonic associations. The Celts had been primarily a hunting people – appropriating hunting gods – and elements of that survived well into their more settled, farming period. These became the Celtic hunter-gods.

Chief among the animals that they hunted were the wild deer and stags which inhabited the primeval forests, and so it is not surprising that at least some of their gods and goddesses should have connections to that animal. Indeed, we do not have to look far to find one in seventh-century-BC Austria, where the cult of an early Celtic hunting goddess held sway at Strettweg. In bronzes found here, the goddess and her soldiers (devotees?) are accompanied by two stags as a symbol of both her hunting prowess and her might. In a bronze from the area around London, the hunting god is accompanied by a stag and two hunting dogs. At Le Donon (Vosges, France), a local hunter-god is depicted as wearing wolfskin and boots decorated with animal heads, and carrying a knife, spear and chopper – transforming him into a kind of aggressive 'wild man' who maintained close contact with nature, perhaps by living deep in the impenetrable forests which still largely covered the land. He rests his hand on the antlers of his fallen prey. It was believed that such woodland gods still continued to hunt there and aggressively protect the lands which they had once controlled.

Many of the names and attributes of such woodland/hunting deities are now lost to us in their purest Celtic form, but what is striking about these early gods is that they often seem to take on some of the characteristics of the creatures that they hunted. For example, some of the deities are dressed in the hides of their prey; others may well have worn the horns, antlers or tusks of their quarry, giving the hunter at least some affinity with the hunted and symbolizing the strong union between man and the forces of nature.

With the arrival of the Romans, several of these deities took on aspects of the incoming culture. The Romans also believed in woodland spirits which had strong links with nature. Such spirits also sometimes had powerful animalistic connections – for example, the satyrs who lived in the Italian woodlands were part-human, part-goat, and they represented unfettered nature in all its hedonistic and libidinous forms. Gradually, the separate Celtic and Roman myth forms began to merge to form hybrid gods such as Nodens Sylvanus, who was offered representations of hunting dogs at his sanctuary in the Severn Valley. Thus, the ancient Celtic hunting aspect of nature began to assume a fairly high place in Hiberno-Roman mythology.

It was the Vikings who completed the picture. Viking mythology was a mixture of lusty battle and hunt. Woden, chief of all the gods, would, from time to time, ride out across the sky mounted on his six-legged horse Slepnir, in a great progression accompanied by the other gods and heroes from Asgard (the Viking Heaven). Their passing was often signalled by rolling thunder and great flashes of lightning, or simply by a rushing wind. Folklore stated that it was best to stay indoors as this cavalcade passed by, because the ancient spirits had the power to take the incautious or curious person along with them.

Like the Roman tales before it, the tale of Woden's Ride was gradually to become incorporated within the overall pattern of Celtic myth and lore. Unrestrained nature, the notion of the riders among the clouds and the remembrance of hunting all became fused in the notion of the Wild Hunt. The ancient Celtic gods frequently hunted their quarry – sometimes animal, sometimes human – across the troubled skies, especially around the 'dark end of the year' (wintertime, when sudden storms were common), making people stay close to the security of their fires.

It is here that the mysterious figure of Herne makes his appearance, as sometime leader of the Hunt, although it is not certain when he actually assumed that role. In all probability, Herne is not a Celtic deity at all, although he does display attributes of the old woodland gods of the early Celtic peoples. Some commentators and folklorists quote Herne as a ghost or the spirit of some Saxon or medieval hunter (indeed, Shakespeare in *The Merry Wives of Windsor* cites him as a hunter who had hanged himself from an oak within Windsor Forest, thus giving him a localized association with Windsor Great Park), but his roots are conceivably much earlier and more widespread than that. St Fergus's cemetery on Inishkeen (County Fermanagh, Ireland), for example, contains an antlered stone head of a pagan Celtic nature divinity, and perhaps Herne is another guise. He is the 'Wild Man of the Woods', the 'Green Man' or a fundamental spirit of nature, living deep in the forest and emerging only when the Wild Hunt is at its height. Some depictions show him as part-stag, certainly hinting at the ancient Celtic hunting deities. Over time, some folklorists have argued, the hunting god was amended and changed, taking on more human characteristics and melding with other folk stories, to form the legend of Robin Hood, the outlaw and huntsman who lived with his band deep in trackless Sherwood Forest.

Herne was, of course, a demonic gift to the early Christian Church as it sought to lay down some sort of formal and unified orthodoxy among its followers. In the figure of Herne, the antlered man, swathed in animal skins, was the very personage of the Devil. It is no wonder, then, that the archetypal fiend is horned, shaggy and sports a long animal-like tail. Here are definite echoes of the early shaman or druid, clad in hairy robes and capering in the caves and isolated earthen forts which dotted the Celtic landscape. Under the influence of the Church, the nature of the Wild Hunt with Herne (or some similar figure) as its master subtly altered. No longer was it simply wise to avoid the Hunt as it passed for fear of being swept along with it – it was now a mortal *sin* even to glimpse the Hunt as it passed. The Hunt was now firmly associated with witchcraft and evil, and those beings who participated in it were either sorcerers or devils. Either that, or they were those who had been placed under some sort of punishment by God for their pagan or diabolic practices.

Some legends concerning the Hunt and dating from medieval and early modern times cite as its leader King Herla – reputedly the last pagan king of Britain – who made an alliance with the final remnants of a goat-footed race who dwelt far under the Pennines, and who, in penance, is condemned by God to ride with his men across the northern British skies until the Day of Judgement. In Porth Chapel and on Bodmin Moor in Cornwall, the spirit of the evil Squire Tregagle hunts through the skies with a pack of demon hounds at his heels.

In all these legends, echoes of the Wild Hunt persist and it was still thought wise to avoid seeing it or, indeed, to have any contact with the near-forgotten Celtic beings rumoured to dwell deep in the pathless forest glades...

Dusk was DRAWING ON and the light was failing all across the forest edge. From somewhere away in the open fields beyond the trees came the thin sound of an evening bell, calling the faithful to the last prayers of the day. Over the trees, dark clouds were gathering and a wind seemed to rise from nowhere, ruffling the branches fiercely as it passed. Away across far hills, great banks of cloud gathered in the increasing wind to signal an approaching storm. The forest creatures stirred fearfully in response – no living thing liked a winter storm. The distant bell called again reassuringly.

By the open door of the charcoal-burner's cottage, the boy watched the far-away cloud banks gather. Leaning heavily on his makeshift crutch, he moved position so that he could get a better view of the strange formations that they made. The hovel stood on the very edge of the forest where the trees were thinnest, and was little more than windowless mud walls thatched with wattle and rushes. High above, the evening clouds rolled closer and closer, assuming an ever more ominous aspect. There was something about them which frightened Peter: the way they writhed and moved, their edges fired with the last of the light, as if they had an intelligence all of their own. Their shapes both fascinated and repelled him. The monastery bell cried warningly and Peter hobbled further back into the confines of the doorway. He had been lame since birth.

The dwelling was dark and smoky. Around the primitive fire in the corner, his mother, brothers and sister were gathered. Some days ago, his father had gone to join the other local burners deeper in the forest and hadn't come back. That wasn't really unusual, for his father was generally gone for days – sometimes as much as a week or more – at a time. As the eldest of the family, Peter had been left in charge, but he knew that with his crippled leg he would be of little use if a massive storm were to break across the forest. His mother was a thin and sickly creature, always coughing and occasionally casting up the bloody flux, and the others were very young.

Peter had gone to the door, as he had seen his father do on countless evenings before, to look at the sky and see what sort of weather he could expect. The rising wind, the rolling clouds and the agitation of the forest animals warned him that the evening could turn from peaceful calm to raging fury, and he hoped that his father wouldn't be too long in the forest. One of the younger children was crying – a high, plaintive cry which matched the continual sound of the distant bell.

'Shut the door, Peter,' instructed his mother in her shrill, complaining voice. 'It's best that we keep it closed on nights like this.' As if in affirmation of her command, the wind soughed and whistled in the doorway. Peter turned around, the point of his wooden crutch skidding awkwardly on the earthen floor.

'I was watching for Father,' he answered rather hotly. He was now the man of the house after all! But his mother ignored his indignation.

'Your father won't travel on this night,' she replied indifferently, as she soothed the crying child. 'None will travel tonight. And it's best that we all keep close to the fire with our door closed and tightly barred – this night of all nights. This is the night of the Wild Hunt.' She was a darkly superstitious woman, brought up in the villages deeper in the forest where, said many, the Old Ways still persisted.

'There are old things still living deep in the woods – far older than any of us can remember – which won't go away,' she went on. Peter nodded, for he had heard this talk before. Something unseen, passing by the open door, pushed at him playfully, threatening to send him sprawling on the dirty floor. 'I even heard one of the Brothers from the monastery talking about the old powers,' she finished, without looking up. Peter pushed the door closed behind him, shutting whatever invisible forces lurked in the dark firmly outside the hovel.

He knew that she spoke the truth. In fact, he had even seen one of those old gods no more than a month ago, as he hobbled home from gathering firewood along the remote forest path. It had been late evening and Peter had passed by the edge of a gloomy glade, half-lit by the smoky fire of the afternoon sun. Shadows came and went across the rotting leaves which carpeted the place, and, among them, strange shapes which were not really seen but glimpsed out of the corner of an eye.

At one end of the clearing rested a large standing stone, dating back perhaps to more pagan times, and it was here that the shadows seemed to cluster most thickly. Standing opposite the ancient monument, part-hidden among the trees, Peter half-imagined, half-saw the dark, man-like, antlered figure which capered and danced close to the stone, gathering its coat of animal skins about it as it did so. He had heard a name for this being, a name that his mother had once whispered to him – Herne. This was, she had told him, the master of the Wild Hunt which raced through the woodlands on the wind, carrying off whatever it met into some distant netherworld beyond the skies. Peter watched the figure as it moved and weaved, now solid, now no more than a shadow against the stone.

'Are you truly the master of the Hunt?' he asked softly, no more than a whisper to himself.

'I am the Lord of all that lives.' the answer was sensed rather than actually heard. 'I am the Lord of the air and of the earth; of the wild woodlands and the peaceful meadows; of the sprouting vines of spring and the dying leaves of autumn. Once all men did homage to me and they will do so again.'

'This is not what the Brothers in the monastery say,' Peter's lips whispered, this time more loudly and defiantly. 'They say that the White Christ alone is Lord!'

'Their religion is young,' answered the shadow. 'Long before they were, I was. Let them have their season. When their faith is gone from men's minds, I will return again to claim what has always been my own.'

'The holy monks say that you are a demon...' began Peter, but the shadow merely laughed – the sound seeming like the whisper of the wind through the bushes.

'That is what their faith says. But then, the holy Brothers have always feared me, for they know that I am always here. Listen for me in the rippling of the stream when it teems with fish in the spring, in the crackle of the gorse fires on the summer hillsides, or in the roar of the wind in the winter storm. Take heed, child, and listen!' And Peter was alone in the glade, with stray strands of sunlight falling on the large stone.

That had been a month ago and now, with the oncoming winter tentatively grasping at the land with its freezing claws, the memory returned to haunt him.

'Watch for me in the roaring winds of winter,' the shadow had said, and with the wind rising outside the hovel, Peter was suddenly afraid. The monastery bell had now fallen silent and all that could be heard was the shriek of a rising storm as it rustled along the forest edge. He placed the great piece of wood which they used as a bar against the door, feeling the wind trying to push around the doorframe as if to seek entry. Then he joined his mother by the low, smoky fire and they all listened for the approach of the storm.

'Herne!' muttered his mother, even without thinking, as the wind began to whistle and bawl outside. As a forest woman, she knew the names of the old woodland gods – those names were still venerated in the villages hidden deep among the pathless foliage. The wind howled around the hovel in response, sweeping and gusting with a growing ferocity. It threatened to blow the flimsy structure over as it passed by. The people in the dwelling drew even closer together. Peter watched the wooden bar against the door as it moved slightly in reponse to the pressure of the wind outside.

Now he thought he heard other sounds – the baying of dogs, the thunder of horses' hooves, the jingle of bridle and stirrups, the blast of a horn – coming from far away but growing closer, ever closer. His mother's thin hand flew to her mouth.

'The Hunt!' she whispered, more to herself than to her children. 'Herne is leading the Hunt and it's coming this way! Oh, my children! Pray. Pray that he'll pass

you by.' Suddenly and inexplicably, the distant monastery bell began to peal. The far-away sounds drew closer, becoming clearer and clearer as they advanced.

'Watch for me in the roar of the winter wind.' The shadow's invitation echoed somewhere in the back of Peter's mind. It was the antlered man, wrapped in animal skins, leading horses and packs of dogs across the darkening sky. The old gods, the spirits of the dead, the half-seen shapes in the woodland, all travelled with him in the Wild Hunt. The rattle of their bridles, the sound of their hunting horns, the yapping of their dogs seemed just above the cottage now – so close, it seemed, that Peter could reach up and touch them as they passed over.

'Pray!' commanded his mother. 'Pray that they will pass us by!' And Peter prayed, part of his mind concentrating on the far-away voice of the monastery bell, but some deep part of him also excited by the sounds in the sky. Some of the other children began to cry, alarmed by the noise and by their mother's reaction to it. Something pushed at the frail door – it may have been only the wind, it may have been something else. The tree-bar held and the mother gave thanks. On such nights, Peter knew, the Wild Hunt had the power to take with it those whom it could snatch away. He concentrated on the faint cry of the bell again.

And yet there was an intoxication deep within his being – something that rejoiced in the thrill of the passing Hunt. It was something that had existed in all men since the dawn of time; he was at one with the wind and with the woods all around him. No longer was he lame and slow – he leapt and gambolled with the clouds and the storm, high above the forest trees. He was a part of the Green Man and the mysterious antlered shapes that danced in the woodland clearing. The night was filled with the blasting of the horn and the loud shout of unfettered nature. It was a joyous, thrilling sensation, unlike anything that Peter had ever experienced.

The ringing of the distant bells now grew steadily more desperate – the monks were tolling them furiously to drive away the storm. And as their peals rose to a crescendo, the sounds of the Wild Hunt began to die away over the forest. By the fire, Peter heard the sound of the hounds, the jingle of the horses' bridles and the cry of the hunting horn fade further and further into the night. His mother looked up from her prayer.

'Christ be praised!' she whispered. 'They've passed us by!' Even the wind was starting to die down, and the monastery bell resumed its slow and monotonous tolling. And yet, as he sat by the remnants of the pitiful fire, feeling the last of the inexplicable excitement drain from his body, Peter knew deep within himself that he had lost something of great value. He knew, too, that the Hunt might never come again, and with the regular tolling of the monastery bell the old shadows of the forest could be gone for ever, fled away as if they had never existed at all. And as he considered this, the tears glinted fresh on his cheeks in the firelight.

The Midnight Washerwomen

Of course, Celtic demons often took on forms, guises and associations other than those connected with animals and the natural world. In many parts of the Celtic world, the dead were treated with both awe and reverence, and it is therefore not surprising that dead ancestors also should assume the role of demons in the ancient mind. Indeed, there was a strong connection between formal Celtic mythology and the dead throughout the prehistoric world.

In a time when life expectancy was especially uncertain due to war, plagues and famine, there was an inherent wish among the ancient peoples for individuals to know the time of their death, so that they could make arrangements for their descendants. This knowledge was the province of the gods and spirits, but it also might be made known to individuals through various means. Later we shall look at the Banshee as a harbingers of death, but this was not the only type of death warning to be found among the Celts.

One of the more traditional of all the ancient Celtic deities associated with death was Clotha, the Washer at the Ford, who gives the River Clyde in Scotland its name. It is possible that this goddess was part of the old notion of the triple goddess of death and slaughter as epitomized by the crow, for she sometimes appears in tripartite form. In most legends, she is portrayed as an old hag (or, in some instances, *three* old hags) continually washing the shirts of those who are about to die in a swift-flowing river. To see her was a sure indication of approaching death.

Clotha appears in a number of ancient Celtic stories. For example, Cu Chulainn on his way into battle sees three ancient crones washing bloody corselets by the side of a river. As he rides past they greet him, but his men who are following him see nothing. Of course, Chulainn is slain before the end of the conflict, while those who have

followed him into battle survive. The belief may come from the ancient custom of washing the dead – the actual bodies of those soldiers who have been slain in battle – so that they can pass into the afterlife spotlessly clean.

The tradition of the deathly washers is kept alive in Brittany. A popular Breton belief concerns *les lavandières de nuit* (or in Breton, *cannard noz*) or the 'midnight/ phantom washerwomen'. While not exactly death warnings, these supernatural creatures are perhaps among the last vestiges of the Clotha belief, and are thought to be either demons or the ghosts of evil women condemned to wash mortuary sheets throughout eternity. The sound of them beating their linen in front of various washing places (always some way from the Breton villages) is usually heard around the hour of midnight and is greatly feared in country areas. The older generation of Bretons state that these beings have an intense antipathy to mortals and will seek to do them harm at every opportunity.

One of their favourite tricks, according to such tradition, is to lure a traveller from his or her path under the pretence of asking for help in wringing out their sheets. The traveller could not refuse, for they might be wrung out like a sheet themselves, with all the blood spilled from their body. If the traveller gave aid, then it was necessary, when wringing the sheets, always to turn in the same direction as the washerwomen, for if by any misfortune they turned in the opposite direction, they would have their arms wrung from their sockets in an instant. It was said that God had condemned these creatures to remain on earth until the Day of Judgement, but if they were to find some mortal who would turn the opposite way to them, they would be released from their toils. Consequently, Breton folklore abounds with stories about them...

I T IS LATE,' said the curé, 'and the light is failing. Perhaps you should spend the night with me here in the Parochial House and set out for home in the morning. No one knows what you might meet on the midnight roads.' Jean Vichon shook his head.

'I am grateful for your offer, padre,' he answered, 'but I have work to do on the farm first thing in the morning and I must get home tonight. Thank you for a pleasant evening.' The curé looked worriedly at the young farmer's son.

'But...' he began, setting down his wineglass. Jean raised his hand. As the eldest son of one of the most prosperous farmers in the district, he knew that his family still had great influence over even the clergy of the region.

'My mind is set, Father,' he answered, 'And I'm bound for home tonight. The corrigans, fees and phantoms which you have me meeting on the midnight roads are nothing more than the drowsy imaginings of old people in front of the fire – they can do me little harm.' The priest, however, still looked worried.

'There are all sorts of evil creatures...' he began, but Jean shook his head.

'I have far more reason to fear footpads and robbers in the dark than the creatures of your imagination, Father,' he said lightly. 'And I have a stout cudgel in my hand and a pistol under my coat.' The priest shrugged.

'It's of your own choosing, then,' he said. 'Go with God, my son, and may He and His angels look down upon you.' And he would do no more to deter him.

The road towards home seemed gloomier and longer than Jean had thought, but he had drunk well with the curé and was full of wine courage, and he strode out purposefully. He had been dining and drinking with the padre at Kerallen, about a mile from Carnac, and had stayed overlong, for as long as the wine and conversation flowed. However, with the moon high in the sky and a small sprinkling of stars scattered between the clouds, it was time to strike out for home, and Jean Vichon could delay no longer.

The road back to Carnac led through a number of scattered hamlets with their ancient bleaching greens and high crosses. At one place it went over a low bridge, where trees hung low across the road creating great pools of shadow and darkness. As he approached the bridge, Jean became aware of a steady, rhythmic sound coming from somewhere close by. It sounded, he thought, as if something were being hammered or pummelled, but though the great moon had lit up the road in front of him as clearly as at midday, he could see nothing there. In fact, the noise seemed to be coming from somewhere near the roadside, close to the bridge. As he drew nearer to the stone parapet it grew louder, and now appeared to come from somewhere below the widest span of the stone structure.

Jean crossed to the very edge of the road and looked down. There, in the shadows, just a little way from the bridge, a number of figures were crouched by the river's edge. They seemed to be women and yet he couldn't be sure, for their forms flitted in and out of the moonlight and seemed vague and uncertain. He advanced towards the parapet of the bridge until he was directly above the shapes by the riverbank, and looked down. There was now no mistake, they were women all right, but they appeared to be dressed in some bizarre and ancient way – the way in which local women had dressed, oh, perhaps a hundred years before. One of them stood in the shadow of a tall willow tree which spread itself out across the riverbank, one actually stood in the river with her dark and ragged skirts hoisted up around her knees in the fashion of peasant washerwomen, and the third was laying out white sheets on the grass above the water. Perhaps they were women from one of the hamlets that he had passed through, although what they were doing washing their clothes at this time of night, Jean couldn't imagine. He strained to see, but the wine and the shadows of the bridge-span made the shapes waver and dance in the moonlight.

One of the women wore some sort of cowl pulled up around her face, another had a shawl wound about her head, while the third had some kind of filthy poke bonnet balanced uncertainly on the back of her head, throwing her face into darkness. The woman in the river bunched a white sheet in her hand and began to pummel it against the rocks of the river – the noise which Jean had heard as he approached. She passed it to her companion on the bank, who spread it out along with the others. What were these women doing, washing their sheets in the river at this time of night? Why, it must be just after midnight and they were still working! Suddenly, as he watched the curious figures below, a frightening thought struck the farmer's young son, driving the last of the wine fumes from his head.

'My God!' he whispered to himself. 'The *cannard noz!*' As a child, Jean had heard of the midnight washerwomen who washed the shrouds of those who were about to die in the rivers around Carnac, but never did he think that he might see them one night. He had heard old people say that merely to glimpse them was an evil enough thing, but for them to see you was even worse! The trick now was to move on down the moonlit road without attracting their attention, or so the legends advised.

Jean turned around and began to creep away from the edge of the bridge, picking his footsteps carefully. The curé had been right: there *were* all sorts of things abroad on the midnight roads! He might have succeeded in his silent journey had not his shoe struck a large stone lying near the middle of the bridge. It bounced away with a loud clatter; and down by the river, one of the midnight washerwomen raised her head in his direction. Jean froze, but he was standing in a stray strand of moonlight and couldn't be missed.

'Behold!' The voice drifted up from the river. It seemed echoing and far away, and spoke in inhuman tones. 'Someone from the world of the living comes to spy upon our work!' The creature standing in the river raised her head as well.

'If he is so interested in what we do, let him come down and work with us!'

Jean turned and was ready to take to his heels, but he remembered just in time that to refuse the call of the *cannard noz* will invariably result in misfortune for those who disobey. Slowly he turned and made his way down from the bridge to the riverbank, where the *cannard noz* stood beckoning him onward.

The woman in the water raised one of the sheets which she was pounding, holding it out in Jean's direction.

'If this mortal takes so great an interest in our work,' she exclaimed, 'let him come and wring out the sheets with us until cock-crow. If he performs his task well, then he will be rewarded, but should he perform the task badly, he will die!'

Jean swallowed loudly. The moon had risen high overhead and he could see the women more clearly. At first glance they appeared to be not all that different from mortal women, but although the moon was high he still couldn't quite see their faces.

'Come forward, child of the living,' commanded the creature in the poke bonnet, beckoning to him with a thin white arm, 'and let us see how well you can perform the task which we set you.' She leaned forward to pass him the sheet, and for the first time Jean could see under her filthy bonnet in the moonlight. He checked an involuntary scream.

At first he thought that she had no face at all, but then, as he looked more closely, he saw the indentations of wide and staring eyes, a nose and a mouth held open in an unending shriek. All these features, however, seemed to be covered with a thin film of skin or some other material, giving her an almost faceless appearance. With his heart stopping within him, he reached out and took the sheet, momentarily touching the creature's hand as he did so. The touch of her skin was as cold as death itself and he quickly withdrew his hand, still grasping the clammy sheet.

'Now,' said his partner, 'we shall dance and wring out the sheet as we do so.' And she began to move gracefully along the bank, twisting the sheet into a long and thick white rope as she did so. Holding the other end very tightly, Jean tried to ape her movements, but the wine had made him clumsy, and anyway, his feet couldn't move as lightly as hers. There was something else which he had to remember as well. Desperately, he racked his brain, but he couldn't recall what it might be. The sheet between them twisted and river water fell from it to the ground in a puddle.

He twisted the sheet between his hands again, then, as he looked down, he saw that it wasn't a sheet at all – rather, it was a funeral shroud. At the other end, the phantom washerwoman screamed in demonic glee, her cry echoed by her unholy sisters.

Suddenly, Jean found himself wrapped up in the sheet that he was holding and it was being wrapped tighter and tighter around him. Claws like talons seemed to tear at his clothes and skin as the phantom washerwomen laughed and mocked him in terrible tones. Their voices held the sound of savage triumph. Then, suddenly, he remembered! When wringing out a sheet, the old ones said, it was essential to turn in the same way as the awful washerwomen – if the assistant turned in the opposite direction, then death would surely ensue. With a sinking feeling in the pit of his stomach, Jean realized that he had turned in the way directly opposite to that of his partner. As the shroud sheet was twisted ever more tightly about his body and the claws of the demons rent at his skin, he prayed silently for a quick death.

'Some sort of stroke brought on by drinking too much wine, I think.' The doctor was a small, bespectacled and bewigged figure who crouched down beside Jean's lifeless body. 'I would also think that he fell from the bridge up there and landed here on the riverbank.'

The curé nodded his head gravely as the doctor stood up.

The first rays of the sun were furtively stealing along the river, catching the water and lighting up the rushes and willows with a beautiful morning fire. It was going to be a glorious day.

'I knew that he had drunk far too much,' agreed the clergyman. 'I did warn him to stay by my fire and sleep it off, but he was obstinate like his father and nothing would do him but to set out on the road. Obviously the drink overcame him and he fell here to his death.' He looked at the fussy doctor. 'A stroke, you say?' The little man touched the cold and lifeless hand. It seemed clammy and slightly wet – and yet he knew that Jean hadn't fallen into the river.

'That is my medical opinion,' the doctor answered airily. The curé looked sadly down. Beside him, his manservant shifted uneasily from foot to foot.

'They say that the *cannard noz* were heard along this very stretch of river last night,' he murmured, half to himself. 'Maybe...' But the curé quickly waved him to silence. Such things were merely superstition and outside the realms of the Church. The clergyman turned his attention back to the body at his feet.

'I suppose we'd better go and tell his father,' he said slowly.

Away along the river, a fowl called with a high cackling sound like an unseen woman's laugh. The noise startled the three men on the bank. Swiftly, the curé's servant threw his coat over the body and the men turned back towards the roadway above. Behind them, in the swiftly flowing river water, something dipped and bobbed and weaved in the current – something which passed unnoticed by any of them. It seemed for all the world like the torn end of a sheet, or of a funeral shroud. Away along the bank, the hidden bird cackled again.

Fairies

Walt Disney and Tinkerbell have a lot to answer for! They have sanitized the fearsome fairy-kind into a child's tale. Fairies are now generally regarded as kindly and gentle gossamer-winged creatures, anxious to aid humans – the type of being who will lead the lost soul out of a dark forest; either that, or merry little figures dancing in a ring of toadstools. Of course, such sanitization stretches back into Victorian times, when our forebears took the terrifying legends of the past and turned them into stories for their children. For the ancient Celts, however, fairies were not such kindly beings, but rather the representation of the elemental forces of nature who, at best, were capricious in their attitude towards mankind and, at worst, were fully prepared to do humans some fatal mischief.

Who were the fairies? 'They are the old gods of the earth,' says the venerable *Book of Armagh*, firmly setting them within their folkloric context. And such an observation is correct, for as the natural gods of the Celtic world began to decline – beaten into submission by the advancing Christian Church – they were replaced by the notion of the fairy-kind. In fact, in many Celtic lands the notion of fairies was little more than a half-repressed folk memory of the ancient gods and spirits which had once inhabited the landscape.

And, of course, the notion of fairies still retained elements of this prehistoric belief. The Irish poet and writer W.B. Yeats made a useful distinction between the trooping fairies (the 'Macara Shee' or fairy cavalcade) and solitary fairies (those who dwell alone in remote and inaccessible places). We shall look at solitary fairies and sprites later, but it is well worth taking a look at the fairy host or trooping fairies now.

In a sense, these were – for the Celtic mind – the last vestiges of the ancient gods who processed across the world at certain times of the year. They were, if you

like, the last remnants of the Wild Hunt (see pages 40–41), which continued to survive in the Celtic folklore tradition of Squire Tregagle and his dogs in Cornwall or the Gabriel Hounds of Wales. Indeed, according to some (admittedly questionable) sources, the name fairy is said to derive from the ancient *fiah ree* (or *ri*) – loosely translated as the 'spirit race', thus attempting to establish clearly their connection with the ancient spirits of former times. They were an unseen host which passed across the countryside – usually after darkness had fallen – in a wild cavalcade, snatching away any and everyone they met on the roads. And it was not only humans they took with them, but also cows from the fields or hens from henhouses. These they cooked in great banquets at the end of each procession, and such repasts – reflecting, as they did, the feasts which characterized Celtic celebrations – frequently became the stuff of rural folklore and legend.

One word of warning, however: such beings usually resented the nomenclature 'fairy', and so it was inadvisable even to refer to them

by that name. Other epithets had to be found – the Good People, the Fair Folk, the Gentry and so on. And it was always wise to have your door tightly locked as the fairy cavalcade passed by.

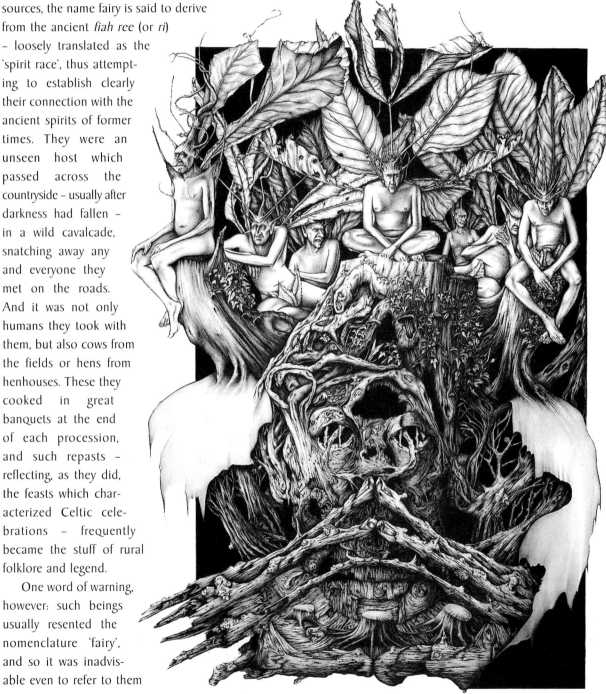

The Laird of Gesto

Arguably, nowhere is the tradition of the trooping fairies more prevalent than in the Highlands and Islands of Scotland. All across the windswept moors and between the lonely islands, large congregations of the creatures were said to travel at ferocious speeds – sometimes visibly and at other times invisibly. In the west, such a grouping was known as the Slaugh, the Spirit Multitude, or the Host. In fact, aspects of the Host have been absorbed into English to give us the word 'slogan' – *slaugh gairn*, the cry or calling of the Host, obviously denoting a battle cry.

In the west of Scotland, the Slaugh is also known as the Na Fir Chis, or Nimble Men – ancient Celtic gods who have been banished to the sky to become the Merry Dancers (or aurora borealis).

As might be suspected, the Host's relations with the humans whom they passed by were frequently not all that amicable. As they rushed past, the Host threw out fairy darts and bolts in order to do damage. These would strike humans at the doors of their houses, break windows or pitchers in the houses, or kill animals as they stood in the fields or about the barnyard. In some cases it was believed that the Slaugh could not themselves directly cause harm (since this was forbidden by God), but that they carried off unsuspecting humans whom they then forced to commit the dreadful acts. The folktales of the Western Isles are full of people being swept up, carried along with the fairy throng and forced to fire fairy darts at their neighbours or at their neighbours' property (usually against their will) at the malicious behest of the Host.

Occasionally, several branches of the overall Host did battle among themselves, a mark of the warlike nature of the fairy-kind. Their blood is spilled on the ground below, to the wonderment of passing humans. In Barra, the drops of blood are referred to as Fuil na Slaugh (the Blood of the Host) and is used to describe the red crotal obtained from the lichenous rocks of the island following a period of hard frost. Tradition says that these are droplets of congealed 'elf's blood' which has gone on to form 'blood stones' – rocks that have special supernatural powers if gathered together.

Quite often, the Slaugh travel about in little eddies of air or mini-whirlwinds which can cross both the land and the sea. If a Christian should see one of these passing by, they must always say 'God bless you', in case some unfortunate is being swept along with them. Upon the mention of the Holy Name, the fairies will be compelled to drop their captive and go in search of some other victim. It was considered an extremely charitable and godly act in the western Highlands to release a neighbour from the grip of the Slaugh. Those who had been taken by the Slaugh and then freed, however, were afterwards compelled to obey the 'call of the Slaugh' and travel with them at any time they were summoned. The Slaugh could take them anywhere, and there are tales of islanders finishing up as far away as Canada and the United States, carried there by the fairy Host. They usually had to find their own way back home again.

Although the fairies could be malicious towards humans, they could also appear quite kindly too, especially to those who approached them as they settled after their wild flight, reflecting the old Highland hospitality. However, one had to be very careful, for their kindness was usually mixed with mischief, as this tale from the west of Scotland demonstrates...

The Laird of Gesto in Skye was travelling, together with his manservant, to visit his kinsman in Benbecula in Uist. He went by boat and, after passing through a particular channel known as Eubhadh Point Channel, they landed at Airigh a' Phuill in Eubhal, from where they set out on foot for Benbecula. They had not gone far, however, when they were overtaken by foul weather and were forced to look around for shelter. Rain and sleet came down in great gusts, and they were caught in the open without even a bothy to keep them from the worst of the weather.

As the two men reached a great depression in the landscape called A' Chlaigeann, they were caught in a particularly driving downpour of sleety snow, and were about to collapse with cold and exhaustion when, directly in front of them, the laird saw a light shining through the blizzard. They made straight for it and were soon standing in front of the brightly lit window of a large house. The laird struck the door with his fist.

'Who knocks at our door?' asked a voice from within. It was full of catches and sobs, as if its owner were just fresh from crying. It didn't sound terribly human.

'It is two strangers sick and weary with the cold who knock upon your door,' replied the laird with all the authority he could muster, given the circumstances and the condition he was in. 'And we demand shelter under the ancient laws of hospitality!' There was a pause on the other side of the door, then the voice spoke again.

'Aweel, aweel,' it said. 'Then come in at once and be right welcome.' And there was the sound of stiff, heavy bolts being withdrawn and the door swung open. The laird and his manservant hurried in out of the rain and snow, hoping to find warmth and cheer.

The house was full of people, some apparently wet with the sleet and snow and all crowded together. At the other side of the fire an old grey man was sitting on a sutty-stool (a three-legged stool) dreaming in the heat. Who had opened the door, the laird had no way of knowing, for it seemed to have opened of its own accord. The old man eyed the strangers curiously, as if wondering what had brought them to the door on such a wild night. The laird made him none the wiser, for secretly he was half-frightened of the old fellow and his queer stare.

'Ye'll be wantin' to eat,' said the old man suddenly, 'and it's a poor house that can't feed its guests.' And he ordered one of the wet-looking men sitting by the fire to go out and get some food for the strangers. The man and several others went out, banging the door behind them, and there was a mighty roar of wind and a beating of wings from outside the house. The manservant's eyes became very wide, for he thought that there might be something just a wee bit uncanny here. The laird thought so too, but said nothing.

Hardly had they gone, but the man and his companions returned again. The old grey man asked them if they had brought anything with them for their guests to eat in the name of hospitality, but the man shook his head.

'We haven't a thing,' he answered. 'We travelled across Lewis and Barra and across Uist, North and South, and as far as Inverness on the mainland, but not a creature did we see that hadn't been blessed and we could do nothing.'

'Bah!' said the old man. 'That's not very good. Go away again and find supper for our guests. I won't have them saying that this is a hungry *brugh* that they've come to.' And so the man and his companions went out again into the storm. It slowly began to dawn on the laird and his lad that this was a fairy *brugh* and that those gathered about them were, in fact, the Slaugh that had troubled the Western Isles for so long. Even then, neither man said anything.

As before, hardly had the men gone than they were back – and between them they dragged a fine tawny cow. The servant's eyes widened, for he knew the creature well.

'Look!' he whispered, pulling the laird by the sleeve of his coat. 'By God, it's Prisaig!' That was the name of the cow. The laird, however, nudged him and told him to keep quiet.

The old man asked the others, 'Where did you get this one?'

One of them replied, 'We came through Gesto in the Isle of Skye and found the dairymaid milking the cows. As she was working, one of the cows lifted its hoof and kicked over the milk pail. The dairymaid got to her feet, lifted a spancel and struck the cow, saying, "You brute! May you never more be milked or driven to the fold and may you take whatever evil fate awaits you! I sincerely hope that the Devil himself flies away with you!" She spoke her curse hastily and in anger, of course, but when we heard it, we pounced on the animal and carried her off with us.'

'Well done!' said the old grey man. 'There's enough flesh on her bones to feed our guests grandly and ourselves forby.' He laughed unpleasantly. 'I'd like to see the owner of the cow when he realizes what has happened.'

'He will never know,' replied the other, 'for we left one of our own kin behind us – him that was old and dead – in the guise of a cow.' And they all laughed heartily, but the laird and his man kept their own counsel and didn't join in the merriment. The Slaugh cooked and ate the cow over the fire and the laird and his servant dined heartily with them on her meat. And never once did the Laird say who he was or that the cow was in fact his, for he had too great a dread of the Slaugh and what they might do to him.

The next morning the storm had passed, and the laird and his man thanked their hosts and set out upon the road for Benbecula. However, although his kinsman was pleased enough to see him, the laird couldn't settle. He kept thinking about his fine cow back in Skye and about how it had been taken by the Slaugh because of a dairymaid's curse. He stayed only a day in Benbecula and then set off for home again.

When he arrived in Gesto, he found all his household there on the very point of death. He soon discovered what was wrong with them – they had found the cow dead and had cooked and eaten it under the impression that it was a real cow. The laird immediately sent for the dairymaid and asked her what had happened between her and Prisaig. She hung her head but told him that nothing had happened.

'I don't think that this is true,' replied the laird, 'for did you not say, "May you never more be milked or driven to the fold and may you take whatever evil fate awaits you?"' The dairymaid was astonished, but admitted that it was so. At this, the Laird told them that they had eaten an old dead fairy man in the guise of a cow and that this is what was poisoning them. He healed all of them, through herbs, potions and purgatives, and soon all were back to fine health. But the dairymaid he dismissed.

This story contains other motifs besides the notion of the Slaugh - notably that of the changeling, which will be discussed later. However, this is the only story I know of concerning a disguised, dead fairy being *eaten* by humans, who then suffer the ill-effects of their unwitting feast.

IRELAND

The Trip to London

Although probably not as strong as its Scottish counterpart, the belief in the Slaugh is to be found in parts of Ireland as well. In some areas of Munster, for example, it was believed that the Slaugh had the power to carry off fresh corpses for their own purposes, and so the funeral bier upon which the coffin had rested was smashed at the end of the funeral to prevent this from happening. The same practice was carried out in the west of Scotland and in the Western Isles as well.

Irish fairies often travelled through the air or along lonely roads in great numbers. It was this 'cavalcade' that Yeats called the Macara Shee, or trooping fairies, and it was ill indeed for the person who met them. They had the power to carry mortals away with them into the fairy realm, never to be seen again.

This same power was held by a homogeneous group of fairy beings which inhabited Irish forts and raths. Although not necessarily specifically referred to as the 'Slaugh', they nevertheless demonstrated some of the same characteristics. For example, they would descend upon some unsuspecting soul and carry that person off with them.

In some country areas, attempts were made to impose a form of order upon this roving group of fairies. They were designated in the rural mind as a procession, travelling only along country roads in some kind of strict formation. Such processions only occurred on certain nights of the year – May Eve and Hallowe'en, for example – when the doors of the fairy raths and forts all over the countryside stood open,

and they were not to be witnessed by mortal eyes. The cavalcade was headed by the king and queen of the rath, with all their courtiers coming behind. A jester – the Fool of the Forth – jumped along beside the procession, carrying a large stick, and it was his mission to keep away any unwelcome visitor. This he did by striking them with his stick and taking away their wits and physical senses. In fact, the medical term 'stroke' may well have come from this particular belief, since it was a stroke that the fairy ministered which often caused paralysis. It was as well to stay inside as the fairy cavalcade – no matter how well organized or spectacularly grand it was – passed by your door.

Fairy processions were also often closely associated with the dead. These were known as 'fairy funerals' and always occurred at the 'dark time of the year' (between Hallowe'en and Christmas). At this time, the souls of all those who had died within the previous year were escorted by the fairies to the very gates of Heaven, as commanded by God. It is worth noting that the fairies themselves, having no souls, were not permitted to enter Heaven, a source of great annoyance to them, and so they were especially dangerous and hostile towards humans around this time. They had the power to take those whom they encountered with them into the next world, simply out of pure spite.

However, it is the swarming fairies – the Irish equivalent of the Scottish Slaugh – whom the Irish call the 'fairy wind', who form the basis of the following story from north Antrim...

There was a man named Thomas McCaughan who lived in the townland of Craig between Dunseverick and Toberkeigh (the blind well). He had a wife and one daughter and they lived in a long, low cottage by the side of the road which led up from Dunseverick village and past the old fairy rath at Ballyloughbeg near Straidbilly. The rath was a dark and gloomy place with queer, broken shadows coming and going there, even on the brightest day. And sometimes at night it seemed to be brightly lit with the lights of the Good People (fairies), who would come and make ceilidh there. It was as well to stay away from the place when these things were happening, but Tom McCaughan was cursed with a curious nature and liked to see what was going on about the countryside, especially at night. It was this curiosity which was to get him into deep trouble.

One evening, around Hallowe'en, just as the sun was starting to set, he took a stroll out to enjoy the night air. He didn't go far, just down to the corner of his house and then to the top of his own yard, where he stopped to light his pipe and look out across the fields to the fairy rath. And as he watched, there seemed to be a great stir down there, with lights darting about back and forth like lanterns and the bushes stirring strangely, even though it was a pleasant evening and there was only a slight breeze. Seized with a great curiosity, McCaughan walked down to the edge of his yard to see what was happening in the rath – and this was his undoing. Suddenly, the stirring among the bushes increased and a great wind rose up out of the rath, seemingly filled with angry, muttering voices. It caught the tails of his coat and was so strong that it lifted him clean off his feet. Up and up it carried him, high over the fairy rath, high over the fields and high over his own house. It was a fairy wind, you see, and as it bore him along, McCaughan was poked and prodded by unseen fingers and his skin was raked by invisible and razor-sharp nails.

The wind carried him onwards, over the houses of Dunseverick village, over the little harbour there and out over the wild Atlantic. He was shouting and screaming, calling for help, but nobody could hear him above the constant roar of the wind and the muttering and murmuring of the angry fairy voices. They were all around him, bearing him along, and he couldn't see one of them. Below him, the waves crashed and pounded and the lights of ships passed far beneath his flying form.

Soon McCaughan crossed the coast of England and only then did the wind begin to slow down, for Irish fairies have only a fraction of their power on English soil. It began to fall away and McCaughan began to drop lower and lower in the air. Ahead of him, he suddenly saw the lights of a grand city, and he was just passing over it when the wind suddenly stopped and he fell like a stone into the streets below him. Battered and bruised from all the poking and buffeting that he'd received, he fell into a darkened lane just off a main thoroughfare and there he lay, groaning, and without so much as a penny in his pocket with which to bless himself.

The city to which the wind had taken him was London, and a grand place it was, if you had plenty of money. But McCaughan was as poor as a church mouse. He knew nobody at all there, and he had nowhere to go and no way of getting back to Ireland. In order to get his boat fare home, he had to look about for jobs and take what he could get. He did all the menial jobs that few people wanted – washing dishes, portering in hotels, cleaning the streets in the early morning. He had to live in the cheapest hostels and boarding houses that he could find, and every penny he had left after he'd fed himself and paid his rent, he put away towards his fare home. It was hard and thankless work, but he saved and and saved and spent very little on himself.

McCaughan lived in London for two years, and at the end of that time, he had enough money gathered together for the fare and a little bit over as well. All the time that he had been in England, he'd never forgotten his wife and daughter back at Toberkeigh, and he had missed them greatly. 'I must bring them something back from England,' he said to himself, 'and, as I've a wee bit of money left over after I've paid the fare, I'll buy them each a present.' So off he went to one of the big stores in London and bought a dress for his daughter and a fine shawl for his wife, both of which he had wrapped up in separate parcels. Then, putting the parcels under his arm, he set out for the boat to take him home.

Hardly had McCaughan set foot on the quayside, than he felt the same wind that had brought him begin to swirl about him again. Once more it was full of whisperings and mutterings, and he felt the fingers of the fairies poking and prodding at him as they had done before. It caught the tails of his coat and was so strong that it lifted him again, parcels and all, carrying him out of the city and into the sky. Higher and higher he rose, until all of London was spread out beneath him like a map. And the wind carried him on – out over the countryside with its thick woods and dreaming farmlands and away towards the coast. Below him, towns, villages and hamlets passed in a wink; once he almost collided with the spire of a church, and another time he passed through a flock of crows going home to roost in a great forest, but soon he could see the sparkle of the sea in the distance and he knew that he was near the coast. As darkness set in, the sea passed beneath him, and once more he could see the lights of ships as they crossed and re-crossed the night-bound ocean.

Then, as daybreak arrived, McCaughan reached the coast of Ireland and still the wind rushed on. When he looked more closely, he could see the old schoolhouse at Toberkeigh far below, and he saw cottages and buildings that he recognized. Soon he was over the townland of Craig and there was his own house, far beneath him. The wind suddenly dropped and he found himself falling towards his own fields. He might have broken his neck, but he fell on to a bag of lime which someone had left lying beside a gentle (fairy) bush at the side of his own yard. Instantly, the murmuring and muttering was gone, as the fairy horde disappeared into the old rath across the fields. Dusting himself down, McCaughan made his way up to his house, still holding tight to the parcels in which he had the presents for his wife and daughter. As he walked up to the cottage, he saw the two women, working away just as they had been doing on the night that he'd been carried off to London. Neither of them even looked up as he came in, nor took the slightest notice of him. If he'd been expecting them to run and put their arms around him with joy, he was sorely disappointed.

'Well,' said he, 'this is a fine welcome home all right. Here you both are, spinning and baking bread just as you were on the night that I was taken away. And neither of you has a word of welcome or kindness for me after my being gone for two long years.' His daughter looked up from her bread-making and laughed.

'Two years!' she replied. 'What's this nonsense that you're talking? Sure you've only been away for two minutes!' McCaughan was staggered.

'Indeed, I have not!' he answered her very hotly. 'I've been away working in London in England these past two years! And I'll soon prove it to you, for I've brought you both some presents from one of the big department stores over there. Here's a dress for you, Molly.' And so saying, he laid the parcel on the table and opened it. There was no dress to be seen and the parcel was full of horse dung. Distractedly, he turned to his wife.

'And I brought a shawl for you, Susan,' but when he opened her parcel, it was the same material.

'Wait!' he cried at last, 'for I can still prove to you both that I was in London. I made a good deal of money while I was there and I still have the fare home in my pockets, for I was carried there and back by the fairy wind! Here, I'll show it to you – it's all English coins.' But when McCaughan opened his pockets they, too, were full of dung mixed with stones, leaves and acorns. That's always the way of it with money which has been touched by the fairies.

Tom McCaughan had been under the fairy influence all right, because of his curiosity about what was going on in the rath. He never got over the experience and it is said that he died soon after. That's what happens if you meddle with the Good People in their forts. This is a story still told by the grandson of Tom McCaughan, who is living near Toberkeigh to this very day.

This story demonstrates another interesting aspect of human–fairy relations – the passage of time. It was said that time passed much differently in the fairy realm to how it did in the human world. In most cases, humans believed that they had only spent a few hours with the fairies, when in fact they had been gone for hundreds of years. This is the only tale that I know of in which time passes in the reverse manner.

The Prisoner of Garwick Glen

It was one thing to be carried off by the fairies (Slaugh or 'fairy wind'), but quite another to break free of their enchantment and return to the normal world. Sometimes abductees were returned after only one night; sometimes they were never returned at all. If they were returned, it was usually at the whim of the fairy-kind themselves, although such releases sometimes occurred through the actions of another human being.

For example, in parts of Ireland, when seeing a fairy whirl-wind it was customary to say 'God bless you', whereupon the fairies would be compelled to release whoever they were carrying. A common story from County Tyrone in Northern Ireland tells of an old man who stood at the corner of his house as a wind passed over it. Above its roar, he heard a child crying. 'Ah, God bless the wee child,' he said to himself, whereupon the child dropped into his arms from out of the sky. The fairies had been carrying it off to a nearby rath, but their power had been broken by the old man's blessing. The man took the child and raised it as his own – not knowing who the mother or father might be – and many people all across Tyrone claim that particular baby as an ancestor.

In Scotland, too, it was necessary to invoke the Holy Name to prevent the fairies from carrying someone off. A sprig of mountain ash attached to the band of a hat or the end of a shawl would usually have the same effect – the fairies would have no power over whoever wore these and, if the wearer was carried off, would be forced to return them immediately. The Holy Cross, a written prayer or a series of holy words would be enough to deter anyone from being carried away by the fairy horde. In order to protect a child from being taken, the father's clothes would be placed across the crib, probably as a signal of human kinship and ownership, and as a warning to the fairy-kind. Even with many of these protections, however, unwary or careless individuals were still spirited away.

The Isle of Man, had its tales about those who were carried off by the *farish* or Guillyen Veggy (the fairy horde), and the efforts of their neighbours and relatives to release them from fairy influence. It was dangerous, said the very old Manx folk, to wander at Cronk-yn-Irree-La on the slopes of Dalby Mountain, for the eerie murmuring sounds of the fairy Host were often heard there at certain times of the year. The Manx called these sounds Sheean-ny-Feaynid – the Sounds of Infinity – and said that they were indisputable proof that the fairy Host dwelt on the mountainside. The following story, which demonstrates this motif, comes from the personal experience of an old resident of Douglas and was recorded around the turn of the century...

Over fifty years ago, I attended a gathering in Laxey which went on long into the evening. It was a grand occasion with plenty of drinking and danc-ing, and I was in very high spirits when I left to walk the distance between Laxey and Douglas. I was in the company of a young girl whom I'd met at the gath-ering and she was returning to Douglas with me. I knew her well, for she was a friend of my sister and was jolly company to be with on such a walk. It was about 12 o'clock when we left Laxey and I hoped that we'd be home well before morning.

When we were about five miles from Douglas, round about Ballagawne School, I heard a noise in the air close by. It was a sound like a good number of people talk-ing and muttering among themselves, although I couldn't make out a word that they were saying. The girl who was with me must have heard it too, for she looked all around her as if trying to see where it might be coming from.

'What's that?' she asked me, but I couldn't tell her, for I was as mystified as she was. It was like being right in the middle of an invisible throng. Then, away in the distance along the road (for it was now getting quite light), I saw a number of figures – maybe about five or six of them – coming towards us, and I wasn't sure at all that they were human. They were coming up the Garwick road to a place where it joined the main road, and if we kept on our present course we would very soon meet up with them. The girl wanted to turn back for she was becoming very frightened, but I said that there was a byroad up ahead which we could take to avoid meeting with them. She took a few steps further, but as she did so the noise in the air became louder and much more agitated. It swirled around us like a cloud of angry bees, and at this my companion became very frightened and tried to turn back for Laxey. She had taken only one step when she was lifted off her feet by invisible hands and carried forward towards the end of the Garwick road and the figures that were waiting there for her.

With a great fear rising in the back of my throat, I hurried on towards the by-road that I had mentioned. Nothing befell me, although I was conscious that the invisible throng travelled with me. The road took me down into a peaceful little valley called Garwick Glen, but though the Glen itself seemed very quiet, it was as if the invisible Host was still all around me, pushing and prodding at me with unseen fingers. I didn't stop in the glen but kept running as fast as I could. At last I began to mount a hill on the other side, and suddenly a strange feeling of quietness and calm came over me, as though I had broken free from the clutches of the unseen horde. I looked back along the glen road, thinking that I might see my companion hurrying to catch up with me, but not a hair of her did I see. The road behind me was perfectly empty. I turned and ran on to Douglas, never looking behind me all the way.

Well, as you can imagine, my companion's disappearance caused a bit of a stir. She had been seen leaving the gathering with me and she had never arrived in Douglas. Her parents waited for a couple of days before coming to see me and asking what had happened to her on the road. I told them as best I could, but I knew by their faces that they didn't believe me. There were some about Douglas who did, though, for Garwick Glen was known to be a place where the Guillyen Veggy (little fellows or little boys – the fairies) were frequently to be seen and heard. Nevertheless, there were still many people who thought that I'd done something terrible to her – maybe even killed her. This rumour was getting about, and I was frightened that it might come to the ears of the authorities and that some law enforcement might be involved, so that I'd find myself in prison in Peel Castle. I thought then that I'd do something about getting her back myself.

So it was that I went back to Garwick Glen a few nights after my original experience there. I wanted to know what had really happened to my travelling companion and this seemed the only way to find out. As soon as I arrived at the head of the glen, the air all around me seemed suddenly to be full of whisperings

and mutterings, as though the hidden throng were well aware of my presence. Swallowing a little (for there was a terrible fear rising in me), I called out the name of my companion across the empty glen. There was no reply, and the road in front of me stretched long and lonely, down through Garwick Glen. I called again, and the muttering around me seemed to increase.

Then, as if from a long way away, I heard the girl's voice calling out my own name. There was a touch of desperation in that call, as if she were being held against her will and wanted to be free. I called again and told her to come to me, but the reply came that she could not. Then I knew that she was being held by the Guillyen Veggy somewhere in the glen in front of me.

Now, when I was young I learned a prayer against the power of the fairies from my grandmother, who was a very wise old woman from Peel. That was the only thing that I could think of to release the girl from their clutches. Just as I opened my mouth to say it, I saw the queer figures that I had seen before. Away down the road in front of me, they seemed to be coming towards me. They were so far away that I couldn't make them out in the poor light, but I was now certain that they weren't human and that they were fairies. Realizing that this was a trick to put me off, I swallowed hard and said:

'*Jee saue mee vosh cloan ny moyrn*' ('God protect me from the children of pride/ambition'), as my grandmother had taught me. Immediately, there was a sound like distant thunder and the road in front of me seemed to waver about and to go in and out of focus. The muttering in the air appeared to grow into a scream

of rage and hatred, and the figures in the road in front of me shrivelled in on themselves and disappeared completely. I looked down the road, and there was the girl coming towards me. She was in a state of great dishevelment and bewilderment, and could remember nothing of what had happened to her or where she had been. One moment, she'd been walking along the road with me near Ballagawne schoolhouse, and the next she was on the road through Garwick Glen. There was no recollection in between.

I took her home, and her parents were overjoyed to see her. She seemed none the worse for her adventure, save for the loss of memory, but people did comment that a great deal of the fun had gone out of her. She sometimes had a dreamy, faraway look about her, as if she were not paying much attention to the mortal world but had her eyes fixed on something that no one else could see. That is sometimes the way of it with those who have been taken away by the fairy Host. A short time after this incident, the girl left the Isle of Man to go and work in America and I never heard tell of her again, even though we had always been very close.

Sometimes, I would go back and look down the road which leads through Garwick Glen. Never again did I hear the mutterings and whisperings in the air, nor did I see anything at all strange there. I'm not truly sure what I saw on that day – the old folks will tell you that my companion was carried away by the fairies and that I somehow saved her from them – but the impression which has been left upon my mind is that the Glen is still inhabited by a race of beings who are absolutely real, but not wholly human. That's what I think, anyway.

Merfolk

Certain ancient Christian traditions relate that when Lucifer and his minions rose in revolt against God, some angels 'sat on the fence', supporting neither God nor the Devil. When the revolt had ended and the Devil was chained, it was considered that these particular angels were neither good enough to be admitted back into Paradise nor evil enough to be consigned to Hell. St Michael interceded for them and asked God to place them between the two, in the world of men. God accepted this plea and so the angels were thrown into the human world – some to dwell in the air (becoming spirits of the air) and some to dwell under the earth (becoming trolls, goblins and so on). The majority, however, were cast into the sea to become the forerunners of the merfolk, who, according to legend, still dwell there. This story is often used to explain the origins of the fairy race and their connection to St Michael (who is the patron saint of fairies), but it is also, more probably, an attempt to 'Christianize' old pagan beliefs concerning the elemental nature of the ocean.

The coastal Celts viewed the ocean with as much awe and deference as their counterparts inland regarded the earthen raths and forts of the countryside. A beneficent sea could give them an abundance of food in the form of fish; an angry and turblent ocean could take their lives and smash their frail craft in an instant. Like the weather, the sea itself had to be placated. This belief bestowed a form of intelligence upon the ocean, which manifested itself in the form of ancient and perhaps localized water-gods. Over a period of time, these gods were slowly transformed into beings (sometimes supernatural) who dwelt beneath the waves. These were the immortal inhabitants, in the early Celtic mind, of Tir fo Thoinn (the Land Beneath the Wave), a wholly separate society from that which lived on the land.

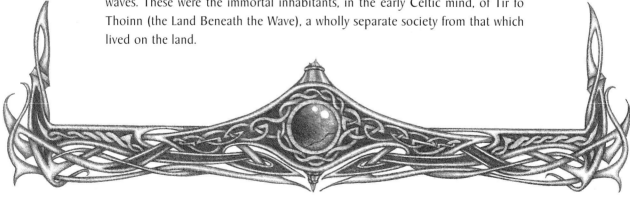

Although no human could live for long in the water, the dwellers of this sub-aquatic realm could reside among mortals if they so chose. Usually, however, they had to discard some memento of their former existence in the sea before they could set foot on land. In some cases, this might be a sealskin cloak, but it might also be something else. Yeats, for example, speaks of a cap made out of feathers known as a *cohullen druith*, which the sea-people wore when in the ocean. If such mementoes were stolen by mortals, the sea-folk could not return to the ocean. Both races – mortal and immortal – could intermarry and have children. In fact, several Irish families – such as the Flahertys and O'Sullivans of Kerry and the MacNamees of Clare – trace their ancestry from such beings. There are many others, too, from places right across the Celtic world, who claim ancestry among the folk of the sea.

Generally speaking, merfolk fell into two distinct categories: the mermaid (who was breathtakingly beautiful and often attracted to human men) and the merman (who was appallingly ugly, argumentative and incredibly spiteful towards mortals). It was, unsurprisingly, the mermaid who usually attracted the most attention and who forms the basis of many folktales throughout Celtic coastal settlements. Tales concerning mermaids and those who have consorted with them provide a great corpus of Celtic sea-going mythology, and who can say – perhaps there is some germ of truth underpinning them. Maybe there is some distant race memory among the Celtic peoples of an ancient race who once lived in or near the sea, all traces of which have been lost to historical record.

The Sea-Bride

Ar bharr na dtonna's fa bheal tra,
Suid chugaibh Mary Chindh's i
ndiaidh an Eirne 'shnamh'.

As I ride on the billows and drift with the tide,
I give you Mary Kinney, who has swum the
ocean* wide.

*Eirne is an old Irish term for the ocean.

The words of a very old Gaelic song, 'An Mhaighdean Mhara' ('The Mermaid'), reveal just how ancient contact between humans and the sea-people is. Although Mary Kinney is (to the best of my knowledge) the only mermaid to be named formally, her story is a common one in Celtic folklore. A fisherman falls in love with a mermaid, and he knows that by taking away her cap (or crown) she will remain on the land and will forget her origins. He does this and hides the cap in an old trunk in the barn. The mermaid forgets her roots in the ocean and lives with him, and together they have a family – a boy and a girl. One day, while playing around the barn, the children open the trunk and discover the cap. Not knowing what it is, they take it to their mother, who places it on her head. As she does so, recollection immediately flood back and she yearns once more for the wild sea. This yearning is so strong and so irresistible that the mermaid, Mary Kinney, leaves her husband and children, who never see her again.

Mermaids in both Scotland and Ireland, of course, were much different from the stylized mermaid (half-woman/half-fish) with which we are all familiar. This is a comparatively recent perception of the sea-folk and comes from English folklore around the sixteenth and seventeenth centuries. The pure Celtic tradition is much older.

There is no discernible physical difference between mortals and mermaids in Celtic lore. However, the mermaid usually travels through the cold sea currents, wrapped in a sealskin cloak and this gives her the appearance of a seal. It is quite common for Irish and Scottish fishermen to confuse the merfolk with these creatures. When she comes on to the land, the mermaid must abandon her cloak, without which she cannot return to the ocean. This means that anyone who finds the cloak has power over the mermaid, since they can control her return to the sea. Because mermaids are so beautiful, certain seafarers felt impelled to hide these cloaks and demand that the mermaids marry them, since they could no longer return to their own realm in any case. Usually there was prodigious issue from such unions, giving rise to a large human/merfolk population in certain coastal areas.

The following story, which is widely told throughout the north of Ireland, usually with a number of local variants, is said to trace the origin of the McCurdy family of north Antrim from one of the most famous sea-maidens – the Raghery (Rathlin) Mermaid...

THERE IS STILL A PLACE UP ABOVE BALLINTOY where you can see the sea-people at their sport. If you stand at the top of a great cliff close to the village and look out towards Raghery (Rathlin Island), you can sometimes glimpse them leaping between the waves and disappearing beneath the swell of the sea – but you have to be quick, for they can be mistaken for seals or great fish, or even a gull diving for food along the ocean surface.

And if you were to climb up as far as Carrick-a-rede and look down across the bays below, you might still see the tumbled ruins of the small fisherman's cottage where Dan McCurdy lived all those years ago. He was a great fisherman in his time and sailed with boats that went as far away as Islay and Bute and to the harbours of Skye and Rum, sometimes even as far as lonely Mingulay away in the west.

They say that he was a good looker, too, but though he sailed to those far-away places and met with pretty girls – both Scots and Irish – he never took a wife. He lived all alone in that low whitewashed cottage, a little way beyond Carrick-a-rede.

One evening McCurdy was taking a pipe by the seashore, as was sometimes his way, just as the sun was touching down on the horizon on its way to bed. It had grown very chilly and a bit of a breeze was blowing in from the sea, and so he had turned up the collar of his coat and taken shelter behind a great rock which stood near the ocean edge. Indeed, he stood so close to the sea that an incoming tide lapped around his feet. He was standing there thinking, when he suddenly became aware of laughter somewhere close at hand. It was a merry and carefree sound, like the innocent laughter of children or young women, and McCurdy's heart was filled with gladness at it. He looked along the rocky coast nearby, but could see nothing except the grim, grey rocks spotted with crotal. Apart from a few lone gulls, nothing moved there. He turned his head, and it now seemed to him that the laughter came from the sea itself. He sank deeper into the shelter of the rock and looked out towards the ocean. His eyes widened in astonishment.

Several large seals were rising out of the tide and moving towards the shore in a line. They seemed just like people treading water – and the similarity didn't stop there, for as they touched the seashore, their skins seemed to crumple and fall away, just like discarded garments. Out of the fallen sealskins stepped several young and beautiful maidens. It was their laughter that the fisherman had heard. They came ashore, still laughing and splashing each other, and it was clear that they were so engrossed in their sport that they didn't see McCurdy where he hid. He stayed where he was to watch what was happening. The girls, still playing, went on along the coast, passing very close to the place where he hid. One of them caught the man's eye – the youngest and most beautiful of them all. She had dark hair which curled about her face in thick coils like seaweed and eyes which were as deep a green as the ocean itself. McCurdy's heart went out to her instantly – but he was fearful of the merry throng, too, for he knew that they were sea-people and that they were not fully mortal. Still, he felt a great longing in his heart for the beautiful woman who had unwittingly passed him by.

There was an old legend which McCurdy had heard from his grandmother that if a mortal were to take the sealskin cloak of a mermaid he would have her in his power and she would have to do as he demanded. A dark plan began to hatch in the back of his mind. Slipping from his hiding place, he went to the spot where she had discarded the cloak. It still lay there, washed by the edge of the tide, and, lifting it, McCurdy slid it under his jacket and took it home with him. There, he placed the cloak up in the skraghs of the house (a small space between the edge of the wall and the thatch) where it could not be found. Then he made himself some tea and bread and sat down to wait.

He waited until it was almost morning and then heard a low tapping at the front door. Smiling to himself, he got up and, on lifting the latch, found the mermaid standing there in the first light of morning. She seemed more beautiful than ever.

'Are you the mortal that has stolen my cloak?' she asked in a soft, slightly timo-rous voice, which reminded McCurdy of the swish of the spring tides across the sand of the isolated bays along the coast.

'I am,' he replied. The mermaid regarded him with her large and languid eyes.

'Then you must give it back,' she told him, 'for I cannot return to my home in the sea without it.' McCurdy appeared to be considering what she had asked. Then he shook his head very slowly.

'It's an enchanted thing,' he said, 'and I've hidden it where no one can find it. I don't think it would be right for me to be dealing with the people of the sea, so I'll hold on to it for a while and see what the priest says about it.' The mermaid's eyes began to fill with tears and looked even more like deep pools between the rocks on the seashore.

'I would beg you to return it,' she said softly. 'I can take you to caves where smugglers have hidden great casks of brandy and tobacco. I can take you to a ship-wreck lying beneath the waves, just a little way off the shore, where gold lies in the hold, piled as high as a man's chest, all of it for the taking. These things I will do if you will return my cloak to me.' Once again, McCurdy seemed to be considering her words, and then once again, he slowly shook his head.

'What would I have to do with smuggled contraband?' he asked her. 'I'd soon be arrested by the local soldiers. And, even if I could swim out with you to the sunken shipwreck, how could I bring all that gold ashore without sharing it with my neigh-bours? Besides, I am content enough here in my little cottage and have no great wish for vast fortunes or expensive things. I think I'll hold on to your cloak and show it to the priest.' There was also an old belief that if a priest so much as touched the enchanted sealskin cloak, it would lose all its power and the mermaid could never return to the sea. Tears were now running unchecked down her beautiful face.

'Please!' she whispered. 'Give me back my cloak so that I can return to my own people. How can you be so cruel, mortal? Is there nothing that I can do for you?' McCurdy appeared to think for a moment, although he had known that this would happen and had planned his answer carefully.

'Well,' he said slowly. 'Since you cannot return to the sea and have now to live on the land...' He paused. 'And since I am alone here and without a wife, maybe you could wed with me. After a while I'll think about the cloak again, and if you've been good to me, maybe I'll give it back.' He had no intention of keeping his word of course, but the mermaid had no choice but to accept his offer. There was indeed no way that she could return to the sea. The tears in her eyes spilled over down her cheeks.

'I have a husband already back in Tir fo Thoinn,' she told him, 'but if you will promise to return my cloak in the future, I'll marry you, since I cannot go back to the sea without it.' And McCurdy gave her his word that he would think about giving her the cloak, though he had no intention of keeping his promise.

So Dan McCurdy and his sea-bride were married. I've heard it said that they were not married in any Christian ceremony (since no mermaid would have anything to do with a clergyman) but in the 'old style' (the pagan marriage of the Western Isles). Afterwards, the mermaid went home to live with him in the little cottage near Ballintoy. She made him a good wife and it was said that none could really tell the difference between herself and any other woman of the countryside, excepting in three things – she never entered a place of worship; she never ate fish; and she had very flat feet. She bore McCurdy three children, two boys and a girl, none of whom had their mother's looks or ways about them at all.

She looked after them all well, and over the years Dan McCurdy grew to love her very deeply, although it was not his way to tell her so. And, for herself, the mermaid seemed happy enough, although some nights when the moon was on the water, she would go to a little point just above Ballintoy and look wistfully out across the ocean. Sometimes, just as the sun was setting, a great bull seal would climb on to a rock and roar towards the land and the woman who stood watching him. Several times he came and several times McCurdy saw him. The fisherman's heart was filled with jealousy, for he suspected that this was her husband from Tir fo Thoinn and that he was calling her back to the waves. He would then go back home and check that the cloak was still there – hidden in the skraghs where none but himself could find it. If his mermaid-wife wished to return to the sea she made no mention of it, nor was the cloak ever mentioned again, and it is reasonable to suppose that in her own way she also loved the fisherman and their children.

One day, when McCurdy had gone with a boat crew to fish off Islay, a great storm blew up. The sea, whipped by a fierce wind from the north, rose high and angry, and McCurdy's boat, bound for home, was forced to take shelter at Raghery until the worst of the weather had passed. Back near Ballintoy, the wind grew wilder and wilder, and McCurdy's wife became greatly concerned that it would lift the thatch from their cottage. Taking a ladder, she went out into the rain to secure the roof and, as she did so, the wind lifted a corner of the thatch and there, lying in the skraghs of the dwelling, she found her sealskin cloak.

On his way home from Raghery with the storm now over, McCurdy sensed that something was wrong and, as the boat touched land, he leapt ashore and ran up towards his house. Even as he approached the dwelling, he knew that his foreboding had been right, for no smoke came from the chimney and the door stood wide to the world. His children were sitting by the empty grate and there was no trace of their mother. Distractedly, he rushed to the corner of the house and looked in the skraghs. The sealskin cloak was gone – she had found it and had returned to the sea.

He never saw her again – at least not in any human form. For many years after, Dan McCurdy lived with his children in the low cottage above Ballintoy. He never took another wife and became strange and solitary in his ways. Often, he was to be seen walking along the beach at low tide, looking longingly out to sea as though searching for something. Sometimes, just as the light was fading, two great seals would climb on to a rock nearby and watch him with an intense, almost human stare. Then one of them would leap back into the ocean, leaving the other to watch the lonely fisherman with a long, lingering gaze. And McCurdy knew that his bride from the sea hadn't wholly forgotten her mortal husband.

His children grew up and the two boys became great fishermen in the area and the girl married a wealthy farmer from Ballycastle. All of them had children themselves and there are many McCurdys living around Ballintoy yet, who claim their descent from the famous Raghery Mermaid. This is a true story for I heard it from the lips of old Lizzie McCurdy – who had more than a hint of the sea in her blood.

The Sunken City

Tir fo Thoinn – the Irish Land Beneath the Wave – is not the only 'lost' or mythical sea-realm in the Celtic world. Scottish, Welsh and Breton traditions also speak of villages, towns and cities all still lying beneath the sea which serve as homes for the merfolk and water-people. Some of these legends may be based upon actual incidents from folk memory, where coastal towns had slipped into the ocean due to continual erosion – places such as Old Findhorn and Fort George in Scotland and Caer Arainrhod in Wales.

Brittany, too, has its fair share of lost towns and submerged landscapes which the sea-people have made their abode. From these sunken places, they venture out to spy upon or torment the land dwellers, and fishermen do well to steer clear of any site that is reputed to be one of their haunts. However, this is not always easy. Sometimes such sunken realms rise to the surface once more (usually every seven years) and sailors are able to land there. The Celtic saint Brendan the Navigator is said to have visited one of these islands on his journey to America – but he was not the only one. John Nesbit, a sea captain from County Fermanagh in Ireland, is said to have landed on the mysterious island of Hy Braseal (or the Island O'Braseal) in 1674. This was supposed to be the Isle of the Blest, which appeared from the watery depths on a fairly regular basis. Indeed, so regularly did it appear and so widely was it reported, that the South American country of Brazil was named after it by certain sailors who mistakenly thought that they had landed there.

All sorts of merfolk lived in the submerged houses and palaces of these realms. In Breton folklore, one of the most famous of these beings was Yann-an-Od (John of the Dunes), who lived in a house of bone, seashell and coral just off the Brittany coast. He is sometimes described as a giant, sometimes as a dwarf, sometimes as an old grey-bearded man in oilskins leaning on the oar of a rowboat. His function is unclear. Sometimes he calls in a strange, hollow, bell-like voice, warning sailors away from his area, or else trying to lure them on to coastal rocks. Once their ships are wrecked, he will drag them down to live with him in his undersea house.

It should be remembered, nevertheless, that Yann-an-Od is only one of a number of Breton mer-creatures who live in the inlets and bays of the French coast. These may be the last remnants of the old Celtic sea-gods who once ruled the waves from the Northern Isles, through the Isle of Man and down to the French coast. Such beings are often very diverse in their physical aspect and powers and are frequently localized in certain seaside areas.

Much more common are the Morrigans – beautiful maidens who more closely correspond to our traditional idea of the mermaid – and who dwell in the sunken city of Ker Ys, one of the most famous lost places of Celtic mythology. Traditionally Ys was lost to the sea about the same time as the inundation of Lyonesse and is said to lie somewhere between the port of Brest and the Isle de Ouessant. There are, of course, many tales of how Ys came to be submerged – the following is only one of them...

I N THE DAYS BEFORE RECORDED HISTORY, the city-state of Ker Ys was one of the most splendid and most mighty in all of ancient Brittany. No other city on earth could compare with the luxury of its palaces and temples or with the architecture of its dwellings, or indeed with the wealth of its inhabitants. It was a merchant port which traded with far-away lands – with dark Ethiopia and yellow Cathay (China) – and its docks were always thronged with ships and produce from many mysterious and exotic countries. It was ruled over by King Gradlon, an ancient but extremely wise monarch, who was assisted in the task by his only daughter, Dahut.

In fact, Ys had but one drawback – a greater part of it lay below sea level. This district contained the palaces and the houses of the wealthy merchants and artisans, which seemed continually threatened by the sea. Yet this was no real problem, for the engineers of Ys had constructed a complicated series of dykes with massive gates and locks which could only be opened by an intricate set of keys. These keys were in the sole custody of King Gradlon himself, and he wore them about his neck on a silken cord, never taking them off once, even to bathe.

Gradlon was an extremely tolerant king. Although his city had once been a pagan port, he welcomed the first missionaries of a new religion – Christianity – into his kingdom and allowed them to set up a small abbey there. Over the years, more and more missionaries arrived in Ys from places like the holy island of Iona, Scotland and Ireland, and the monastery became larger and more prosperous. Gradlon himself converted to Christianity and made the local abbot, St Guenole, his royal adviser. The abbey at Ys – the Abbey of Ker Ys, together with its attendant shrine – became one of the most important in all of Brittany.

Soon came the time for Dahut to be married. It has to be said that, although she was very wise (almost as wise as her father, despite her comparative youth), she was also rather plain-looking. Few suitors came forward for her hand and those who did were quite unworthy of it. It looked as if Dahut would spend the rest of her days as an old maid – a prospect which filled her with no great cheer.

Then, surprisingly, an eligible suitor came forward. Not much was known about him and he gave his name simply as Cado, the Dark Prince of Kernow (Cornwall), on the other side of the sea. Although dark and saturnine and with a narrow, feral face which hinted at intense cruelty, there is no doubt that the Dark Prince was exceptionally handsome and Dahut fell for him almost at once. Gradlon was delighted with his daughter's apparent happiness but St Guenole, the king's adviser, was not so sure. He had the suspicion that this Cado might be the Devil himself, or else some sea-spirit come to harm the king, his daughter and his city. He advised Gradlon against the marriage, but the king would hear none of the holy man's words. He encouraged the lovers to be seen about and concerned himself with making arrangements for the betrothal ceremony.

The saint, however, had been correct in his assessment, for Cado was nothing more than an evil sea-spirit whose intent was that Ys should be swallowed up by the raging ocean. Knowing that Dahut was infatuated with him, the demon urged her to bring him the keys to the flood-gates of the protective dykes around Ys.

'They will be mine in any case when I am your king,' he assured her, and the silly girl was so taken with him that she agreed to help him. The demon promised her that the keys would form the centrepiece of a great pagan revelry at which the old gods of the sea would be honoured, and that both of them would plight their troth in marriage.

While the old King Gradlon slept deeply, Dahut entered his chambers and removed the keys from around his neck, taking them to Cado, who left straight away to open the flood-gates. The sea began to rush in, overwhelming the lower part of the city. Sensing something was amiss, St Guenole rushed to the old king's room.

'Great king, arise!' he shouted. 'The flood-gates are open and the sea is no longer restrained!' Blearily, Gradlon rose from his bed and looked out of the window. He saw only the splendid buildings of Ys vanishing beneath the waves and the beautiful temples crumbling before the onslaught of the ocean. The holy man grabbed his arm and led him to the stables. 'There is nothing that can be done to save Ys,' the saint advised him. 'We must save ourselves and flee to the high ground.' The two of them mounted their steeds and fled from the doomed city.

Everywhere there was confusion. Merchants, artisans and commoners thronged the main streets in panic and the king and his companion found it difficult to make progress because of the crush. Thoroughfares which had once been open to them were now closed because of the sea, which had flooded most of Ys. However, they struggled through and had soon reached the outer walls of the city.

As soldiers worked to open the perimeter gates and keep back the near-hysterical mob of refugees also trying to flee, Gradlon heard a cry from somewhere behind him.

'Father! Don't abandon me here! Help me!' Turning round, he saw the frightened face of his daughter among those of the citizens whom his guards were trying to hold back. The demon Cado had abandoned her and had returned to the sea in his true guise as soon as the flood-gates had been opened. Now she was left to die in the ocean-wrecked city in the midst of a cataclysm that she herself had brought about. Gradlon paused. Even though she had done an evil thing and had destroyed Ys, she was still his daughter. Bending down, he scooped her up on to the back of his saddle as his soldiers finally opened the gates and allowed them to gallop through. And they were not a moment too soon for, with a mighty roar, the sea finally overwhelmed the entire city.

Riding towards the highlands beyond, Gradlon looked back and saw a great lake where the city of Ys had once stood. But there was worse, for the lake was spreading quickly towards them as the hungry sea claimed most of the land round about. And it was gaining on them. Desperately, the king looked towards the saint, who had already seen their predicament. By now the sea was almost upon them both.

'Throw into the sea the demon that you carry behind you!' shouted Guenole. 'Let Cado take that which is his own anyway!' For a second, Gradlon hesitated. Dahut was his daughter, after all, and he had saved her from the doomed city.

'Throw her now!' screamed Guenole. 'She belongs to the sea demons now and is no longer your daughter! Throw her to the ocean or we are all lost!' With only a moment's hesitation, Gradlon hurled his screeching daughter from the saddle and the sea swallowed her up with a triumphant roar. In the waves, the old king thought that he saw the face of Cado and of a thousand other sea-demons, howling in savage ecstasy. Then the ocean began to recede, and the king and St Guenole rode on to safety. Soon they were in the high-lands, where they were taken in by simple shepherd folk and were well treated. Gradlon went to dwell with his kinsmen in Britain and St Guenole went on to found a new holy house – the celebrated Breton shrine at Landevennec. But Ys was completely destroyed and still lies beneath the sea off the French coast. From time to time, the bells of its great abbey can still be heard tolling gently in the ocean swell.

And what became of Dahut, the king's daughter, who had brought such a catastrophe about? It is said by many old Bretons that she still lives somewhere in the deepest ocean and that on occasion she haunts the submerged ruins of Ys. Fishermen declare that they have seen her, sitting on a rock combing her hair and singing softly to herself in the place where her father flung her. To see her is an evil omen, for it usually portends shipwreck and danger. In Brittany she is well known as Marie Morgan, the daughter who sings amid the sea, luring voyagers to their doom. Some tales also say that she is the queen of those who were drowned when Ys was flooded and that she hates the living with a passion, seeking only to do them harm. Who knows – for there are more things lurking amid the waves than we can even dream about.

The legend of Ys is both very ancient and extremely confused, with many variants around one original tale. It is told as an explanation of the origin of the Morrigans – the Breton sea-people. According to tradition, the city was supposed to stand in the area now occupied by the Bay of Douarnenez, Finisterre, and was one of the greatest centres of learning and religion in Dark Age France. The saint mentioned in the tale, St Guenole, has been identified with the Gallic St Winwaloe, who lived around AD 457 and certainly founded the Christian shrine at Landevennec. Although born in Brittany, his lineage is given as 'son of Fracan' and *cousin* to Cado, Duke (or King) of Kernow (Cornwall). Having become one of leading preachers of his time, Winwaloe established a Celtic Christian monastery on the island of Thropepigia in what is now Brest harbour. Although the monastery was a success, Winwaloe was, in the first instance, a missionary, and so he decided that he should carry his message on to the mainland. Taking the hand of one of his disciples, the saint boldly stepped out on to the sea and began to walk towards the land, some distance away. The tide, so legend states, drew back before each step, and so Winwaloe and his brothers were able to proceed to the coast completely dry-shod, when previously they had been forced to use a boat. It was this miracle that reputedly brought him to the attention of King Gradlon, who immediately sought him out as a royal adviser. Gradlon himself also certainly existed, as his carven image appears in the old church at Quimper.

The destruction of Ys is also commemorated in an old Breton poem which ends:

The sea opens its abysses and Dahut is swallowed up by the deep,
The king's horse, now lighter, reaches the shore,
Dahut, since then, is calling sailors to be wrecked.

The Mermaid of Zennor

As regards relations between merfolk and mortals, the mermaid of Celtic tradition is a somewhat ambiguous creature. In some folktales, no other fairy being so actively seeks out human relationships – even going so far as to marry mortal men – while in other stories, the mermaid is the harbinger of death and destruction, hating humans with a poisonous passion. This ambivalence may, of course, be partly explained by Christian attitudes towards the children of the sea.

In earliest times, the sea-maiden was the embodiment of the traditional Celtic ocean deity, who may have mated with mortal man as her whim dictated – indeed, in popular legend, such unions were to be encouraged, as they ensured a bountiful supply of fish and also, perhaps, fine fishing weather throughout the year. After all, it was a holy thing among ancient peoples for gods to mate from time to time with their worshippers. However, the coming of the rigours of the Christian faith changed all that. The sea-people were now seen as agents of the Devil, seeking to lure the godly away from their devotions through their wiles. Thus, mermaids became beautiful temptresses whose only purpose was to lure the unwary Christian men into the ocean and drown them. Then their human souls would become the property of the mermaid herself and also of her master, the Devil. It is hardly surprising, then, that stories of mermaids luring seamen to their doom on the rocks were a common theme in folklore from all over the Celtic world. The siren songs of the merfolk

were used to explain shipwrecks all along the coastline of Britain, Scotland, Cornwall and Brittany.

Not only this, but mermaids were also used in these same areas to explain accidental drownings along the seacoast. Travellers, it was alleged, had been lured from coastal paths by the siren song of the creatures or by their lascivious invitations, for mermaids, taught the Church, were extremely sensual beings. Indeed, it was commonly believed that it was dangerous even to fall asleep on a beach within reach of the sea for fear of being carried away by the merfolk. If one did so, it should only be within the sound of church bells, which would, hopefully, drive away such Satanic demons.

In fact, there are few tales of merfolk ever venturing on to Church property, since the holy precincts would remind them that they had no souls and, therefore, could not enjoy Eternal Salvation. Most mermaids – as in the case of the Raghery Mermaid cited previously – chose to avoid setting foot within a church or chapel, and most of them tended to give priests and clergymen a wide berth. However, there were notable exceptions to this rule.

The most famous of these was the Mermaid of Zennor in Cornwall, and it is her story which shows the ambiguous way in which the sea-people viewed mortals. The mermaid was greatly attracted to a mortal man but also wished to drown him in the ocean. Perhaps there are some echoes of Freudian symbolism there...

With evening now drawing on, the lamps were lit in the little church at Zennor, on the very tip of the Cornish shore. It was late in the year, and gales lashed the coastal rocks and outcrops while the wind roared ceaselessly through the gullies and inlets both night and day. In such weather, the fishermen kept close to their villages and hamlets, not daring even to venture out on any fishing expedition. Instead, they went to their churches and prayed for an end to the fearsome gales.

As the wind swept along the Cornish coastline, the little congregation of Zennor raised their voices in song, their music rising high over the shrill voice of the storm. At the front of the church, beside his long-bearded father, Matthew Trewella lifted his hymnal and sang louder than any in a clear, lusty voice. The lamps guttered and threatened to go out, but still the people of Zennor continued to sing and pray.

Matthew was the eldest of his father's sons and was one of the most handsome fishermen to be found anywhere in Cornwall. It was said that his mother – now long dead – had Spanish blood in her veins, and this was reflected in the young man's dusky good looks. His dark hair hung down in ringlets above his collar, framing a broad and pleasant face that had been tanned by the sea winds until it was almost mahogany in colour. His eyes were dark and mysterious and seemed always to be twinkling, as if to match the half-smile that continually played around the corners of his generous mouth. Many girls around Zennor and beyond loved Matthew Trewella and sometimes he favoured them with a smile or a dance, but none seemed to have taken his heart. He continued to live with his father and two younger brothers in a little low cottage which lay between Zennor hamlet and the ocean.

Although they were simple fishermen, the Trewella family had a long and distinguished history. It was said that they had once been squires and ladies in Zennor parish – indeed, there was still a Squire Trewella living not all that far away – but some of them had taken to the fishing and had preferred that life. The neighbouring Squire Trewella had never married and so was childless, and it was rumoured that, as he was a distant kinsman to Matthew, the young man might be in line to inherit his estates. This, of course, made Matthew all the more desirable as a catch in the eyes of the young ladies round about. Nevertheless, he displayed no favours at all to any of them and they were at a loss as to how to snare him.

There was, however, one way to his heart, if the maidens around Zennor but knew it. Matthew Trewella was extremely fond of music and singing – particularly of church music. He sang in the choir in Zennor church and was sometimes to be found walking along the cliffs above nearby Pendour Cove, singing to himself – some hymn tune or sacred refrain. Now, with the dim lights flickering in the tiny church, his voice rose heartily as if to drown out the elements which raged outside.

Away across the ocean beyond Pendour, thunder boomed and the wind increased. The doors of little Zennor church suddenly blew open but only the wind swirled in, howling up the nave like a Banshee and drowning out the singing of the congregation. Old Sexton Redruth struggled against the blast and pushed the doors shut again before returning to his seat. And yet, when he looked up, he saw that someone else had joined the little group in the church.

Away in a corner, only half-lit by the flickering lamps, was a darkened pew. It had been carved from oak and had its own door. It was said to have belonged once to a very ancient seafaring family from the Zennor district, and the carvings along its door and sides reflected this. There were strange, tall boats and queer sea-serpents rising up out of the ocean; there, too, were drowned sailors and shipwrecks, hinting at trade in distant and turbulent seas. The last scion of this old merchant family was long since dead and the pew had stood empty and unused for many years.

Now somebody stood there. It was a young girl, dressed in fine clothes as befitted a person of wealth and status, and, even in the poor light, the old sexton could see that she was extremely beautiful. She stood with her head bowed as though in prayer, copper tresses falling about her shoulders, half-listening to the music of the hymns. Old Redruth tried to focus on her to see if he knew her, but his failing eyesight betrayed him. Sometimes she seemed to be a living person, other times she seemed to be no more than an insubstantial shadow cast by the flickering light.

At the end of the service, the sexton made his way to the pew and opened the door for the girl to descend into the church. She came down, moving as gracefully as any great lady should, and even the old man could see that she was very pretty. He was not the only one, for many of the young men in the congregation had also noticed her, and they thronged around pew to walk with her to the church door. She favoured many of them with a dazzling smile, but it was noticeable that her eyes flitted inevitably towards Matthew Trewella.

Old Redruth asked her name and she replied in a light and silvered voice, giving the name of the ancient family whose pew she had stood in. She was a distant relative, she explained, who had come to stay in Zennor as a child and who now occasionally returned to the area. This the old sexton found incredibly strange, for the family house of which she spoke had long fallen down and the land on which it had stood was now used for farming purposes. There was certainly more to this mysterious lady than met the eye, the old man decided!

If Sexton Redruth had serious reservations about the young lady, the young men who crowded around her pew did not. Indeed, most of them seemed to be under a kind of spell which she cast, offering to carrying her prayer book or to walk her home – both offers she declined. Matthew Trewella hung back in his usual shy way, but all the same, he never took his eyes from her. Despite the urgings that she should not walk home alone but should have an escort, the girl left the church on her own, taking the road that led down from Zennor towards Pendour Cove. Sexton Redruth watched her with an increasingly wary expression stealing across his wrinkled face, for the road that she took lay directly opposite the lands of the family whose scion she claimed to be. In actual fact, she was walking away from the place where she claimed to be staying. In the old man's mind, the mystery deepened.

For many days there was no other topic of conversation among the young men of Zennor than the beautiful girl who had turned up at the church. Since that visit, nobody had seen hide nor hair of her, and although several young gallants had hung about the crossroads and taverns hoping to catch at least a glimpse of her, they were disappointed. It had begun to dawn on several of them that the address that she had given no longer existed, and speculation about her origins was rife throughout the community. Some said that she was a grand lady from another parish, some that she was a run-away from a noble family further north who had gone to live among the gypsies who sometimes congregated near Zennor as the days drew shorter. But nobody knew for sure. If Matthew Trewella had any suspicions as to who she was, he kept them to himself. He was not the type of man to join in the tittle-tattle of the countryside anyway. Still, the girl had made a distinct impression on him, for he found himself thinking of her more and more and even sometimes dreaming about her too. Still, he put such thoughts to the back of his mind and helped his father with the fishing. Weeks went by and the strange beauty was not seen at Zennor church.

News now reached Zennor that Squire Trewella – Matthew's distant kinsman – lay gravely ill and was likely to die. He had been hunting and had taken a fall from a horse which had badly injured his leg. But it was not this that had caused his illness. Rather, as he had lain far away from his house, a heavy rain shower had come on and drenched him. By the time he was found, he had been soaked to the skin and had developed a raging fever, which now threatened to kill him. The doctors came and shook their heads and said that he wouldn't see out the month. There was great speculation that Matthew would become his heir and would be entitled to whatever estates he possessed. Although they were not vast, they were substantial, and would certainly set the young fisherman up for the rest of his life. Matthew, however, merely smiled and waved the suggestion away. He was happy enough where he was.

The following Sunday, the strange lady returned to Zennor church. Another fierce storm had been brewing far out to sea and winds whistled inland, keeping the fishing fleet in port and rattling the doors and windows of the fishermen's cottages as they passed. A tiny congregation had gathered to pray for the passing of the season of storms and for a bountiful harvest of fish. It was a service purely for fish-erfolk and yet, when Sexton Redruth raised his eyes, there was the young woman standing in her accustomed pew, her head bowed. The wind caught the edge of the now open door, making it rattle, and Redruth made his way to the back of the church to close it, wondering how it had opened in the first place. He was sure that he had pushed it tightly closed against the elements.

Once again, the service over, the young men of Zennor gathered around their beautiful guest and offered to escort her home on such a stormy night. She declined their offers, albeit with a dazzling smile, and told them that she was well used to storms where she came from. However, her eyes kept wandering to the face of Matthew Trewella and his to hers, and old Redruth had the impression that if the young man had offered to go with her, he might not have been turned down so easily. Even so, she continued to flirt with the other young men as far as the church door, before finally going out into the storm and taking the road which led down to Pendour Cove once more.

The storms passed and the Zennor fleet put out again, returning laden with fish. Such was the joy in Zennor at the fine catch that it was suggested there should be a service of thanksgiving the following Sunday. Because he had such a fine singing voice, it was widely proposed that Matthew Trewella should sing the solo. At first he refused, but gradually they won him round and he agreed, on the understand-ing that he should be allowed to rehearse with the choir that Wednesday night.

Wednesday itself was a dark and gloomy day, with large banks of clouds gathering far out to sea and the threat of another storm sweeping in on the huddled fishing villages. The wind blew cold from the north and the sea thundered and threw great salty breakers against the rocks in the normally quiet bays and inlets. Word had come to Zennor that Squire Trewella, who had seemed to be rallying for the last week or so, was now in rapid decline and was not expected to last more than a couple of days. Lawyers were already circling his bed like crows and it was expected that Matthew would inherit the squire's estates quite soon now, tying him and his descendants to the area for ever.

That evening, Matthew made his way to the church for choir practice. Many of the young girls of the countryside were there, some of them aware of Matthew's prospective inheritance and all of them certainly trying to attract his attention. He paid them all no heed. Once more, old Sexton Redruth lit the lamps and the choir began to sing. Soon it was Matthew's turn. Stepping forward, his clear voice rose high and loud over the roar of the storm outside. And, as he sang, his words were answered by a beautiful, bell-like tone which seemed to come from somewhere close at hand and within the ancient church itself.

All heads turned. The sound was so sweet and pure that none of the choristers had ever heard anything like it, for it rose and fell like the tide and hinted at the deep, green, fish-filled caverns far beneath the ocean, and they all wished to know who was singing. There in the shadows of her usual pew stood the strange girl, and there could now be no doubt as to upon whom her attentions were fixed, for her gaze never seemed to leave Matthew Trewella. The young man appeared to be in a trance, captivated by the beautiful singing. The lady spread her cloak as if to embrace him, and slowly the young fisherman began to move through the church towards her as if in a dream. None moved to stop him, for all were held in the thrall of the song that she sang. He drew close to her and she swept her cloak around him like a wave of the sea. The doors of Zennor church suddenly burst open and the wind and rain howled in. Like shadows, Matthew Trewella and the girl were gone and, as those who were present came to themselves, both of them vanished into the midst of the storm outside. Only then did several of the choristers run forward to stop them, but the wind from the door drove them back into the body of the church. By the time the gale had dropped, Matthew and the girl had long departed.

It was old Sexton Redruth who eventually surmised what might have happened to the young fisherman. Some days later, the old man made his way down to Pendour Cove, and there in the sand he saw a single line of footprints stretching out into the incoming tide. Those footprints, he believed, belonged to Matthew Trewella. The grand lady who had lured him away from Zennor church, the sexton told himself, had been nothing less than the spawn of the ocean.

The day after Matthew's disappearance, the news reached Zennor that Squire Trewella had died in the night. As expected, Matthew had been named as his heir and was due to inherit the squire's estates. Lawyers decreed that Matthew should present himself and take possession of his new-found property, but he never did. In fact, no trace was ever seen of him again. Nor did the grand lady ever again come to sing in the tiny church at Zennor, and it was widely assumed that they had run away together. Some said that Matthew was seen in London, others that he was seen in York, others still that he was living in Exeter or St Ives, but no man could be sure. Old Redruth kept his own counsel for many years, never voicing his suspicions.

That is not quite the end of the story. A good number of years after Matthew had vanished and his name was all but forgotten in the district, a foreign ship waited out a storm a little way off Pendour Cove. Although her crew was mainly Spanish, she had an English captain, who ordered that the ship had to be made fast with a heavy anchor if they were to ride out the gale. All of a sudden, one of the crew glimpsed something off the port bow.

A mermaid had risen from the depths and was calling on the captain. The man came in answer to her call and she told him to remove his anchor and lower it somewhere else, as it was blocking the entrance to her house and she could not get in to tend to her lover and her children. Her lover, she told the sea captain, had been a mortal like himself but was now one of the sea-people. His name, when he had lived on land, had been Matthew Trewella of Zennor. The seaman gave a sharp intake of breath, for he had heard of an old legend of a youth who had vanished many years before. The anchor was raised, and when the gale had passed, the ship put into Pendour Cove and the captain went ashore to inform the inhabitants of Zennor that he knew what had happened to their long-lost son. The congregation of the church thought long and hard about the occurrence, and old Sexton Redruth – then approaching his dotage – revealed that it had confirmed his darkest suspicions. He warned that another young man might be carried off in the future, for the rocks around Pendour Cove were the haunt of mermaids and strange sea-things. Many in Zennor church agreed with him, and so they decided to carve the warning on the pew where the ocean woman had sat.

Those who enter Zennor church, even to this day, will be struck by the strange figure of the mermaid carved on the end of the pew. She has long and flowing hair, and holds a mirror in one hand and a comb in the other – the symbols of vanity and heartlessness. But if the curious were to walk along the sands at Pendour Cove where poor Matthew is said to have vanished, there is nothing to be seen – only the tide running back and forth to and from the shore. It is still said, however, that Matthew can be heard there, singing loud and long as he was supposed to do that night in Zennor church. But, again, there is really nothing to be heard, only the crash of the breakers against the rocks, coupled with the endless murmur of the ocean.

CDonSTeRs

Monsters in Celtic folklore and mythology arguably fall into two categories. The first would appear to be actual creatures which did exist or may have existed in some former time but lingered on in the memory of the people – great serpents, bears, wild pigs. These formed the basis of stories concerning dragons, monstrous boars and shaggy half-human beings which littered both the great Myth Cycles and the hearthside tales of the Celtic peoples. The second type of monster was purely of the supernatural kind and may have been a representation of ancient hunting gods. Some of these god-monsters were recognizable creatures – gigantic horses, monstrous wolves etc. – while others were queer, ill-defined beings which sometimes contained elements of both human and animal. Many of these entities were larger than life and they were incredibly dangerous.

As the embodiment of ancient gods, some of these monsters were worshipped, but that didn't mean that they were especially beneficent towards their devotees. Many were capricious and vacillating in their ways and expectations, perhaps reflecting the natures of the animals which they represented – sometimes tame, sometimes wild and feral.

An example of a monster which combined both animalistic and supernatural aspects was the boar. In fact, this animal was incredibly important to the ancient Celts because, together with the stag, it was perhaps the most hunted animal but was also one of the most ferocious when at bay. The Celts also found boar meat incredibly succulent and it often formed the centrepiece of their banquets. Pork was also the meat which was believed to be most frequently consumed in the Celtic afterlife, and so the boar took on a special significance in both life and death, becoming the symbol of war and hunting on the one hand and hospitality and feasting on the other. As a further symbol of greatness and strength, the best piece of pork at a banquet was named as the 'champion's portion' and was awarded to the greatest warrior present. In this, the strength and cunning of the god was passed on to the most deserving mortal, thus forging a link between the

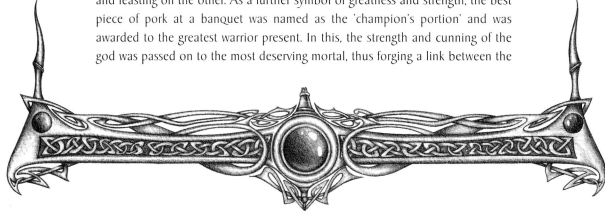

natural world and the realm of the gods. An example of this practice is to be found in the Irish mythological Bricriu's Feast, where the great heroes of the land squabble furiously over the 'champion's portion'.

And, of course, the boar also took on supernatural aspects as well – the Irish hero Diarmaid has a foster-brother who takes the form of a wild pig, which the hero hunts and by whom he meets his eventual death; in the Welsh tale of Culhwch and Olwen, the creature Twrch Trwyth is a formidable monster transformed from an evil king. In many cases, monstrous entities – boars, stags, horses and more – were also used as lures to draw ancient heroes into the Otherworld, which existed just beyond mortal sight.

Boars and other animals, many connected to the ancient Celtic hunter-deities, formed the basis for many of the monsters that preyed upon the Celtic mind, but there were others which, while having animalistic attributes, were also supernatural. Many of these were associated with the dead and haunted the graveyards of the Celtic world. Many are almost formless, half-described things which terrified the unwary after dark. All of them had some sort of supernatural quality about them and were not easily destroyed. Only the very brave or those protected by the power of Christ (saints, priests or holy men) could stand against them, and the power of the Cross would often drive them away.

This, of course, was a thinly disguised attempt to demonstrate the force of the Church over the powers of pagan darkness. Ancient forces stemming from a Devilish past, the Christian faith taught, still lingered in the remote places of the countryside, coming into their own as soon as the sun set and darkness fell across the land. Such things were fearsome to behold, had a taste for Christian blood and were truly monstrous in every sense of the word. Gradually, these night creatures, too, found their way into legend and folklore and came to be feared throughout the settled world as the last vestiges of an awful, ungodly tradition. Is it any wonder that monsters lurked somewhere in the depths of the Celtic mind, just around the corner of everyday vision, waiting to pounce on the unwary or the unholy? Monsters, said the Celtic priests and monks, were everywhere, if we only had the faith to see them...

The Last Serpent

Is it not strange that in a country such as Ireland, which is bereft of snakes, the motif of the serpent features very heavily in both art and folklore? Representations of serpents appear both on pagan stones (the so-called 'serpent-stones') and in the artwork on certain Celtic Christian engraved crosses. Further, almost every Irish schoolchild can recount the legend that it was St Patrick who drove the snakes out of Ireland in the fifth century. A suggested explanation for the Irish fascination with snakes and serpents is that the Celts, being an Indo-European people whose religion was heavily fragmented into localized cults, may have brought with them serpent cults as part of their overall belief system.

The serpent, of course, held an immense fascination for the ancient mind the world over. It was the symbol of both good and evil – its venom being used in the preparation of medicines as well as being a deadly poison. Snakes were venerated from earliest times – even by the ancient Egyptians, when they were worshipped in the person of the god Set. Latterly, Christianity turned the snake into a creature of evil and personification of the Devil, probably because of its prehistoric/Egyptian associations.

In Ireland, the suggestion of snake cults would seem to be borne out by certain symbols which they appear to have left behind. For instance, in the corner of a remote field at Glenshesk, north Antrim, we find a large cult stone depicting what many have interpreted as a rearing serpent, marking the edge of an ancient prehistoric (and later Christian) enclosure. It was probably not actual *serpents* which St Patrick drove out of Ireland, but rather serpent *men*, the remnants of the old snake cults that had existed within the country.

Nor was St Patrick the only Christian saint in Celtic folklore to drive out the deadly snake or the abhorred serpent cult: there were several such holy men and women. St Cado of Brittany expelled great snakes; St Clement vanquished the Dragon of Metz; St Romain drove the terrible serpent Gargouille out of Paris; St Kevin is commemorated in a panel in Glendalough Cathedral for setting his dog Lupus on to a monstrous serpent in County Wicklow; even St Columcille is said to have obliged his followers by driving out a terrible dragon from Donegal.

The belief that it was specifically St Patrick who drove them out dates back to the twelfth-century writings of Giraldus Cambrensis, who states that: 'St Patrick, according to common report, expelled the venomous reptiles from it [Ireland] by the Beculum Jesu [the historical holy staff or rod of the saint].' The saint was said to have fasted for 40 days and 40 nights before performing the deed and so gained miraculous power. The feat is further attested by a Welsh monk, Jocelyn, writing around the same time (1185), who states that the expulsion occurred at Cruachan Aigle, a mountain in western Connaught. The saint 'gathered together the several tribes of serpents and venomous creatures and drove them headlong into the Western Ocean'. Other sources state that this event took place on the island of Inis Mura (Inishmurray), off the coast of Sligo.

In the north, the most famous Draconis Extinctor (killer or destroyer of serpents) is often cited as St Murrough or Marriagh O'Heaney of Bannagher, a local saint who was reputed to have been baptized by Patrick himself. St Murrough is especially famous for driving out the fearsome Lig-na-Baste or Paiste, the last of the great serpents, in north Derry. Paiste is, the ancient Irish name for dragon or reptile, the equivalent of the Saxon wyrrm, and usually refers to some scaled, snake-like monster. Incidentally, the term is also widely used throughout the Western Isles and is still evident on Mingulay through the name Ravine of the Paiste, an inlet on the island's coastline.

In Ireland, the monster was not utterly destroyed, but was driven down from the highlands by St O'Heaney and into Lough Foyle, where it now creates the fearful and unpredictable tides that swirl about the coastal area there. Other versions of the same tale relate how the Paiste entered the sea in north Antrim near the village of Ballintoy. Whatever the location, the story is widely told and often widely believed as well...

In the days just after the death of the Blessed St Patrick, the lands which bordered on Lough Foyle were tormented by a terrible creature which the people called the Lig-na-Baste, or Paiste. This was one of those ancient creatures which had been left over from the foundation of the world and was probably the last of its kind left alive. It was certainly a fearful animal, and the people of the countryside were very afraid. It destroyed the crops all through the farmlands round about, and ate cattle and sheep on the mountain slopes. There were some along the shores of Lough Foyle who said that the Lig-na-Baste could also breathe out fire and that it could burn houses and castles that were many miles away. The beast lived in a narrow, dark glen along the Glower River and nobody would go near the place, so terrified of the monster were they.

In the end, some of the country folk went to St Murrough O'Heaney, a very holy man who lived alone in a little cell up in Bannagher, away above Lough Foyle. He had a great reputation for supernatural powers and they asked him if he would get rid of the serpent for them. Finally, the saint agreed and prepared to do battle with the serpent.

St Murrough fasted and prayed for nine days and nine nights and then went down to the edge of the Glower, where he cut himself three thin rods from the reeds that grow along the riverbank. Then he made his way up to the glen where the serpent lived. The monster rose up as soon as the holy man came near it – and it was a terrible sight indeed. The creature was well over 11 feet tall when it was fully reared and had horns on either side of its head, curled like those of a ram. It was covered in armour-like scales, each as large as a dinner plate, and its long tongue was as thick as a black rope and fairly dripped with a green venom. Its fangs were as thick as the stalactites which hang down from the roofs of caves.

'Well, my little manling,' it demanded, 'what brings you to my lonely abode? Are you some sort of offering, come to be devoured?' And it laughed unpleasantly. In those far-off days, serpents could still speak, for did not the serpent in the Garden of Eden tempt our mother Eve with its honey'd words? Yet its voice was like the hiss of steam escaping from a cauldron and was very dreadful to hear. St Murrough wasn't afraid of the creature, however, for he had the power of the Living God behind him.

'I've come to ask a favour,' said he. The Paiste lowered its head until it was almost level with the face of its visitor, and its yellow eyes seemed to look deep into the saint's very soul.

'Speak then,' it hissed, 'and tell me your request. Mayhap I may be in a mood to grant it before I utterly devour you.' St Murrough remained unmoved by the monster's threat.

'It is an ancient task which I must perform,' he told it, 'which is part of my Christian teaching. It is the laying of three rushes across your back. Grant me this request and I'll trouble you no further.' Now the holy man hoped that the monster knew nothing of Holy Scripture, for there is nothing in the Christian canon regarding such a practice. The Paiste reared itself up even further until it towered above the saint, its upper portions nothing more than a dark shadow among the low-hanging clouds. Black and fetid smoke belched from its nostrils. It seemed to be considering St Murrough's proposition.

'You are either very brave or extremely foolish, man-creature,' it said at length. 'I assume that it is your belief that makes you so. Very well, I am in the mood for levity and will allow you to place the rods upon my back in order to perform your religious task. After all, what harm can three thin sticks do the likes of me? But then be assured that I will devour you!' And it gave yet another of its unpleasant, roaring laughs. St Murrough inclined his head in apparent submission.

'As you will,' he replied. The serpent lay down upon the dark earth of the glen, half-coiling itself around some large rocks nearby, and, very carefully, St Murrough laid the thin rods upon its scaly back. Assuming that his task was now done, the Paiste heaved a great sigh and made to rise.

'Now, holy man, prepare to be devoured!' But the saint held up a restraining hand.

'Wait just one moment more,' he asked, 'for in order to complete my ritual, I must say a prayer over these rods.' The serpent fairly seethed with irritation.

'Truly, you test my patience, holy man,' it roared. 'A patience which I warn you is not infinite! Very well, mutter your meaningless gibberish over the rods, much good may it do you. But do not delay putting off the moment of your doom any further!' Once again, St Murrough seemed to make a submissive bow and the serpent relaxed slightly.

Kneeling beside the great, scaly hide of the monster, St Murrough O'Heaney prayed. He prayed as he had never prayed before and with all the supernatural might at his command. And his prayers were answered, for, all of a sudden, the thin reed rods seemed to lengthen and twist themselves around the monster's thick body. Even their very nature changed, for in a moment they had wrapped the Paiste completely, like great bands of supple steel. Realizing what was happening, the creature tried first to shake them off – they wouldn't move – and then to break them by expand-ing and contracting its great body. The bands wouldn't give in the slightest. The Paiste realized that it had been tricked and that it was now the saint's prisoner.

'Betrayed!' it howled in a most awful

voice. 'You have betrayed me, holy man! For this you shall perish most horribly!' But St Murrough raised an admonishing hand.

'You are a foul creature of darkness that has no place in the Christian world,' he told it. 'Your time is long past. No more will you attack or torment God's children in this or in any other part of the land. This is my command! Give me your word that you will accept it!' The Paiste struggled, but each time it did, the steel bands seemed to draw more tightly about it, threatening to crush the very life from it.

'Very well!' it roared. 'I give you my word. Now release me from your trap!' But St Murrough shook his head.

'How am I to trust the oath of such a creature as you?' he asked. 'But I shall let you go eventually, although not until the Great and Holy Day of Judgement when One more powerful than I shall loose your fetters. Until then you must remain imprisoned!' He looked around him, out over the countryside. 'You shall depart this glen and go on your belly across the land and into the waters of Lough Foyle, there to remain until it comes your time to be released! This is my further command to you!' And, raising his holy staff, St Murrough pointed to the monster the way it should go. Once more the Lig-na-Baste shook itself, trying to get rid of its fetters, but to no avail.

'I will *not* go,' it hissed. 'For it is not given to you to command such as I!' Again the saint shook his head and made a motion in the air with his staff. The grim bands about the serpent tightened even more and the Paiste howled in agony.

'My commands are in the Name of the Living God,' said St Murrough solemnly. 'All creatures, whether they walk or crawl, must obey His will.' He raised his staff even higher into the air and shook it threateningly. 'Now go!' And, faced with such supernatural might, the Lig-na-Baste had no other choice but to obey. It went grudgingly, roaring, hissing, swearing and issuing fearful threats as it did so. When the Day of Judgement came, it warned, it would return to its dark glen and would ravage utterly the countryside between Lough Foyle and the Glower River and beyond, and would devour all the people still living therein. This it solemnly swore. But St Murrough was unmoved, for he knew that he would not live to see the Great Day of Judgement but, when it did come, he would be counted with the Blessed. Thus the serpent's awful threats held no terrors for him.

The creature entered the sea at Lough Foyle and soon sank out of sight beneath the waters. But it is still there to this very day, trying to free itself under the ocean from the bands which St Murrough O'Heaney placed around it. Fishermen from north Derry and from Donegal have always spoken of the queer tides which run along that stretch of the coast – unpredictable tide, which no man can explain by ordinary means. And that is proof, if proof were needed, that the monster is still struggling down in the depths, patiently waiting for the Great Day of Judgement.

The Buggane of St Trinian's

Even with the coming of Christianity to the Celtic lands, folk memories of ancient powers dwelling within the landscape, powers which were sometimes embodied in physical form, did not necessarily die away. They continued to lurk in the darker corners of the Celtic mind, growing more and more monstrous over the course of time, and not even the light of the Christian Gospel could dispel them. Some of these dimly remembered forces became associated with old pagan mounds and raths, others with wells and caves, and some of the more frightening ones were even strongly connected with abandoned early Christian burial grounds.

The unquiet ghosts of the holy dead became fused with Celtic nightmares, often taking on a frightening aspect in which they could literally tear mortals limb from limb. Many old graveyards and ruined churches, in both Ireland and Scotland, have such legends associated with them. Vicious ghosts pelt passers-by with stones, rocks or with any other missile which comes readily to hand, and may even tear their clothes and skin, while Welsh legends speak of the monstrous hands of the dead reaching from the earth, to cling to the feet of those who traverse their final resting places.

The Isle of Man, too, has its stories which connect monsters to the places of the dead, and none more so than tales concerning the ancient church of St Trinian, in the barony of the same name at Marown. The church itself, which stands on one of the hillside farms of the barony, has a mysterious history. It is certainly one of the oldest churches on the island and is said to have been founded originally by a Scottish saint, Ninian. Certainly the lands belonged to the Priory of Whithorn in Galloway (St Ninian's foundation) during the twelfth century. Several churches bearing the name 'Trinian' (taken as a corruption of Ninian) have also occupied the location.

Old Manx people sometimes still refer to the site as Keeill Brisht or the Broken Church, because they state that the construction of the last building was never actually completed. When its foundations and walls were laid on the site of an ancient pagan graveyard around the fifteenth century, so the legend goes, a terrible Buggane, or demon, 'with eyes like torches' rose from the ground and brought them all crashing down again. The story has parallels all through the Celtic world – the ancient and roofless church of Templastragh on the northern Irish coast is associated with a similar tale, as are several ruined churches in Argyll.

It is more probable that the building of St Trinian's was halted for a much less supernatural reason. In the fifteenth century, Sir John Stanley, to whom the barony belonged, summoned the Prior of Whithorn Abbey to come and do fealty in return for his Manx possessions. The Prior was given 40 days' grace to do so, but, as ancient texts record, 'he came not'. Consequently, his lands on Man were forfeit and all building on the church stopped. The legend of the frightful Buggane, however, still persists in many parts of the island.

The term 'Buggane' sometimes has an ambivalent meaning – it can (and usually does) refer to a hideous monster in the supernatural sense, but it can also mean a tyrannical ruler or attacker. In this sense, it could be applied to Richard de Mandeville, who, in 1316, landed on Man, together with a band of ruthless Irishmen, and plundered the country for about a month. A few years later, he came again – this time with 'a multitude of Scottish felons' – and ravaged the island. He is said to have been responsible for many of the broken (ruined and roofless) churches all across Man and might rightly be termed a 'Buggane'.

The supernatural Buggane has, of course, a longer and much more complex history, and it is just as likely an explanation for the non-completion of St Trinian's as any of the above. It is unquestionably a folk memory of an ancient Celtic god of some disestablished religion who showed its disapproval at the building of a Christian precinct on land previously sacred to itself. Many such tales exist in Celtic legend, where strange fires and inexplicable storms destroy the foundations of a church built on pagan land. These stories serve to demonstrate the conflict within the Celtic mind between the acceptance of the incoming Christian religion and the innate reverence for the much older pagan sites.

It is perhaps worth noting that some folk historians, such as the Reverend Sabine Baring-Gould, argue a Slavic origin for the notion of the Buggane (and probably for the 'boggarts' and 'bogles' of northern Britain as well). Baring-Gould derives the name from the Slav word *bog*, meaning a provincial god or local deity. The word, he suggests, may have crept on to the Isle of Man during the time of the

Viking occupation there. The word 'Viking', should not be taken to cover only Scandinavians as among their number they no doubt included other races, perhaps some Slavs. The word *bog*, according to Baring-Gould, may have gradually become debased – as happened with other local spirits or forces in the Celtic world during Christian times – simply to mean 'demon'. The Manx themselves may have further debased the word by adding the diminutive suffix '-*ane*' (meaning 'little') to it, thus giving the concept of 'little demon' – probably referring to a local supernatural force of limited power.

Whether or not the Buggane had merely limited power, it was certainly terrifying to most people – excepting, perhaps, a few hardy souls...

NEARLY EVERYBODY ON THE ISLE of MAN has heard of the Buggane that dwells over in the ruined church of St Trinian's at Marown. And, years ago, nearly everybody was afraid of it as well, for it was supposed to be an awful dead thing with great saucer-like eyes, terrible clashing teeth and huge claw-like hands that could tear apart anyone who saw it. Nobody would go near the old church after nightfall when the Buggane was at the height of its powers, for fear of what might befall them there. Over the years, however, it became a great 'dare' among the islanders to spend a whole night at Keeill Brisht (as St Trinian's was called) – but it was a dare that even the strongest and boldest person in the whole of Man would never take up.

There was a tailor living in Marown at one time and, although he was certainly extremely good at sewing, cutting and making up clothes, he was also a rather boastful fellow, especially when he had some drink in him.

'I've no fear of the old Buggane at St Trinian's,' said he one night when he was well into his cups. 'And it wouldn't cost me a thought,' and he snapped his fingers for effect, 'to spend the whole night in that old church and to see what rises up to meet me at the stroke of midnight.' All this, of course, was said to impress those around him, particularly several fine-looking girls who had gathered to hear him.

'Well then,' said one of the other lads with a laugh. 'Let's make a wager. You spend the whole night in the old church and if you should happen to survive the awful Buggane, I'll personally pay you seven gold sovereigns and you can have a kiss from whatever girl takes your fancy among the company here.' There was a general murmur of approval from the others, for they all wanted to see if the tailor would take up the challenge. The wager was, of course, too good to pass up.

'Right!' said the tailor, slapping his thigh very loudly. 'Let's make it tonight that I stay there and I'll have seven gold sovereigns from yourself–' he indicated the fellow that had made the wager– 'and a gold sovereign apiece from the rest of you. Oh, and I'll have two kisses from whatever girl here takes my fancy!' And so it was agreed, for everybody thought that their money and kisses were safe and that, for all his grand talk, the tailor would never go through with the bet.

Now, as far as the tailor was concerned, all his boasting had been nothing more than the drink in him talking, and it's one thing to make grand boasts and bets when the drink-courage is on you and you're among a crowd of friends in a well-lit tavern, but it's quite another thing to reflect upon what you've wagered when the drink has left you and you're all alone on the dark road leading up the hillside towards St Trinian's. That was the way of it with the tailor. Soon, whatever drink-courage he had in him was gone and he found himself not too far from the ruined church, with his friends watching him from a distance. He had called into his own house on his way there and had taken some material with him for sewing in order to pass the night. All the same, he was terrified.

'What have I done?' he moaned to himself. But it was his own tongue that had got him into the trouble and he now had to go through with it. There was no other way.

'The sewing will make the night pass quicker,' he said hopefully, 'and before I know it, morning will be here.' Yes, the sewing would take his mind off the gloomy church all around him – at least, that was what he thought.

If the night outside was dark, then Keeill Brisht was even darker. Only a little moonlight filtered through its broken walls, and when it fell on the flagstones which lined the floor it created large and dangerous-looking pools of shadow which ran away to the far corners of the old building. There, too, were ancient tombs of those who had requested to be buried close by the old place at some former time and, somewhere in the darkness, a bird called with a high, chattering sound. The tailor's friends, who had been following him to make sure that he actually went to the haunted place, now wisely stayed back and left him alone.

Swallowing hard, the tailor took up a position, sitting cross-legged as tailors were wont to do, in the very centre of the ancient nave. Then, taking up his material, he began to sew, looking neither right nor left, up nor down. He sewed and sewed, working at a long seam, and gradually the hours began to creep by. Soon midnight had passed and all was still silent within the tumbled ruin. The tailor was just congratulating himself for not yielding to any silly superstition regarding a Buggane when he thought that he heard a faint noise. He listened intently and the sound came again. It was a low and echoing moan which seemed to come from the very earth beneath him – from somewhere far below the stone flags on which he sat.

'It's nothing!' the tailor told himself, and began stitching all the more. 'It's only the wind!' But the sound came again, louder this time, and there could be no mistaking it. It was now a long, long moan, as though somebody (or something) were stretching upon wakening. The sound echoed round and round the old church and was certainly terrible to hear. The tailor tried to pay no attention to it and still kept at his sewing, looking neither left nor right, up nor down. Away across the countryside the sky seemed to lighten a little, although it was still very dark. There was a scratching and a movement which seemed to come from beneath the flags nearby. Trying to keep himself from screaming in fright, the tailor stitched even more quickly. His fingers fairly flew across the seam that he was working on, so intent was he.

There was now the loud and unmistakable noise of a flagstone being drawn back and, looking up for an instant, the tailor saw that one of the stones had been slightly raised up on its side like a trapdoor. A mighty voice, deep and brassy as any bell, suddenly boomed through the ancient building.

'I hear movement in the upper part of this church!' it declared. 'And it appears to me that some bold mortal has trespassed upon my ground! He will soon learn the folly of his ways, for I shall instantly destroy him!' And, as it spoke, shadows wheeled and danced all along the length of the nave. As for the tailor, he made no move, but continued to sit cross-legged in the middle of the floor. Fear had apparently rooted him to the spot. 'Is there anyone up there who can hear the sound of my dreadful voice?' And there was silence as the unseen monster waited for an answer.

'Yes!' said the tailor, hoping that his own voice didn't tremble too much. 'I can hear your words!' Again there was a long pause and, somewhere close by, the nightbird called again with its chattering cry.

'Oho!' replied the monster at length and with an evil-sounding chuckle. 'A mortal has dared to enter the precincts of Keeill Brisht after nightfall, when I am at the height of my powers! Do you know who I am, foolish mortal?' The tailor swallowed hard but kept on with his sewing, never lifting his eyes from the seam that he was stitching.

'I think so,' he answered, still trying to keep his voice from faltering. 'I think that you are the famous Buggane of St Trinian's.' Again there was silence for a moment, then the awful voice spoke once more.

'You speak truly, mortal. I *am* indeed the Buggane whom those on this island have feared for many centuries. Do you know that the very sight of me can sometimes strike mortals blind? Do you wish to see me before I destroy you?' The tailor cast a glance through the ruined windows of Keeill Brisht. Away in the east, the sky seemed to have lightened a bit more but it was still very dark.

'If it is *your* wish,' he said. The monster gave a great and booming laugh which reverberated from the shattered walls and hollow flagstones round about. The tailor's heart fluttered and threatened to fail with fear.

'Very well! You shall see me! But I warn you, I am not a pretty sight and those who gaze on me usually die from terror. Are you sure that you wish to see me?' The tailor kept his eyes fixed on the garment seam in front of him.

'I am,' he replied, still trying to keep his voice as even as he could. The great flagstone was raised even further and several large and bony fingers crept up over the edge of the pit beneath it. They were dark grey in colour, covered in ropy tendrils of black hair and had great rending talons, curved like hooks, instead of nails. They were like the fingers of some gigantic dead man. The Buggane laughed mockingly.

'Do you see my great fingers?' it asked. 'They are long and horny, are they not? And look at the nails. Did you ever see such talons? They will rend you to pieces without much effort. They are most terrifying, aren't they?' But the tailor didn't look in the direction of the great fingers, but continued to concentrate hard upon the sewing in front of him.

'They are indeed,' he replied, indifferently. 'I'm almost terrified at the sight of them.' Deep in its lair, the Buggane roared angrily at his seeming lack of fear and pushed the flagstone up even further, so that its huge head could come at least a little way through the aperture in the floor. Like the fingers, it was slate-grey in colour, with great wreaths of black hair hanging from the forehead like moss on a stone wall. Eyes, as big as saucers, blazed in the gloom like foglamps. The tailor refused to look but kept on sewing.

'Do you see my mighty head?' bellowed the monster. 'Do you see my eyes as big as saucers? See how they blaze like great burning fires! Are they not frightening?' The tailor now wanted to scream and run but, somehow, he held his nerve. In the east, the darkness was slowly beginning to fade and the sky was now as grey as the Buggane's skin.

'They are indeed,' he replied. 'Truly, I'm almost frightened!' The Buggane was by now growing more and more frustrated, because the tailor seemed to have no fear of it at all. It raised itself up even further, pushing back the great flagstone as far as it could. Now its terrible head was actually clear of the floor and the sight of it would have driven many other men mad but the tailor didn't look at it. His eyes never shifted from the material in front of him.

'Do you see my awful teeth?' roared the Buggane, clashing them loudly for effect. 'They can cut a man in two with their sharpness and grind his bones to a fine powder between them. Aren't they fearful?'

'They are indeed,' replied the tailor. 'In fact, I'm almost afraid!' And, as he spoke, he moved his gaze to the window of the Broken Church. There was a hint of redness in the eastern sky but it was still very faint. In great anger, the Buggane heaved itself up out of the pit and towered above the little man. It was a gigantic creature, so tall that its head stretched high above the standing walls of the roofless building, with skin the colour of dead flesh and hands and feet that were no more than long and tearing claws. The merest glimpse of it would have quelled even the stoutest fighter on Man. The tailor, however, did not look at it, but kept on at his work, even though his heart was fairly failing within him.

'Now look upon me as I am!' howled the monster. 'Look upon me and go insane with terror!' The tailor's needle and thread flew along the seam as never before. Quickly, he stole a glance towards the window and saw that the sky to the east was growing a dull, angry red which seemed to deepen and increase by the minute. Dawn was not all that far away now.

'Just wait one moment until I finish this seam,' he told the creature. 'Then I'll look at you. I've work to complete here!' With a ringing cry of fury, the Buggane took several steps forward, its claws outstretched to grab and tear apart this foolish and impertinent mortal. As it did so, the tailor finished the last stitch on the seam.

'There!' he said. 'Now I'm done.' Just then, the sun thrust its head over the horizon, filling the land with a ruddy daylight. Dropping his work on to the floor,

the tailor made a run for it. The Buggane made to follow him but, because of the sunlight – which can destroy all monsters and dead things – it couldn't venture outside the church ruins. Without a backward glance, the tailor darted through the door and out into the day. With a furious shriek, the Buggane had to draw back and seek the cool gloom of Keeill Brisht.

The tailor made his way back down the hillside to where his friends were waiting for him, astonished that he had survived the terrors of Keeill Brisht and the attentions of its Buggane. Even though he was a bit boastful, he had still shown great courage and bravery.

Cheerfully, the tailor collected his various wagers and took his kisses and, ever after, there was a slight twinkle in his eye and a kind of half-smile upon his lips every time he passed the ruined church on the hillside. But he never ventured in there again.

The Buggane, however, was not so happy at its victim's escape, and in the darkness of its lair it swore dreadful vengeance on any other mortal who dared to venture into the ruins of Keeill Brisht after dark. So, if you should wander through the tumbled stonework of old St Trinian's when the moon is up, and if you should hear a sound that has nothing to do with the night wind, don't say that you haven't been warned!

The Water-Bull and the Nightmare Horse

It is hardly surprising that in a culture such as that of the early Celts, in which animals were often imbued with god-like qualities, certain beasts also sometimes took on demonic or monstrous aspects. Animals which were admired for their strength and virility might have a darker side to them, too, and could kill and maim when the mood took them. Contained in this belief was a race memory from more primitive times, when aboriginal man competed with the wild animals for food. Some of the creatures with whom he competed – many of which are now long extinct – were undoubtedly truly monstrous. Even today we find palaeontological evidence of our ancestors' battles with great elk, bears, immense wolves and gigantic moose and bison. Doubtless, some of these conflicts were enshrined in the stories and legends which passed from one generation to another in the primitive world.

Arguably, no creature embodied the elements of strength, ferocity and virility to ancient peoples more than the untamed bull. In many cultures, it was considered to be sacred and even played a part in early mystery religions and cults – for example, it was strongly connected with Mithraism. From earliest times the Celts both admired and revered the bull, and there is much evidence of bull-veneration right across Europe from as early as the seventh century BC. Bull figurines have been found in graves at Hallstatt in Austria, at Lexden near Colchester in Essex, and at Byciskala in the Czech Republic. There is even evidence that the humble domesticated ox was venerated both as a symbol of agricultural wealth and prosperity and for its undisputed power as a labouring animal.

Evidence further suggests that bulls may also have been one of the earliest sacrificial animals. Bulls and oxen were certainly sacrificed to other gods during the Iron Age. Elderly cattle were slaughtered and buried, probably as offerings to gods who dwelt deep underground and who feasted upon their butchered flesh. In other cases, bulls and horses that had died naturally were not butchered but offered in their entirety to the gods of earth and air. Bull sacrifice among the Celts is recorded by Pliny the Elder (*Natural History XVI: 95*), who describes the ritual slaying of two white bulls by Celtic druids at the time of the crescent (or horned) moon, and it is reasonable to suppose that such rituals were quite widespread throughout the Celtic world. This accorded to the animals a kind of supernatural status which eventually found its way into Celtic iconography and legend.

One of the greatest tales in Irish mythology, for example, concerns the Donn Cuailnge, or the Brown Bull of Cooley, and is embodied in the Ulster Myth Cycle as the Tain Bo Cuailnge (the Cattle Raid of Cooley). This enchanted bull and its counterpart, the White-horned Bull of Connaught, are the catalyst which provokes a bloody war between the provinces of Ulster and Connaught and the conflict is only ended by the deaths of the two creatures, once more demonstrating the supernatural aspect of the bull in Celtic mythology.

Bulls also appear in Scottish folklore, but in a slightly different guise. Here, they are usually fairy creatures who are associated with water – with the lochs and rivers which cut the Scottish countryside. The foremost fairy creature is the water-bull, a ferocious animal which lives in deep lakes and which can dwell if it so chooses both on land and in water. Its favourite trick is to emerge from a loch and mix with a herd grazing nearby, unnoticed by the farmer. Then it will lead the herd away into the loch, never to return. In this way, it is said, the fairies replenish their herds of cattle beneath the waters. Consequently, no farmer will allow his cattle to graze anywhere near a loch or swift-flowing river for fear they may be spirited away. Water-bulls can often be known, according to folklore, by their peculiar markings or by the curious shape of their ears.

The following story, concerning the fairy creature and linking it with another enchanted animal, was once widely told all through the west of Scotland, though its probable origin is to be found on Islay in the Inner Hebrides. It was so common at one time that the great Scottish folklore collector J.F. Campbell included a version in his *Popular Tales of the West Highlands...*

t the NORTHERN END of one of the Scottish islands (probably Islay), there lived a reasonably wealthy farmer who had a large stock of cattle. One year, a strange calf was born among them which caused great alarm, for its markings were not those of a normal cow and its ears were an odd shape. Just to be sure, the farmer brought an old woman, wise in the ways of the fairies, from the inner island to have a look at it and see what she thought. No sooner had she laid eyes upon it than she declared it to be indeed a fairy thing, a water-bull, and she recommended that it be put in a house by itself for seven years and fed on the milk of three cows during that time. All was done as the old woman advised, but that was not the end of the story. The calf grew to a ferocious size in a matter of days (a sure sign that it was a fairy creature) and became very wild, hurling itself against the door of the house as it tried to break out. All were greatly frightened of it, including the farmer himself.

A few weeks later, a servant girl went as a cowherd to tend a number of the farmer's cattle which were grazing on the banks of a nearby loch. While the cattle were so engaged, she sat herself down on a nearby bank and fell into a light doze. It was not long before she was wakened by the sound of someone coming up the bank towards her and, opening her eyes, she saw a strange man in rather grand clothes walking along its edge in her direction. His hair, however, was an untidy mess and hung in long tails and strands about his face. Stopping directly opposite the spot where she sat, he asked her as a favour to *fasg* (arrange) his hair for him. Reluctantly she agreed, for although she was suspicious of the stranger and didn't like his bold ways, he still seemed to be a gentleman of some quality and she was frightened to refuse him. Getting down beside her, he laid his head upon her knee, in the fashion of Continental lovers and their ladies, and she began slowly to untangle his locks. However, it was more difficult than she had imagined, for among the strands of hair was a green substance which wound around each individual lock. To her horror, the girl realized that this substance was 'Liobhagach an locha', a slimy water-weed which comes from either the sea, a lake or a river. The smell of the man's clothes was also salty and brackish, like something which has lain for too long upon the loch bottom.

The servant was terrified, for she now knew that the stranger was not at all human, but she also realized that if she screamed, it would be the end of her. So she stayed silent, continuing to plait the hair gently, until the stranger fell asleep on her knee. As soon as he began to snore, the girl undid her apron strings and lowered the apron to the ground with the sleeping burden still upon it. Then she fled as quickly as she could to the house of the wise woman, who lived nearby. Only once did she look behind her, and when she did she saw that the stranger had turned into a great horse-like beast (a kelpie or 'river horse') and had risen up to come after her. She screamed very loudly.

The wise woman had come to her door to see the commotion and in an instant she realized what was happening.

'Go to the farmer's house,' she commanded the girl, 'and to the place where he keeps the fairy bull. There you must open the door and let the bull out. Don't be afraid, for it won't touch you – it has other things to attend to.' The girl ran on and up towards the farm, with the nightmare fairy horse after her.

Soon she had reached the house where the farmer kept the fairy bull. From inside the place came the sound of crashing and roaring, for the bull was still desperately trying to break out of its confinement. The girl hesitated, for she was frightened of the monster within the house, but, looking behind her, she saw the horse coming after her and changing colour as it went, and she feared that even more. With a trembling hand, she shot the bolt which held back the door of the house and leapt aside.

There was a crash and a loud splintering of wood as the door was smashed away. Out came the fairy bull, snorting and bellowing and looking around it with red and menacing eyes. Terrified of being trampled to death by its hoofs, the girl flung herself on the ground, but the water-bull paid her no attention and charged straight for the nightmare steed that had been following her. The two enchanted creatures met in a crash of dust and stones and began to fight each other. They fought and fought, moving so quickly that no one who saw could determine who was winning. Soon both were nothing but a blur which began to travel across the countryside, wheeling and spinning like a whirlwind. Soon the pair of them had come to the loch from which the kelpie had originally emerged to torment the servant girl; however, they didn't stop there, but whirled straight on and into the loch, still fighting until the waters covered them up and they were seen no more. And still no man could tell which one of them was the best, so close had their contest been.

Several days later, however, the body of the bull – all torn and bloodied – was washed up on the loch shore and it crumbled to dust as soon as the rays of the sun touched it. But the terrible horse was never seen again. And, although the girl went back to the bank above the loch on several occasions afterwards, she wasn't troubled by the fairies any further.

Halflings

Within Celtic mythology and folklore there are certain creatures and entities which do not correspond to any specific category of mythological being. These might be brought together under the title 'halflings', because many of them contain both human and supernatural elements. Some, such as the Banshee, are not easy to define at all – for example, are they human, spirit, god or fairy, or do they contain aspects of all these?

Many of these beings are probably fragmentary memories of ancient gods or of demons which characterized the belief systems of the prehistoric world. In a number of ancient Myth Cycles, supernatural beings actually mated with mortals – in classical Greece, the god Zeus, in a number of elaborate disguises, showed a particular interest in sexual liaisons with mortal women; in early Hebrew tradition, the Nephilim or 'sons of God', mated with the daughters of men and spawned a race of giants. In more primitive and less developed religions, the union between human and Divine usually took on ritualized elements.

In the early Celtic world, too, with its particular emphasis upon fertility and regeneration, there is little doubt that the mating of both the natural and supernatural played an extensive role. For example, the first Celtic kings, who were thought to be the actual physical embodiment of the lands which they ruled, underwent a symbolic and ritualized copulation with the earth in order to assume their royal status and to ensure prosperity for their people throughout the coming years. Naturally, within folklore such couplings sometimes were believed to have produced actual offspring. It is thought that, in early hero tales at least, some of the mighty Celtic champions (for example, the Irish Cu Chulainn) derived their great powers from some form of supernatural ancestry. Not only this, but many ancient religions also believed in unions between humans and beasts – the more ferocious the better – in order to imbue offspring with bestial strength and attributes. Sometimes, according to folkloric traditions, such offspring were more bestial than human.

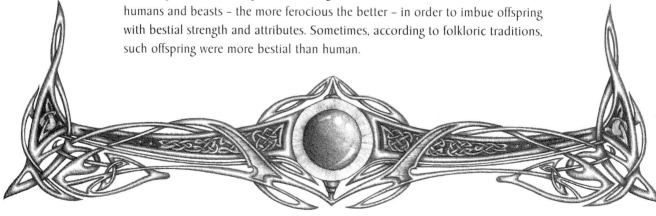

Not all unions between supernatural beings and mortals were successful. Several gave rise to ghastly misshapen creatures which were full of malicious intent towards other mortals. These, taught the Christian Church, were more commonly the result of unions between extremely lustful women and the 'demons of the air'. Such beliefs may well have been used as explanations for deformed births, which undoubtedly occurred among our ancestors. Of course, anyone who looked either different or 'odd' was often regarded with suspicion or credited with supernatural powers. An aura of mystery and fear hung around them and they were widely avoided by other, more 'normal' people. Gradually, tales concerning them passed into the folklore and legend of a particular area – unquestionably exaggerating their differences and heightening their supernatural powers.

Legends concerning the halflings, then, are a mixture of the fragmentary memories of ancient deities and forces which our ancestors once worshipped. They may also be distant recollections of our badly deformed fore-bears. In many respects, such stories still linger somewhere in the dark recesses of our conscious-ness, even today.

The Love of Aoibheall

No other Irish mythological/folkloric being is as mysterious or complex as the Banshee. As far as folktales go, it is often impossible to determine what manner of entity she is. For example, is she a fairy, a ghost or a spirit, or even a human being? Or does she contain attributes of all of these?

We are, of course, all familiar with tales of her appearances. She is the harbinger of death and destruction, who announces her presence prior to a calamatous event by loudly wailing and weeping. Sometimes she is seen, other times she is not. Even descriptions of her vary widely. Sometimes she is an old hag, at other times a matron, and at other times still a beautiful young girl. This, of course, reflects the Celtic notion of the triple goddess, sometimes also embodied as the scald or Royston crow (see page 36).

The Banshee is said only to appear to certain Irish families – those with a respected status or lineage in the Gaelic world. She was believed to attend those with the prefix 'O'' before their names (since that was often taken to imply a noble ancestry), although latterly she is said to have appeared to other families as well. Nevertheless, for a family to have an attendant Banshee is still considered in many parts of Ireland to be a mark of breeding.

So what manner of creature is the Banshee? Not even her name gives us a clue, for 'bean-Sidhe' simply means 'Woman of the Fairy', but it does not specify whether this is a woman from the fairy world, a mortal woman whom the fairies have imbued with specialist knowledge and power, or a woman who has come from the union of mortal and fairy. Again, there is confusion here, for one of the earliest references to a Banshee occurs not in Ireland at all but in medieval Scotland and it involves a mortal woman.

In 1437, King James I of Scotland was approached while processing on his way from Edinburgh to Perth by an Irish woman, who cried out as he passed her near the town of Leith, 'My lord king, you may pass by this water but you shall never return again alive.' The nobles who were with James drove her away, describing her as 'an Irish soothsayer or Banshee', and telling the king not to take any heed of her wild prophecies. The king did as they told him, but he would have done well to listen to her words, for soon after he was slain by the Earl of Atholl and his followers. In this case, the Banshee was completly human and was to be regarded as no more than a prophetess.

References to further similar Banshees are to be found in Scottish and Welsh gypsy lore, where bands of Irish vagrants, working at the various harvests, each had their own Banshee or 'wise woman' travelling with them. This person seems to have been something akin to a fortune-teller and/or healer.

Other folklorists have classed the Banshee as an ancestral spirit, the ghost of some former person connected with the family to whom she appears. In this respect, they have noted two separate aspects of the being – one a welcoming young maiden who sings sweetly in order to warn of an approaching familial death; the other a screeching hag who roars in triumph as one of the family dies. This is explained by recourse to the history of the family concerned. The welcoming Banshee is said to be the ghost of a guardian ancestor who gently guides the departing spirit into the afterlife; the other is a person against whom the family have done great wrong in times past, and who howls in savage satisfaction and glee as one of their number dies.

And what of the fairy aspect of the Banshee? Perhaps that is the oldest aspect of all, stemming from a time when the Sidhe and mortals both shared the land of Ireland. The following story is said to date from the twelfth century and concerns the relationship between a fairy woman and a mortal. It is set earlier, at the time of the final conflict between Celtic and Norse influence in Ireland – the Battle of Clontarf, on 23 April 1014. During this battle, the Celts, under their king Brian Boru, broke Norse dominion in the southern lands of Ireland for ever. The fairy woman who is mentioned here, Aoibheall, certainly appears to have existed, for she is mentioned in certain other ancient texts as being the Banshee of the Royal House of Munster...

HE SUN WAS SLOWLY BEGINNING to set and the gathering of great dark clouds along the horizon signalled the end of the day. The army had camped close to a swampy hollow between two low hills and the mist which had begun to gather there was now riven with the light from their cooking-fires. War-bothies, too, had been raised, sheltering men and animals, and beyond them were the tents of great Brian and his generals, looming like avenging ogres in the gloom. From somewhere far away, the oncoming evening echoed with the distant blast of war-horns from the Viking encampment to the west. The next day would herald a great battle, and war-weary soldiers needed to rest and sleep.

Stretched in front of his campfire, Dunlang O'Hartigan – one of the foremost of Brian's commanders – chewed on a piece of nearly burned meat which he had snatched from the blaze. It was salty and tasted strongly of woodsmoke, but it was food and a soldier like O'Hartigan couldn't afford to be choosy. On the other side of the fire, several other of Brian's generals lay half-asleep, their hands on their swords. The heavily bearded youth who lay opposite him, sleeping on his shield, was O'Hartigan's own son Turlough, and another youth who lay to one side of him, Brian Boru's son Conlaig. The High King's other son, Murrough, half-crouched before the flames, his hands on the pommel of his longsword, staring deep into the centre of the fire. Its light made his face seem ruddy and charged with blood. O'Hartigan knew that, in his own way, each man dreamed of the battle on the morrow and that, in his own way, each man also feared it. There would be great slaughter. From far away, the Viking war-horns blared against the oncoming dusk. It was a trick to unsettle Brian's army and by the gods it was working! O'Hartigan gulped down another piece of the meat and offered the remainder to Murrough, but the warrior shook his head.

'There will be much death tomorrow!' The older man chewed on the gobbet of gristle, allowing juices to run down into his beard. 'There is talk that we won't be able to drive the Norse curs back to the sea. They say that there are over 1,000 of them added to what Irish troops the renegade Maelmore has brought with him from Leinster.' Conlaig shifted, moving nearer the fire.

'They say that the Norse have brought giants with them from the Northern Isles as well,' he said slowly. 'And that they'll use them as warriors against us!' O'Hartigan snorted contemptuously.

'All old wives' tales,' he replied. 'Great Brian has brought warriors from all over the Celtic world and there's no match for any of them. The Mormaer of Ce has brought nearly 2,000 troops from Dalriada across the Sea of Moyle and I've heard that Breton troops are arriving by the day from Armorica. We'll give those Norse curs something to think about tomorrow.' The younger men remained unconvinced.

'Even so,' said Conlaig uncertainly, wiping his beard, 'the Vikings are hardened fighters – there are Manx men among them whom, they say...' O'Hartigan silenced him with a wave of his hand.

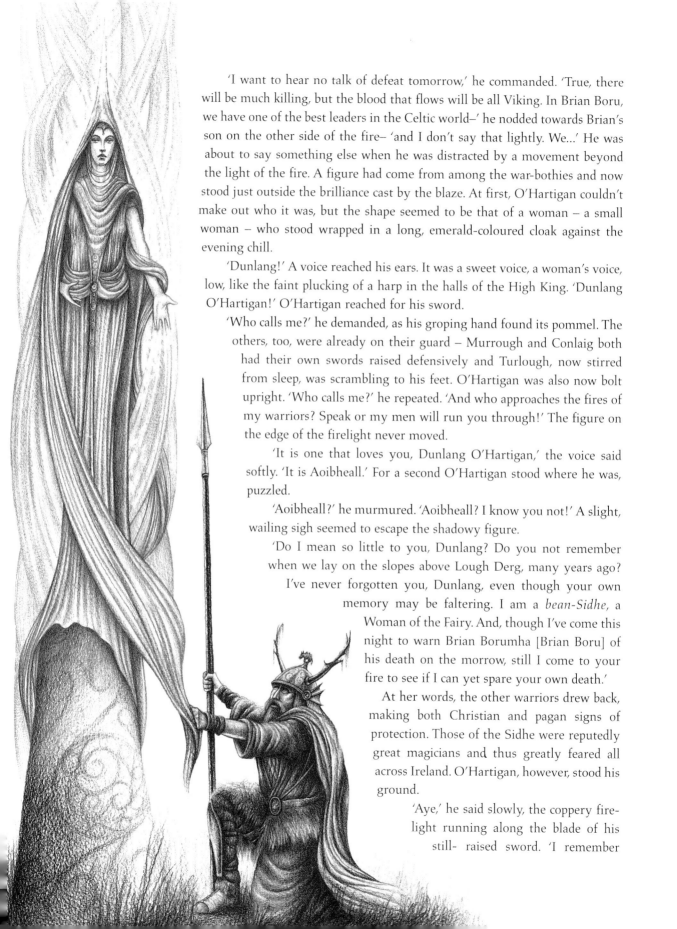

'I want to hear no talk of defeat tomorrow,' he commanded. 'True, there will be much killing, but the blood that flows will be all Viking. In Brian Boru, we have one of the best leaders in the Celtic world–' he nodded towards Brian's son on the other side of the fire– 'and I don't say that lightly. We...' He was about to say something else when he was distracted by a movement beyond the light of the fire. A figure had come from among the war-bothies and now stood just outside the brilliance cast by the blaze. At first, O'Hartigan couldn't make out who it was, but the shape seemed to be that of a woman – a small woman – who stood wrapped in a long, emerald-coloured cloak against the evening chill.

'Dunlang!' A voice reached his ears. It was a sweet voice, a woman's voice, low, like the faint plucking of a harp in the halls of the High King. 'Dunlang O'Hartigan!' O'Hartigan reached for his sword.

'Who calls me?' he demanded, as his groping hand found its pommel. The others, too, were already on their guard – Murrough and Conlaig both had their own swords raised defensively and Turlough, now stirred from sleep, was scrambling to his feet. O'Hartigan was also now bolt upright. 'Who calls me?' he repeated. 'And who approaches the fires of my warriors? Speak or my men will run you through!' The figure on the edge of the firelight never moved.

'It is one that loves you, Dunlang O'Hartigan,' the voice said softly. 'It is Aoibheall.' For a second O'Hartigan stood where he was, puzzled.

'Aoibheall?' he murmured. 'Aoibheall? I know you not!' A slight, wailing sigh seemed to escape the shadowy figure.

'Do I mean so little to you, Dunlang? Do you not remember when we lay on the slopes above Lough Derg, many years ago? I've never forgotten you, Dunlang, even though your own memory may be faltering. I am a *bean-Sidhe*, a Woman of the Fairy. And, though I've come this night to warn Brian Borumha [Brian Boru] of his death on the morrow, still I come to your fire to see if I can yet spare your own death.'

At her words, the other warriors drew back, making both Christian and pagan signs of protection. Those of the Sidhe were reputedly great magicians and thus greatly feared all across Ireland. O'Hartigan, however, stood his ground.

'Aye,' he said slowly, the coppery firelight running along the blade of his still-raised sword. 'I remember you, woman of the Sidhe, but that was years ago when I was a young man. I have a wife now and sons of my own. What is it that you want with me now, in my declining years?' The shadowy figure sighed once more and took a step nearer the fire. The warriors drew back slightly, murmuring fearfully as they did so. O'Hartigan could see Aoibheall more clearly. She hadn't aged at all, for she was as he remembered her those long years ago, small and intensely beautiful, her long dark locks flowing over the shoulders of her green cloak, her face narrow and with large staring eyes which always seemed filled with wonder. Her skin was as pale as the untrampled snow, accentuated by the darkness of her garments. She was, every inch, one of the Sidhe. Behind O'Hartigan, the warriors murmured even more fearfully among themselves. Aoibheall paid no attention to them, but kept her dark, almost pupil-less eyes fixed on Dunlang.

'I loved you then, Dunlang O'Hartigan,' she said in her low, melodic voice, 'and I love you yet. I have always loved you. When you rode into battle against the forces of Leinster, I watched you from afar; when you pledged your sword to the Borumha, I looked upon you from the shadows; and when you married and your wife gave you strong sons, I watched and wept. I make no demands upon you but have come with an offer. It is an offer made in love, Dunlang. It is an offer of life. Although great Brian must die at the hands of the Norsemen, the Sidhe have agreed to spare your life and that of your sons, but you must submit to my request.' The warriors now clustered around O'Hartigan in an almost protective circle, their longswords drawn.

'Careful, Dunlang,' hissed Murrough, 'it could be a Norse trick. I even sense Maelmore's hand in this.' Turlough, however, was not so sure.

'Hear what she has to say, Father. Ask her what her offer is. If the Sidhe will help us, we may live to fight for ever.' O'Hartigan's face narrowed.

'Speak then,' he snapped. 'For I'll hear what sort of offer you want to make. But take note, whatever it is, it'll not deflect me from my service to Brian.' Aoibheall shook her head.

'After night has fallen tomorrow, Mael MacDomnhaill will sit as High King of Ireland,' she said, 'and the Borumha will be king no more. But if you set aside fighting for just one day – do not take up arms on the morrow – the Sidhe will promise you and your sons 200 years of life on the earth. But you must not fight, for if you do, you will surely die. Aye, and all your household as well. And I would not have that, for I still love you.' O'Hartigan's breath escaped in a fierce hiss.

'See,' whispered Murrough at his elbow. 'It's a Norse trick, Dunlang. They seek to make us put up our swords and deflect us from the conflict, so that they can overrun our camp and slay great Brian. Our own armies and those of our enemies are too finely balanced. For one of our commanders not to fight would undoubtedly give victory to the Norse! Tell her to go about her business and pay her no heed! If needs be, kill her where she stands!' O'Hartigan stroked his beard thoughtfully.

'You speak of killing far too impetuously, Murrough. As one of the Sidhe, she poses no real threat to us,' he said at length, 'and her business is with great Brian himself. What she says may be true regarding his death tomorrow, but I am a warrior and can serve Mael MacDomnhaill as my king as well as I can Brian Borumha. I further sense that she speaks truly with regard to the 200 years of life which she offers me and my sons. Let her go on her way and utter her prophecies to the High King, but as for her offer, I think that we can turn our backs on that. The battle tomorrow against the Norse will be fierce and bloody and every sword will be needed. Any man who will not fight for Brian in such a conflict deserves to be branded as great a craven traitor as Maelmore. Such a name will not hang upon Dunlang O'Hartigan or his brood.' He turned to the Banshee, who still stood in the light from the fire. 'Go with my blessing and issue your prophecy. As for myself, I would rather die in a day on the field of battle than live for 200 years as a coward.' Aoibheall's dark eyes widened and appeared to fill with tears.

'There is no way that I can change your mind, my love?' she enquired, but O'Hartigan shook his head.

'Now go!' he commanded. 'Brian awaits your news of his fate. I will take whatever I am given in the field tomorrow – whether it be glory or death.' Still grieving, Aoibheall turned away. But Turlough caught the edge of her cloak.

'Tell me this, *bean-Sidhe*, since you have the gift of prophecy – by the setting of the sun tomorrow, will Brian's army be victorious against the Viking foe?' Aoibheall looked at him long and sadly as if considering a response to his words.

'They will be victorious,' she answered with a great weariness in her voice, 'but you will not see it.' And, in an instant, she was gone, as though she had been no more than a shadow or a flimsy fragment of smoke from the fire. The warriors looked at each other uneasily.

Brian Boru was sitting in his war-tent, deep in thought, when Dunlang O'Hartigan approached him. The Irish High King started suddenly as the warrior's shadow fell across him. Seeing Dunlang, the old man broke into a slow and relieved smile.

'Forgive me, Dunlang. I thought...' but O'Hartigan was able to finish the sentence for him.

'You thought that the *bean-Sidhe* had returned with further prophecies for the morrow,' he said. Brian looked at him in wonder, his aged brow becoming increasingly furrowed.

'How...' Then some light of recognition dawned behind his eyes. 'You too!' O'Hartigan nodded. 'She has long gone,' went on the High King, 'but she told me that I shall die tomorrow by the hand of a Manx king and that my distant kinsman Mael MacDomnhaill will be High King after me. She says that I shall not live to see the final outcome of the battle.' O'Hartigan nodded. 'And what did she prophesy for you, my captain?' Dunlang swallowed.

'She promised me and my sons 200 years of life if I would put aside fighting for my king for a single day on the morrow. This offer I refused, even though she claimed to love me.' Brian smiled wearily.

'You should have taken it,' he replied. 'It is not often the Sidhe offer the gift of 200 years of life to a mortal soldier.' O'Hartigan looked away, unable to meet his king's sad gaze.

'My king, it's true that I've given up much. I've given up a life without death, without cold, without hunger, without thirst and without decay. I've given up the delights which being loved by a fairy woman can bring. But remember, Brian, that several years ago I swore an oath of loyalty to the High King of Ireland that I would stand by his side no matter what foe he faced and that I would not turn from this duty. And what greater delight for a warrior than to die on the field of battle and on the same day as his king and friend.' Tears were now flowing freely from Brian's tired eyes as, standing up, he stretched his hand forward and gripped Dunlang's broad shoulder.

'Truly,' he said, emotion clouding his voice, 'with a warrior like you, I am the most fortunate of kings.' Dunlang bowed his head so that Brian would not see his own tears.

It was the morning of Good Friday 1014, and the hills overlooking Clontarf were black with Celtic soldiers. Many were fresh from Mass and had been marked with the cross of the White Christ on their foreheads. Striding up to where the rest of his company stood, Dunlang O'Hartigan looked across to where the Norse army was still massing.

'What do you see?' he asked Murrough, who had been scanning the Norse army for a few minutes. The warrior grunted.

'I see the standards of Sigurd Hulversson of Orkney,' he reported, squinting slightly against the morning sun, 'and those of Sygtrygg of Dublin.'

'And to the west, the pennants of the traitor Maelmore and his contingent of Leinstermen,' added Turlough, spitting in the dust. 'Theirs is truly a mighty host. As big as the stories have said.' O'Hartigan gave a laugh which lacked mirth of any kind.

'All the more to perish before our swords then,' he replied. 'All the more to be cut down like wheat before a scythe.'

'And above it all,' whispered Murrough, 'I see the Morrigu, wheeling like a ghost in the air overhead.' Dunlang snorted.

'Enough superstition! We'll...Hello, something's happening.' There was a movement further along the Celtic line and the war-horns of the Vikings blared. From behind Dunlang came a mighty roar from a group of Dalriadic Scots from Ce, slightly further up the hill. They mocked the Vikings across the valley.

'It seems we're ready for battle,' murmured Dunlang. 'Great Brian has given the command.' And suddenly he was running, a loud scream tearing from his throat, down the hill with Irish and Scots on either side, towards the Viking enemy.

Thus the two great armies from both the Norse and Celtic worlds met at Clontarf on Good Friday. And as they fought, the air above them turned black and seemed to be full of wheeling spirits as the Sidhe came to watch. Fiercer and fiercer grew the battle, while darker and darker became the sky. It was a red and butchering day, with both forces almost equally matched, and as the sun set among bloody clouds the battlefield lay black with the corpses of the fallen, where great hooded crows strutted and pecked. From time to time, women wrapped in shawls would wander, looking for lovers or husbands and sending up great cries of grief when they found the bodies.

Among these camp-followers and hunters of the dead was one wrapped in an embroidered cloak of emerald green. She moved between the crumpled bodies and broken and abandoned weapons, looking – constantly looking. Suddenly, she paused above a particularly mutilated heap of corpses. Reaching down with a pale hand, she pulled one away, sending its head rolling across the blood-soaked ground. Murrough's sightless eyes stared up at her. To the left lay the tattered remnants of what had once been Turlough. Of Conlaig there was no sign, but she knew that he, too, was dead.

Yet it was the torn body before her which she sought, and as she knelt beside it, lifting the broken war-helm from its bloodied head, she sent up a great howl of anguish and despair which far outdid the keens of the other woman on the battle-field. Reaching down, Aoibheall began to clean away the blood from the dead face of Dunlang O'Hartigan with the edge of her cloak. And when Dunlang's own mortal wife came to reclaim his body, the Banshee stole away, returning to the slopes above Lough Derg, where her eerie song can still be heard today, pining for her lost love.

At Clontarf, the Celtic forces of Brian MacCennetig (or Borumha or Boru – 'of the tributes'), Lord of the Dal Cais and High King of Ireland, completely broke Norse power in the country. The victory was not without its price, for Brian's army, although triumphant, suffered severe and heavy casualties. Among them was Brian himself, slain in the door of his tent as he waited for news of victory by an axe which had been thrown by the Manx-Norse warlord Brodr. At the time of his death, Brian was 72 years old and had taken no part in any of the fighting. His successor as High King was his distant kinsman, Mael MacDumnhaill.

The Changeling

Legends concerning changelings appear throughout the Celtic storytelling tradition, especially in Ireland, and are usually the focus of great fear and suspicion. Changelings were stunted, complaining, wizened and unhealthy creatures who were believed to have been substituted by the fairies for normal healthy children which they had stolen away. In some traditions, the changeling was itself a fairy which had been driven out by its own kind; in others, it was a half-human/half-fairy being, the spawn of a prohibited union between the Sidhe and mortal worlds and shunned by both. Whatever its origins, it was regarded as a 'cuckoo in the nest' of the mortal family to which it was attached. In many instances, it was supposed to bring ill-fortune, reducing the family to poverty and destitution.

The belief may partly have its roots in the advance of Christianity across the Celtic world and from its teaching to have young children baptized into the faith. Any child which had not received the sacrament of baptism, according to Church teaching, was especially at risk from the attentions of demons. Only the sprinkling of the baptismal waters could protect it from their wiles. Preachers pointed out the high instance of infant mortality in the early world – those who had been baptized into the Church were holy innocents and their souls were now with the Lord, but the souls of those who had not were snatched away by infernal spirits and condemned to the torments of Hell. It was a natural progression to incorporate this religious belief with Celtic folk tradition and to transform the swarming demons which crowded around the crib of the unbaptized child into the trooping fairies who desired mortal children for their own.

Later the story was modified so the fairies not only took the child with them, but left one of their own – a nasty, bad-tempered and complaining imp – in its place. Such changed children did not live long (usually no more than 12 or 13 years, although some appear to have lived longer) and during their brief lives they required constant attention. In many cases they had a deformity or disability which set them aside from other people. Some couldn't walk, others were dumb, others still had cleft palates, peculiar squints, or were blind. Nevertheless, changelings often exhibited both wisdom and cunning beyond their years. It was their love of music, however, which sometimes gave them away, because, coming from the fairy tradition, they were inordinately fond of music and had an ear for a good tune. Many were particularly fine musicians, despite their crabbed looks and sullen ways.

It is, of course, not hard to see that the changeling beliefs were frequently used to explain the onset of a natural illness and physical defects in small children. Tuberculosis, for example, produced many of the symptoms which characterized the changelings – pinched, pale features; continual crying and irritability; loss of appetite (refusal to take the breast); and so on. The notion of changelings was particularly widespread in Irish areas such as the Burren in County Clare, which is believed to have suffered periodic epidemics of tuburculosis during the mid- to late nineteenth century. The belief served to explain why beautiful, robust children detriorated, almost overnight, into whingeing, unhealthy creatures and why they subsequently continued to decline, until death. Even when a baby died, the belief offered at least *some* consolation to the anguished parents – after all, it was not really *their* baby who had died but a substitute from the fairy world. Their own offspring was still a prisoner of the fairies and might yet be returned to them at some future date. If nothing else, the belief provided some psychological hope for them. Nevertheless, looking after the mewling 'fairy' creature in the crib was a daunting task for any mother.

Babies, therefore, needed to be protected from such evil substitution. This could be done in a number of ways. The most effective, as we have already noted, was to have the baby baptized as quickly as possible. However, in remote rural areas this was not always possible, so other protective measures had to be invoked until baptism could take place. A crucifix or St Brigit's Cross placed above the crib would serve to keep the fairies at bay until a priest could arrive. Failing that, an older remedy would suffice. The father of the child would place an item of his own clothing across the crib in which the infant lay sleeping. By doing this, he reminded the fairies that the little one was, in fact, human and belonged to him. Such measures, however, were not always effective and children still seemed inexplicably to sicken and wizen. This was often attributed to the formidable dark powers operating in a district. Where protection failed, it was sometimes believed that the changeling could be 'driven out' of a house and that if this were effected, the fairies would be compelled to return the child which they had originally stolen away.

There were many suggestions, for the 'driving out' of a changeling and the restoration of an abducted mortal child, some of them quite horrific. One was to trick the changeling into admitting its age, which would probably be longer than any mortal span (for, even though they resembled children, changelings were already supposed to be hundreds of years old), thereby confirming that it was indeed a fairy creature. On such an admission, the being would be forced to flee, returning the mortal child at the same instant. This method forms the basis of the popular Irish folktale *The Brewery of Eggshells*. It has to be said, however, that this means of exposure was frequently extremely difficult. True to its disguise, the changeling often refused to speak and therefore could not be lightly trapped in this fashion.

Other disposal methods, were less pleasant. One was to feed the infant on a mixture of lusmore (foxglove) and warmed milk. Traditional lore held that fairies feared foxglove and that its introduction into the child's food would, 'burn out the entrails' of the supernatural creature. With foxglove being a natural poison, it may certainly have achieved this effect!

The most effective method to rid the house of a changeling, however, was to place it on the iron blade of a shovel and hold it over a raging fire. During this operation, the following incantation was to be repeated: 'Burn, burn burn – if of the Devil, burn; but if of God and the saints, be free from harm.' Terrified by the flames, the changeling would immediately rush up the chimney, for there was a strong belief among the Celts that fire was the greatest enemy of all sorts of ghosts and phantoms. All that would be left on the shovel blade would be a blackened bit of stick, and the true child would be returned within the hour. Although this sounds like appalling behaviour on the part of any parent, there is little doubt that it was tried on many occasions in the remoter parts of Ireland, Wales and Scotland.

In some exceptional cases, it was not a small infant who was taken at all but a mature adult. A 'stock' or substitute would then be left, which to all intents and purposes *appeared* to be the person concerned (albeit in a rather sickly state), but to the trained eye was indeed a fairy creature. Priests' housekeepers, relatives and friends were especially at risk – Lady Wilde, for example, tells in her *Visions and Beliefs in the West of Ireland* of a priest's sister (who was also his housekeeper) in Kilcloud, County Sligo, who in the latter part of the nineteenth century was taken and held by the fairies for a period of seven years before being returned. During the time in which she was 'away with the fairies', a representation of her sat on a piece of rush matting in a corner, refusing to speak or eat, and simply drawing a bit of a veil over its face when approached (presumably to prevent others from looking too closely at it) and moaning to itself in a low, strained voice.

At the end of the time, the woman unexpectedly 'came to herself' and resumed her housekeeping duties. She remembered nothing of what had happened to her during the seven-year period. It was simply assumed that she had somehow returned from the fairy world and that the 'stock' or shape which had taken her place in the mortal sphere was now gone. Nowadays we would look for some mental cause to explain her odd behaviour – a breakdown of some sort, perhaps – but this was not really an option for the people of the time and in the locality. For them, the notion of the 'fairy abduction' served just as well.

Incidentally, a similar notion of fairy abduction provided the foundation for the last 'witch burning' in the British Isles. This occurred in Ballyvadlea, near Clonmel in County Tipperary, Ireland, in 1895, when Michael Cleary, convinced that his wife, Bridget – who was very ill at the time – was actually a changeling creature (the real Bridget, he believed, was being held in nearby Kylegranagh Hill), held her over an open fire in order to drive the evil being out of his cottage and bring his true wife back to him. In this he was assisted by Bridget's own father and several of his neighbours, indicating just how strong the changeling belief was in certain rural areas of Ireland. Bridget, of course, died from her ordeal and was secretly buried near her house to encourage her true, mortal self to return. This particular case has been well documented and is worth studying as an example of the changeling tradition.

Although extremely widespread throughout Ireland, the notion of the changeling also occurs elsewhere in Celtic tradition. In England, for example, the belief appears in Shakespeare's *A Midsummer Night's Dream* (Act 2 Scene 1), while in Spenser's *Faerie Queen* (Book 1 Canto 10):

A Fairy thee unweeting reft,
There as thou slept in tender swadling band,
And her base elfin brood there for thee left,
Such men do changelings call - so changed by fairies theft.

The following story comes originally, I believe, from the Isle of Man, but variants of it are quoted by folklorists from other Celtic areas as well...

A family named Cubbon, living near Dalby, had a poor idiot baby which was continually crying and making a nuisance of itself in the house. Even when it grew up to be a man of about 19 or 20 years old, it still lay on a mat before the fire like a small infant would do. The father was a good-hearted farmer who worked very hard for all his family, but no matter how hard he laboured there was just no satisfying this idiot being. It lay upon its mat and howled for food, and when something was brought to it, it was speedily gobbled up and the creature shouted for more. It couldn't speak like a normal person but made strange, grunting shouts which frightened everybody in the house. There was no clothing it either, for it grew out of everything that was put on its back and still needed more. The mother and father worked themselves to distraction, but the harder they worked, the more this creature wanted from them.

It was a wizened and pinched-looking thing and it seemed to grow all awkwardly – a bit growing here and there and other bits not growing at all – so clothes were difficult to buy for it and the mother had to have them specially made, which cost more money, of course. But they never stinted, even though they had very little luck after the child was born. It was just as if this big baby was taking all the luck out of the house, as well as the food and clothes. Still, the parents looked after it extremely well and Mrs Cubbon even hired the services of a travelling tailor to help make the idiot's clothes. As they couldn't pay much, the tailor had his keep with them and soon became very friendly with the family. Indeed, he became such a good friend that he looked after the house for them when they were out and took care of the idiot, for he had no fear of it as some others did.

One day, the tailor was sitting in the kitchen, working at the table. Mrs Cubbon had gone out of the house on some message or other and had left the idiot on its mat in front of the fire as usual. It seemed to be watching the blaze very intently. As the tailor worked, he whistled a dancing tune that he'd heard on his travels across Man, and a very lively tune it was. And, as the tailor whistled, he idiot seemed to be paying more and more attention to the melody. All of a sudden, it sat bolt upright and looked all around it. Looking at the tailor very craftily, it spoke. Its words took him by surprise for, in all its life, it had never spoken before, only gurgled and mewled like an animal. Its voice was cracked and ancient-sounding, like the tones of a very, very old man and there was a slyness in its words, too.

'That's a very good tune that you're whistling!' said the idiot.

'It is indeed,' answered the tailor, still greatly astonished. 'It's played at a good many dances all over the island.'

'Well,' said the idiot, 'if you don't tell anybody when they come back to the house, I'll dance that tune for you!' Now this took the tailor even more by surprise, for the idiot had never walked, let alone danced, since the day that it had been born. He began to suspect that there was something strange about it and that it mightn't even be human at all. Still, he kept his nerve and answered it.

'Go on then!' said he. 'For I'll not believe it until I see it myself.' Whereupon

the idiot got up from the mat and began to caper about the floor, while the tailor whistled the tune and clapped his hands in time. And a fine job it made of the dance, for it could certainly step out well enough. Then, when the tune was finished, it lay down on the mat once more and never moved. But it kept watching its companion out of the corner of one squinty eye. The tailor, although a bit shaken by these mysterious events, kept on at his work, and at length began to whistle another tune – a mournful lament this time. The idiot pricked up its ears once more.

'That's another fine tune,' it said suddenly, 'and if you don't tell anybody when they come back to the house, I'll play it for you on that fiddle up there.' And it indicated its father's fiddle, which hung above the fireplace. The tailor was now even more taken aback, but still he held his nerve.

'Do it then!' he told it. 'For I'll not believe *that* until I see it with my own eyes.' The idiot got up from its mat, took down the fiddle and began to play. The tailor had never heard such sweet and melodic music before. And when it had finished one tune, the idiot struck up some more – old, old tunes that the people had long forgotten. So the tailor and the idiot spent a very enjoyable afternoon together. But, as soon as Mrs Cubbon came to the door, all the music and jollification stopped and the idiot lay down on its mat again in front of the fire, just like a big baby. All was as it should have been.

'You've a fine chap there!' said the tailor as soon as the mother came in, indicating the idiot. The woman smiled wanly.

'Yes indeed,' she said with a great weariness in her voice. 'It's a great pity that he'll never be right, for he's a bit of a handful, even at the best of times.' And as if in response, the idiot squinted up its eyes like those of an old man, watching her from under the lashes. The tailor laughed and shook his head.

'Oh, but he and I have had a fine time this afternoon,' he replied, 'and he was great entertainment.' He paused. The idiot now shifted its gaze to look at him warily. 'What with his fine dancing and all.' The mother looked at him, wide-eyed with astonishment.

'Oh, but the poor thing could never even walk,' she protested as she went to place some more wood on the fire. 'He's been lame since birth.' Once again, the tailor shook his head.

'Ah, but he can play the fiddle as well,' he went on. 'So I'd stoke up the fire, good and hot, for I think that we've something not quite right here – something supernatural, maybe.' And so more wood was thrown on the blaze and it roared up, sending out great reeking clouds of smoke. All the while, the idiot mewled and gurgled, making stranger and stranger noises and frenzied signals with its hands. Mrs Cubbon was by now becoming very frightened and would have turned and run, but the tailor motioned her to stand where she was. He fixed the idiot with a steely gaze as it thrashed and wailed in an alarming manner on the mat.

'Maybe you should stop this,' suggested Mrs Cubbon, 'for we seem to be frightening him. He's not a well child, you know!' By this time, the idiot was practically howling, but the tailor threw another log on to the fire.

'All this is for you,' he said to the idiot. 'For I think that you are a changeling and only fire can drive one of your kind from a house.' The idiot watched him with its squinty glare. There was now a queer 'knowing' manner about the way that it watched its mother and the tailor. Without warning, it pulled a little black ball out of its pocket and threw it on to the floor, where it went rolling across the flagstones. And, as its mother and the tailor watched, the idiot jumped to its feet and ran after it. Out of the door and into the road outside went the ball with the idiot close behind. Over the hills it went and was soon lost to view, never to be seen again. It was as though a great, dark cloud had been lifted, for the family began to thrive and prosper again. They had many more children, but never again were they plagued by the demands of a changeling. But they'd had a lucky escape, all right, thanks to their friend the tailor!

The Lady of the Forest

It was not only the spawn of gods and fairies which constituted the halflings of ancient Celtic folkloric tradition, for there were also certain tales of the offspring of mortals and animals. Such stories may have had their origins in what sociologists now refer to as 'feral children' – that is, children who have been raised in the wild. There is little doubt that at least some ancient and medieval societies were less stable than our own. Tales of children being abandoned in the wild by parents who were subsequently slain in raids or who simply couldn't cope with the pressures of family life are legion in folklore and may hint at an actual, darker, historical truth. In many such stories, the children are raised by wild animals who look after them and care for them. In early Latin folklore, for example, the twin founders of Rome, Romulus and Remus, are so abandoned, but are raised and suckled by a she-wolf.

This belief may be a continuation of the ancient religions which inextricably linked men and animals with unions between the two. The offspring of such unions then took on some of the attributes of their animal-parent (an extension of the notion of totem in many early societies), becoming brave like the wolf or strong like the bear.

There is no doubt, however, that many children *were* abandoned in the wild at times of societal crisis – indeed, the practice still continues today in some parts of the world. Such children sometimes turned up again, exhibiting the characteristics of the wilderness which distinguished them from 'normal, settled' people. Faced with a 'wild boy' or 'wilderness man', it was but a small step to believe him imbued with supernatural powers and to attribute supernormal feats to him. This may be the actual origin of the idea of the werewolf – the half-man/half-wolf who dwelt in the forest and only appeared when the moon was full. There is also, in certain parts of eastern Europe, the idea of the Wolf or Animal Master – a human who shares a natural affinity with animals (particularly wolves), which he or she commands. Such beliefs were also, at one time, widespread in parts of rural France, and it is worth noting the high incidence of werewolf trials in certain French regions during the sixteenth and seventeenth centuries as an indication of the intensity of this phenomenon.

But wolves and bears are not the only creatures with which human beings have been linked. We have already considered the serpent (see page 86). At one time, the ideological connection between snakes, serpents and human beings may well have been extremely strong and very complex. This connection has translated itself into local folklore, particularly in Brittany, where tales of serpent-women – sometimes women who had mated with serpents – once abounded. This was the ultimate halfling, the monstrous fusion of human with reptile, and was greatly to be feared. The following story, which is a variant of an old Breton legend, is a good example of the continuance of this particular belief...

IGHT WAS NOT FAR away, and already the setting sun was sending strange shapes and shadows scuttling along the forest track. Touched by the final rays of its gloomy fire, the trees on either side of the narrow trail took on dark and monstrous forms which appeared to tower over and threaten any traveller who made his way home through the deep woodland. Here and there, a nightbird called eerily to its mate, before fluttering away through the overhanging branches to its nest, and a light if chilling breeze swirled about the trackside tree-boles, touching low shrubs and bushes with its cooling breath.

At a forest crossroads, the chevalier reined in his horse and tightened his cloak around his shoulders at the oncoming night cold. He had hoped to be through this forest and back in his castle before nightfall, but now this didn't look entirely possible. The woodlands had a particularly sinister reputation: they were rumoured to be the haunt of ghouls and werewolves. They were further said to have been a place where the Celtic druids had conducted particularly foul rites – the ruins of their circles and temples still littered the deep forest areas, and it was believed that certain of the things which these ancient witch-men had worshipped still lingered in secret places deep among the pathless tangle. Why, only recently one of his own woodsmen had brought back the grey and matted pelt of a creature which he claimed to have slain deep in a forest glade – a creature which had promptly turned into a man and vanished before his eyes. And he had spoken to others who had seen things between the woodland trees. These had been no more than shadows but they had, he was told, no parallel in the sane and wholesome world – a gigantic man-like creature known as Le Grand Bissetre, which hovered and howled at certain pools in the trackless waste; tiny, luminous and malignant sprites – *lutins de nuit* – which lured unwary travellers into hidden marshes among the trees; and beings which took on the form of great dogs – *meneurs de loup* – in order to attack and savage innocents who were abroad on the forest roads after dark.

All this the chevalier remembered, as he felt the forest chill seep through his heavy cloak and faintly touch his bones. Still, he hoped that it wouldn't be too long before he was sitting once more in front of his own roaring fire, shielded against the night by the walls of his own stronghold – if only he could find his way out of this damned forest. He certainly had a notion as to where he might be, but the forest trails seemed to move and change, and he was growing more and more unsure of his direction by the minute. Still, he didn't want to admit, even to himself, that he was lost and at the mercy of the supernatural things which might dwell deep in this woodland. Desperately, he looked around for the hut of a forester or charcoal burner – these, he had assumed, were always to be found at crossroads – where he might confirm his road, but each way he looked he saw only an empty trail lined by monstrous and shadowy trees. All about him the forest grew darker, as the sun declined and the evening shadows grew longer and thicker.

From seemingly far away he heard it – faintly at first, then becoming slightly clearer, as though the source of the sound were slowly moving between the trees in another part of the forest. It was the sound of someone singing – a woman – her voice rising over even the high fluting calls of the late birdsong. And, as he listened, the chevalier knew that he had never before heard anything quite so sweet. He partly recognized the song – it was a very old tune, long out of fashion – and it reminded him of his youth. Listening to it, he recalled youthful hopes and lost loves; adventures attempted and then abandoned in some former time; of attachments formed and then lost for ever. Bereft of lute or other musical instrument, the sound of it seemed to swoop and dance between the ancient trees of the forest and away to the countryside beyond. It was both achingly sad and hauntingly beautiful at the same time.

'I must see who it is that sings so sweetly at this hour of the evening,' muttered the chevalier to himself. The sound was rising and falling between the trees – now dying away, now rising clearly again, so that he couldn't really determine its origin. Still he urged his horse forward and off the track, in what he assumed was the direction from which the singing came. At first the animal seemed unwilling to go, but gradually it began to move slowly and haltingly between the trees. The sound of singing seemed to grow nearer and the chevalier guessed that he was now drawing near to she who sang.

The forest suddenly thinned out and the horseman found himself on the edge of a clearing somewhere near the heart of the woodland. A single but relatively strong shaft of the fading daylight flooded the place with a dull, grey brilliance which revealed a large pool in its centre, surrounded by badly overgrown ruins, obviously from some distant and antique period. The pool and the ruins had undoubtedly formed part of some extremely ancient complex. But it was not the fallen stones that held the horseman's astonished gaze, for sitting on the crumbling, green-grown steps which led down to the very edge of the pool was a young woman who sang softly and sweetly to herself.

The chevalier was staggered, for never before had he seen so beautiful a woman. Her dark hair fell in light and flowing ripples across her shoulders, framing a small, heart-shaped face from which large and faintly luminous eyes looked up. She wore a long flowing dress of the softest green, which cascaded down the time-worn steps to the edge of the pool below her. At the sight of the singing woman and the ancient ruins, the horse shied and refused to go any further, forcing the chevalier to dismount and step into the glade. Uncertain of himself, he drew his sword and moved forward.

At his approach, the woman looked up.

'Who is it who approaches me at this hour with his sword drawn?' she demanded. 'Are you a robber, sir, come to slay me for anticipated wealth? If so, I doubt you will find anything of value here, for these ruins are old and conceal only moss and forest rot.' The chevalier lowered his blade.

'Forgive me, madam,' he said, bowing low, 'I mean you no harm, for I'm no bandit. I am a traveller in these woodlands, drawn here by your wonderful singing.' The woman regarded him warily.

'I am glad to hear that you are not a robber, sir,' she replied, 'for I am a woman here alone and without any to protect me! I am also most gratified that you should find my poor song so pleasing. If you wish it, you may stay with me and listen to further melodies, for I am accustomed to come here and to sing from this hour until the sun has finally set.' She motioned to a creeper-covered mound. 'I pray you, sit a while.'

And so, even though the darkness was creeping across the forest, the chevalier sat down and listened to the strange forest woman sing. The melodies that she sang were both ancient and very beautiful – songs of loves from long ago, of great exploits and near-forgotten sadnesses. Her voice was as clear and pure as the sound of spring water bubbling from the mouth of a stone jar. The chevalier was spellbound, for the tunes awoke in him other memories from times long past. As she finished, he applauded her loudly.

'Bravo, madam!' he cried. 'I've never heard melodies of such rarity sung in such a beautiful way.' The lady blushed slightly and prettily lowered her head.

'Oh tush, sir!' she answered modestly. 'I'm sure that there are many girls about your castle who can turn a tune much prettier than I!' The chevalier shook his head.

'None can sing as well,' he protested. 'Not even the professional singers in the theatres, I declare! Will you sing to me some more before I set out for home again?' The girl kept her head lowered.

'Alas, sir. The moon is already out and I must away to my own bed. But if you should come this way again and at this hour of the evening, I will sing you some more of my poor tunes.' The chevalier quickly declared that he would be back to hear her the very next night and she smiled approvingly at him, the first strands of moonlight touching the side of her beautiful face with its silver fingers. He asked her for directions back to his castle and she gave them without hesitation and then, crossing to where his horse still grazed under the trees, he mounted and left her sitting by the pool. He should have realized, as he rode away, that although the moon was up and flooding the forest with its wan brilliance, the lady by the pool cast no shadow in its light.

He found his way back to his castle without any trouble – it was almost as if his horse knew where to go – and was soon sitting in front of the roaring fire which he had imagined earlier. He should have been content. And yet he was troubled, for he could not get the strange forest maiden out of his mind. He only had to shut his eyes to see her face and, as it rushed by the turrets of his stronghold, the wind seemed to sing with her clear voice. He could barely wait for the next evening to come around.

Once again, he rode into the forest as the sun began to sink down towards the far hills at the end of the day. Soon he had reached the little crossroads, where he reined in his mount and paused to listen. The strange woman's voice came drifting between the trees, and he had only to follow its sound to arrive at the woodland pool once more. There, amid the ruins of some former time, sat his companion of the previous night, a looking-glass in her hand, combing her long tresses with a golden comb. She had dressed herself in another garment of emerald green, which was held in place by amulets and clasps of pure wrought gold, and great bangles and chains of antique reddish metals hung from about her neck and arms. Setting aside the comb and mirror, she welcomed him once more and motioned him to the mound close to her side, where he sat until the moon was riding high among the clouds, listening to her songs.

And so it was that each night, for several months, the chevalier left his castle at sunset and rode off into the forest to be with the strange singing woman. He mentioned her several times in conversation with his servants, much to their alarm and disquiet, for the woodland had a sinister reputation. One old woman who had worked for his father gripped his arm as he made to fetch his horse.

'Stay away from the forest, young master,' she warned, 'for the sake of your father and for the sake of she who bore you. There are many tales of strange creatures which dwell in those woodland depths – some of them not natural things. The land was once inhabited by the druids, who performed terrible rites there – rites frowned upon by our Mother Church – and it's said that the awful beings which they summoned might still linger there. Therefore, stay tonight in the protection of your castle and close to your own fire.' But the chevalier would have none of this. He was already falling in love with the wonderful singer and was not to be denied a chance to meet her.

'Sheer superstition!' he scoffed. 'Cease your prattling, old woman. No harm has yet befallen me among those forest trees, nor shall any. I'm off to meet with my friend in the glade.' And, despite her protestations, he rode off.

The old woman's warning had, however, made up his mind for him. No longer did he intend to travel into the darkening forest at night; he would ask the girl to marry him and bring her back to his own castle. That would silence those who whispered about him – those who said that his new friend was a witch! He was now resolved on the matter and put his proposal to her that very evening. At first she seemed dumbstruck, then appeared to be seriously considering his request. Then she gave a beaming smile.

'I will wed you indeed,' she answered, 'and I will dwell in your castle, for I have loved you since I first saw you.' The smile faded and her eyes became very serious. 'But I would place three conditions upon our marriage if we are to live together in happiness. First, we must not be wed in any church, for I have a great fear of such places. Being a child of the forest, I was raised outside holy teaching, and now that I am grown I see no need for it. Second, you must never ask me anything regarding either my family or my relations, for it is a long time since I saw them and to think of them again would only cause me pain. Thirdly, and most importantly, I must be allowed to leave your keep one night in the month and to remain away from you until dawn. You must never ask me where I go, nor make reference to my departure in any way. Nor must you follow me or have me followed. If you obey these restrictions then I will be your wife and we shall enjoy a happy existence together. Promise me now!' The chevalier was so smitten with the girl – who called herself Elvira – that he agreed to her terms immediately.

And so it was that they were secretly wed and she returned with him to his castle. However, it was noted that wherever she went in the castle grounds, dogs howled and horses shied and the servants were most uneasy about her. The chevalier himself simply put this down to superstition on their part and paid it no heed. And one night in each month, his wife would leave the safety of his castle, venturing along the road towards the forest, never returning until morning. She told him nothing about where she went or whom she met and he, true to his word, never asked her about it. However, the servants muttered among themselves. Her ladyship was not very well liked by them, for she seemed proud and haughty and,

unlike her husband, had little to do with her vassals. They began to talk about her strange ways with some relish.

Soon the lady's disappearances had become something of a scandal. The chevalier now knew that his servants laughed at him and said things about the marriage behind his back. They said, for instance, that the lady had a lover in the forest and that he was no more than a cuckold. Nevertheless, he bore their whispers with at least some grace. Elvira was a kind and loving wife and, although his moods grew blacker with the servants, he seemed to cling more and more to her. There was also the problem of children, for soon they had been married for well over a year and still no baby had come. The servants whispered that Elvira had already borne a child to her lover in the forest.

Matters came to a head one day when the old servant woman – the one who had served the chevalier's father – took him aside.

'There is much talk,' she told him, 'not only among the servants in your castle but among the neighbouring villagers as well. They say that you are a cuckold and that your wife has had several children to other men – even the tenants on your own lands.' He swung on her fiercely.

'Then they lie!' he snapped. 'Now I will hear nothing further against my wife – not from you or anybody.' The old woman looked at him with some concern.

'But have you never wondered where your wife goes on the one night of the month?' she asked. 'If you knew for certain, then you could put an end to these rumours.' The chevalier paused, for he had indeed been wondering about his wife's nocturnal wanderings. He saw the wisdom of the old woman's words, and then and there made his mind up to follow her the next time that she went back to the forest.

Three nights later, she left the stronghold and took the road which led to the woodland. Her husband watched her from an upstairs window and, as soon as she was out of sight, he donned his cloak and, leaving the keep by a side door, set out to follow her.

It was a dark and blustery night with large clouds rolling back and forth across the sky. Even so, there was just enough moonlight to illuminate the road in front of him, and as he hurried along after his wife, the chevalier could just see her form a good way ahead of him. She was following the path which led directly to the forest.

On the edge of the tree-line, she paused and looked around her, making her husband dive into the shelter of a gatepost, from where he continued to watch her. Then, suddenly, she was gone once more into the woodland depths and he had to run to check for a sign of her direction. She seemed to heading for the tiny forest crossroads where he had first heard her, but he could not be sure. Arriving there, he paused and listened. Over the rising wind and the low whisper of the trees, he heard her voice singing an old, old song. It was just as he had heard her on that first night. Making his way through the trees, he reluctantly drew his sword. If she was there, singing to some other lover, then it was best to be prepared to confront them both! Gradually, the trees thinned out on the edge of the glade and the chevalier stepped through and into the moonlight beyond.

Like the last rays of the sun, great shafts of moonlight fell into the forest clearing, lighting up both the pool and the surrounding ruins. The chevalier stared, open -mouthed, at the sight which confronted him, and his sword dropped from his nerveless fingers.

She who was his wife still sat on the weed-choked steps which led down into the pool, but now she was greatly changed. She had discarded her robes and was naked. The upper part of her body was certainly that of a mortal woman but – horror of horrors! – her lower parts were those of a great scaled serpent, which lay with its tail curled in the water below. In one hand she held the mirror while she combed her hair with the golden comb. Then, as if she realized that he stood there, she looked up and he saw that her eyes were red and pupil-less and that a great forked tongue flickered around the edges of her full red lips. With a hiss of fury, she opened wide her mouth and he could see two great fangs, positively dripping with venom. He froze where he was – unable to move.

'So, mortal!' the creature by the pool hissed – its voice low and rasping and totally unlike the dulcet tones of his wife. 'You have disregarded my warning and have broken your solemn word to me. Now you see me as I truly am and in a form which I had hoped that you would never look upon!' Somewhere, in the back of his throat, the chevalier found words to reply.

'Who – what are you?' he stuttered. The creature hissed and reared up above the water. To the chevalier, it now seemed both monstrous and alien and he was terribly afraid.

'I am the last of the beings who once dwelt in these forests,' it answered. 'My people were worshipped by the druids, at this temple, in times long past, but with the coming of the Christian faith they had to slink away into the deep mountain caves and the forest trails. Over the centuries they have all died out, until only I am left. Alone in this dreary forest, I craved company, even the company of humans, and so I sought you out as a husband. In my human guise, I would have been a good wife to you, but humanity is difficult to maintain and from time to time I must slip away back to my true home amid these ancient ruins and resume my original form. I had hoped that you would never see me so, and you had given me your word as a Christian. Now you must pay the price for your curiosity, for in my original form I hunger for human flesh!!' And while the chevalier stood, mesmerized, the serpent-woman glided from the pool towards him, her scales rustling as she did so. Her awful mouth opened above him and the last thing that he saw were her terrible fangs as she slithered her coils around his body. The forest rang with his final cry of despair.

The Green Children

Celtic folklore is littered with tales concerning lost and mythical lands, populated with strange beings, sprites, ghosts or fairies. From time to time, it was believed, the creatures which inhabited these realms would pass across into our own, where they would often cause both great wonder and great mischief. There are myriad stories, for example, of mysterious people coming from an enchanted land far beneath the sea, to live and marry among the dwellers on the land; there are stories, too, all across the Celtic world, of strange beings falling from ships or from towns in the air and being forced to live on the ground. (Such tales may, of course, be a much later invention than the lore of the Celts, and may have more to do with early Christian theories regarding fallen angels. Furthermore, the strange patterns of clouds sometimes resemble ships, castles, cities and towns, and it is only natural that some old medieval wonder tales should be connected with these.)

Strangers who arrived in small, tightly knit communities were usually treated with great suspicion. The early Celts, being extremely territorial, counted people from other areas as hostile and untrustworthy, and so it is no surprise that the concept of the stranger crept into folklore as a creature of mystery with, perhaps, supernatural powers. This was particularly true if the strangers behaved in odd ways, or if they spoke in an unknown tongue. Sometimes, the stranger did not have to have come from all that far away from the community in question. To illustrate this point, the French peasant author Emile Guillaumin, writing in 1904 concerning the recollections of his grandparents, tells of a little swineherd who met a stranger on a lonely heathland path. The stranger spoke to him in an unfamiliar language and the swineherd was absolutely terrified: 'I saw this big dark person who was not from any of the three neighbouring farms, I was so terror-struck that I could not move.' The stranger turned out simply to be an itinerant tree-feller looking for somewhere to fill his water flask. However, this encounter serves to demonstrate the closeness of localized groupings (a distinct feature of early Celtic society), and the utter rejection and terror of the unidentified individual which persisted in such narrow communities. Doubtless, the little swineherd thought that the tree-feller was the Devil himself, or some evil spirit come to torment him or do him harm. Such fear, suspicion and wonder were usually accorded to *all* strangers as soon as they entered the lands of a community. To justify these emotions, the descriptions of the interlopers were often exaggerated in order to make them more fearsome and threatening, and such awesome descriptions very often became part of the folklore of a community. Indeed, this was a common feature of Celtic communities.

The following story *may* have an element of truth in it, or it may be based upon one of these exaggerated folktales. It may also owe more than a little to the imagination of the medieval writer Roger of Coggeshall, who was famous for his rather tall and unsubstantiated stories. In essence, the legend concerns two children, both coloured bright green, who appeared in Norman Suffolk, close to the village of St Mary's by the Wolf Pits, near Bury, during the reign of King Stephen (1135–54). Both children were captured by local peasants, and as they could not speak English of any sort but 'babbled in some queer foreign tongue', they were taken to a local knight and landowner, Sir Richard de Colne, who was a noted traveller in foreign parts and considered to be an extremely wise man.

It was a time of civil war, when the forces of the king fought with those of Matilda – Henry I's daughter, also known as Empress Maud – for the English throne (a period described by one commentator as '19 years when Christ and his saints slept') and, in the unquiet mood of the time, the children were regarded as objects of fear and superstition – perhaps portending the end of the world. They were considered to be some form of halfling – human in shape but with definite unearthly origins. It might even be further advanced that, during a time of unrest, they could be seen as coming from some long-forgotten Celtic Otherworld...

'GREEN CHILDREN?' The voice reverberated all through the draughty castle hall. 'Green children? What nonsense is this? The land is torn in pieces by strife and warfare and you come to me with some fanciful tale about green children!' Edric the peasant and his son Osric huddled closer together, more out of fright than anything else. They feared the Norman knight even more than they did the peculiar infants that they'd found. At least *they* were only children; Richard de Colne was a powerful landowner *and* their feudal lord.

'It...it's true, my lord,' mumbled the elder of the two, gathering his ragged and mud-stained jerkin more tightly around his skinny frame, as if to shield himself from his master's sullen glare. 'They are queer, sorcerous children whom we found down by the Wolf Pits and they are bright green in colour. By holy St Edmund, I swear it, lord.' He was almost crying now. Sir Richard towered over them, an elderly, balding man with an enormous pot-belly hanging over the belt of his breeches. 'We brought them to you as quickly as we could, seeing that you're a great and learned man, much travelled in far countries in the course of holy wars. If any man knows who they are and from whence they've come, it's yourself, sire.' He had hoped that the abject flattery would please his liege-lord. Sir Richard merely snorted as though he were far above such fawning ways.

'And where are they now?' he asked. Edric smiled, showing the last stumps of rotten teeth which lined his discoloured and disease-ridden gums.

'They wait your pleasure outside in the yard, my lord,' he answered in the same fawning tone. 'We've left them in the care of your falconer. They are both weak and fainting with hunger and will surely give him no trouble.' Sir Richard scratched at his filthy beard.

'And where did you find these...these green children?' he enquired warily. 'This is not some sort of devilish trick to hoodwink the forces of the king and favour the Empress Maud, is it?' But Osric quickly shook his head, desperately trying to reassure the knight as to their good intentions.

'Oh no, my lord! They came up from some deep realm out of a large hole in the earth near to our village...' Sir Richard held up a hand to stem his excited babble.

'Which is?' he asked, trying to bring some sort of order to their jabber. The two looked at him uncomprehendingly. 'What's the name of your village, you dolts?' At last a glimmer of understanding began to register on their blank peasant faces.

'It's called St Mary's by the Wolf Pits, lord!' replied Edric, anxious to please as ever. 'On account of the little church there. You've probably ridden through it many a time on your way with your hounds.' Sir Richard nodded a little. He remembered the 'village' – little more than an untidy and haphazard cluster of low mud-hovels, together with the 'little church' close to the roadside. If a horseman were to blink while riding along that road, he might be past it and never know.

'And just where was this hole from whence they came?' he enquired caustically. He still suspected some sort of trick, engineered for some unknown purpose by Empress Maud's followers. His sarcasm was lost on the two peasants.

'On the very edge of the village, sire.' The oafish pair were being as obsequious as possible, hoping no doubt that their lord would reward them. 'There was a great storm about two or three nights ago and the wind uprooted a mighty oak tree just beyond our furthest house. Where it had stood, there was now a great hole which seemed to us to lead down into a dark cave into which none of our villagers would go. Our priest told us that there might be demons lurking down there!'

Sir Richard eyed them with some amusement. He was well aware of the superstitious fears of the tenants living on his land. In truth, they saw demons lurking everywhere around them – peasants, he had once remarked, were afraid of everything, even of their own shadows on the ground behind them.

'Later, however, while Osric here was looking for a pig which had escaped from my house and which I was saving to pay your rent, my lord, we saw these two strange beings crawl out of that very hole, just as the priest had said. They seemed to have no idea where they might be and jabbered in a foreign, bird-like tongue which we couldn't make head nor tail of. We took them prisoner – they didn't put up much of a fight, my lord, nothing we couldn't handle ourselves – and brought them here for your lordship to see.' Sir Richard considered for a moment.

'And what of this hole out of which they crawled?' he asked, almost half-mockingly. 'Is it still there? Mayhap a score of armed knights may also appear in our world and lay waste your village – eh?' But the two men shook their heads.

'Not at all, sire! For shortly after we'd taken them, there was a great underground cataclysm – the sides of the great hole had been weakened by days of constant rains and fell in upon themselves. The hole was sealed with clay and rocks, so that now no trace of it can be found.' Consistent with the sort of fabulous tall tales which these villagers tell, thought the knight. Nevertheless, he looked all around him as though half-expecting some mysterious monster to leap at him from the shadows. There was no doubt that the peasants' tale had unnerved him.

'Well!' he snapped. 'Well! Let's see these fabulous creatures which crawled from a hole at St Mary's by the Wolf Pits!' He spoke almost sneeringly, for he'd heard peasant tales before and knew there to be hardly a grain of truth in any of them. There was a movement by the doorway and two small figures – a boy and a girl – were thrust into the centre of the hall by Sir Richard's falconer. They seemed smaller than natural children. The boy wore a bright green doublet and hose, and the girl a loose, shapeless gown of a darker hue. The colour of their skins was completely green – a dark, deep, emerald shade. But it was their eyes which held the attention. They were also green, but were wide and slanted in an oriental kind of way, giving them an almost mysterious and inscrutable appearance. Nevertheless, they shrank down fearfully in front of Sir Richard, who regarded them openmouthed with wonder.

'They do not understand what we say?' he asked, finding his voice at last. 'For you say that they speak only in a foreign tongue?' Edric and Osric nodded vigorously together.

'Nor will they eat any of our food, lord, for we offered them apples and a cooked piece of hare, but although the boy tried some of the apples, they made him sick like to die. Neither of them would touch the hare at all, even though it was fresh. We asked them what they would have to eat, but they didn't seem to understand us at all.' Sir Richard scratched at his beard once more. By St Edmund and Our Lady, this was a most wonderful and perplexing problem indeed.

'They have none of the Saxon English, hey?' he said at length. 'Well, perhaps they'll speak Norman French, then.' And he launched into two or three sentences of the tongue. The girl looked at him uncomprehendingly, but the boy answered in some kind of high, fluting language which it was almost painful to hear.

'God's wounds! Enough! Cease your shrilling!' Sir Richard cried, clasping his hands to his ears, and the boy fell silent once more. 'Let's try something else.' He pushed his broad and bearded face close to that of the girl, who recoiled from the foulness of his breath. 'Food! Do you want food? What kind of food do you eat?' The girl shrank further back, obviously very frightened by his manner. 'There is one word that all God's creatures understand – ' Sir Richard turned to the still-huddled peasants by way of explanation – 'and that word is "food". I've yet to meet any being, no matter how strange, that didn't know how to fill its belly.' And he gave a guffawing but humourless laugh. The children still looked at him uncomprehendingly. 'Food!' He paused. 'Here! You! Servant! Bring me the cold roast fowl from the kitchen. That'll make their mouths water, I'll wager!' The servant hurried away to obey

the command, returning in a moment with a large cold chicken on a metal platter. Sir Richard tore off a broad leg and thrust it towards the boy, who turned his head away slightly as though disgusted by the cold flesh.

'Here! Eat! Food!' the knight urged. The children peered curiously at the chicken leg but made no move to eat it. Sir Richard turned back to the servant. 'No matter! Maybe they're not meat eaters – I've heard of how some religious cults in far-away lands forgo the eating of meat of any description. It is a common practice among some of the heathen Saracen. Bring me some cheese…oh, and some grapes as well!' Lifting the cold chicken, the servant hurried back to the kitchen, returning with yet another platter on which were several small pieces of cheese, some apples and some grapes. The children looked at these, prodding them with their green fingers, but refused to eat anything. The boy spoke again in the same high, fluting tones which nobody could understand. Once more, Sir Richard clasped his hands against his ears to shut out the sound.

'Enough, I say! God's wounds, I'll declare that you'll both eat a piece of cheese before the day's out, for there's no harm in such good food!' he snapped angrily, tearing off a morsel of the food and thrusting it towards the girl. She drew back and looked as if she was going to be sick. 'Obviously, these people do not enjoy cheese,' Sir Richard snarled in frustration, 'but, by St Edmund and Our Lady, what *will* they eat? God's teeth, they must be sorely famished!' Desperately, he pointed to his own bloated paunch, but still the children gave not even the vaguest sign that they understood the gesture.

While this bizarre exercise was going on, it so happened that an old serving woman had just entered the hall on her way through to the kitchen, carrying a large basket of long green beans under one arm. As soon as they saw the beans, both children commenced a loud and delighted racket, waving wildly and expectantly towards the heaped beans. With a loud scream at the sight of the two green beings, the peasant woman dropped the basket and fled back to wherever she had come from. The green children, on the other hand, fell upon the wicker container and began to split open the bean pods, cramming the raw beans into their mouths as quickly as they could. The knight and the two peasants stood watching them in amazement.

'Well,' observed Sir Richard, 'it seems that we now know what they'll eat. Green beans. Ah yes, green beans for green children!' And he gave a dutiful half-laugh at his own joke, to which his tenants didn't respond.

When they had eaten, the children seemed more content. They actually smiled at Sir Richard, and the boy made a few fluting noises of thanks. They were, however, still a marvel and a puzzle.

'What are we going to do with them now?' the knight asked, more to himself than to the two peasants, who still watched the green children with great awe. This was indeed a question which no one could answer, but since the children showed no inclination to leave his castle, it seemed that he was stuck with them for the foreseeable future. He took them both as his wards, declaring that they would remain with him for as long as they desired. He brought a priest, Father Anthony, to try to communicate with them and teach them English. And he fed them, too, although for many months afterwards the children refused to eat anything except long green beans.

The summer came and went and the winter followed soon after. Fairs and markets passed in the surrounding countryside. The children visited them all and were held as a marvel by all who saw them. Father Anthony declared that they must be baptized into the Christian faith, and so they were, at a special service which only Sir Richard and his household attended. They now came to Mass and, under the priest's tutelage, began to adopt more civilized and Christian ways.

Gradually, they also began to eat other foods besides beans, and started to speak in a halting form of English which only those who knew them well could follow. The girl showed a greater aptitude for the language than her brother, who often seemed stubborn and hostile to his new environment. He refused to answer questions, made little attempt to speak except in his original fluting voice and accepted the Christian religion with a barely concealed ill-grace. His sister, on the other hand, took to the new ways with ease, showing a special interest in both music and poetry. Soon she was able to flirt prettily with all the young swains who came about Sir Richard's estates.

One winter, almost two years after the children had appeared at St Mary's by the Wolf Pits, Sir Richard de Colne called a grand meeting in the hall of his castle. At such gatherings, it was customary for a minstrel to play for the entertainment of his master's guests, but this time Sir Richard raised his hand and turned away from the minstrels' table.

'We have something special for your entertainment tonight,' he announced, gesturing to the green-skinned girl who sat at the head of his own table like a daughter. 'Many of you here will recall that almost two years ago, two green children were brought to me. To this day, no man has been able to tell me from where they came, and they themselves spoke such an odd and foreign language that I was unable to ask them. Nevertheless, I placed them under my own care and protection and began their instruction in our own ways and tongue. And now...' he turned towards the girl, who returned his smile – 'one of our guests at least has learned enough of our language to tell me where she comes from and I have asked her to share her recollections with you tonight.'

There was a general rustle of excitement among the guests. The girl rose and walked over to the seats where the minstrels usually sat. The light from the torches and the sconces on the walls above fell against the side of her green face, making her appear all the more strange and alien. She turned to look at her audience, who waited expectantly, and at last she spoke – in poor, halting words but enough to make herself understood. And, as she told her story, her brother sat at the head of

Sir Richard's table, sullen and silent and clearly wishing to take no part in the proceedings. The green girl loudly cleared her throat.

'I come from what seems to be a far, distant country,' she began, 'and yet it might not be so far away at all, for I believe that it may lie under your very feet. Its people call it St Martin's Land.' A murmur of utter astonishment rippled around the hall. 'It is a land that has been lost to your knowledge since the times of the Celtic peoples who once ruled this country, for there are legends among my people of trade and commerce between our two dominions in times long past. In my country, everything is green. The land is green, the people are green, the animals are green – why, even the very sky is green. In most respects, my country is very much like your own – the people live by farming and they dwell in small villages along the sides of great and rapid rivers which break up the land.

'The sun never shines in my country, nor is there any distinction between day and night. There is always a faint and constant green glow which seems to come from just below the horizon, and this gives us our light. Nor are there seasons, neither winter nor summer, although there seem to be heavy rains at certain times, sometimes so heavy that we have to move some of our settlements for fear of flooding. Thankfully, these downpours come very infrequently and mostly we have no more than a light, misty drizzle, just enough to supply whatever crops we may plant.

'Neither is there any formal religion or belief among my people – apart from the understanding that all life, no matter how lowly, is to be prized. Consequently, although our cows give us milk, our sheep give us wool and our hens give us eggs – just as they do in your lands – they are not, themselves, eaten. Indeed, we find it abhorrent to devour any animal which shares our world with us. We subsist on pulses, most of which are planted during our season of rains. Now, I have told you that there is no formal religion among us and this is so, for we have neither priest nor prelate. There are, however, old stories that at one time we worshipped gods very much like those of the ancient Celtic peoples, and evidence of that worship still litters our countryside in the shape of ancient forts and raths. There are even yet, it's said, some among us who would follow strange, old ways.

'From the high hills of my own land, I can sometimes see another, much brighter domain divided from ours by a broad and fast-flowing river. I have never been there, nor has anyone else in my village, and we know nothing about it.' The audience listened in awe – never had they heard such wonderful things before.

'But how did you come to our world?' asked Sir Richard wonderingly. 'I've had my men search for months to discover the hole from which you crawled and they found nothing at all.' The girl looked at him very sadly.

'Alas, we cannot say how we came to your land,' she answered. 'But I can tell you this. My brother and I were tending our father's sheep on a very high hill in our own country. We had been playing – I had been trying to see the bright, shining country on the other side of the river from some very tall rocks – and we had accidentally allowed the sheep to stray. Fearing our father's anger, we ran after them and began to round them up again, but one had strayed into a deep cave on the very mountaintop. It was an exceptionally large cave and, strangely, one that we had never noticed before. A cold and eerie wind seemed to be blowing from it continually, making the pair of us very afraid. Even so, we feared our father's fury more than we did the gloomy cave, and so we went in to bring back the sheep.

'It had wandered deep into what now seemed to be a great cavern, which was growing darker and darker by the moment. Still, we advanced forward into the darkness. All of a sudden we heard the sound of bells – soft bells, loud bells, treble bells, silver bells and brass bells, all ringing and ringing – a beautiful sound to our ears, for bells are seldom heard in my own country. It seemed to us that the sounds came from the furthest end of the cavern, and so we decided to go on and find out where they came from. Indeed, we had no option, for the bells were so sweet and melodic that they had an almost hypnotic effect upon us, drawing us towards them. And so, forgetting the sheep and all else, we made our way towards that sound, venturing deeper and deeper into the cavern.

'At first the ground beneath us was flat, but soon it began to grow steep, aye, and very steep at that. But the sound of the bells drew us onward, ringing and still pulling us towards them. Then, far away in front of us, we saw a bright light – brighter by far than anything else that we'd ever seen in our own gloomy green world. It was so bright that it was almost white and it nearly blinded us with its brilliance. It was from this brilliant light that the sound of bells seemed to be coming and so we made our way, rather hesitantly, towards it. And the nearer we came, the more dazzling the light grew, until we stepped out of the cavern and into the brightness. The ringing stopped as suddenly as it had begun and your daylight knocked us senseless. It was as though a great and unseen weight had been dropped upon our shoulders and we were barely able to carry it. How long we lay in a swoon, I have no way of knowing, but it must have been a long time, for when we came to we had been bound and restrained by two of your people, who brought us to this castle.

'Here we have lived for two years – I find it strange to talk that way, for there is no idea of changing time in our world. We simply sleep and work when we wish it. The invisible weight of which I spoke still remains upon our shoulders, although it has grown slightly easier to bear of late. I find the air thick and difficult to breathe, although that, too, grows steadily easier. My poor brother, however, is constantly sick – in my own country it is generally the women who are the stronger gender while men, although the rulers and officials in each village, are the most subject to illness. My brother heartily dislikes your world. He is homesick for our own climate and our own country and he still finds your world very strange. If you were surprised to see green children, think how odd it must be for us to be constantly surrounded by pink men and women!' There was a burst of general laughter at this.

'My brother detests having to eat cooked meat,' went on the girl. 'And he finds the changeable weather most distressing. I fear that if we stay here much longer, he will die.' And she looked sorrowfully across to where the green boy sat. 'Thus, and with the help of our kind and generous guardian, Sir Richard de Colne, I have searched for the hole which will take us back again to St Martin's Land. I have searched long and hard, but have found nothing. Any trace of the cavern through which we came now seems to have been swallowed up and we are trapped within your world.' The assembled company sighed and nodded their heads. 'But, lest you think us ungrateful, let me say that you've all shown great kindness to us both. However, I must tell you that if we should find the entrance to the cavern, we will be obliged to return home. Although I am very happy here among you all, I can do no other, for the sake of my poor brother.' And she walked back to her seat. That was just the beginning of the evening, for one question from the guests didn't wait on another. The girl tried to answer them as best she could and they all talked of many bizarre things, long into the night.

Several months later, the green maiden's dire prophecy came to pass. In the colder days towards the end of the year, the green boy became extremely listless. He wouldn't eat, he took no interest in his lessons, nor did he take part in anything to do with play of any kind. Sometimes he was to be found down by the Wolf Pits, looking longingly at the ground. And, as winter tightened its grip on the land, turning the ground into hard iron, he began to sicken seriously. Father Anthony did what he could – he offered prayers and sent to the abbey at Bury for the sacred water from the Well of Our Lady there – but all to no avail. As Christmas Day approached, the boy contracted an inexplicable fever and died.

His sister lived on in the castle of Sir Richard de Colne for a time. She began to behave like any other girl, she ate the foods which everyone else ate, she spoke English much better albeit with a peculiar accent, and she began to love drinking and dancing. She became very flighty in her ways and many of the swains of the district began to pursue her for she was steadily growing more and more beautiful. Gradually, her skin lost its greenish tinge and turned to a dull coppery colour, while her hair became more and more fair. She seemed, to all intents and purposes, happy enough with her life in the castle, and yet fieldworkers would often see her walking down by the Wolf Pits alone. They didn't approach her, for they knew that she must be very lonely and sorely missing her own people.

In time, she left the charge of Sir Richard de Colne and married one of his squires. They went to live at Lenna, near King's Lynn. But even then, on occasion, she would leave her husband and return to St Mary's by the Wolf Pits, looking as lost and lonely as ever. Then, one day, she simply vanished.

There were many rumours concerning her disappearance. Some said that she had actually been Sir Richard's mistress and had borne him several children in secret, and that his own jealous wife had murdered her by poison and made away with the body; some said that she had been swept up in the savage conflicts which still raged through the countryside. Others affirmed that she had found her way back to the underground realm of St Martin's Land; still others declared that she had run off with someone else and was living in Norfolk, where she eventually died, a very old woman. What truly became of her, no one will ever rightly know. Nor since that distant time has anyone else appeared from that queer, green country that is said to lie somewhere far beneath our feet.

Although there are a number of different legends concerning the green children, there is no real attested historical record as to their existence. Nevertheless, there is such a wealth of stories concerning them and their relationship with Richard de Colne that there may be *some* historical truth in them. For example, there are persistent tales of a book which was copied down by a scribe and dictated by the green-skinned girl concerning some of the 'ancient religions and practices' of St Martin's Land. This volume was reputedly read by Sir Richard's confessor – alternately referred to as Father Anthony and Father John – who found it so shocking that he hid it away, declaring that 'Christian eyes would never look upon what was writ therein'. The book is still said to be somewhere in the vicinity of Bury St Edmunds.

There are, too, references in some of the medieval literature to 'Green Jack's Children'. It is never properly specified what these 'children' were, but it may be that they were remnants of a pagan Celtic woodland cult which practised fertility rites well into early modern times. It *might* just be that the green children were *not* from a subterranean world at all, but were really members of this cult – the description 'green children' perhaps arising from the oversight of some medieval writer and later elaborated upon by subsequent authors – who were either captured or sheltered by a Norman knight.

The most interesting and plausible explanation, however, is put forward by the Fortean writer Mike Dash, who states that the tale may have a more mundane interpretation as a tale of two malnourished waifs from the Suffolk village of Fornham St Martins – St Martin's Land – who were caught up in the war between Stephen and Matilda and arrived in the vicinity of St Mary's by the Wolf Pits after walking through passageways in the Neolithic flint mines that run under Thetford Forest. Their 'greenness' was actually a disease known as 'green chlorosis', caused by severe under-nourishment, while their 'unintelligible language' was merely a thick and unfamiliar local accent. However, it must be said that all this is no more than speculation. For all we know, the eerily twilit realm of St Martin's Land might really lie far below the ground.

Solitary Fairies and Sprites

We have already looked at the fairy Host – the Slaugh or Macara Shee. These, of course, were not the only types of fairy to inhabit the gloomy and mysterious world of the Sidhe. From all over the Celtic realm, there are tales of solitary spirits or sprites inhabiting a whole range of locations, ranging from the wild and isolated mountaintops to the relative comfort of a hearthside. These are, of course, as much a part of fairy influence as the trooping horde, indeed perhaps even more so.

Many of these fairies and sprites probably have their point of origin in the ancient idea of a *genius loci*, the spirit inhabitant/protector of a specific place or locale. Many early Celtic beliefs stated that certain places or geographical features were the haunts of forces which looked after them and were often hostile towards mortals who tried either to settle in them or to desecrate them for agricultural purposes. Trees, wells and even great stones were the favoured abodes of such forces, and the belief encouraged a healthy respect for the land within the Celtic mind. If wells were filled in or trees cut down, then the action would inevitably have severe repercussions upon those who carried out the act. Small wonder, then, that the Celts treated the land with a large degree of awe! Spirits were everywhere.

Gradually, however, these forces changed subtly in character. No longer were they simply god-like spirits and localized powers; they were now individual fairies and goblins, living in the remote and isolated places which had once been a more spiritual abode. Irish tree-spirits, for example, became *skeagh-shee* (*skeagh* referring to an isolated tree), protective fairies who would often take revenge upon those who either uprooted or damaged their tree-charges in the interests of

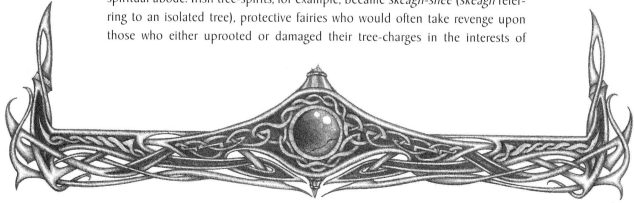

progress'. These also appeared in Britain as Oak-shees (specifically attached to oak trees). Other ancient forces simply became the fairies of stones and wells. Fairies could now rightly be described as the 'old gods of the earth', as the venerable *Book of Armagh* had declared.

Because the ancient gods had been of a diverse aspect, this was also reflected in the *types* of fairies which were described. There were, for example, gnomes and goblins who lived deep underground, perhaps echoing the chthonic deities which certain of the early Celts worshipped; there were water-sprites, the personification of ancient river- and lake- gods; there were house-hold spirits which harked back to the protective gods of home and hearth-side; and there were sprites of the air, commemorating those aerial gods which had been worshipped in the high places, such as moun-taintops, all across the Celtic world. All had their origins in Celtic antiquity.

Many of these fairies also had strong associations with specific locations – dark glens, gloomy lakes, remote islands – all places where ancient and voracious gods had once been worshipped. There was, for the country people, little that was comforting about the fairies. For those who lived and worked upon the land, they were still the personification of primal forces

which had never completely been driven away by the emergence of Christian belief but which still, some-how, maintained an uneasy existence alongside it. And, like the natural spirits of old, fairies were to be found everywhere in the Celtic landscape.

The Fairy of Lanascol

One of the most common of all the solitary fairies was that which attached itself to a house. In pre-Christian times, even the Romans had such beings, which they called *lares* and which were supposed to safeguard the dwelling, bringing good luck to the family who lived there. Indeed, many of these household spirits were well treated - almost as members of the family - with libations of milk or wine, together with small pieces of food, being left as an offering for them by the side of the hearth. In that way, the spirit remained in a building and the family concerned were ensured of health and prosperity for the foreseeable future.

The Romans were, of course, not the only ancient people to hold such beliefs. The Celts, too, held hearthside spirits in awe, and there is ample evidence of bones (both animal and human) being buried at the corners or under the hearthstones of dwellings in order to attract such spirits to a house and hold them there. Hearths were regarded as extremely important, because the fire burned there, giving out both light and heat, and so they were considered to be the very heart of the household and a suitable dwelling-place for beneficial forces. Over the years, such household gods were slowly transformed into household fairies, most of whom remained in their former habitats by the hearthside. It was common for Celtic households to continue to supply votive offerings to these fairy beings - a piece of bread or cake, or a glass of milk or beer each night was usually enough. The relationship between the family and the house fairy was usually well established and reasonably amicable. Many such fairies were considered to be feminine, thus further reflecting both the 'motherly and wifely' aspects of the ancient home-maker.

In Brittany such hearthside fairies were known as *lutins*, and they demonstrate a rather mischievous aspect to human–fairy affairs. The *lutins* appear to be genial tricksters for, besides looking after the well-being of the family, they love to play tricks upon the woman of the house. They hide things, which she is sure she left in a safe place but now cannot find; they break plates when she is not looking by causing them to fall inexplicably from the dresser; they move the milk pail so that it accidentally collides with her foot, overturns and spills all over the kitchen floor. In short, these *lutins* are actually responsible for the myriad small accidents which occur around the house in the course of a day. Nevertheless, despite their perverse nature, there is no harm in them and they are generally even-tempered and good-natured. However, if libations or offerings are forgotten, they can bring a terrible misfortune on a house, for they are capricious beings and can be just as malicious as they are genial and mischievous.

And what happens when the family moves on and the house is abandoned? In some cases, it is thought that the household spirits move with the family to their new abode. It is more commonly believed, however, that the fairies remain where they are in the style of the *genius loci* because, it is argued, they are attached to the *building* and not to the family itself. Even when houses are deserted and left to fall down, the fairies are forced to stay where they are. All throughout Brittany there are stories of old and empty houses which are 'fairy haunted' and are held in superstitious awe by the local populace. The tale of the Fairy of Lanascol is a good example of this belief...

You WILL HAVE HEARD, no doubt, of the female fairy which inhabits the old Château of Lanascol in lower Brittany, for I've heard that stories concerning her are widely known all across France and beyond. She is something of an enigma, for some people say that she's not a fairy at all in the accepted sense, but some kind of being – half-fairy, half-human – with strange and supernatural powers.

The Château of Lanascol hardly deserves to be called a 'château' at all. Much of it is simply a ruin, badly overgrown and falling down. It was, in times past, the manor house of an important local family, whose name I've forgotten but who

owned several of the nearby villages. The villages themselves aren't all that prosperous, for their population seems to be composed of peasant farmers who are
sometimes sailors and sailors who are sometimes peasant farmers. What became
of this family or where they went, I can't really say, but they abandoned the
manor house and left it to crumble. Over the seasons, the rain and wind took their
toll on the stonework and the ivy began to swallow up the entire building.
Gradually the roof fell in, leaving only a few supporting walls standing, swathed
in ivy and wild creeper.

However, in its heyday the manor house at Lanascol must have been an imposing place with extensive grounds, wide avenues and walkways. In fact, the remnants
of those ancient paths are still to be seen, although they disappear year after year,
beneath a carpet of wild grasses and foliage. The most impressive of all these walks
is, naturally, the great driveway which leads to the ruined house itself, lined as it is
with rows of copper beech whose great leafy branches are reflected in splendid
pools nearby. From the driveway, other little paths wander off and are soon lost
among the overgrown brush which has now taken over the once beautifully mani-
cured and well-tended lawns. On autumn evenings the colours of the estate are
something to behold – fading greens tinged with autumnal golds and yellows,
decaying russets mixed with a still-verdant emerald – the perfect place for a late
walk before bedtime. And yet none of the villagers will venture there as soon the
sun begins to dip towards the horizon, for it is then that the Groac'h Lanascol or La
Fée de Lanascol – the Fairy of Lanascol (sometimes simply referred to as 'the Lady')
– is to be seen taking her own evening stroll.

Descriptions of her vary, although she is frequently to be seen in clothing of
various hues which usually match the colourful riot of her surroundings.
Sometimes, she is seen as an old woman, walking very bent, with both hands leaning on the stump of a crutch with which she often stirs the dead, fallen leaves on
the path. The leaves which she stirs suddenly become bright golden in colour and
chink against each other with the undeniable sound of metal, at which the Fairy
chuckles softly to herself. In the locality, however, it is considered an exceptionally
unlucky omen to see her in such a guise as it can portend death for the viewer or a
general calamity in the district. Slightly better is to see her in the appearance of a
young and beautiful princess, gaily adorned in striking colours, skipping along the
avenue and followed by several curious, small, silent black men.

Sometimes, the Fairy advances along the driveway with a sedate, queenly bearing and it seems that, as she passes, the ancient copper beech trees bow down, as if
to receive her commands. If she should look into any of the nearby pools, it is
reported that the water will tremble from the potency of her gaze. Her very glance,
while in this form, is said to have the power to paralyse those who venture into the
old estate, so that they may be taken to the ruined château by her mysterious
servants. Far better, then, not to see her at all and to avoid completely the haunted
ruins and their shadowy surroundings.

However, this is not always so easy, for sometimes the Fairy appears to be able to leave the overgrown estate of her own volition, and thus the following story is told about her on one of these occasions.

The estate of Lanascol had become a wilderness and the old manor house, greatly weakened by years of rain and snows, had more or less fallen in on itself. Weeds and creeper grew everywhere and the whole place had become something of an eyesore. The people of the village decided to do something about it. First of all, through the local priest, they traced the owners of the estate, but whether that family no longer wanted anything to do with such an ill-reputed property or were simply indifferent to the villagers' pleas is not known. They told the representatives of Lanascol that they could do what they liked with the ruinous estate.

The villagers approached the public notary at Plouaret and asked him to auction it. The notary shook his head and told them that, even if they could obtain the permission of the owners to do so, the estate had such a notorious fairy-haunted reputation that no one would buy it. Nevertheless, the villagers were insistent and told him to contact the owners to obtain permission to sell, with half the profits going to the village. The owners, surprisingly, agreed – the overgrown estate was of no consequence to them and better to get some money for no trouble than to try constantly to maintain such a squalid piece of land. The notary was forced to put the estate on the market.

The day of the bidding dawned and, it seemed, a number of purchasers had arrived – some from quite far away. There were farmers who intended to demolish the ruined château and plough up the estate for agricultural purposes; there were property speculators who planned to pull down the house and turn the land over to builders; and there were those who simply wanted to build new, even grander houses for themselves on the estate. The bidding between all these interested groups was hot and heavy, and soon the property had reached its reserve price and looked to go further. It seemed to be going to an agent from Paris who was representing a great property consortium. The estate was just on the point of being knocked down when, on the last appeal of the auctioneer, a female voice, very gentle but at the same time very imperious, spoke out.

'A thousand francs more!' it said. There was great commotion in the hall and everyone looked round to see who had spoken. The property agent was outraged and scanned the sea of surrounding faces for that of a woman. It could only have been a woman who spoke, after all – the tones were too delicate and feminine to be those of a man – and yet there was not a single woman present in the hall! Summoning all the dignity he could muster, the notary drew himself up to his full height.

'Who was it that spoke?' he demanded. The voice gave a slight chuckle. It now seemed to come from somewhere near the back of the hall, although there was no one – let alone a female – to be seen.

'It is the Fairy of Lanascol who speaks,' it said.

There was now general confusion in the hall and the bidding broke up without result. From that day onward, no purchaser would come forward to acquire the

haunted property and soon the entire estate was removed from the market. There was no reason why it should remain for sale. The grounds and the crumbling manor house were allowed to revert to their true owner – the Fairy of Lanascol.

The notion of the Fairy of Lanascol appearing in a number of differing physical aspects – an old woman with a crutch or a beautiful young maiden – has echoes, of course, of the Irish Banshee. Indeed, the idea that to see her in such forms heralds either death or misfortune is extremely Banshee-like in tone and probably contains at least some echoes of the ancient Celtic triple goddess. Certainly, there is no doubt that she is some sort of folkloric survival of a belief in an earlier regional goddess.

Nor is this fairy unique in Breton folklore. Many ruined châteaux and manor houses are strongly associated with the fairy-kind. Indeed, Professor Anatole le Braz, author of such works as *La Legende de la Mort* and *Au Pays des Pardons*, clearly states: 'Brittany has always been a kingdom of Fairie. One cannot even travel a league without brushing past the dwelling or habitation of some male or female fairy.'

Bridget and the Leprechaun

Arguably no fairy has come to symbolize Ireland more than the leprechaun. He appears on tea towels, mugs and ashtrays; tourists can buy china statuettes of him in any gift shop between north Derry and south Kerry. Yet although he is Ireland's national (tourist) spirit, 'leprechaun' was originally used only in the north Leinster area. In Ulster, for instance, the term for such a fairy was *lurachmain* (leprechauns are still sometimes referred to as 'langremen' in south Armagh); in Connaught, it was *lurican*, and *lurgadhan* in Munster. At the beginning of the twentieth century the north Leinster name spread across Ireland and is widely accepted in all parts of the country today.

Leprechauns are invariably male; if there are any females, they are never seen. Individual leprechauns are secretive about their origins and there is much speculation as to how they reproduce! Some say that leprechauns are the result of a mating between mortals and fairies, disowned by both and cast out of their respective worlds. More than any other form of fairy, leprechauns typify the notion of the *genius loci*, for they are only to be seen (or heard) in isolated or inaccessible places - sometimes in remote and difficult glens, at other times in low caves or under the tangle which grows over a deep ditch.

According to all accounts, they take the form of aged, diminutive men who function as fairy shoemakers. This indeed has provided the popular name for the creature - it may have been derived from the Irish *lieth bhrogan* (shoemaker), although some authorities claim that the Irish word *luacharma'n* (pigmy) is the source. They are further described as being roughly three feet in height (although many are much smaller), incredibly ugly, dressed in a shabby green frock coat with red knee breeches buckled at the knee, and with woollen stockings and wide-brimmed green hats which are often askew to one side. The general impression is that of untidiness and extreme surliness, for the leprechaun is certainly not an entirely sociable being. Additions to his garb include a dudeen - a remarkably foul-smelling pipe which he continually smokes - and a blackthorn stick with which he beats off unwelcome attention. He lurks in sheughs (gullies) and behind bushes or under low-hanging trees. The only indication as to his presence is the tapping of his hammer on the heel of some shoe that he is mending.

But leprechauns are more than simply cobblers. They are, in fact, the bankers of the fairy world because they know where all the ancient treasure of Ireland, including gold brought there by the Norsemen, is hidden. In fact, there is no site in a particular location which the leprechaun *does not* know, because he has lived there for a long, long time. Consequently, when the rather more fickle trooping fairies (the Macara Shee) need money in order to dispense largesse to those mortals whom they meet, it is to the leprechaun they must go. And this fairy, with a heart as hard as any bank manager, will consider their request. It should be remembered, however, that a leprechaun is a natural miser and does not easily part with the money of which he considers himself the guardian. Nor has he any particular love for the fairy horde, whom he usually regards as flippant and feckless. More often than not, the leprechaun refuses to give the fairies the wealth which they have requested - again, his bank-manager instincts are to the fore!

Leprechauns tend to avoid contact with humans because they regard them as foolish, flighty creatures who will undoubtedly attempt to steal the wealth which the leprechaun has so carefully catalogued and hoarded. Despite his squat and stocky stature, the leprechaun can move with surprising speed and can be gone quicker than mortal eye can follow him. If caught, however (and leprechauns are seldom caught), he will promise great wealth in order to gain his freedom, but he is an exceptionally tricky character and not to be trusted.

It can be seen from this that the idea of the leprechaun - the foremost of Irish solitary fairies - is an attempt to personify (and to some extent sanitize) the idea of the *genius loci*. There are glens and hollows where leprechauns are said to live which were undoubtedly the sites of early Celtic spirit-worship in times long past. The many comical tales concerning leprechauns, coupled with their dishevelled appearance and peculiar ways, are perhaps an attempt to remove the enigmatic and forbidding aspects of many of the localized deities and 'humanize' them. It seems to have worked, judging by the popular tourist image.

The following story comes from County Kildare and uses the local name for the leprechaun - lurikeen. It serves to show the tricks the creature can play if caught by a human hand...

There was once a girl called Bridget Fahey, living in sight of the ancient Castle Carberry, near Edenderry, long ago in my grandmother's time. She looked after an old, blind mother and a couple of sisters in a little mud cottage by the roadside and she was a right decent and polite child, for all her hardship.

One evening, she set out to go to a neighbouring well for some water, just before the sun would set. She hadn't gone far along the road when she thought she heard a sound coming from under an old, low-hanging thorn bush, halfway up a grassy bank. It was a 'tap-tapping' sound, like a cobbler might make when he's working. Bridget was greatly puzzled and began to climb the bank to see where the sound was coming from. She moved very quietly over the grass until she had reached the bush. There, directly under the thorn, sitting in a sheltery nook, was a lurikeen, working with a vengeance on the heel of an old brogue which was only big enough to fit the foot of a fairy like himself. Bridget looked hard at him to make sure that she wasn't dreaming.

But no, there he was – a little old man, no more than a foot tall, in a long green coat with patched red knee breeches which looked as if they had been made from an old petticoat, and with a foul-reeking dudeen rammed into a corner of his mouth and a jug of porter jammed into the thorn roots by his side. He was boring holes in the leather, jerking his waxed ends, and sewing away like fury. Indeed, he was so busy at his work and so taken up with singing a ballad in the old, old Irish that he was not even aware of Bridget, until she reached down and caught him by the scruff of the neck and he couldn't get himself free of her grip. She had seized him to make him reveal the where-abouts of his hoard of gold and so bring an end to her family's hardship.

'What d'ye think ye're doin'?' he cried, spitting out the pipe and turning himself around slightly in her fist. 'Grabbin' at a poor cobbler who's tryin' t'make an honest shilling for himself. Ah, what's the world coming to when a pretty colleen sneaks up on a decent soul, like a fox coming into a hen roost? Worse than a rogue or robber, she is! Now, put me down Miss Bridget and we can take our ease, have a chat and enjoy the evening like two sensible creatures.' But Bridget was not to be hoodwinked so easily for she knew that as soon as she set him on the ground he would be gone, quick as a wink, under the thorns and bushes, and she'd never see him again.

'Ah Mr Lurikeen,' she answered. 'I don't care a wisp of a borragh [broom] for your politeness or how badly you think you've been done by. I know that you have a crock of gold hidden somewhere and I'll not set you down again until I have a good piece of it.' The leprechaun snorted derisively.

'Ah, sure I have no crock of gold,' he protested, 'that's only an oul' saying among folks that don't know any better. Sure, I'm only a poor tradesman, and if you let go my arms I'll turn my pockets inside out for you and give you leave to keep any halfpenny you can find there.' But Bridget guessed that this was yet another trick, for as soon as she lifted her eyes from him, he would vanish away like an evening mist.

'I'm not falling for your mischief,' said she. 'So hurry up and tell me where you've hidden the money, or else I carry you all the way into Edenderry in my fist and then you'll have plenty of eyes to watch you instead of just mine. Now make haste, Mr Lurikeen, and tell me where you've hidden your crock!' The leprechaun thought for a moment.

'Well, well,' he said at last. 'Never was a poor artisan so plagued in his work. Never was there such extortion in all the decent lands of Ireland since the days of Black Cromwell, bad cess to *that* name...'

'Hurry up!' urged Bridget, 'for my patience is running out very fast!'

'It'd make you wonder,' went on the leprechaun, as if he hadn't heard, 'that such a dear, comely girl such as yourself – a girl who's always first to the altar rails at Mass, I shouldn't wonder – could abuse an honest toiler of what money he has put by him for the cold times ahead.'

'Save your complaining!' snapped Bridget in frustration. 'For you'll get no sympathy from me. Everyone knows that lurikeens have great stores of gold put by and you'll hardly miss what I'll take from it. Now hurry up and take me to where you've hidden it and don't take up my time with your blarney!' And she tightened her fist around the leprechaun's middle, making him cough and splutter.

'Easy! Easy, my girl!' he gasped. 'I was only having a bit of light conversa-tion with you. Is it gold that you're after? Well, if there's any to be had – and I don't say that there is – it'll be under old Castle Carberry itself. But we'll have to walk a piece to get it. Now put me down and we'll be on our way. Come on! The gold is waiting for us!' But Bridget was still very wary of his tricks.

'Put you down indeed!' she snapped. 'And as soon as I put you on the ground, you'll be away like a hare. No, if it's all the same to you, Mr Lurikeen, I'll carry you up to Castle Carberry in my hand.' The leprechaun gave a hearty laugh which almost unsettled Bridget, for this was her first encounter with the fairies.

'For a bright and pretty young colleen you're very suspicious,' he taunted, 'and sure what harm could I do with yourself standing over me? Well, have it your own way. Let's go up to Castle Carberry. Do you see it over there?' Bridget was about to turn her eyes from the little man up to where she knew that the castle stood, but she bethought herself in time. It was yet another of his tricks to get her to take her eyes of him. 'I know where it is right well,' she told him. 'So let's get up there without any more of your shenanigans.' The little man shrugged his shoulders.

'As you wish Bridget, but if you're going to keep your eyes on me, then watch your feet, for the path's very uneven and you might trip over a root or a stone and hurt yourself badly. I couldn't help you, you understand, for it's not given that the fairy-kind should help mortals, even such a pretty one as yourself.' Bridget ignored all his flattery.

'I'll take my chances on the path,' she answered. 'Now let's get going.'

They went up the pathway, over heights and hummocks, and the leprechaun seemed quite reconciled to his situation and even laughed and joked with his captor. However, as soon as they reached the brow of a little hill, his manner changed. He let out a loud screech and threw up his hands.

'Oh, but we'll find no gold at Castle Carberry this day or any other!' he shrieked. 'The whole place has gone up in flames! It's on fire! Oh, murder! Murder!' Instinctively, Bridget gave a great start and looked up towards the castle. It stood, just as it had always done, in the last strands of the setting sun and with no flames about it at all. At the same time, she missed the weight of the leprechaun in her hand and when she looked down at her fist, he was gone without a trace. She never saw him again. The whole thing now seemed like a dream to her and she went back to the well and home again to her blind mother and sisters.

However, the leprechaun had left her one reminder of the adventure. When she opened her hand, right across the palm where she had gripped him, there was a great red mark about the size of a shilling. This stayed with her until the day that she died and served as a warning not to go messing with leprechauns. This is a true story, for my grandmother saw the mark herself when she was only a child and Bridget Fahey was an old, old woman.

CORNWALL

The Tolcarne Troll

Great supernatural powers of varying degrees were often attributed to the fairies, perhaps reflecting their miraculous powers as local gods. Some fairies, for example, had the power to turn leaves, shells and other rubbish into the semblance of gold coins which reverted back to their original form as soon as they were taken out of the fairy's sphere of influence. It was extremely unwise, therefore, for mortals to accept fairy money since it was, in all probability, worthless. Other fairies certainly had the power to heal both humans and animals and were sometimes associated with wells or rivers; still others even had the power to manipulate time and would often lead mortals 'astray' – keeping them away from home for long periods. Fairies could also affect the crops or sometimes the births in a locality, and all those in a community who died without confessing their sins belonged to the fairy-kind.

In short, fairies enjoyed all the powers which had once been held by the ancient tribal gods of a district – powers which stretched back into Celtic antiquity. Some even had the power to see the past and future clearly, giving them the gift of prophecy and also confirming their god-like status in the mortal mind. Arguably, nowhere was this belief more strongly held than in Cornwall.

Cornish fairies (or pixies) were often given to prophecy, and warnings. For instance, in certain Cornish tin mines, 'knockers' – tiny, subterranean pixies – would foretell of imminent catastrophes such as cave-ins by tapping on the mine walls or making strange noises. This often served as a warning to the miners that they should vacate the workings. In return for this service, saucers of milk or beer were often left for the 'Good People'. If these were not left, it was feared that the helpful 'knockers' might quit the mine.

Similarly, seagoing pixies would aid fishermen in the Mousehole and Sennen Cove areas by calling out, 'Poor times and dirty weather,' across the waves, as a warning not to put to sea as a storm was coming or that the day's catch would be bad. Although many people heard the call, which was spoken in ringing tones like the sound of a brass bell, nobody could ever determine where it came from, except that it seemed to originate from somewhere in the ocean. This warning, incidentally, was also sometimes transmitted by Manx sea-fairies and was usually accompanied by a strange, thick mist rolling towards the shoreline. The voice usually came from the centre of this fog.

All over Cornwall, there was (and still is) a firm belief that the fairies were the last remnants of some ancient Celtic tradition. A Mr Herbert Thomas, once editor of four Cornish newspapers, is cited by Evans-Wenz in *Fairy Faith in Celtic Countries* (1911) as stating: I should say that the modern belief in pixies, or in fairies, arose from a very ancient Celtic or pre-Celtic belief in spirits. Just as among some savage tribes there is a belief in gods and totems, here there was belief in little spirits good and bad, who were able to help or hinder man.'

The idea that fairies are spirits who are able to determine both the past and future is reflected in this old Cornish story, which also displays both Middle Eastern and Norse elements which are probably almost as old as the Celts themselves...

ON A HILL, JUST ABOVE THE VICARAGE at Newlyn, stands a strange outcropping of greenstone which locals try to avoid as much as they can on account of the weird tales that are often told about it. It is known as Newlyn Tolcarne and was said, in times past, to have been a place where the ancient Celtic druids carried out their awful and mysterious rites. But there is no doubt that, at one time, a fairy dwelt there and was greatly feared by some in the Newlyn district. He was known as the Tolcarne Troll and had lived there for as long as anyone could remember. In fact, he was supposed to date back to the time of the Phoenicians, who had come to Cornwall trading in tin. He had spent his early years voyaging on various ships which sailed between Tyre (which was a big Phoenician city) and the coast of

Cornwall, and it was said that he had assisted in the building of Solomon's Temple in Jerusalem. He had also acted as an oracle to Hiram, who was the king of Tyre, for he was able to see both the past and the future whenever he chose.

The Troll had come to Cornwall on a galley which was trading along the coast and had fallen out with its captain, who had abandoned him on the shore, sailing back to Tyre without him. So he had taken up his abode at Tolcarne to wait for another ship, but none had ever come. Some people called him the 'Wandering One' or 'Odin the Wanderer', after an old god of the Vikings.

The Troll was usually described by those who saw him as a little old pleasant-faced man, dressed in a tight-fitting leather jerkin and with a great hood over his head. Most of the time he was invisible and lived either in or close to the rock, making his presence known only by tiny sounds and grunts. But when he chose to he could make himself visible, sometimes startling anyone who came around the place with the suddenness of his appearance. Sometimes he could be summoned to appear, although it was really up to him as to whether he did so or not. Aunt Betty Grancan, who lived near Tolcarne, said that he could be called up by holding up three dried leaves – one of the ash, one of the oak and one of the thorn – and by pronouncing a certain incantation or charm. The words were in ancient Cornish and could only be passed from one believer to another, through a woman to a man and from a man to a woman alternately. If the charm was passed to a sceptic then it was lost for ever and the Troll would never appear again.

There were good reasons for summoning the Troll, because in his right hand he would usually hold the Mirror of Ages, a glass which could show the present, the past and the future. It was said that this mirror was an extremely holy thing, forged by angels back in the dim and distant days at the very start of the world, and that whatever it showed was either true or would come true. It was reputedly a gift from Heaven, sent with an angel by God to celebrate the completion of Solomon's Temple and to increase further the knowledge of the great and wise king of Israel. It was stolen by the Troll and carried on board ship to Cornwall, where both the mirror and he who had stolen it had been abandoned for fear of Divine retribution. Other stories said that the glass was a pagan thing, created by either the old Phoenician or the old Celtic gods, and that it was more concerned with the great Cycle of Rebirth in which the ancient Celts believed. It was further said that if a man looked into its depths, he could see previous lives that he had lived and future lives which he was likely to experience, and the great Wheel of Life inexorably turned. It was even said that you could name the time or period and the Troll would grant you the ability to relive your past life therein all over again.

There is a story that a rather grand solicitor from Penzance was sure that he had been a great and powerful landowner in some past life and was anxious to prove it to his disbelieving friends. He had heard from Aunt Betty Grancan and several others about the Troll living at Newlyn Tolcarne, and of his miraculous mirror.

'That'll prove how grand I was in all my past lives to those who laugh at me,' he said, 'and it'll allow me to live my great past lives all over again.' And he set off for Newlyn Tolcarne to find the Troll. As instructed by the very old people of the area, he had taken with him three dried leaves of different types – ash, oak and thorn – and he had learned a little rhyme in ancient Cornish (he was not a natural Cornish speaker). Passing by the vicarage, he made his way up the hill towards the little greenstone outcropping. When he reached it, he paused and brought the dried leaves from his pocket and, holding them aloft, he recited the little charm that he'd been taught. Nothing happened, although the day darkened a little and dull-looking clouds began to scud in from the east. There was a bit of a wind getting up too. Again the solicitor repeated the charm, with much the same result.

Then he recalled what Aunt Betty Grancan had said. 'If the Troll doesn't appear to you at first, empty a tot o' dark rum on the ground. That'll bring him!' And so, heeding her advice, the solicitor brought out a little bottle from his hip pocket and poured a small libation on the ground. Libations of beer and spirits were always good for bringing out the fairies – and this time it worked! Around the side of the greenstone mound came a very pleasant-looking little fellow – no more than three feet tall – with a cherry-red and smiling face, dressed in a leather jerkin with a hood and licking his lips at the thought of the rum. Under his right arm, he seemed to be holding a fairly large mirror. The solicitor knew that this was the Tolcarne Troll. He held up the rum bottle by way of a further offering and the little fellow's eyes lit up.

'Well,' he said, 'what can I do for you?' The solicitor's eyes never left the mirror beneath his arm. The Troll laughed loudly.

'Oh,' he said. 'I see that like many of the other sons and daughters of Adam, you wish to see what the future may hold for you. Is that the way of it?' But the solicitor shook his head.

'I'm not terribly concerned about the future,' he told the Troll loftily, 'for I've money enough put by which'll see me quite comfortably into a grand old age. No, I'm told that your mirror can show me what I was in a previous life and that you can even allow me to live as I did then.' The Troll seemed to be considering his words. At length he nodded, still smiling to himself.

'That's quite so,' he answered. The solicitor's eyes lit up.

'I'm convinced that I was of great importance in all my former lives,' he told the fairy, 'and I'd like to pick one of them at random and relive the highlights of it. Can that be done?' The Troll never ceased smiling.

'It can indeed,' he replied. The solicitor became even more excited.

'Then hold up your mirror,' he demanded, 'and let me see my lives long past – maybe I shall be a Roman Emperor or a Norman king.' Still smiling a queer smile, the Troll held out his mirror for the solicitor's inspection.

'Then look,' said he, 'but keep your wits about you, for in this glass the aeons move swiftly like storm clouds in a summer sky. A hundred centuries are but an instant to those who are immortal.' And he was telling no word of a lie, for, as the solicitor looked, centuries rolled past within its depths more quickly than he could follow them. Roman soldiers ran across a grassy plain; Viking ships rode at anchor off a distant coast; Norman galleys landed on a beach, discharging horses and armoured men. The scope and swiftness of it all fair took the other's breath away.

'Stop!' he cried as medieval knights galloped past, just beyond the surface of the glass. 'I'll live my life here in this grand feudal time.' And he pointed towards the unfolding scenes in the mirror.

'So be it,' said the Troll, snapping his fingers. 'Be as you were then.' And there was a roar like the wind and the hilltop at Newlyn Tolcarne was gone. Instead of standing beside the Troll, the solicitor found himself in a sea of mud and filth. And he was wallowing in it, too! His body felt strange and unwieldy, and as he looked down he saw to his horror that instead of hands and feet, he had trotters. And just as he realized this he saw, looking up, a swineherd coming into the stone-walled pen all around him. Lifting a long stick, the swineherd struck him across the back and proceeded to drive him towards the gate of the pig enclosure. He tried to cry out – to warn the dolt away – but his words came out in a single squeal.

'Come on pig!' cried the yokel, hitting him again with the stick. 'Let's get you down to the slaughterer. His lordship fancies fresh pork for his table very soon!' Again the solicitor cried out – a cry which once again turned to a squeal. He shut his eyes and when he opened them, he was standing on the top of the hill again with the little Troll in front of him still holding up the mirror.

'Well?' he said cheerily. 'Did you enjoy your previous life as a pig in medieval times?' The solicitor snorted as the visions in the glass began to move again with an increasing swiftness.

'There must have been some mistake!' he blustered. 'Let me try Tudor times. No doubt I was a grand noble then – maybe even at the court of the king!'

'So be it,' cried the Troll, snapping his fingers once more. 'Be as you were then!' And the hilltop at Tolcarne was suddenly gone and the solicitor found himself looking at rows and rows of heavily booted feet. He was crouched uncomfortably under a table, from which scraps of bread and meat were falling. Beside him a couple of dogs were lying, watching expectantly for every scrap that fell. And as a half-eaten chicken leg fell to the ground, he felt himself start forward. With a shock, he realized that he was a dog as well! A boot caught him a blow on the hindquarters.

'Lie down!' snapped a voice from above, as the solicitor stuck his long, doggy nose out from his shelter and into the rank and fetid air of a roadside tavern. 'If I see you stirring again, I'll beat you like the ignorant whelp you are!' There was no doubt that he was a mangy, beer-house mongrel. He cried out in protest but all he could do was to bark loudly. The boot struck him again.

'Shut up!' shouted somebody. The solicitor closed his eyes again, and on opening them found himself on the hilltop beside the Troll. The little man looked at him quite pleasantly.

'Any more?' he asked laughingly. 'Would you like to live your life as you were in some other time?' But the solicitor shook his head. His body still ached where the swineherd's stick and the tavern-man's boots had struck him. He felt very chastened and the pride was certainly knocked out of him. The Troll laughed once more.

'So,' he said cheerfully, 'you've seen your past lives as a pig and as a dog. Well, at least you can tell your grand friends that you've advanced but a little. You're now a solicitor!' And with another laugh, he was gone.

Although this is a fairly humorous tale, frequently told against the legal profession (who do not appear to be well liked in Cornwall, given the number of derogatory stories told against them), it does not fit in well with the Celtic (or Cornish) notion of reincarnation. Under this belief, human rebirth must remain within the mortal race and the transmigration of souls into animals is expressly forbidden by Divine decree. However, even the holy decrees of the Infinite should not be allowed to ruin a good story, should they?

Witches, Wizards and Wise Women

Although, as far as we know, the ancient Celtic peoples observed no formalized religion, this does not necessarily mean that they had no forms of worship. The description 'druid' has been applied to a relatively mysterious body of holy men and women who presided over Celtic devotions, but historians have argued that such a term may have been used to include a multitude of functionaries – judges, religious leaders, poets and so on. Nor does the word itself give us any clues as to the shadowy people who made up the druidic numbers. The most common meaning and concept of the druid is taken from Pliny the Elder, who makes a connection with the Indo-European word *dru*, meaning 'oak' (the oak being a central element in Celtic supernatural belief), thus giving us the idea of druids as being 'men (or women) of the oak'. Many scholars, however, now believe that the word simply means 'wisdom', giving a much wider context than that of a simple religious or cult leader.

Early Celtic religion would appear to have been guided by shaman-like figures through whom the supernatural world of gods, ghosts and spirits was linked to the material, mortal one. This may have been done, as in other tribal societies, through 'spirit possession' – where the god or force occupied the body of the shaman for a time in order to conduct its affairs. It was through such persons that the spirits made their will known and that their worshippers made requests. They were healers and performed magical arts and/or miraculous feats. In many ways, it is reasonable to suppose, the early Celtic shamans functioned in the same way as, say, North American Indian medicine men. Because of the fragmentary nature of Celtic religion, such shamans functioned only at a local level and were the vessels and interpreters of largely local deities.

This rather loose, 'shamanistic' religious format seems to have taken on a more formalized, ritualistic and austere aspect at some point. Julius Caesar, writing about his campaign against the Celts in Gaul (France) mentions in his *Gallic Wars* (Book IV), says:

> Throughout Gaul there are two classes of men of some dignity and importance...One of the two classes is that of the Druids...[who] are concerned with the worship of gods, look after public and private sacrifice, and expound religious matters...They have the right to decide nearly all public and private disputes and they also pass judgement and decide rewards and penalties in criminal and murder cases and in disputes concerning legacies and boundaries.

Caesar and his contemporaries, then, portray these 'holy people' as enjoying an extremely high status in Celtic society – comparable to the rank of '*equites*', or knights, and as a rank of the nobility directly below tribal royalty.

Nor was the rank of druid simply a male preserve. We have references to several '*drui-ban*' (female druids), particularly among the Gaulish Celts. A questionable work known as the *Scriptores Historiae Augustae*, speaks of two third-century emperors, Aurelian and Diocletian, both of whom had encounters with female druids acting very much in the style of oracles or prophetesses, while Caesar remarks that Germanic women had divinatory powers in the fashion of Celtic female druids. Even in the Christian tradition, the notion of female druids continued. St Bridget of Kildare was said to be a '*drui-ban*' (and was herself the daughter of a druid) before converting to Christianity.

With the expansion of the Roman Empire in the west, the notion of druids as purely Celtic magicians and miracle-workers appears gradually to have died out. (It was, however, later to be revived as a romantic ideal during the Renaissance, when druids were depicted as the custodians of a lost but essentially noble wisdom). The gods which they had worshipped were now largely replaced with Roman or Romano-Celtic deities, whose ceremonies were administered mainly by formal priests. By the time of the collapse of the western Roman Empire in the fifth century AD, literary references to druids in both Britain and Gaul had all but come to an end.

In Ireland, however, the writings of the early Christian Fathers remained full of allusions to druidic lore and practices. Mythic texts such as the *Ulster Cycle* contain references to druids, although now more in the role of prophet rather than miracle-worker or channel of the gods. There is no doubt that the idea of druids was not completely eradicated from the Celtic mind. In Ireland and Scotland especially, their role seems to have been largely taken over by the Filidh (poet-seers), who continued there until almost the seventeenth century.

The druidic tradition of miracle-working and magic continued in a localized setting. This usually concerned itself with local issues – the healing of sickness, the curing of animals, ensuring that the weather was good, interpreting signals and signs concerning the future. The magical element of these operations was handled by strictly local practitioners who were well known to and part of the communities in which they served. The very word 'magic' (which had never been used in connection with the druids) became exemplified in terms like the 'gift', 'cures' and 'charms', thus taking away the underlying perception of formalized witchcraft and firmly integrating the paractitioner within the local society. Thus, the local healer didn't practise 'sorcery' as such – he or she simply had 'a gift' which was, in all probability, passed down through the family line. There were, of course, darker sides to this gift as well – the power to do neighbours and their possessions great harm, for example – and, through time, this also became integrated into the expanding folklore concerning such people. They had connections with the 'fairies' and they obtained their powers from dark spirits.

Gradually, a rich tapestry of 'fairy doctors', 'spae women' and 'gifted' people began to emerge, bringing the world of the Celtic supernatural with them right up to the present century. Certain of these people still exist in isolated pockets of rural society, where they perhaps continue to work their miracles in limited ways, largely oblivious to the steady march of modern technology and thought.

The Madness of Myrddin

Undoubtedly, no wizard of the ancient world is better known than Merlin. His name has been closely associated with primal sorceries and magics, from the stylized Victorain romantic literature up to the Disney cartoons of the present day. He is cast in the role of chief adviser to Arthur, king of the ancient Britons, and also of the enchantress Vivian's besotted lover (although some British sources state that the witch Morgan le Fay – Arthur's half-sister – was the only love of Merlin's life). In the final analysis, he is represented by the oak tree (into which he heartbrokenly turned himself following Vivian's rejection), the symbol of Britain and steadfastness. An actual oak – the Priory Oak in Carmarthen – was strongly associated with Merlin, although it was removed by the local authority in 1978.

Despite his widespread renown, however, Merlin's origins are somewhat obscure and were most probably Welsh (although Ireland, Brittany and Scotland lay claim to him as well). Indeed, one of the *Trioedd Ynys Prydein* (*Welsh Triads*) tells us that the country of Britain was originally known as Clas Myrddin – 'Myrddin's enclosure' – before it was inhabited. Historians such as Professor John Rhys have suggested that Myrddin may have been a localized deity who was worshipped at Stonehenge, which according to some traditions (particularly those recounted by Geoffrey of Monmouth) was actually magically transported to Salisbury Plain by him from Ireland. (Other sources, as we saw in Chapter 2, cite that the stones were transported by the giants Gog and Magog on the orders of King Vortigern.) If Myrddin was in fact a spirit or god, then he also had some human elements about him, for he fled in the face of oncoming Christianity, accompanied by nine attendant bards and followers, to Bardsey Island off the Lleyn Peninsula, taking with him the 'Thirteen Treasures of Britain'. In his godly form, Myrddin has been identified with the Hellenistic god Kronos (Chronos) – an extremely ancient Mediterranean fertility deity and father of Zeus.

Much later, Myrddin became a figure of Celtic legend, taking on quasi-druidical attributes and changing his name to the Latinized 'Merlin', and with this he also seems to have crossed the border into Britain. Part of this may be attributed to Geoffrey of Monmouth's *Libellus Merline* (*The Little Book of Merlin*), written around ad 1135, which is the first fully developed account of him. This also formed the basis

for Geoffrey's allegorical Latin poem 'Vitae Merlini' ('Life of Merlin') written in 1150, which is a complex and prophetic text, arguably in the style of the early Welsh bards. Indeed, apparently drawing upon early Welsh sources, Geoffrey also links Merlin with the bard Taliesin, and the two certainly seem to be entertwined in the Welsh mind. One Welsh tradition says that Merlin actually had three incarnations – one as a wild man of the forest, another in King Vortigern's time (hence the connection with Stonehenge) and yet another as Taliesin himself. The idea of a multiple Merlin is found again in the works of the early medieval scholar Geraldus Cambrensis (Gerald of Wales), who states that there were two Merlins – the sage and the wild man – demonstrating both sides of human nature.

Nor was Arthur the only ancient British king with whom Merlin was associated. We have already mentioned Vortigern but there are also strong links with King Gwenddolau, a king of Britain who may have had druidic connections. This British prince or ruler fought against his own cousins – Gwrgi and Peredur – at the Battle of Arfderydd in ad 575, during which he was killed. Welsh tradition states that Gwenddolau was Merlin or Myrddin's liege-lord (Geoffrey of Monmouth disputes this, saying the Merlin actually fought on the opposing side), and that Merlin and his brothers formed part of one of the 'six faithful companies of Britain'. The companies continued to fight on for six weeks after Gwenddolau was slain but were eventually overwhelmed by superior numbers. During those six weeks, all Merlin's brothers had also been slain and Merlin himself went wild with grief, dwelling in the deep forests with his sister Gwenddydd, living on wild berries and uttering dire and insane prophecies. During this time he was known as Merlin Wyllt, or the 'wild man', touched by the forest spirits. Later, he was to settle down, incorporate the knowledge he had learned in the wild woodlands and become the sage Merlin Emrys, who was almost druidical in his wisdom and intellect.

It was the Renaissance which transformed Merlin yet again into the classical enchanter, wise in the ways of ancient Britain, and 'played up' his distinctly Celtic flavour. The thirteenth-century *Auchinleck Manuscript* – possibly a combination of much earlier sources – had linked Merlin to Ulthar Pendragon, father of the famous Arthur. This link had been strengthened by Sir Thomas Malory's *La Morte d'Arthur*, written between 1469 and 1470. In the sixteenth and seventeenth centuries, writers fell upon this connection, making Merlin a wise, all-knowing sage, confidant and magician in the style of later occultists such as John Dee, William Lilley, Marcilio Ficino and Ananasius Kircher. The template for Merlin as the consummate wizard had been set.

And yet his pagan roots still lay in Merlin Wyllt, the near-bestial man of the forest – intoxicated by knowledge and touched by the ancient Celtic woodland forces. He was one of the last of Gwenddolau's followers, driven mad with anguish at the death of his brothers at Arfderydd. The name, incidentally, means 'lark's nest', and it is said that Gwenddolau's campaign came to an end in the nest of a lark – probably the important ancient British harbour at Caerlaverlock, which translates as Fort Lark...

At Last the din of battle had almost faded away and he was alone in the forest. Myrddin paused and listened, but could hear nothing except the far-away shouts of soldiers, rising above the sporadic birdsong, as they combed the forest edges looking for the last survivors of Gwenddolau's army. Gwenddolau himself lay with most of his forces, away beyond the tree-line, slain by the sword of Rhydderch Hael, the powerful king of Strathclyde and Myrddin's own brother-in-law. Now his soldiers hunted along the forest edge for any stragglers from the pagan king's followers. Myrddin was fortunate indeed to have escaped their clutches, although a sword blow to his side had almost killed him and he was bleeding seriously from numerous cuts across his body.

Seeing that Gwenddolau and his army couldn't possibly win against the forces of his own cousins, Gwrgi and Peredur, aided as they were by the military might of Strathclyde, Myrddin had fled into the forest to escape capture. And as he ran, he had actually seen Gwenddolau fall in battle, struck down by an imposing figure which could only have been Rhydderch Hael, commander to the Strathclyde forces.

And then the scenes of battle and slaughter had fallen away behind him and he was deep into the dark and concealing woodlands. Yet he still heard the shouts of the dying and smelled the acrid tang of woodsmoke, as his enemies set fire to the scrub along the edge of the forest in order to smoke out rebels. He thought that he heard the whinnying of horses as mounted warriors tried to follow those who had fled among the trees. They wouldn't catch him, however.

Myrddin had now come to a clearing in the woodlands where a river formed a large pool between low-hanging bushes. Throwing himself to the ground, he pulled off what remained of his shattered helmet and war-mask and, hurling aside his blood-stained sword, plunged his head beneath the water. The pool was cool and clear, but it soon reddened with the blood which flowed from the numerous cuts across his body. Hoisting himself up, he moved unsteadily to the other edge of the clearing and fell down upon the fresh sweet earth. His muscles ached and his belly rumbled for want of food but there was little to be had, not unless he ate leaves and berries like the wildfowl around him. He laughed silently to himself. Only madmen did that – those crazy, red-eyed hermits who lived away in the forest and who were sometimes seen mouthing strange prophecies at the corner of some village square. He had heard some say that these 'wild men' had actually been 'touched' – specially favoured – by the powerful spirits which dwelt in the deep woods and that they had a queer magic about them, but Myrddin wasn't so sure. Their life of seeming madness was not for him – he was a warrior after all!

Despite the relative calm of the day, the woodland somehow seemed on edge. Everywhere there were furtive movements and scufflings as forest creatures sought new hiding places among the foliage. It was as though the whole place seemed to be waiting for something – Rhydderch Hael's soldiers to come and set it completely ablaze, perhaps. Still, Myrddin was weary – he had just fought a battle – and he needed rest, no matter what happened. He shut his eyes and was soon breathing deeply and restfully. The sun played on his face in shafts and the angry shouts of the pursuing soldiers suddenly seemed too far away to be heard.

Myrddin was ever after unsure whether what followed was simply a dream or a vision. He was conscious that someone passed between the sunshine above and his face. A shadow passed and was gone, but it was coupled with a movement of water as though something had climbed from the splashing pool and had come out on to the land to look down upon him. The day suddenly darkened as though the sun had disappeared behind heavy clouds. Myrddin opened his eyes. The glade around him was still empty, although eerie, broken shadows came and went everywhere. He was aware, too, of something else – close by. It was a heavy, musky stench – the reek of wet fur drying in the evening air. He groped for his sword but couldn't find it. There was now no sound in the evening except for the faint echo of birdsong. The cries of Rhydderch Hael's warriors seemed to have gone completely, swallowed up by an almost oppressive woodland silence, broken only by the infrequent and feeble cries of hidden birds.

'Who's there?' Myrddin was sure that he was being spied upon. The hairs on the base of his neck fairly prickled from the sensation of being clandestinely watched. There was no reply to his challenge but the sensation grew stronger, as if those who watched drew slightly closer to him. Fearful that it might be an enemy, he tried to get to his feet, but the pain in his body and his loss of blood made him unsteady and he collapsed again with a groan. A darkness swam around him, but he was conscious that something touched him. The musky scent was now almost unbearable, filling his nostrils like acrid pond-water and almost making him retch and gag. And yet the touch was soft, like the hand of a maiden, gently caressing his brow.

'Rest!' whispered a voice, close to his ear. 'Rest, for you have a great destiny before you.' It was the voice of a young girl and it reminded him of his sister Gwenddydd, kind and gentle. Yet although the tone was soft, it stirred up unaccountable echoes which swirled and reverberated around him like the cries of battle.

'Who...' he began. The touch came again, like the soft brush of rain across his forehead.

'Shh...' replied the voice. 'Close your eyes. All will be explained, but first you must rest.'

'No!' Myrddin tried to shake himself free of the swimming darkness to see who spoke. He vaguely glimpsed the glade around him, as if through a film of water, and

it still appeared empty. 'I must get back to the battle. My three brothers...'

'All your brothers are dead,' the voice told him hesitantly, 'slain with Gwenddolau beyond the forest. You have been spared because of your destiny.' The warrior shook his head, unable to take in the dreadful news. 'Now rest, for your journey back to life is a long and difficult one.'

'Who...who are you?' Myrddin found himself growing weaker and the darkness about him increased. 'Let me see your face!' The echoing voices around the glade gave a low chuckle.

'We are the spirits of the woodland,' the reply came. 'We were already here when your Celtic forefathers came to this place and we have dwelt here in spite of them. We have no face that we can show you.'

'Then what is this destiny of which you speak?' Myrddin felt his mouth filling with blood. 'Why is it that my brothers have been slain and yet I have been spared?' There was silence for a moment. Birds called to each other with fractured shouts in the gloom.

'You have been spared death in battle so that you can die and be reborn in this place,' the voice said at length. Despite his pain, Myrddin laughed, hot blood trickling from the corners of his mouth. He tried to wipe it away with the back of his hand, but it wouldn't obey him. The wound in his side throbbed unmercifully.

'What sort of madness is this?' he asked, more to himself than to the owners of the voice. 'How can I die and be reborn again?'

'All things die and are reborn,' the voice patiently explained. 'This is one of the great truths of the Celtic faith. But not all are born as they died. Some are born in different forms, others as different persons. So it will be with you. The warrior in you must die so that your true form may be released in order to fulfil the destiny which we have ordained for you.' Myrddin attempted to laugh once more and blood gushed from his mouth and down across his beard. The laugh gave way to a bout of painful coughing.

'What destiny is this? My king is dead and I'm badly wounded and like to die myself. There's little destiny for me here.'

'The destiny lies with a king other than Gwenddolau. Lie back and close your eyes and we shall show you both your own future and that of Britain.' Slowly Myrddin closed his eyes and sank back on the ground. Images rushed into his mind like tumbling water. He saw himself, as part of Gwenddolau's army, fighting alongside his brothers against the forces of Rhydderch Hael and being slowly driven back. Swords clashed, horses screamed, men shouted in pain. Then the scene subtly altered. It was another battle for another king – a battle in which he took no part. He saw himself again, much older this time and in the robes and cowl of a druid. He was standing on a hilltop, leaning on a staff of yew wood, sagely surveying the conflict below him. An army charged and voices roared the name of their king. And the name that they shouted was 'Arthur'.

'What does this mean?' he heard himself ask.

'It means that Myrddin the warrior must die so that Myrddin Emrys – Myrddin the Sage – can come forth. The king whom he will serve will be the greatest these

ancient lands have seen, because he will have our blessing and you shall be our instrument. You shall be Arthur's adviser.' It was all too much for Myrddin to take in.

'No!' he protested. 'I'm a soldier – a warrior. I led a company of Gwenddolau's army! I have no learning like that of a sage or druid. I...' But the voice cut across his outburst, gently but firmly.

'You are our instrument,' it repeated, 'and we shall guide you. We shall give you the words that you must say to Arthur, so that his kingdom can become the greatest this country has seen and will see. This is the way of things. Already to the north, there are other kingdoms rising...'

'Aye, that of Strathclyde and of my accursed brother-in-law Rhydderch Hael!' Myrddin spat out more blood. As the light in the clearing faded, it seemed that he was growing weaker still.

'No!' chided the voice. 'These kingdoms lie in other lands. The Saxons of the north shall rise and overthrow even the descendants of Rhydderch Hael, when his name is but a memory. They shall reduce the land to ashes and only the might of Arthur will be able to stand against them and hold them in check for a time. And you shall be our eyes, ears and tongue at his court. You shall guide Arthur's hand in our ways and according to our desires. Even though you will not fight, yet will you shape the courses of battles with your wisdom and magic, and, ultimately, the future of Britain. This we have seen. And even when the northern Saxons rule the land in the dim future, your name coupled with that of great Arthur shall provide an inspiration for men of true Celtic blood!'

Visions now flooded into Myrddin's mind like an unstoppable tide. He had fleeting glimpses of a man pulling a mighty sword from a rock; of horsemen riding across the land, looting and burning as they went; of great dragon-prowed ships riding at anchor off the coast, their crews storming ashore to bring havoc to the shoreline settlements.

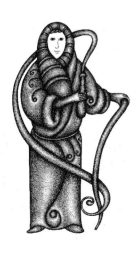

'These things are decreed and will come to pass.' The voice hesitated suddenly, as if unsure as to how to go on. 'There is one more thing that we would show you. In a time in the future a new invader shall come, not with sword or armour but with a book, and we will be powerless against it.' Now Myrddin knew that he was crazy. How could any army win battles armed only with a book, he asked himself? He seemed to be looking now across open countryside where a body of men, clad only in brown robes and carrying a wooden cross in front of them, advanced through a driving sleety rain.

'These are not warriors,' the voice went on, 'but priests. They are the followers of the White Christ and against Him we have no power. Their weapon is called the Word and it will change men's hearts so that they will turn their backs upon us. We will be forced to dwell in the dark places of the forests and mountains, our names little more than legend. When you see these men arrive, you will know that both your time and our time is done for a season.' Once again there was a pause. 'Such things are set in the Wheel of Time and cannot be changed. But as the Wheel turns our time may well come again, and this hope shall live on in your name – the name of Myrddin Emrys, or as men shall then call you, Merlin.'

'No!' Myrddin was having none of it. He knew he was bleeding heavily again and that death was not too far away. 'I am a warrior, not some trifling druid. Show me that I can come again as a fighting man and I shall die happily enough.' There was only silence.

'Such things are set, now and for ever. We have gifted you with visions of the future – prophecies of that which is to come. You will become a great seer and the future shall be as clear to you as the present. You will become immortal in men's minds. Is this not a far better destiny than that of a warrior?'

Myrddin made to answer, but the darkness overwhelmed him and he was too weak to make any reply. He closed his eyes more tightly, shutting out the far-away birdsong and the other sounds of the forest. And the voice.

'Shhh.' The evening breeze and rain caressed his brow. 'Rest!' The forest around him sighed. 'Rest and be reborn!'

It was morning when he opened his eyes again and sunlight streamed everywhere through the forest glade. The pool nearby gurgled merrily and wildfowl cried and twittered in the surrounding foliage. The shadows and voices of the previous evening were gone. Blearily, Myrddin climbed to his feet. The pain in his side had completely gone and no further blood flowed from any wound on his body. A sword, coated in rust, lay nearby, and as he looked down at himself he saw that his clothes hung in rags around him and that his metal corselet was covered in mould. Unsteadily, he tottered over to the pool and stooped to wash his face. It had subtly altered. While his features still remained the same, the face seemed to have lengthened and taken on a leaner, more fantastical aspect. Both his beard and his hair had grown and now flowed across his back and chest in a matted, greying cascade. His eyes, too, which had always been fierce and angry, were now infused with an awful passion which veered between wisdom and madness. It was the face of a forest hermit. Wiping away the last of the water from his brow, Myrddin cast off the remains of his war-harness and made his way over to some nearby bushes. He was achingly hungry. Reaching among the brambles and chasing away a bird who was nesting there, he began to pluck at some wild berries, which he quickly crammed into his mouth.

Ancient traditions state that, in this wild state, Myrddin left Britain shortly after Gwenddolau's defeat and went to Scotland, where he lived in the Caledonian forests as a hermit for some time. There, he became something of a prophet or seer, still intoxicated by the woodland spirits and issuing prognostications very much in the frenzied style of the ancient *kahins* (oracle-mongers) of eighth-century Arabia. He eventually travelled south again, now a wandering druid and using the name Myrddin Emrys, to settle at the court of the British warlord Uther Pendragon, who was, of course, the father of Arthur. The Merlin of classical antiquity was already being born.

The Brahan Seer

One of the most important functions of the early Celtic druids was to predict the future. If a local king was to go into battle or embark upon some potentially hazardous enterprise, it was advisable to know the outcome before such an undertaking began. If a community was to face, say, famine or some other hardship in the course of a year, it was as well to be prepared. The prophetic abilities of the druid were therefore of paramount importance in Celtic society.

This need to know the future through supernatural means continued right down to the early years of the present century. Nowhere was this more evident than in western Scotland. In the western Highlands and in the Isles, there were a group of men and women who were 'gifted' (some of them would argue that they were 'afflicted') with the *Taibh-searachd, taibhs* or *taish* – commonly known as 'second sight'. This was the ability to see events long before they happened. Usually it was confined simply to local issues – a birth or, more commonly, a death in the immediate community. Sometimes those so gifted were able to predict with reasonable accuracy whether the harvest would be good or whether a newborn calf would live to adulthood. These were the humdrum predictions of everyday life. However, this ordinariness did not take away from the supernatural nature of the act of foretelling, and those who had the *taish* were often regarded with awe and reverence by those around them.

How did the 'sight' or gift of prophecy take hold of an individual? Although it was widely believed that it was conferred at birth – something akin to a natural musical talent – there are tales of certain people not acquiring the gift until old age. Nor was it voluntary, for the visions usually came without warning or choice. Women, according to Highland tradition, did not usually make good seers. It was not that they didn't experience the visions, but that they were incapable of interpreting them correctly. When in a state of prophecy, the seer's eyes rolled upwards in the head and breathing became harsh and laboured. According to Martin Martin in his invaluable *A Description of the Western Isles of Scotland in 1695*, 'The eyelids of the person are erected and the eyes continue staring until the object vanishes. There is one Seer in Skye whose eyelids turned so far inwards that he had to draw them down with his fingers or get others to do so.'

In an area such as the Scottish Highlands, where the clan system was still extant and local families were often bloodily feuding among themselves, again it was vitally important to know the outcome of disputes and disagreements. The result of a clan war could, of course, mean a redrawing of the territorial boundaries through conquest or the murder of an important chieftain. In this case the prophecies took on a highly 'political' flavour, making the prophet or seer even more sought after in some parts of the country, particularly the western Highlands.

In some cases, it was even believed that the seer could also somehow *influence* the future. This was undoubtedly due to what we might describe as the 'supernatural aura' which, in popular belief, attached itself to these people. There are numerous stories across the Highlands and Islands of the 'seer's curse', perhaps visited upon a clan chieftain who had angered the seer in some way, or even upon a whole clan, which then caused them to lose their lands.

Undoubtedly, one of the most famous prophets in Scotland was Cionneach Odhar – Dun-coloured Kenneth MacKenzie (also described as 'Sombre Kenneth of the Prophecies' – Cionneach Odhar Fiosaiche), more popularly known as the Brahan Seer. This seer was a rather shadowy figure, living in Scotland around the seventeenth (or possibly the sixteenth) century, but to many Highlanders even today his name is as familiar as that of the prophet Isaiah or Nostradamus.

There are many disputes surrounding the Brahan Seer's origins and life. However according to Alexander MacKenzie, however, who collected and published the prophecies of the Brahan Seer in 1877, he was born on MacKenzie land at Baile-na-Cille in Uig, on the Isle of Lewis. Somewhere between 1660 and 1675 he came to live near Loch Ussie in Ross-shire, where he worked on the Brahan estate of the Seaforth MacKenzies. It was here that he began to utter prophecies concerning not only local events but also more national events involving the fates of certain clans and of the Highlands as well.

Like many other of the Celtic wizards and wise women, Kenneth had an object upon which he sometimes focused and which was said to give him his power. In Kenneth's case, it was a blue stone which he had inherited from his mother. The stone, it was said, had been given to her by the ghost of the daughter of the king of Norway and supposedly had miraculous powers, including that of conferring the gift of accurate prophecy upon its owner. Kenneth used it to great effect. The stone was supposed to have been round and smooth with a hole all the way through its centre like the access for a spindle. Kenneth raised this hole to his 'predicting eye' and through it saw his visions. Most sources agree that this particular eye was 'cam' (blind to normal vision). This would place him among the 'scryers', or 'crystal gazers', who had characterized the late Elizabethan period in England.

As with all tentative historical figures, this story is a disputed one. There are other references to a Coinneach Odhar prophesying in Skye which place him a century earlier. Just to confuse matters, there are two historical references in which a Coinneach Odhar is accused of witchcraft in 1557/1578. It is, of course, quite possible (indeed probable) that these accounts refer to different individuals, but if that is the case, then it shows the power and significance of the name, as well as the awe which surrounded gifts of prediction right down to the eighteenth century.

Some of the Brahan Seer's predictions became widely famed in the Highlands. The majority of them refer to the clan MacKenzie, particularly to the Seaforth MacKenzies, but some more general ones are attributed to him as well. For instance, it was said that he prophesied the building of the Caledonian Canal 150 years before it was built, by saying that ships would one day sail around the back of Tamnahurich Hill (the Hill of Yew Trees) at Inverness. It is also believed that he foresaw the Highland Clearances and the eventual breakdown of the Highland clan system. On each hillock across the Highland moors, he foretold, an English white house would be built – these were the shooting lodges of the English and Anglicized Scottish aristocracy.

His most venomous prognostications were saved for his employers. There would come a time, declared the seer, when ravens would gorge themselves on the blood of the clan MacKenzie on top of a standing stone known as Cloch-an-t-Seasaidh near the Muir of Ord. The MacKenzies would be decimated in a battle nearby, he went on, and the remnants of the clan would be taken to Ireland in an open fishing boat. Later, the prophecy was altered in such a way that it no longer referred directly to the MacKenzies but to the MacRaes of Kintail – and in this context, it actually came true. Regarding another stone – Cloch an Tiompain (the Stone of the Lyre) – Kenneth said that one day ships would tie their cables around it even though it was many miles

from the sea. This came about in the nineteenth century when another canal was built in the area.

Throughout his life, Kenneth MacKenzie seems to have been a somewhat gloomy and sarcastic character, frequently getting into trouble with his employers because of his caustic, malicious wit and doom-laden prophecies. It was his scathing humour and insolent attitude that led to his eventual death. He was invited by the Seaforth MacKenzies to a convivial gathering of the local nobility in Brahan Castle. One of the party remarked to Kenneth (within the hearing of Lady Seaforth) that he had never seen such a grand gathering of gentlemen's children. The seer sneeringly answered, '*Is mo th'ann do chlann ghillean-buird agus do chlann ghillean-stabuil no th'ann do chlann dhaoin uaisle*' (he saw more in the company who were the children of footmen and grooms than the children of gentlemen). This, of course, cast aspersions on the parentage of everyone present and was a calculated insult to both the company and the host. Enraged, the company ordered him to be seized and punished. After eluding his infuriated pursuers for a time, he was eventually apprehended.

Seeing that there was no escape, Kenneth MacKenzie once more resorted to his magic stone, which he raised to his eye and prophesied the eventual end of the Seaforth line. He then threw the stone into a cow's footprint which was filled with water at the time and uttered a final prophecy. He declared that a boy would be born in Scotland with two navels and six toes on each foot, and he would one day find the stone inside a pike and would thus inherit the abilities of the Brahan Seer. It is said that the water in the cow-print began to spread and rise without relenting until it formed modern-day Loch Ussie. The seer, however, was taken to Chanonry Point, where, under the stern eye of the Church authorities, he was burned for witchcraft, seated on a tar barrel. Even so, the Seaforths did not escape the seer's prophecy, for on 11 January 1815 the last Lord Seaforth died without issue, pretty much as Kenneth had foretold. Although there is a Brahan Seer today, the boy with two navels and six toes on each foot has not yet come forward to claim the magical blue stone.

The above is, of course, only one account of Kenneth MacKenzie's end. Because of the dramatic character of his prophecies and because so little is known about the shadowy figure who issued them, legend has built up around the Brahan Seer, who is perhaps one of the last examples of the prophetic Celtic druid. The following are various testimonies to his supernatural skills, taken during the 1800s across the western Highlands...

There are many stories told about Coinneach Odhar, the MacKenzie Seer at Brahan, about his drinking and dark ways, but there's no doubt that he was a great prophet. Everything that he foretold came true, no matter how queer it seemed at the time. He prophesied that a mighty natural stone arch – the Clach tholl – near Storehead in Assynt would fall with a crash so loud as to cause the Laird of Leadmore's cattle – 20 miles away – to break their tethers in fright. Everyone thought that he was mad, for the arch had been there for as long as anyone could remember – and anyway, how could a crash be heard by cattle grazing so far away? But it came to pass all right in 1841, when the laird's cattle, having strayed from home, wandered away as far as Clach tholl and were grazing within only a few hundred yards of the place. Suddenly, the arch fell with an almighty crash which sent them back home in a terrible fright, tearing everything before them.

Many of his prophecies concerned people as well. There was an old woman living at one time in the village of Baile Mhuilin, in west Sutherlandshire. She was known locally as Baraball n'ic Coinnich (Annabella MacKenzie) and she was about 95 years old. There was a story about her that when she was a young slip of a girl, the Brahan Seer had prophesied that she would die from a severe bout of measles. Her mother and father had protected her, keeping her well away from any place or person where the measles were. She had lived all through her great life without ever taking measles at all and, because of her advanced years, everyone thought that she was far beyond the reaches of the disease. The villagers laughed at the old prophecy and said that, for once, the Brahan Seer had been wrong.

But wait! One year – Baraball was almost 100 at the time – a great plague of measles went through Sutherlandshire, touching young and old alike. Thinking that she was beyond taking the sickness, Baraball went about in her usual way, but the measles came calling at her door. She was so sick with them that she couldn't get out of her house at all, and as she lived alone she had nobody to look after her. Within two or three days she was dead, just as the seer had predicted. There are those who will tell you that Barabell n'ic Coinnich died during the early 1800s and that the seer's prophecy concerning her had been issued over 100 years before she was even born!

Another story concerning Kenneth also features an old person. In the early seventeenth century, during the seer's lifetime, there lived in Kintail an old, old man named Duncan MacRae who was very curious about the manner by which he should come to his end. He went to see a local seeress, who informed him that he would die 'by the sword' (*le bas à chlaidheamh*). MacRae distrusted the prophetess and her prognostication seemed highly improbable for such an old man. Indeed, Duncan MacRae had always gone out of his way to avoid trouble and had really

taken no part in the clan disputes which had raged through Kintail. He decided that he would refer the matter to a higher authority, the Brahan Seer, Coinneach Odhar himself, who was at that time living close by in a house of sods. He made his way up to the seer's sod-house, where in the smoky half-light streaming in through the door Kenneth was smoking a pipe and drinking from a jug of spirits.

'You have come to ask me how you are to die,' said Kenneth, without looking up from the burning peat embers in front of him. Old Duncan MacRae was astounded.

'Indeed, seer,' he replied'for I've been told by a spae-wife in Kintail that I'm to die by the sword but I'm an old, old man and I've never fought a battle in my life. I believe that I'll die in my bed. Am I right?' The seer didn't answer for a moment but sat leaning on his stick and looking into the dying embers of his fire.

'The spae-wife is right,' said he, taking another swig from the jug and spitting into the fire. The flames leapt up. 'I've seen you die through my stone and with my cam eye of prophecy. It will be by the sword sure enough and the cause of your death will be words. Now go and leave me, for I've much thinking to do this day.' And with that, he squarely turned his back on old Duncan MacRae and would say no more.

The prophecy was long discounted in the neighbourhood, and by none more so than old Duncan himself. Even so, he kept well clear of fights and never became involved in any dispute.

In 1654, the Cromwellian General Monck (later Duke of Albermarle) came to Kintail and set up a camp there, and his soldiers rode all through the countryside, hunting out Catholics and outlaws. Duncan, anxious to stay out of the way of any fighting, left Kintail and went to live in a house in Glenshiel. One morning, he was out for a walk through the hills, his dog by his side, when several stragglers from Monck's army came over the hill. These were not regular army men, but rough southerners who had broken away from the main force in hopes of plunder. Seeing Duncan, they enquired where they were – but they spoke in English, and Duncan only understood Highland Gaelic. Desperately, he protested that he couldn't under-stand a word that they said, waving his arms and shouting in Gaelic and with his dog barking beside him. Thinking that the old man was cursing them, one drew his sword and ran Duncan MacRae through. He died by the sword, as the seer had said, and the cause of his death was words. This story is quite true, for it was written down by the Reverend John MacRae of Dingwall in his *Genealogy of the MacRaes* in 1702.

These were just some of the prophecies of the Brahan Seer which came to pass, but there is no doubt that he saw things that other men could not. Didn't he prophesy that the great MacKenzie stronghold of Fairburn Tower in Ord should pass from their hands and that a sow would farrow within its grand hall, a calf would be born in its upper chambers and a rowan bush would grow from its walls – and it all came to pass?

(Incidentally, exactly the same prophecy or curse was reputedly issued against the Erskines of Alloa Tower in Clackmannanshire by Thomas the Rhymer: 'The family will become extinct and their lands given to strangers...Horses will be stabled in its hall and a weaver will throw his shuttle in the Chamber of State. But when an ash sapling springs from the topmost stone, then the curse will have run its course. This also allegedly came true.)

Two of the Brahan Seer's more famous predictions actually refer to the present century. 'The day will acome when a king shall be born but never crowned. Three years after there will be trouble-some times' – a well-known prophecy in Skye in 1908. Three years after the abdication of Edward VIII in 1936, the second World War broke out. Another prophecy states: 'When there are three queens in Scotland, winter will be turned into summer and summer to winter.' This prophecy was particularly well known all through the Outer Isles. In 1953, when Queen Mary, Queen Elizabeth the Queen Mother and Queen Elizabeth II were all alive for nine months, the winter was excep-tionally mild and the summer exceptionally harsh.

The Death of Biddy Early

Although Ireland can boast the first and last witch burnings in the British Isles – Petronella of Meath (the maidservant of Dame Alice Kytler) in Kilkenny in 1324 and Bridget Cleary in Tipperary in 1895 – formal witch trials are extremely thin on the ground there. This is not to say that there were not 'witches' of a sort – rather, that methods of dealing with them may have been slightly different from elsewhere. If there were formal witch trials (and we do know that there were some in Kilkenny and at least one in Youghal in Cork), records of them may have been lost, or the women involved in alleged supernatural activities, particularly in rural areas, were never formally brought to trial. It is more probable that witchcraft may have been viewed differently among the Celtic Irish than, say, in England or on the Continent. Unlike Scotland, where most of the agents of supernatural power were men, Ireland had a strong tradition of 'wise women', who sometimes crossed the line into accusations of witchcraft.

Celtic society had a very strong impression of female power. Indeed, many of their deities were female and certainly women played a central role in Celtic community life. We have already noted that among the druids were a number of *drui-ban* (female druids). Many of these were undoubtedly healers with a vast knowledge of herbs and natural lore. This knowledge was probably passed down from woman to woman across the generations until fairly recent times. Even when the notion of the female druid died out, communities still looked to the women in their midst for their arcane knowledge, healing powers and general practicality. Slowly, the *drui-ban* became the 'wise woman' of the community. This was probably especially true in rural areas, where the old Celtic ways and beliefs still lingered.

Here, wise women functioned as doctors and midwives and often as veterinarians too. They were an indispensable facet of Irish country life.

But, as the Christian Church took a firmer grip on rural communities, questions began to be asked as to how these women had obtained their powers. Gradually, explanations were given – usually by the clergy. They trafficked with fairies, with ghosts, with dark forces which still lurked in the landscape; their ways were evil and not Christian. This stance was adopted because many of the women concerned showed a particular disdain for Church authority and for priests. Many behaved in what were considered to be 'unfeminine' ways. In a past age when women were expected to be subservient and to show respect and reverence for men and the Church (the officials of which were also men), rural 'wise women' flouted such expectations. Many of them displayed a fiercely independent streak – they smoked, drank and gambled, just as men did, and they were forthright in their opinions – and in many instances, their opinions contradicted those of the Church. Being the last repositories of the ancient Celtic wisdoms which had been handed down, they were an alternative to the ecclesiastical authorities. Small wonder, then, that they were denoucned from the pulpit as witches and harlots.

Several names, of both men and women (but especially women), gained notoriety across Ireland as wise men and women and fairy-doctors, respected in their own communities but denounced by the religious authorities. Among the men was the famous Maurice Griffin, the fairy-doctor of Kerry, who, it was said, could cure a sick animal simply by looking at it. He had obtained his powers through drinking the milk of a cow which had eaten grass touched by a fairy cloud. His fame as an animal healer was well known, even far beyond the borders of Kerry. The Church, however, left him pretty much alone and reserved its most scathing condemnation for women. Nevertheless, in many cases the clergy had little success in diminishing the often widespread fame of these individuals.

The names of two women stand out from the rest – Moll Anthony from the Red Hills of Kildare and Biddy Early from Kilbarron Lake in Clare. The 'Rale Oul' Moll Anthony' did not, of course, live at the Red Hills at all, but at the bleak Hill of Grange between Milltown and Rathangen in Kildare. And, just to complicate matters further, it's possible that her name wasn't Moll Anthony at all but Mary Leeson, who originally came from Punchesgrange. She had contracted her name from Mary to Moll and had taken the Christian name of her father – believed to have been one Anthony Dunne – as her surname. There is no doubt that local people considered her 'well in with the fairies', for her house was said to stand on a fairy path between the Hill of Allen and Donadea's Green Hill. Whoever she was and whatever her connections, there is no doubt that she was a great healer, of both humans and livestock. In some cases, sick animals were cured at the moment the owner came to Moll for a consultation. Such tales only increased her supernatural reputation, as well as her standing in the community, and she was alternately loathed and feared by the Kildare clergy. Despite her great powers and the awe in which she was held, Moll remains a hazy and mysterious figure. No one can say for certain, for example, when she was born, when exactly she lived or when she died. She has become one of those timeless figures who seem to have lived in every age. Sir Walter Fizgerald, however, sets the date of her demise in 1878 and states that her power to cure was passed on to a relative named James Leeson. Certainly, records show that a James Leeson lived 'in a comfortable slated house' on the Hill of Grange where Moll's old mud-walled cabin had been, but no one can say whether or not he had a 'cure' about him. There is a great deal about Moll Anthony that we don't know.

We do know a little more about her counterpart in Clare, Biddy Early – but not that much more. She was born Biddy O'Connor (Connors) at Faha, near Kilanea, County Clare, in 1798. At the age of 16, she appears to have moved from Faha to Carheen or Ayle (there is no record of her family moving there with her), where she lived 'in a haggard' (outhouse), working as a servant to some of the landlords round about. Around 1816, there was a rather gruesome murder in Ayle. One of the landlord's agents – a Mr Sheehy – was cut to pieces with scythes and billhooks by tenants on

his employer's estates, and several large houses round about were put to the torch. It's not clear whether Biddy was herself somehow implicated in these disturbances, but she left Ayle shortly afterwards and moved to Kilbarron.

Around this time, she may also have changed her name to Early. It is possible that she may have married a certain Tom Early or that she may have moved in with him in Kilbarron. If she was indeed married, then the details of the union are unclear. It's extremely hard to follow Biddy's matrimonial history with any degree of certainty, as she was married at least four times (probably more) – the longest period being to Tom Flannery of Carrowroe, whom she wed some time in the early 1840s. This, of course, doesn't count the men who lived with her right into her old age.

The framework of Biddy Early's life is not at all easy to follow in any chronological or ordered manner – large gaps and contradictions in the account remain everywhere. But we do know certain things about her. Factually, we know that she appeared in court in Ennis in 1865 on a charge of witchcraft; that she married for a fourth time, extremely late in life and to a much younger man named Meany from Newcastlewest (although it appears that she had previously been living for a long time with a man named O'Brien from Limerick); that she ended her days extremely poor by lonely Kilbarron Lake; and that she died in 1874. And we also know other things about her by repute – that she was frequently drunk and had a vicious tongue; that she was greatly disliked by the local clergy; and that she ran several card schools in the area (she herself was believed to have been an excellent card player). Is it any wonder that such a woman, who spent her days drinking, swearing and playing cards, and who married men much younger than herself, drew allegations of witchcraft and fairy magic about her? She was supposed to have put the 'glamour' (power of illusion) upon young men to draw them to her bed even when she was very old.

Like the Brahan Seer, Biddy was connected with a particular artefact which was supposed to be the source of her miraculous powers. In Biddy's case it was a small blue bottle which she always kept about her, usually in the drawer of an old dresser. Some said that she had won it in a game of cards with a fairy man; others said that she had been given it in a fairy rath by the ghost of her dead husband Tom Flannery.

But even the longest and most colourful life has to draw to a close, and so it was with Biddy. She died in her lonely cottage by Kilbarron Lake in April 1874. Many churchyards in Clare lay claim to be her burying ground but, as with any figure of myth, no one can really be sure where she lies...

It was a BEAUTIFUL EVENING, soft and warm, with the russet sun throwing long and broken shadows across the pale lake waters. Somewhere in the evening a waterfowl called, probably from long rushes around the edge of the lake. Its sad cry drifted up from the water and to the window of the tiny cottage on the height. Biddy Early sat up a little bit on the narrow, creaky bed, gathering her bits of old blankets about her.

'It's callin' for my soul,' she said feebly. 'I'm not long for this world.' One of the two old neighbour men who sat near the edge of the bed moved forward, taking the pipe from his mouth.

'Ah now, Biddy. There's no need for talk like that. You'll outlive us all!' The unseen bird cried again by the water's edge. The old woman on the bed shook her grey head.

'I've seen it, Pat,' she answered him. 'One night as I sat beside the peats with my little bottle in my hand, I dreamed of myself, lying stretched out in this cottage with all my neighbours about me. You were there yourself, Pat Loughnane, and so was Tim Minogue over ther–' she indicated the other old man– 'and William Connors. All of you were sitting in my kitchen having a sup to my memory. Death was hovering over my stiff body like a winding sheet and the door lay open for my soul to depart. That was what I dreamed, Pat, with the fairy bottle in my hand.' Pat Loughnane looked at her, not really knowing what to say, for he knew that Biddy's prophecies usually came true.

'I know that it is near my time and that I'll not get better with this sickness. But I'm resigned to that. Very soon my soul will be going to live among the waterbirds on Kilbarron Lake.' And she gave a bit of a harsh laugh which rapidly turned into a barking cough. 'There's no other help for it.'

'Is there anything that you want us to do then, Biddy?' asked Tim Minogue from the other side of the bed. There was a slight catch in his voice, for it was widely held that of all her neighbours and many men friends, he had loved her most and for the longest time. Biddy thought for a moment, fiddling with the ragged edges of the blankets. Her eyes moved here and there like bright insects in the gathering evening gloom.

'There's one thing comes to me, Tim,' she said gently and thoughtfully. 'I've been thinking in these past days about myself and the clergy, and about how I'd like to have the rites of the Church about me when I die.' The two men nodded, for they had been thinking the same thing themselves. It was an unwise thing, it was said, to die with your soul unshriven, especially if you'd lived such a life as Biddy Early's. And of course there was the fairy bottle which was thought to be the source of her strange powers – just owning that was enough to condemn a soul to Hell.

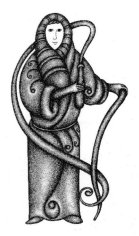

'It'll not be an easy road,' sighed Pat Loughnane, 'for the clergy have never liked you, Biddy. Do you remember when you trapped the Feakle priest in the river?' Biddy gave another faint laugh.

'Aye, Pat, I mind it well. He was only a young curate but he spoke out against

me from the pulpit in Feakle. Then he came riding past my house to curse me and I waited till he'd come to the river ford and threw "the powder" at the flanks of his horse, so that it wouldn't go neither forwards nor backwards and he had to stay there until I chose to release him. Oh, I mind that all right.'

'He didn't take it at all well,' Pat reminded her. 'He was a curate, after all.' But all the same, the three of them laughed at the memory.

'They say that there's a new priest in Feakle,' said Biddy at last. 'Will you go, Tim, and bring him up to me? I'd like to make my peace with God.' Tim Minogue rose and left the room. Biddy listened until she heard the sound of his ass-cart moving away. Pat Loughane got up to go as well but, leaning forward in the bed, Biddy grabbed his arm.

'Wait a minute, Pat, for I've something to ask you.'

'Ask it,' he told her.

'It's said that your grandfather, oul' Pat Loughnane, was a great man and one of the best that ever came into Feakle. And that's true, for I dimly mind him as a child. I mind that he had an undertaking [he was an undertaker]. They said that he used to bury a lot of people for nothing, them that couldn't pay. I've no money about me for my funeral, but will you bury me, Pat?' He looked down at her very sadly.

'I will,' he said.

'Then you can have my haggard and my house if you do,' Biddy told him, 'and I'd give you my blue fairy bottle as well, with all its cures, but that has to be given back on the hour of my death.' But he shook his head, for he wanted nothing to do with fairy things.

It was the following evening that the priest came all the way up to Kilbarron from Feakle. He was a middle-aged and severe-looking man and he came with his vestments, stole and Holy Book. Biddy had rallied a little that day and was now sitting right up in her bed as he ducked in under the door.

'I've come to hear your confession,' said he rather stiffly, putting on the stole. Biddy nodded and the priest sat on the end of the bed to hear what she had to say. And, as she began to speak, a crow alighted on a bush just outside the window and began to 'caw caw' very loudly, as if it was purposefully trying to drown out her words. After the confession, Biddy turned to the priest.

'Father, will you lift that crow in and bring it to the end of my bed?' she asked. The priest looked at her curiously.

'I'll try, anyway,' he said. He reached out of the window, but the crow eluded his grasp and hopped to another branch, well out of his reach. The priest now began to read from the Bible, but the crow on the bush kept up a steady 'caw caw', always trying to distract him, and he had to set the Holy Book down for a minute.

'I'll bring it in,' said Biddy, hoisting herself up even further in the rickety bed. And, lifting up her pillow, she took the small blue fairy bottle from under it and whatever she said or whatever she did, the crow flew in through the window and perched at the end of the bed, watching both her and the priest with dark and intelligent eyes.

'That's what you couldn't do,' said Biddy to the priest. 'Now will you put it out again?' The priest made a grab for the bird, but it slipped out of his grasp and flew up into the rafters, from where it continued to watch them both. The priest made to pray but he was continually interrupted by the crow, which 'caw cawed' mockingly down at him and he couldn't go on.

'I'll put it back out again,' said Biddy, and she held up the bottle in her hand with the neck of it pointing towards the crow. The bird immediately flew out of the room, through the window and alighted in the bush once more, from where it continued to 'caw caw' at the clergyman. Reaching forward, Biddy gave the bottle to the priest.

'At the moment of my death, I'm supposed to give this back to those who gave it to me. But I'm frightened that they'll take my soul as well, Father. 'Tis for you now – it's better in the hands of the clergy – and if you keep it about you, you'll have all the powers that I had.' The priest took it from her and slipped it under his cassock. On his way back to Feakle, however, he threw it from him and into Kilbarron Lake, where it lies to this very day. Even so, the priest (it's said that his name was Father Fawley) was said to have great powers and was even supposed to be able to light the altar candles by the power of his prayers. His name is still spoken with reverence in the Sixmilebridge district.

When he had gone, Biddy lay down again on the bed for a little while and some of her neighbours came in to sit with her. A few of them had gathered in the little kitchen next to the bedroom and were drinking glasses of poteen (illegal spirits) to toast the soul on its way from the world. After a time, at her own request, Biddy was propped up against a couple of pillows, but she was very frail. Pat Loughnane and Tim Minogue and a couple of other fellows had gathered in the bedroom – the overspill from the kitchen. They gave Biddy a glass of poteen but she could only sip at it and couldn't throw it down her as in the old days. She sat and slept in the bed while they talked around her in low whispers.

The light was beginning to fade, and although lamps and candles were lit in the kitchen, the bedroom had become very dark and shadowy. The crow had come back again to the bush outside the window and called from time to time in a harsh, croaking voice. It was answered by waterfowl calling up from the lake at the end of the day.

A man put his head round the bedroom door – Seamus Merriman from Tulla.

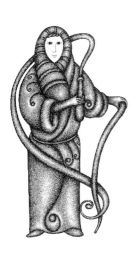

'How are you, Biddy?' he asked. She muttered something to him and fell back on the pillows once more. The men came and went from the door to the fire and back again, talking softly among themselves as they did so. Suddenly there was a whoosh from the fireplace as though something had been dropped down the chimney. The men started back and a ball of fire or light passed by them and out through the cottage door. The crow on the bush outside the window cawed loudly and flapped its wings. Although they were all shocked by the suddenness of it all, the men were full of poteen and soon settled again, wiping at their faces with dirty handkerchiefs and talking quickly among themselves. Nobody had paid any attention to Biddy Early for a moment. Daniel Minogue, Tim's brother, looked into the room. Biddy was still sitting bolt upright in the bed, propped against the pillows.

'Are you all right, Biddy?' asked Daniel, but there was no answer from the figure in the bed. The crow on the bush flew away across the lake, cawing loudly as it went. Tim Minogue himself jumped up from his seat at the foot of the bed.

'Biddy!' he cried. 'Are you all right?' No answer. He looked at Pat Loughnane. 'Is she dead?' Pat shook his head.

'She could be, go and see.' Daniel went out and, lifting a candle from the kitchen, brought it back into the darkening bedroom. He held it close to her face and saw that the eyes were wide and staring. Biddy Early was stone dead. Her passing had been a quiet one. Slowly, the narrow cottage on the height above Kilbarron Lake began to fill with the weeping of the men.

She made her way towards a bunch of bushes between the cottage and the lake below. There was somebody standing there and she knew him by the way that he stood. It was Tom Flannery of Carrowroe, her husband for the longest time and the only man that she'd ever truly loved. How long had it been since she'd laid him in the clay? She couldn't remember. He was not the old sick man that she'd buried, but the young handsome fellow that she'd married long ago. Suddenly she felt very sprightly, as light as a young girl on the road to her first dance, as she ran towards him and threw her arms about him.

'Hello, Biddy! I've been waiting here for you. I've been waiting an awful long while.' He put his own arms around her tightly.

'Oh, Tom,' she cried. 'I haven't got the bottle for you that you gave me all those years ago. I gave it away to a priest. I didn't think that I'd see you again.' But he only smiled sadly and shook his head.

'It doesn't matter,' he said. 'Come on and we'll go down to the water. Listen, the birds among the rushes are calling to us.' And so they were. He took her hand and together they walked, like young lovers, down the slope towards Kilbarron Lake in the final rays of the fading sun.

Ancient Heroes

As in the mythologies of other ancient cultures, the tales of the Celts had their heroes. Initially being a warrior society, Celtic culture placed great emphasis upon fighting, honour and bravery. In the Celtic mind, those who demonstrated such attributes often transcended the boundary between mortals and gods and, perhaps, even became the centre of a localized warrior cult.

In a society which, in its early stages at least, was primarily geared towards conquest and warfare and whose fractured nature often meant that many disputes were decided by conflict, the figure of the warrior assumed a central position. Both classical and vernacular literary sources portray a heroic Celtic society which appears to have been based upon a warrior élite, and where frequent displays of combative skill and feats of bravery were considered as much a part of everyday life as general toil. They describe a society where both soldiers and hunters were accorded an almost legendary, god-like status.

The link between warriors and gods was a strong one. Many Celtic tribes existed on land whose boundaries were protected by a tribal deity which not only looked after the land but also warded off attackers. Over time, this function was taken on by a warrior caste which, to all intents and purposes, became the instrument and embodiment of the god. It is not an immense leap of logic, then, to present the foremost warrior, soldier or hunter of any social grouping as the physical aspect of the deity. This was explained, perhaps, through a miraculous birth or through some form of supernatural (or life-changing) experience befalling this warrior, inextricably linking him to the deity or deities. The Celts, of course, were not the only culture to do this, and similar examples exist in both early Hellenistic and Mesopotamian societies.

Some great warriors were special to the gods, who went out of their way to imbue them with supernatural powers, thus ensuring success in fights or battle.

Some ancient heroes were protected by special, magical artefacts, others were equipped with a fierce battle prowess. This latter skill was common among Celtic warriors. Many of the legends in the Myth Cycles tell of warriors (a good example is Cu Chulainn) who were overcome by 'battle-spasm' or 'intoxication' in the heat of a conflict. This frenzy was believed to be a gift of the gods, and when it came upon a warrior during a conflict he was all but invincible and slew the enemy in what might be described as a 'killing spree'. Some believed that they were actually possessed during these times by the battle-god, creating a bridge between mortal flesh and supernatural power.

Not only were the warriors themselves linked to the gods, but so were their weapons. Indeed, in many cases it is the weapon itself which provides the link between the warrior and the god. In some folklore, an individual receives a special weapon from the gods which transforms him or her into a mighty and fearsome warrior. Similar ideology still persists to the present day with the comic-strip superhero who receives often supernatural or superhuman powers in miraculous ways and sometimes connected with a personalized artefact such as a belt or a ring.

This link between weaponry and the supernatural realm is clearly demonstrated from as far back as the Bronze Age. Even then, worshippers deposited valuable items of metalwork, mainly martial equipment, in bogs, rivers and lakes as votary offerings to the gods. Some had even been ritually damaged to demonstrate supposed use in battle. Many Celtic shrines contained weapons offerings – for instance, at Cournay-sur-Aronde at Oise in Brittany, and at Hayling Island, Hampshire, and South Cadbury, Somerset, both in Britain. These weapons were probably offered as 'bribes' to the gods, to ensure that these worshippers were on the winning side in any forthcoming conflict.

Tales of battle-frenzied warriors and supernatural weaponry have become entwined with the fabric of Celtic myth and legend and have provided the basis for the great Myth Cycles. Even today the name of some ancient warrior such as Cu Chulainn or Arthur can provoke great feelings of patriotic pride as we salute and still, in our own way, pay homage to the powerful Celtic heroes of yesteryear.

BRITAIN

The Sword in the Lake

No ancient hero has the power to stir British passions more than King Arthur. Even though Cornwall, Wales and even Scotland and Ireland lay claim to him, Arthur has always enjoyed a special place in British mythology. In fact, he is often regarded as the mystical protector of the country, not dead but merely asleep and ready to rise in Britain's hour of need. He is alternately described as a great and noble king, a ravaging Celtic warlord, and Celtic Britain's most able defence against the invading Saxons.

So was there an Arthur outside of all this mythology and folktale? The simple answer is that we don't know, for the time of Arthur belongs to a period known as the Dark Ages – between the departure of formal Roman forces and the full flowering of Christian Britain. He dwelt, so the legends suggest, in the sixth century, which historians have often called the 'silent century' because little is known about it and few texts from it survive to state what was going on. Indeed, the only contemporary text to mention a great Celtic king is a monk named Gildas, who, writing about AD 540, makes reference to such a ruler while mounting a forthright attack on the princes and bishops of his own time. Things, he says, are not as good now as they were in the time of that particular king. He praises the government of the king but he does not name him. The earliest mention of Arthur by name is in a seventh-century tribute to a warrior who had died at least 80 years previously. The anonymous poet praises the warrior's prowess, but adds 'still, he was no Arthur'. In the middle of the same century, the last of the Celtic British lowland armies was destroyed and the poets of the day referred to the men as the 'heirs of great Arthur'. In both these instances, the poets are looking back to an already legendary figure somewhere in the past and not of their own time. The name refers to some powerful commander – probably Celtic – who led his people to a number of great triumphs and, in doing so, proved himself a great hero.

The name itself, however, says something of Arthur's origins and reputation, for it is not a Celtic name at all. Rather, the name Artorius is a common Roman Christian name. It is not previously reported in Britain until, apparently, after Arthur's death when roughly half a dozen Celtic rulers gave their children the Romanized name Artorius or the Celtic form of Arthur. Thereafter, it simply dropped from

use and is not known to have been used by anyone for about 600 years, when the Norman romances brought it to popularity once again – a popularity which has never faded.

In the sixth century, however, Arthur appears to have been a name which was much venerated – and probably for some time after as well. Documents from the eighth and ninth centuries seem to suggest that tales concerning Arthur were still being told in Britain, Brittany and Ireland. There were reputed to be some records of his exploits too, but these seem to have been destroyed because from the ninth century this ceased to interest the British and Irish scholars, who remembered only his name. And Arthur's name must have become a byword for stable government during the upheaval of the Dark Ages. Later, Arthur would become a potent symbol of Celtic resistance to the Saxon invader – however, it is highly probable that his government had a quite different practical aim from that of the Celtic peoples – and this was to restore and revive the already collapsed Roman Empire in Britain.

Almost as famous as Arthur himself was his sword, Excalibur. Across the years, the weapon has assumed magical qualities which provided both the foundation and the authority for Arthur's reign. Weaponry, as we have already noted, was venerated from earliest times as a link with the warrior-gods, and none more so than the commonly used sword, which provided a link with its owner and sometimes the gods as well. In fact, swords became a central feature to many mythological and legendary tales, becoming a quest item for many aspiring heroes.

One of the fabled lost Thirteen Treasures of Britain was Dyrnwyn, the sword of Rhydderch Hael, the powerful king of Strathclyde (see pages 152–7), which was supposed to burst into flames from hilt to point if anyone save Rhydderch drew it. Stories concerning the sword Excalibur may well have been based upon legends of Dyrnwyn. It is, however, a much later addition to the Arthur legend and probably dates from medieval times, most likely from Geoffrey of Monmouth, who gave the crude Celtic tales a medieval romance and structure. It is in Geoffrey that the tales of chivalry and courtly honour have their origin, perhaps together with the notion of Excalibur.

From its very inception in folktale, the sword has mystical and supernatural attributes. It is drawn by Arthur from a stone – in fact, Arthur is the only person who could perform such a feat. This contains echoes of the sword of Rhydderch Hael, which was only useful to the Strathclyde king who was its owner. And yet, the entire folkloric episode may owe its origin to a mistranslation. It may be that some monk, writing in Latin about Arthur and his resistance to the frequent invasions of Celtic Britain during the Dark Ages, stated that Arthur was the only man who could take the sword 'from the Saxon' (i.e. defeat them – *ex Saxono*). A copyist, coming along much later, misread the text and wrote that Arthur was the only man who could take the sword 'from the stone' (*ex saxo*). From this copying error flowed a folktale, and thus the legend of the sword in the stone may have been born.

With the death of Arthur, Excalibur had to be returned to its supernatural owners. Following a catastrophic defeat round AD 515 at the hands of his illegitimate son Medraut – born out of Arthur's incestuous relationship with his half-sister Morganna – at Battle of Camlann (the name means 'crooked/blind glen' and has been tentatively, though not conclusively, identified with Birdoswald, near Hadrian's Wall), and with his forces dead or scattered, Arthur orders that Excalibur be thrown into a nearby lake. This has connections with the ancient Bronze Age rituals of earlier times and marks Arthur as having at least some connection with the Celtic world.

So, who was Arthur? To answer this, it is probably best to set aside notions of a chivalrous medieval king seeking the Holy Grail or a proud Celtic prince repelling Saxon invaders. Arthur *might* well have been a Romano-Celtic warlord, grabbing and holding territory in the desperate scramble for land and power in the period which immediately followed the departure of the Roman legions from Britain. This, of course, is not to diminish his historical stature in any way. Through *might* of character and force of arms, he maintained a stable government in a chaotic country; for a time, he subdued the Germanic peoples who threatened to invade Britain and who elsewhere mastered Europe; and, for a brief time, he prevented a remote corner of the Roman world from slipping into total barbarity. He was the last great Roman emperor in western lands and the first powerful king of a newly forged England. He justifiably deserves his place – both mythological and historical – as one of Britain's greatest heroes.

A LIGHT MIST HUNG OVER THE CROOKED GLEN, making the shapes of the trees in the valley bottom seem distorted and indistinct. Somewhere nearby a raven called, perhaps summoning others of its kind to come and feast on the bloody carcasses of men which lay everywhere in the aftermath of the battle.

They had carried him to a hillside, high above the slaughter, where he could rest and gain some temporary respite from his wounds. And those wounds were serious. Arthur knew as he stared down at his shattered breastplate of Roman armour, now red with his own seeping blood, that he was unlikely to survive very much-much longer. He raised a hand in front of his face and saw that it was stained with gore – his own gore. A shape came out of the haze and knelt beside him. It was Baedwr, the last and one of the most loyal of his followers. Desperately, Arthur tried to rise, but the effort was excruciating. Baedwr urged him to rest. He sank back to the ground, exhausted.

'How many of us are left?' he asked, his words little more than a cough. He felt a slow trickle of blood fall from the corner of his mouth and into his beard. No, he would not survive this last battle. Baedwr shook his head.

'All your army is scattered, Arthur,' he said softly. 'Scattered or dead. Medraut's forces surprised us as we came into the glen down there. They came streaming down from the hillside all around and caught us at the lower end like pigs in a trap. Most of your men are crow food. Bors, Gawain, even the Armorican (Breton) companies are destroyed and their leaders killed.' He looked sadly at his dying lord.

'I'm all that's left, Arthur.' The fallen warlord groaned and tried to wipe the blood from his mouth.

'And Myrddin?' he asked. 'By the gods, I could do with his healing ways now!' Baedwr looked away.

'Dead,' he answered. 'I've seen his head hanging from the saddle-bow of one of their horses.' Arthur tried to laugh, but blood clogged his throat.

'So, not even his supposed druidic arts could save that old schemer's life!' he said. 'And Medraut is triumphant and now is king in my place!'

'Medraut himself is dead!' said Baedwr quickly. 'Killed in the fighting. His general Maelgwn now commands what's left of his forces.' Arthur groaned.

'Then Britain is surely doomed,' he said, turning his head away. 'At least Medraut had some sort of humanity about him. Maelgwn is an animal and a butcher. He'll grab my lands and set himself up as a tyrant to oppress whoever he can. A black day true enough.' There was the sound of a war-horn down in the glen and Baedwr started in fright.

'Arthur, my lord, I have to go. Maelgwn's horsemen ride everywhere, seeking out stragglers. I'm heading for Cymru [Wales] and safety. I only came here to see if there was anything that I could do for you before I left.' Arthur considered for a moment, then a light came into his glassy eyes.

'There's one thing,' he whispered. Baedwr moved closer.

'Name it, lord.' With a gory hand, Arthur gestured to where his sword, Excalibur, lay, a little way off. It had fallen from his scabbard when they'd carried him up the slope and now lay with its point towards them. The edges of the blade were stained with dried blood and its hilt had been slightly broken but it was still a fine weapon. 'Excalibur must not be allowed to fall into Maelgwn's hands – it's the symbol of my authority and my power. Maelgwn would only use it to rally forces to him and then devastate the land. He would only use my blade for evil and this must not be allowed to happen. No, Excalibur must be returned to the gods who gave it to me. There's a small lake near here. If you want to do something for me, take it there and go to the centre of the lake – you'll find a raft waiting for you there – and drop it into the water. That'll be your last service for me!' Baedwr leapt to his feet.

'It's as good as done, my lord!' he replied, lifting the sword. Painfully, Arthur rolled over on to his side.

'Now,' he muttered. 'I need rest.'

As he hurried to the lake, Baedwr felt the sword nestling comfortably against his side. It was a remarkably fine blade, he told himself, too good to hurl into a lake. As Arthur had said, it was the symbol of power and authority in the area and if he were to keep it himself, then he could rally Arthur's battered forces to him and begin resistance to Maelgwn and, perhaps, take part of Arthur's lands for himself. He didn't know which thought appealed to him most.

The mist seemed thicker about the lake. It curled in wreaths around the reeds at its edges and had gathered in thick, almost impenetrable clots close to its centre. Baedwr found the raft as Arthur had said, pulled in among a bank of reeds, together with its long guiding pole. He made to push it into the water but suddenly somewhere to his left a waterfowl called in harsh, broken tones. Baedwr paused and looked at the sword. All the temptations came back to him. He saw himself as a future leader of Arthur's people, rallying opposition against Maelgwn and his followers, and finally defeating the tyrant to become a king of Britain. He examined the sword – the hilt was cracked but that could be fixed and the weapon felt good in his hand. He checked out the balance – it seemed perfect. Without hesitating, he slipped Excalibur under a covering of reeds, to await collection later, and turned back towards the hills above Camlann.

Arthur was fading fast, the ground beside him reddening with spilled blood. A great crow had landed close by and was eyeing the dying warlord with a beady eye. Baedwr chased it away and it rose, cawing protestingly into the misty air.

'Did you throw Excalibur into the lake as I asked?' With an effort Arthur hoisted himself up on to one elbow. Baedwr crouched beside him.

'As you told me, Arthur,' he lied, unable to meet his chieftain's eyes. Arthur coughed – a harsh, racking sound.

'And what did you see as you threw it into the water?' he asked. Baedwr was suddenly wary.

'Nothing, Arthur. I only saw a few strands of mist among the reeds and the surface of the lake stirred by a small breeze. Other than that...' With a shrug, he let the sentence hang. Arthur's eyes narrowed.

'Don't lie to me!' he snapped angrily, more gouts of blood spilling thickly down his beard. 'You've kept Excalibur for yourself. And I thought that you were my most loyal of followers! Go immediately and throw it into the lake as I told you to do. Go quickly! Maelgwn's forces are everywhere and I don't want to see you caught by them!' Swiftly, and rather shamefacedly, Baedwr hurried to carry out his leader's instructions.

Between Camlann and the lake, he was forced to hide as several horsemen thundered past, all with Maelgwn's colours fixed to their spears. They didn't see him in the misty evening and, as he huddled behind a bush, Baedwr watched them disappear into the fog with a mounting fear. This was what the future held for him – to be hunted like an animal by enemy forces. Even in Cymru he might not be safe – Maelgwn's claws were very long. If he had a sword like Excalibur, though, he wouldn't have to fear those who came after him. He could set himself up as a petty ruler beyond the Cymru border and dare Maelgwn and his soldiers to take him. But he would need the sword to do that – the sword that was the symbol of Arthur's power.

It still lay under its covering of rushes by the lakeside where he had left it. He took it in his right hand and weighed it, considering all the options. From the reeds nearby the waterbird called again, its tones harsh and ringing. Its cry seemed to make up Baedwr's mind for him. Better to live like a king with a powerful sword than to die like a fugitive without one. He slid Excalibur back under the reeds and hastened back to the hillside above Camlann.

At first he thought that Arthur was dead, for the war-lord lay very still in a puddle of blood. Several large birds – three of them crows – had gathered about his feet and one had actually hopped on to his chest and watched Baedwr's approach defiantly.

'Arthur?' Baedwr was afraid to shout too loudly in case Maelgwn's soldiers were somewhere close by. The body stirred and the crow flapped its wings uncertainly. Arthur raised a feeble and bloody hand and the bird rose, followed by the others. Only a large hooded raven remained close by, taking an interest in what was going on.

'Did you do as I asked?' Arthur croaked weakly. 'Is Excalibur at the lake bottom?' Baedwr was still unable to meet the dying man's gaze, but he nodded.

'As you commanded,' he answered. 'I pushed the raft out to the very centre of the lake and dropped Excalibur in.' Arthur sighed almost contentedly.

'And what did you see as you tossed the blade into the water?' he asked. Baedwr had expected the question and was ready for it.

'The water stirred, great Arthur, and a huge cloud of fowl rose up from the reeds by the lakeside and flew off into the mist. Other than that there was nothing.' Arthur hawked and spat bloodily.

'That's the second time that you've lied to me!' he retorted with all the force that he could muster.

'No, my lord. I...' Baedwr tried to bluff it out but Arthur waved his protestations of innocence away.

'Am I to be surrounded by fools and traitors?' he growled throatily. Baedwr hung his head. 'I might just as well have handed Excalibur to Maelgwn and have done with it.' There were angry shouts from the mist down in the valley bottom. Maelgwn's men were advancing up the hillside towards them, calling to each other in the fog. 'Now we've very little time, thanks to your scheming, for Maelgwn's army's almost upon us. They're looking for stragglers and they'll soon find me here and finish me off. Go back to the lake and throw Excalibur into the water as I asked. I cannot pass beyond until that's done. The future of my spirit rests with you, Baedwr. Go now, before they catch you!' Baedwr turned away as the shouts seemed to recede a little way down Camlann valley.

This time there could be no deception. Somehow Arthur knew each time he lied. Making his way back to the lake, Baedwr had already decided that this time he would obey his lord. The lake edge was still misty and clogged with reeds, but Baedwr quickly found the raft and pushed it out on to the water. Taking Excalibur from its hiding place, he grabbed the steering pole and began to propel the raft towards the thick clots of mist in the centre of the lake. Further and further out he poled, and soon the lakeshore was gone in the mist behind him. Still, he guided the raft out towards the spot where the mist gathered most thickly. As he approached it, he lifted Excalibur and prepared to throw it. A twinge of remorse and uncertainty caught him – it was a beautiful sword, the grip and the hilt could soon be repaired... No, Arthur depended upon him! And yet it was too grand a weapon to be consigned to the weedy depths of a lake...The unseen bird in the reeds called again. Baedwr shook his head as if to clear it of unworthy thoughts and, pushing the pole into the water, urged the raft forward. Lifting Excalibur, he threw it towards the centre of the seemingly solid mist.

The hand which rose out of the water to catch the flying weapon took him by surprise. It was not so much a hand but more of an almost skeletal claw, its nails long and ragged, the fingers twisted and gnarled and the arm hung with weed and lake-scum. Excalibur seemed to fall towards it as if the weapon actually knew where it was going. The hand from the lake opened to catch the falling sword and grabbed it around the damaged hilt. And, as Baedwr watched, a shaft of golden fire seemed to run along the entire sword-blade from point to now seemingly repaired grip. The whole weapon flared up, even brighter than the sun, driving the last shards of mist from the waters of the lake and making Baedwr shield his eyes from its brilliance. Slowly and deliberately, the shining sword was withdrawn beneath the water, which seemed to bubble and hiss fiercely, sending up tiny spurts of steam. Then Excalibur was gone and the lake was silent. The mist wreathed back again. Terrified, Baedwr turned the raft around and began to pole furiously for the lakeshore.

Arthur still lay on the hillside above Camlann, but he was not alone. At first Baedwr thought that Maelgwn's troops had found him, and he allowed his hand to fall to his own sword, ready to rush to defend the body of his fallen lord. Then he hesitated. Those who stood around Arthur's torn body were not soldiers. In fact, he couldn't really make out what they were, for they wore long blue robes with cowls pulled around their heads. Nor did they seem to be attacking the dying king, but almost kneeling before him. There was a faint quivering sound in the air, like the shimmering noise of heated blood in the ears before a battle or on a drowsy summer's day. Arthur had, once again, raised himself on an arm and seemed to be accepting their ministrations. Looking up, he saw Baedwr still standing in the distance.

'You have given Excalibur back to those to whom it rightfully belongs?' he asked. His voice seemed somehow stronger and held tones of its old authority once more. Baedwr nodded slowly, still uncertain of the strangers a little further up the hillside.

'And what did you see when you threw it into the lake?' asked Arthur. Baedwr swallowed, still unable to comprehend what he'd seen...what he was seeing.

'A hand, great Arthur,' he answered. 'It rose from the water and took it. And the sword burned, brighter than the sun, and made the lake-water boil and bubble.' Arthur sank back slightly on the grass.

'Finally, you have done as I asked,' he sighed. 'Now I can go to join with my forefathers. Go now, loyal Baedwr, and flee to Cymru as you'd planned. Don't

worry about me. I shall always be with you.' The figures gathered around him more closely, bending over him now and several raising the edges of their robes as if to mask him from view.

'But how...who...' Baedwr was mumbling now, but Arthur signalled him to go.

'Quickly now! Maelgwn's soldiers are everywhere. Already they're moving back up the valley and they'll find you here if you don't get on your way! I'm going to a far better place, a place from where I can watch my kingdom grow and change. And when the time is right, I'll return and claim my own. Now, go and waste no further time!' One of the blue-clad figures turned towards Baedwr and its cowl fell back slightly. The warrior saw that it had no face, simply a ball of shining light where its head should have been. Realization suddenly hit Baedwr like cold lake water.

'The Tuatha!' he whispered to himself. 'The Sidhe! The old gods of Britain.' The glimpse only lasted for a moment and then the being lifted the cowl of its robe once more. Another raised the corner of its robe in front of Arthur and there was a faint singing sound in the air. Light seemed to flicker all around them, as bright as it had been when Baedwr had seen Excalibur drawn down into the lake. Once again, he threw his hands across his eyes to protect them. The light faded. Baedwr lowered his hands and found himself alone on the hillside above Camlann. There was no trace of either Arthur or the strange beings who had clustered about him, there was only a large pool of drying blood on the ground where his lord's body had lain. No faint singing noise in the air now, but there were other sounds. Shouts echoed from away down in the valley, drawing ever closer. Maelgwn's soldiers! He couldn't stay here any longer. Turning, he began to run across the hillside. About an hour later, he came on a wounded horseman, slowly making his way from Camlann's slaughter. Baedwr killed him and took his horse. Soon he was thundering on his way towards the borders of Cymru.

Maelgwn's reign did not last long, for soon Arthur's lands were overwhelmed by the yellow-haired Saxon armies, marching from the west – 'like moving fields of wheat' – under King Hengist. Unable to hold the lands he had taken from Arthur, Maelgwn and his forces were defeated and driven back to the sea. Saxon kings now ruled in Arthur's stead and yet, somewhere in the hearts of all true Britons, Arthur still lived on, waiting to return and reclaim his lands, Excalibur still in hand.

The King of Rathlin's Daughter

Unquestionably one of the greatest heroes of Irish myth is Cu Chulainn – the Hound of Culann. The title *cu* (hound) was commonly given to a warrior in early Celtic literature, denoting fierceness and aggression, and Chulainn appears as a champion of Ulster who predominates in a series of mythological tales known as the *Ulster Cycle*.

Chulainn is a designation rather than an actual name. It was probably a cult name, since it is highly possible that he was worshipped as a warrior-god in certain parts of ancient Ireland. Early sources tell us that his given name was Setanta, which, coincidentally, corresponds with the Setantii – a Celtic tribe dwelling in Britain. His favoured weapon, the javelin, is described as the *gae bolg*, which evoked the name of the Belgae, an extremely important tribe in western Europe, while the name of his father-in-law, Manach, suggests the Manappi, a Gaulish tribe. It has been suggested that Cu Chulainn is actually of Gaulish descent, his forefathers coming to Ireland via Britain and settling in Muirtheimhne (County Louth), which is frequently given as the hero's birthplace.

The first reference to him is to be found in the epic *Tain Bo Cuailnge* (*The Cattle Raid of Cooley*), thought to be largely a seventh-century work, in which he almost single-handedly defends the province of Ulster from the invading forces of Queen Meadhbh of Connaught. In this, he is depicted as a mighty warrior who, in the heat of battle, undergoes some sort of supernatural transformation known as a *riastradh* or 'spasm', which turns him into a frenzied monster. One eye becomes large and red, while the other becomes incredibly small; his hair becomes spiked, metallic and glowing; while his enormous fanged mouth throws out sparks and flame like a dragon. His whole face and forehead become enveloped in the 'warrior light' and he is gifted with fantastic strength and battle prowess. Faced with this prospect, is it any wonder that armies flee before him?

Cu Chulainn also has supernatural attributes about him. According to the *Tain*, his Otherworld patron is Lugh, the Celtic god of light, who guides his steps and comes to relieve him when he is weary, causing him to sleep for three days after a particular battle. This, of course, demonstrates the connection in the Celtic mind between warriors and local gods and may hint at a religious cult which had built up around around Chulainn himself.

The supernatural element may have been 'watered down' slightly by the eighth century, for a text from that time tells of his conception and birth, still maintaining some unearthly connections, but also closely linking him by blood to the Ulster king Conchobhar mac Nessa. This text seems to have been amended again later in the century to include more godly attributes and connections for the hero. His 'mother' Deichtine, King mac Nessa's sister, reputedly took refuge from a storm in a strange house where a woman was giving birth. At the same time a mare dropped two foals, just as the child – a boy – came into the world. Deichtine took charge of the baby and nursed it, and she and her retinue stayed the night in the house. In the morning, the dwelling had gone and they found themselves in a great rath, alone but for the boy and the foals.

Deichtine took the child back to her brother's home at Eamhain Mhacha, but the baby grew ill and died. Heartbroken, Deichtine took a drink and a tiny creature slipped into her mouth and down her throat. That night, she dreamed the Lugh came to her and revealed that he was the father of the child. It was not dead, she was told, but awaiting rebirth through her. When she became pregnant, it was suspected that her brother, the king, was responsible. In order to allay such accusations, Conchobhar gave her in wedlock to one of his foremost warriors – a soldier named Sualdamh. She miscarried but almost immediately became pregnant again – this time, it was said, by her husband – and gave birth to a son, the very image of the child that she had nursed in the rath. She called him Setanta.

Here the legend becomes confusing, for the next story concerning Chulainn shows him as being given by his mother to a blacksmith called Culann. It is possible that the blacksmith was to be his tutor and raise him in the ways of the warrior. For a child, even from infancy, he showed both great soldierly attributes and almost supernatural strength. While at play, he accidently killed Culann's hound.

'I'll be your hound,' said a remorseful Setanta, thus earning himself a nickname *and* a title, Cu Chulainn.

A number of versions of Chulainn's life are given by a variety of texts, some of them dating from as late as medieval times. Accounts of his death, for example, were already circulating in manuscript form by the tenth century. One of these versions shows how he was lured away into the Glen of the Deaf, where nothing could be heard, so that he would not take part in the war against Connaught. Unaware of the din of battle which was raging a short distance away, he took his ease until one of the children of another warrior – Cailitin – came and told him that he was needed in the conflict. During the course of the battle, Chulainn was severely injured by a javelin thrown by Lughaidh, the son of one of Chulainn's enemies, Cu Roi. The injury was so bad that the hero's intestines fell out, tripping him up as he went to drink from a nearby lake. Seeing that he would not survive, Chulainn gave a great laugh and stated that he would not fall but would face his enemies standing up. Using the intestines, he tied himself to a great standing stone and there continued to fight. However, not even a hero could withstand such an ordeal, and at some point in the battle, Chulainn seems to have died. So feared was he that for three days none of his enemies dared to approach him to see if he still lived. At last one of Cailitin's sorcerer-daughters changed herself into the shape of a crow and lit on his shoulder. Realizing that he was dead, the forces of Connaught came up and tried to remove the sword from his hand. Chulainn held it so tightly that no man could prise it free and so Lughaidh severed the veins around the hero's wrist, forcing the hand to open. The sword fell, cutting off Lughaidh's own swordhand as it did so. Even in death, Chulainn was able to wreak vengeance on his enemies.

It is possible that Chulainn is an amalgam of a number of Celtic heroes – men with, perhaps, supposedly Divine or supernatural attributes – who have come from different parts of the Celtic sphere of influence. It is also possible that fragments of other old hero tales were added by those who copied down the stories from predominantly oral sources. Whatever his origins, he has exerted quite an influence on Celtic imagination and literature. Such an influence exists right to the present day, appearing in the work of such Irish literary figures as Lady Gregory, Standish James O'Grady, Austin Clarke and Thomas Kinsella, and even extending as far as modern-day Irish comic books.

The following tale forms part of an ancient Gaelic poem, 'Tochmare Emhire', which links the hero with the northern coast of Ireland and with Scotland...

DARK DAYS HAD faLLeN UPON THE WHOLe coastLINe of IReLaND, both north and south. Raiders were sweeping down from the northern seas and ravaging Irish coastal settlements without mercy or hindrance. No king or local ruler was fit to stand against them, for they came in waves and when one was driven back, another arrived and took up the fight once more. Some kingdoms tried to make peace with them, but they demanded tributes of increasing size and value until no ruler, save the High King of Ireland himself, could deliver up what they asked. And all the while, their raids increased with astonishing severity.

The kings of the Isles of Western Albyn (the Hebrides – the Western Isles of Scotland) called a great *kabol*, or war-council, to see what could be done about these raiders. Their lands were being devastated, too, and their people made homeless because of the attentions of these pirates. They brought the famous Irish hero Chulainn to speak to them, but although they debated with the champion for seven days and nights, they could not arrive at any resolution to the problem. At last, Chulainn decided to go home. The war-council was going nowhere and he had business to attend to in his uncle's house at Eamhain Mhacha. Climbing into his boat, he bade farewell to the Albyn chieftains and set sail for Ireland.

He was sailing southwards, along the northern Irish coast, when a fearful thirst came over him. He mouth was dry and sore, and as he had no water on the boat, Chulainn looked around for somewhere that he could land and drink from a well or spring. He didn't want to land on the mainland, for he had been told in Albyn that some of the tribes along this part of the shore were fearsome giants and, worse, man-eaters. Now, while Chulainn was not frightened of giants, the thought of cannibals turned his stomach. Then, ahead of him, he saw a small and pleasant-looking little island, a little way from the coast. He landed there, in the hope of finding a spring close by.

Clambering over the rocks, he made his way to the top of the island, where he thought there might be a well. He had only gone but a few yards when over the top of a huge boulder he saw the tip of a fair head on its other side. Crouching down, he crawled forward and, peering over the lip of the rock, saw a young maiden chained to the ground by massive iron links. She was weeping silently to herself.

There was nothing to fear from a young girl, so Chulainn scrambled down beside her.

'What are you doing on this lonely island by yourself?' he asked. 'And why are you chained to the ground?' The girl looked up at him with tears still filling her eyes.

'Leave me, sir,' she instructed. 'For if you remain here with me, you'll surely be killed.' But Chulainn shook his mighty head.

'Tell me anyway,' he said. 'For I'll free you if I can.' But the girl stood aghast.

'Oh, don't try to do that! If you do, you'll doom my people.' Tearfully, she composed herself and told the hero her story.

'I am the daughter of the king of Rechru (Rathlin Island). For many years now, my father's lands have been devastated by fierce raiders coming down from the north in sleek ships, who have burned many of the villages on the island and carried away our women and cattle back to their own dark lands far to the north. Over the past four or five years, these raids have increased until my father and his people can no longer bear them. In an attempt to save our island, my father tried to make peace with these savages. He told them that he'd give them whatever he could if they'd stay away and

leave Rechru alone. The chieftain of the raiders agreed to this and demanded 200 sheep each year as a tribute, and my poor father was forced to agree for the sake of his people. But the raiders were greedy and each year that they came back, they demanded more and more tribute. At first it was 200 sheep, then it was 300; then it was 300 together with 200 cattle; then it was all of this together with 100 slaves. There was no satisfying these robbers. My poor father was at his wits' end. In desperation, he sought the advice of the druids, who told him that if he left his daughter as an offering to the raiders, they might cease their unreasonable demands. I was to be chained on an island off the coast and simply left. The raiders would come and take me and, perhaps, leave Rechru alone. So I wait here for their coming.' And her head sank to her breast and she gave way to uncontrollable sobbing. Chulainn was moved by the pitiful tale.

'Is there no champion on Rechru who can stand up to these raiders?' he asked. 'Is there no hero on the island who can defend your honour against these barbarians?' But the girl shook her head.

'Rechru is only a small country,' she told him, 'and the raiders have killed most of our young men in their attacks. There's no one on the island who'll take them on. All we have left are women and old men.' Chulainn shook his great head in disbelief.

'Then I'll defend both your island and your virtue!' he declared. 'I'll be your champion!' The girl looked at him, hope mixed with terror in her eyes.

'But sir...you cannot...you do not even know my people...' But Chulainn had seized one of the chains that bound her to the ground in his great hand. The warrior-strength came upon him, and with a single motion he broke the heavy iron chain in two.

'No, sir!' protested the princess. 'You really can't...' But it was now too late. A number of ships had dropped anchor off the island and the raiders had arrived. They swarmed ashore, weapons at the ready to receive their tribute, only to be met by Chulainn, his own sword drawn and ready to fight. The two factions met in a clash of steel which reverberated all around the tiny island. The Ulster champion cut the first of them down with ease but further waves of pirates rushed up the beach and hurled themselves into the fray.

For most of the long day, Chulainn and the raiders fought, the champion throwing the bodies of pirate after pirate back into the ocean. In the end, the remnants of the shattered raider force turned tail and fled to their ships, to sail back to wherever they had come from.

Striding up to the princess, Chulainn reached down and broke the final chain which bound her. She noticed that he was badly out of breath from his exertions and that blood oozed from a sword-slash high on the upper part of his arm.

'You're wounded,' she said, as he sank on to the rocks beside her. The hero ran a hand through his great mane of hair.

'It's nothing,' he answered. 'It'll heal in its own time.' But the princess was insistent. Tearing a strip from the hem of her dress, she dipped it in a small spring nearby and bound up the champion's arm. Then she urged him to stay a while with her and rest. Chulainn waved away her invitation.

'I've urgent business elsewhere,' he told her, 'and must return to my uncle's palace at Eamhain Mhacha. Your own people will see to you, for I must be on my way.' And so saying, he made his way back to his boat and set sail. In the distance, he noticed the sails of ships coming from Rechru to see what had befallen their princess. They would rescue her from the island and take her home, where she would be safe. Chulainn was sure that the raiders wouldn't trouble the people of Rechru again. He sailed further south, but after a while his body began to grow weary from the day's fighting and he pulled into a tiny, friendly coastal settlement in order to rest.

Meanwhile, the princess had returned to Rechru, much to the joy and delight of her father. In fact, he was so delighted that he decreed that a grand banquet should be held to give thanks for her safe return, with the hero who had rescued her as the guest of honour. But who was this hero? The princess hadn't asked his name and really had no idea as to who he might be. A proclamation was therefore issued from the court in Rathlin for the stranger to reveal himself. A number of the great heroes of Ireland came forward, each claiming to have rescued the princess. She didn't recognize any one of them.

Away along the coastline, Chulainn heard of the banquet and decided to make his way to Rechru and join in. The hall was packed and there was a great noise when he arrived, as the heroes of Ireland were all boasting of their mighty deeds and of how they had saved the king's daughter from the raiders. The princess sat in a corner, looking particularly glum, but as soon as she saw Chulainn she brightened up.

'There is the hero who saved me!' she exclaimed. 'And look, he still has the piece of my dress which I wound around the wound on his arm. This is the mighty champion who defeated the raiders!' Faced with such evidence as the fragment of the dress, there could be no doubt. Chulainn was fêted and brought before the king of Rechru, who offered him both his daughter's hand in marriage and a portion of the island to rule as his own. But Chulainn declined both of these.

'While I'm flattered by all your attentions and by your kind offer,' he told the princess, 'I'm already promised to another. Nor can I stay here and rule the portion of the island which your father would kindly give to me. I must return to my uncle's house at Eamhain Mhacha, for he has great need of me. His druids have foreseen a great battle to defend the citadel in which I must take part. This is my destiny and it cannot be changed. But rest assured that I will always remember you.' And, as the banquet reached its height, Chulainn turned and made his way back to his boat. As the princess watched, he sailed away to the south. She watched him go until he was no more than a speck on the horizon.

In some versions of this tale, the raiders are described as 'Vikings', perhaps because they are alleged to have come 'from the north'. This is unquestionably a later addition to the story, since it would place the event in the ninth or tenth centuries, when the Hound of Culann was dead and well outside the main corpus of the Myth Cycles.

The King of the Otherworld

In many of the ancient Celtic tales, the hero must undertake a quest into a mysterious, dangerous or supernatural realm in order to fulfil some objective. This undeniably linked the mortal warrior with the gods. In some cases, too, the warrior took on various aspects of the gods while in the realm and was no longer the same when he returned to the mortal world. Some returning heroes had the gift of prophecy, others the ability to talk to the dead – an ability also accorded to certain of the early Christian saints.

Perhaps no Celtic hero was more closely associated with the Otherworld – the world of gods, spirits and the dead – than the Welsh champion Pwyll. He is renowned for being the husband of the Welsh sorceress-queen Rhiannon and also the father of Pryderi – a Welsh king strongly associated with the supernatural – but there are great stories regarding Pwyll, too.

One such tale appears in an ancient Welsh text, *The First Branch of the Mabinogion*, and it demonstrates clearly the interchange between gods, spirits or demons and men. Pwyll is originally described as a lord of Dyfed, a kingdom in ancient Cymru (Wales), and also as a great huntsman. One day, while out hunting, he sees a strange pack of dogs which pursue and eventually overpower a fleeing stag. Driving off the dogs, he sets his own hounds to attack the body of the fallen animal. While they are so engaged, a horseman suddenly rides up, mounted on a black and snorting steed, and reveals himself as Arawn, king of Annwn, the Welsh Otherworld, which is reputed to be far beneath the earth (indeed, it is described in some early religious texts as being the Welsh equivalent of Hell). Both the stag and hounds belong to him, he tells the dumbstruck Welsh king, and for his impertinence Pwyll has earned Arawn's eternal enmity.

Terrified, Pwyll asks how the anger of the demon-king may be revoked. Arawn considers the question for a moment and tells him that there is a way, but it is a dangerous one. Still fearing the demon's wrath, Pwyll promises that he will do anything if the hostility can be removed. Arawn tells him that both of them must exchange physical forms and identities for the space of a year. Arawn will rule in Dyfed as Pwyll, while Pwyll himself must take on the guise of Arawn and rule Annwn for the specified time. At the end of a year, Pwyll, in the form of Arawn, must also meet and kill the demon-king's greatest enemy, Hafgan. This enemy is truly a supernatural creature, combining the elements of warrior, giant and sorcerer. He must be killed with only one blow. If Pwyll should strike him a second time, Hafgan will recover and fight again with renewed vigour.

Pwyll is frightened, but the anger of Arawn frightens him even more, so he agrees. There is a flash like the most brilliant lightning and the two beings exchange physical forms and identities. They then set off for each other's kingdoms.

For a year, Arawn rules in Dyfed and no one suspects that he is not Pwyll, while for the same year, Pwyll rules in the dark, underground kingdom of Annwn, again without suspicion. Both reigns pass without any great incident, but Pwyll fears the approaching end of his term in the Otherworld, when he knows that he will have to face Hafgan. Eventually the dreaded time comes and Pwyll, still wearing the appearance of Arawn, prepares to meet the frightful Hafgan...

ALL was DARK AND GLOOMY within the rock chamber and no light filtered in from the better-lit caverns outside. The only illumination was a tall and burning torch which had been pushed into the sand that made up the cavern-floor. Its pallid and flickering light sent shadows wheeling and leaping around the rocky walls, but revealed very little of the chamber itself. A circle had been drawn close to the brand, just under a large upright which seemed to support the roof above and, Pwyll assumed, this would probably be where the fight would take place.

He was aware of others sitting in the shadows and dark areas of the cave, all unspeaking but simply watching. These would be the Elders of Annwn, the druid priests who watched and guided every aspect of life in the underground kingdom. Among them would sit Teyrnon, the old druid who had been his royal counsellor and adviser throughout his year-long reign and who, he suspected, knew that he wasn't truly Arawn. If he did suspect, the old priest had never said. He wished that he had Teyrnon by his side now, to seek the old druid's help against the unknown enemy, but he knew that under the ancient laws of this land Teyrnon was not allowed to intervene in any way. No, he must fight Hafgan himself and on his own terms.

So they waited for the enemy to appear. There were faint scufflings, coughs and soft mutterings in the darkness beyond the torch-glow as the druids moved and settled. But no one spoke and Pwyll found the silence more disquieting than anything else. Back in Dyfed, he had been used to the shouts and roars of his warrior comrades, even before the battle. Here there was just an aching and fearful silence.

So he waited, his sword ready. Only one blow, Arawn had told him. And that blow must kill the monster. If you should happen to strike Hafgan twice – even by accident – he will recover and become twice as vicious. Even with all your warrior's skills, you will not be able to stand against him then. Pwyll checked his sword, moving it from hand to hand to test its balance while he waited.

There was a sudden blast of trumpets from the outer darkness and figures moved along the edges of the torchlight. Pwyll was aware of a faint commotion among the druids who had been sitting in the gloom. His heart rose into the back of his throat. As if in response to the noise, the torch itself seemed to flare momentarily, and as it did so, Pwyll saw a form step into the circle.

At first he thought that Hafgan wore some kind of all-covering body armour, but as the light glinted on the body of his enemy, Pwyll saw that it was covered in heavy scales. Despite this, Hafgan seemed at least partly human in that his shape was man-like, if very tall, and that he had arms and legs like any other man, albeit his fingers were crooked and clawed like the talons of a great bird. He was dressed only in hide breeches and with a leather war-harness about his upper torso which held a small array of weapons. Pwyll was armed only with a sword.

Halfgan's head was completely hairless and seemed to be smoothly rounded and grey-looking, like a coastal rock that has been washed for years by the sea, the mouth nothing more than a thin and lipless slash which curled in a perpetual and evil-looking sneer at its corners, while the eyes seemed sunken in the forehead and regarded Pwyll with a mixture of arrogance and contempt. Although he was taller than his opponent, Hafgan seemed slightly stooped and hunched, a thick mane of fur spread across his shoulders. Pwyll noted with a shudder that in his right hand the creature held a large spiked club, with which he made threatening motions in the air.

'So, Arawn.' Hafgan's voice sounded somewhere between human tones and the croak of a raven and was certainly not at all pleasant to hear. 'We meet as ordained. Only one of us will walk away from this place, so the prophecy says, and I intend that it should be me. Are you ready for the conflict with me then, king of the Otherworld?' The creature gave a thoroughly unpleasant laugh. 'Are you ready to die?'

'Not by your hand!' cried Pwyll, springing forward, his sword at the ready. One sudden blow before Hafgan was ready might do it, he reckoned. But despite his size and armoured bulk, Hafgan appeared extremely swift on his feet, dodging the blow and leaping to one side. Pwyll went sprawling in the dust. In an instant Hafgan had spun round and was standing over him as Pwyll scrambled upright once more.

'You'll have to be much quicker than that, Lord of the Otherworld,' he taunted. 'I may look clumsy but it's just an illusion, for am I not a master of magic and shadow-play? Nothing is as it seems with me! I could have killed you there but I think I'll let you live. Believe me, your death will be a slow one! This, I promise you.'

So saying, he lashed out with the spiked club. Pwyll quickly danced back but Hafgan followed, his red jaws open in a fearful roar, revealing long and rending fangs. Darting to one side, Pwyll managed to avoid the creature's rush. Hafgan was suddenly past him in a blast of stinking wind and was skidding round in the sand to face him once more. Pwyll straightened up to face him, and behind him in the darkness the druid audience moved and whispered among themselves. Obviously, they did not give much for Pwyll's chances against such a foe. Nor did the warrior himself, for he was battling against a foe who used the very shadows of the cavern against him. How could he hope to win?

'One blow,' Arawn had told him, 'but it must be well struck. You will not get another chance!' Desperately Pwyll tried to focus in the flickering torchlight, trying to find a weak spot on Hafgan's armoured hide. The creature now swung the mace threateningly in the air and, as Hafgan raised his arm, Pwyll thought that he saw a soft spot underneath.

'One blow will be enough to kill him,' Arawn's words echoed somewhere in his head. 'Take it quickly!' With a triumphant roar, Pwyll ran forward, his sword raised to deliver the final blow. Hafgan's monstrous form seemed to ripple and change in the feeble light, becoming an impossibly tall skeleton, clad in a rusting helmet and mouldering, rotting armour. The hideous skull-face opened its mouth to reveal long, vampire-like teeth. Sweat stood in great beads on Pwyll's forehead. He'd heard of Otherworld shape-shifters in legends but this was the first time that he'd ever seen one.

'So, Arawn!' roared Hafgan in savage triumph. 'You truly thought that you had the measure of me! But once again, you were wrong. Take this for your impertinence!' And the spiked club struck Pwyll in the ribs as he hurtled past, momentarily knocking the wind from him. Pwyll fell his full length on the sand, hearing the whispering of the druids close by above the blood which was singing in his head. The spiked mace came whistling down again and he rolled aside to avoid it. The

skeleton-thing was now chasing him as he climbed to his feet once more and made to move away, keeping the length of his own sword between them.

'You're only putting off the evil moment!' The Hafgan-creature spoke with a terrible, bleating laugh. 'Surrender to me now and die like a warrior!' Pwyll took a couple of steps backwards and collided painfully with the nearby rock pillar which supported the roof. He felt it move a little as his weight slammed against it and a light shower of dust cascaded down about his shoulders. The stone pillar appeared a bit unsteady! But he had no time to think about this for Hafgan was on him again, the great spiked club in one hand and a short, stabbing knife in the other. Almost arching himself in two, Pwyll avoided both. Hafgan, however, merely laughed.

'You can't keep this up for ever, Arawn!' he roared. 'Soon you will tire, your reactions will slow and then I'll have you. No mercy for you, so-called Lord of the Otherworld!'

'The creature has him now!' he heard one of the druid priests whisper from the dark behind him. 'Arawn cannot afford to strike more than one blow and that's his downfall.'

'But if he were to use his surroundings,' said another voice, one which he recognized as Teyrnon, 'then he might make that blow count as *more* than a single stroke.' Pwyll thought desperately. Maybe his old mentor was trying to give him some sort of hint – but how could he use it? There was little about the gloomy cavern, except...A crazy plan began to form in the back of Pwyll's mind – so crazy that it might just work.

He was brought back to harsh reality by a passing blow against the side of his helmet. The world flashed suddenly out of focus and he had to shake his head to restore his vision. The skeleton-thing rippled and changed once more. Now it had become a towering shadow – black as night and with curling, shadowy horns on either side of its mighty head. Slanted eyes glowed redly at its victim.

'I'm growing weary of this battle,' snarled Hafgan. 'Let's finish it now! Surrender or be killed!' Spitting dust and blood from the corner of his mouth, Pwyll shakily raised his sword in what he hoped was a defiant manner, worthy of the true Arawn.

'Then you'll have to kill me, monster!' he shouted, reversing into the gloom. With a roar, Hafgan rushed towards him. Thrusting forward, the king of the Otherworld struck the shadow a light blow on his side, sending him reeling off balance and into the stone pillar. Hafgan collided with the upright and tumbled to the ground. Instantly, he was on his feet again, weapon at the ready and reverting to his original form.

'A squalid trick!' he sneered, shaking off the fine dust that had fallen on his furry shoulders. 'But you've wasted your blow and done me no harm. Now you truly *will* die!' And he made to move forward.

From somewhere far above them came a low groan. Dust began to fall like a curtain across the torchlight, this time coupled with tiny bits of rock. Alarmed, Hafgan looked upwards, to see even larger chunks of stone fall from the cavern roof as the pillar into which he had blundered slowly gave way. The druid audience, too, made a dash for the door of the cavern and Hafgan began to follow them – but it was already too late.

Pwyll squeezed himself into a crevice in the wall as rock tumbled down, swallowing up his adversary in a roar of rubble and dust. In an instant, it was all over, and as Pwyll emerged from his hiding place in the rock cleft, all that remained in the fragmentary light which flooded in from outside was a pile of stone. From beneath this, Hafgan's claw-like hand hung limply. His opponent was quite dead.

'So,' said Pwyll softly to himself, 'only one of us will walk from this place alive. Just as the prophecy said.' And without a backward glance, he made his way to the mouth of the cavern and out into the lightless kingdom beyond.

At the end of a year, Pwyll and Arawn once again exchanged both bodies and identities and resumed their own lives, each ruling his own kingdom. Arawn's wrath was lifted, and indeed, the king of the Otherworld was so delighted at the death of his enemy that the two kings became good friends. In gratitude for Pwyll's slaying of Hafgan, Arawn sent many gifts to the king of Dyfed's palace. One of these was a pig, which was originally an underworld animal. This, say the Welsh, explains how the pig came to be in our world and why it is always rooting in the earth. Pwyll went on to further exploits and deeds, including the capture of Rhiannon, who was to become his bride, and became one of the first great heroes of Wales.

Select Bibliography

Anon, *The History of Witches, Ghosts and Highland Seers* (Berick, 1803)

Baker, Margaret, *Folklore and Customs in Rural England* (David and Charles, 1974)

Bottrell, William, *Cornish Witches and Cunning Men* (Oak Magic Press, 1996)

— *Traditions and Hearthside Stories of west Cornwall Collected by William Bottrell* (privately printed, 1873)

Bottrell, William, Hawker, R.S., and Hunt, Robert, *Strange Tales of the Cornish Coast* (Tor Mark Press, 1997)

Campbell, J.F., *Popular Tales of the Western Highlands* (Edinburgh, 1860; Paisley, 1890)

Carmichael, Alexander, *Carmina Gadlica* (Floris Books, 1997)

Crossley-Holland, Kevin, *Folk Tales of the British Isles* (Faber and Faber, 1991)

Cunliffe, B., *The Celtic World* (Constable, 1992)

Curran, Bob, *Banshees, Beasts and Brides from the Sea* (Appletree Press, 1996)

Curtin, Jeremiah, *Myths and Folk Tales of Ireland* (Dover, 1993)

Dash, Mike, *Borderlands* (Arrow, 1997)

Grant, I.F., *Highland Folk Ways* (Berlinn, 1993)

Green, Miranda, *Celtic Myths* (British Museum Press, 1993)

Gregory, Lady, *Visions and Beliefs in the West of Ireland* (Colin Smythe, 1970)

Hawker, R.S., *Hawker's Tales of Ghosts and Witchcraft* (Oak Magic Press, 1997)

Hunt, Robert, *The Drolls, Traditions and Superstitions of Old Cornwall* (Llenarch Press, 1997)

Jones, Prudence, and Pennick, Nigel, *A History of Pagan Europe* (Routledge, 1995)

MacKenzie, A., *The Prophecies of the Brahan Seer* (Golspie, 1972)

MacLellan, Angus, *Tales from South Uist* (Berlinn, 1997)

MacNeill, F.M., *The Silver Bough* (3 vols., Glasgow, 1957–61; an abridged version of this work was printed by Canongate Publishers, Edinburgh, 1988)

MacPhearson, John (The Coddie), *Tales from Barra Told by the Coddie* (Berlinn, 1992)

Montgomerie, Norah and William, *The Well at the World's End* (The Hogarth Press, 1956)

Morris, John, ed., *Nennius: British History and the Welsh Annals* (Phillimore, Chichester, 1980)

O hOgain, Daithi, *Myth, Legend and Romance: An Encylopaedia of Irish Folk Tradition* (Prints Hall, 1991)

O'Rahilly, Thomas, *Early Irish History and Mythology* (Dublin Institute for Advanced Studies, 1946)

Owen, Elias, *Welsh Folklore* (1887; reprinted by Llenarch Press, 1996)

Pennant, Thomas, *A Tour of Scotland and a Voyage to the Hebrides* (London, 1774)

Polson, A., *Scottish Witchcraft Lore* (Inverness, 1932)

Rhys, Sir John, *Celtic Folklore* (Oxford, 1901)

Skene, William F., *The Four Ancient Books of Wales* (2 vols., Edinburgh, 1868)

Thompson, Francis, *The Supernatural Highlands* (Robert Hale, 1976)

Welch, R., ed., *W.B. Yeats: Writings on Irish Folklore, Legend and Myth* (Penguin Books, 1993)

Wentz, W.Y. Evans, *The Fairy Faith in Celtic Countries* (Oxford University Press, 1911)

Yeats, W.B., *Fairy and Folk Tales in Ireland* (Picador, 1979)

Zipes, Jack, *Victorian Fairy Tales* (Methuen, New York, 1987)

Index

Albion, King of Celts 13, 19
Ambrosius, Aurelius 20
angels 66
Anthony, Moll 164
antlers 40, 41, 43, 45
Antrim, Ireland 58, 60
Aoibheall (Banshee) 102, 104–8
Arawn, King of Annwn (Welsh Otherworld) 185, 186–9
artefacts, magic 164, 171
Arthur, King of Britain 14, 17, 151, 154–6
    reputation 172, 173
    sword (Excalibur) 172–9

Badbh Catha (battle raven) 36
Badbh (goddess of battle and slaughter) 36
Baedwr, follower of Arthur 17, 18, 173–9
ball 113
Banshee (Woman of the Fairy) 102, 104–8, 138
baptism 109
battle crow/raven 36
battles 103, 107–8, 152, 154, 173, 183
bean-Sidhe (Banshee) 102, 104–8
beans 126, 128
Bedwyr *see* Baedwr
bells 37–9, 129
    monastery 41, 42, 44–5
    sanctified 39
Benbecula, Uist 54, 57
boar *see* pig
bog (god or demon) 90–1
bottle, magic blue 164, 167–8
Brian Boru/Borumha, King of Ireland 102, 104–6, 108
Brute, King of Celts 13, 19
Brythonic Celts 8
Buggane of St Trinian's 90–6
bulls 97, 99
Bury St Edmunds, Suffolk 122, 131

Cado, Dark Prince of Kernow 74–5, 76
Camlann, Wales (battlefield) 173–9
cannard noz (Brittany) 48, 50, 51
cap (mermaid) 67, 68
Cape Telamon, Battle of 6–7
Carnac, Brittany 47, 48
Castle Carberry, Co Kildare 140–2
Cathubodua (raven goddess) 36
cavern 129, 130, 189
Celts
    Britain 7–8
    invaders 8–9
    Po Valley 6–7
changelings 57, 109–13
charcoal burners 41–2
Chateau of Lanacol, Brittany 134–8
chevalier 114–21
children 114, 122–31

Christ 156
Christianity
    impact of 9–10, 28–9, 30
    and merfolk 77
Chulainn, Cu, Ulster champion 46, 100, 171, 180–4
cloak (mermaid) 68, 69–71, 72, 82
Clontarf, Ireland 102, 107–8
Clotha, Washer at the Ford 46
club, spiked 186–8
cohullen druith (mermaid's cap) 67, 68
comb 34, 35
Conlaig, son of Brian Baru 103, 104, 108
Cormoran, Lord of St Michael's Mount 13, 19
cow 56–7, 58
crows 31–5, 36–9, 167–8, 176
Cruachan Aigle, Ireland 36–9, 86
Cubbon family 111–13
'cuckoo in the nest' (changeling) 109
Culhwch ap Cilydd, Welsh hero 14–18

Dahut, daughter of Gradlon 73–6
Dalby, Isle of Man 111
Day of Judgement 89
deformity, humans 101, 109
Deichtine, mother of Chulainn 180
demons 28–51
dogs 115, 147, 185
drui-ban (female druid) 149, 163
druids 115, 119, 121, 148–50, 186
dykes, Brittany 74

Eamhain Macha 184
Early, Biddy 164–9
Edric the peasant 123–4
Elvira, serpent-woman 119–21
Excalibur (King Arthur's sword) 172–9

Fahey, Bridget 140–2
fairies 52–65, 132–47
    cavalcade 52, 58
    forts and raths 58, 59, 60
    funerals 58
    hearthside 134–8
    prisoners of 109–10
    protection from 109–10
    shoemaker (leprechaun) 139, 140
    wind (Slaugh) 54, 56, 59–60, 62, 63
fiah ree (spirit race/fairies) 53
fiddle 112–13
Filidh (poet-seers) 150
flood gates 74–5
Fomorii (one-eyed giants) 14
forest 41–5, 114–21
foxglove (lusmore) 110

Galatia 7
genius loci (spirit protector) 132, 139
Geoffrey of Monmouth 19, 151, 172
Gesto, Skye 54, 57
giants 12–27
    brothers 19, 20–3, 24
    dance of 19–23
    human remains 12
    one-eyed 14–18
gnomes 132, 133

goblins 133
gods 28–30, 177–9
    battle 170–1
    earth (fairies) 52
    sea 65–7, 73
    woodland 44–5
Gog, giant 19, 20–3
Goidelic Celts 8
gold, crock of 140–1, 142
Goleudydd the witch 14, 17
Good People *see* fairies
Gradlon, King of Ker Ys 73–6
green chidren 122–31
'Green Jack's Children' 131
Green Man 41, 45
Griffin, Maurice 163–4
Guildhall, London 23
Guillyen Veggy (fairy horde) 62, 63–4
Gwenddolau, King of Britain 151–2, 154–7

Hafgan, supernatural creature 186–9
halflings 100–31
Hallowe'en 58
hand 177
healers 163–4
hearthside fairies 134–8
Hengist, King of Saxons 19, 179
Herla, King of Britain 41
Herman, giant 24
hermits 30, 157
Herne, master of the Hunt 40–1, 43–5
heroes 170–89
Hickathrift, Tom 24
Hill of Poison, Islay 35
hoodie (crow) 31–5
horse 97, 99
Host (fairies) 54, 63, 65
Hound of Culann *see* Chulainn, Cu
hunting 40–5, 185

Imhar the Landwaster/the Raven 31
Islay, Scotland 31–5, 97, 98–9
Isle of Man 24, 62–5, 90

James I, King of Scotland 102
javelin 180, 181

Keeill Brisht, Isle of Man 91–6
kelpie (river horse) 99
Ker Ys, Brittany 72–6
keys 74
Kilbarron Lake, Co Clare 164–9
Killaurus Mountains, Ireland 22
Kinney, Mary (mermaid) 68
Kintail, Scotland 160–2

lake 174–9
Lammas Fair 30
Lanascol, Fairy of 134–8
language 7–8
leaves, dried 144, 145
leprechaun 139–42
libations 134, 145
Lig-na-Baste (Paiste) 86, 87–9
London 20–3, 59–61
Lough Foyle, Ireland 87, 89

Loughnane, Pat 165–7
lurachmain see leprechaun
lurikeen *see* leprechaun
lutins (hearthside fairies) 134

Macara Shee (fairy cavalcade) 52, 58, 139
MacCumhaill, Fionn, Irish giant 13
McCurdy, Dan 68–72
MacDomnhaill, Mael, King of Ireland
    105–6, 108
MacKenzie, Annabella (Baraball n'ic
    Coinnich) 160
MacKenzie clan, Kintail 159
MacKenzie, Kenneth (Cionneach Odhar)
    158–62
MacRae, Duncan 160–2
madmen 152
Maelgwn, Welsh general 174–6, 179
magic 150
Magog, giant 19, 20–3
Marcus Valerius Corvus (the Raven) 31
Market-jew (Marazion), Cornwall 25
Marown, Isle of Man 90, 91
mating, human and supernatural 100–1
Maud (Matilda), Empress 122, 123
Medraut, son of Arthur 173–4
Menw, British champion 17
merfolk 66–83
    mermaids 67, 68–72, 77–83
    merman 67
Merlin *see also* Myrddin
    wizard 24, 151–2
Mhor-Ri (Great King) 30
Minogue, Daniel 169
Minogue, Tim 165
Mirror of Ages 144, 145–7
mischief, fairies 134
monks, writings 9–10
monsters 84–99
    animalistic 84–5, 97
    Buggane 90–6
    serpent 86–9
    supernatural 84–5
    water-bull 97–9
Morrigan (Phantom Queen, goddess) 36
Morrigans (mermaids) 73, 76
Murrough, son of Brian Baru 103, 104,
    106–7, 108
musicians 109, 112–13
Myrddin (Merlin), wizard 151–7, 174

Nephilim, giant race 13
Newlyn, Cornwall 143–7
Noah, descendants 13
Nodens Sylvanus, woodland god 40

oak tree 151
Odin, All-Father (Norse god) 14
O'Hartigan, Dunlang 103–8
Old Denbras of Towednack 24–7
Olwen, daughter of Pencawr 14, 17, 18
oral tradition 10–11
Osric, son of Edric 123–4
Otherworld (world of spirits) 185

pagan beliefs 9–10, 28–30

Paiste (reptile) 86, 87–9
Pencawr, Yspaddaden (Welsh cyclops)
    14–18
Pictish guard 20–3
pigs 84–5, 146–7, 189
pixies, Cornwall 143
Po Valley, Italy 6–7
Polyphemus (cyclops) 14
pool 116, 152
pork 84
priests 156, 167–8
princess, Rechru 182–4
prophecy ('sight') 158–62
prophet 157, 158
protection, from fairies 62
Pwyll, Welsh champion 185–9

queens, prophecy about 162

Raghery (Rathlin) Island 31, 68, 72
    princess 182–4
Rathlin Island *see* Raghery Island
ravens *see* crows
rebirth 154, 157
Rechru *see* Rathlin Island
Redruth, Sexton 79–83
Rhydderch Hael, King of Strathclyde
    152–7, 172–3
Richard de Colne, Sir 123–30
Robin Hood 41
rock fall 189

sacrifices 28, 29, 30
St Bridget/Brigid of Kildare 39, 149
St Guenole of Brittany 74, 75–6
St Ives, Cornwall 25, 27
St Martin's Land 128, 130, 131
St Mary's by the Wolf Pits 122, 123, 127,
    130, 131
St Michael 66
St Murrough O'Heaney 86, 87–9
St Patrick 36–9, 86
St Trinian's Church, Marown 90, 91–6
St Winwaloe 76
satyrs 40
Saxi, giant 24
sea-bride 68–72
sea-gods 65–7, 73
seals 68, 69, 72
seanchi (men of lore) 10
'second sight' 158
seer (prophet) 157, 158–62
serpent 86–9
    driving out 86
serpent-woman 115–21
Setanta, warrior-god 180
shamans (Celtic priests) 148–9
Sheean-ny-Feaynid (Sounds of Infinity)
    62
sheets, washing 46–51
Shetland Islands 24
shoemaker, fairy (leprechaun) 139, 140
shrouds 48, 51
Sidhe (gods) 179
    see also bean-Sidhe
singing 115–17, 121

skeagh-shee (Irish tree spirits) 132–3
skeleton (Hafgan) 187–9
Slaugh (fairy wind) 54, 57, 58, 59–60, 62, 63
Slepnir (six-legged horse) 40
snake *see* serpent
solicitor 144–7
spirits 28–30
    countryside 53
    woodlands 40, 153–7
sprites 115, 132–47
stags 40
'stock' (substitute) 110
stone
    arch 160
    circles 19, 22
    magic 158–9
    and sword 173
Stonehenge 13, 19, 22, 23, 151
strangers 122
sword 172–9, 181, 186

taibhs/taish ('second sight') 158
tailor 91–6, 111–13
Taliesin 151
time, and fairies 61, 65
Tir fo Thoinn (Land Beneath the Wave) 66,
    71, 73
titans 13, 14, 19, 24
Tolcarne Troll 142–7
Trewella, Matthew 77–83
Trewella, Squire 78, 81, 82
Trithick, Tom 25–7
Trojans 19
troll 142–7
tuberculosis 109
Turlough 103, 104, 106, 108

Vichon, Jean 47–51
Vortigern, King of Celts 13, 19–23, 151

warriors 152–6, 170–89
washerwomen 46–51
water-bull 97–9
water-weed 98
weapons 171, 172–9, 180, 181, 186–8
werewolf 114, 115
Western Highlands, Scotland 159–62
Western Isles, Scotland 31–5, 54–7, 68–72,
    97–9, 158–9, 181
Wheel of Time 156–7
Wild Hunt 40–5, 53
wind, fairies 54, 56, 59–60, 62
wise women 148–50, 163–9
witchcraft 150, 163, 164
wizards 148–57
Woden, Viking god 40
wolf 114
Wolf Pits 130
women, wise 148–50, 163–9
woodland 152–7
woodland spirits 40, 44–5, 153–7

Yann-an-Od (John of the Dunes) 73
Ys *see* Ker Ys

Zennor, Cornwall 77–83